PENGUIN BOOKS
One December Day

Rachel Marks studied English at Exeter University before becoming a primary school teacher. Despite always loving to write, it wasn't until she gained a place on the 2016 Curtis Brown Creative online novel writing course that she started to believe it could be anything more than a much-loved hobby. She lives in Gloucestershire with her husband and their three children. *One December Day* is her fourth novel.

One December Day

RACHEL MARKS

PENGUIN BOOKS

PENGUIN BOOKS

UK | USA | Canada | Ireland | Australia
India | New Zealand | South Africa

Penguin Books is part of the Penguin Random House group of companies
whose addresses can be found at global.penguinrandomhouse.com

First published by Penguin Books 2023

001

Copyright © Rachel Marks, 2023

The moral right of the author has been asserted

Set in 12.5/14.75 Garamond MT Pro
Typeset by Falcon Oast Graphic Art Ltd
Printed in Great Britain by Clays Ltd, Elcograf S.p.A.

The authorized representative in the EEA is Penguin Random House Ireland,
Morrison Chambers, 32 Nassau Street, Dublin D02 YH68

A CIP catalogue record for this book is available from the British Library

ISBN: 978–1–405–94905–7

www.greenpenguin.co.uk

For Dylan, the best cuddler in the world.

16th December 2004

LAURA

The crowd is packed so close that we have to fight our way towards the stage. I struggle to keep hold of Sarah's hand and pull at the neck of the Christmas jumper I had to wear to gain entry. I struggle out of my jacket as we move through the room, the change in temperature from the icy wind outside to this tiny club causing my face to burn.

'I think we might get a bottle smashed over our heads in a minute,' I shout into Sarah's ear as we reach the front, acutely aware of the hundreds of eyes boring into the back of my skull.

'It's fine, it's fine. We're VIPs,' Sarah says, waving up at Luke on the stage. He smiles and nods his head in acknowledgement, his hands glued to his guitar, his mouth up against a microphone that's wrapped in tinsel.

And then, he sings – his gorgeous raspy voice filling the room, his deep brown eyes fixed on me. And I'm ashamed to admit it but my knees actually feel *weak* – a properly 'Bambi learning to walk' level of unstable.

'They're really good, aren't they?' Sarah shouts over the top of the music.

They are. I've read the articles online. 'University Band Bursts on to the Music Scene After Being Featured on Radio One'. They're picking up rave reviews, becoming the talk of the town. But I was still worried that they were going to be crap. That I was going to have to lie to Luke when he asked me at the end of the gig what I thought of it.

I nod in response to Sarah, embarrassingly lost for words and unable to break eye contact with Luke. The fact that he is wearing glasses with two reindeer waving out the top of them should make him less appealing, but, worryingly, it doesn't.

'God, you two.' Sarah moves her head in front of mine and points two fingers into her mouth.

I elbow her and then we turn back to the band to listen to the music. We watch the whole set – a mixture of beautiful lyrical ballads where it feels like the room falls silent except for the sound of Luke's voice coming out of the speakers, and rousing guitar-heavy numbers where everyone seems to move in time with the music, no longer aware of where they are. When they end on 'Last Christmas', there's such a joyful festive atmosphere that even *I'm* nearly swept up in it.

Eventually, to the sound of hysterical screaming, the band leave the stage and, along with the rest of the crowd, Sarah and I head to the bar. When we finally get to the front, both of us order two drinks so we won't have to rejoin the queue for a while – Sarah going for the 'Scrooge-Driver' while I opt for the 'Mistletoe Margarita' (because of course drinks must have cringey Christmas names throughout the month of December).

'I'm surprised you didn't go for a "Bah Humbug Highball"', Sarah teases as we take our cocktails (adorned with Christmas tree straws) over to a corner of the club.

There are no free seats, so we lean up against the wall,

finally able to hear each other talk without shouting quite so loud.

'So, what did you think?' Sarah asks.

'Yeah, they were pretty good, weren't they?'

She laughs. 'I reckon if Picasso had asked for an appraisal, you'd have said, "not bad".'

I roll my eyes. 'The last song was a bit of a low point. Plus having to wear this.' I run my hands over my jumper, accidentally causing Rudolph's nose to start flashing.

'I saw you singing along.'

'Never.' I smile. 'Must've been a twitchy nerve in my lips.'

'Ah, so that's what it was.' Sarah scans the room. 'God, I'm going to miss all this. The course, I mean.'

She's doing a masters in music performance at the local university – it's how she met Luke – and she's only got just over a month left.

'Still the best thing you ever did?'

'Composing all day? It's felt like a bit of an indulgence, to be honest. I mean, what's the likelihood of finding a career off the back of it? But I've loved every minute.'

'It's not an indulgence. You've been following your passion. I'm jealous.'

Sarah started playing the piano aged three. By the time I met her in primary school, it was already clear that she was hugely talented. And not only can she play, she writes the most beautiful scores. When she's sitting at the piano, her fingers like ballet dancers on the keys, it's like she travels somewhere else.

'You'll find your passion, too.'

I wrap a strand of hair around my finger, a habit my mum loves to berate me for.

'Hmmm. I hope so. It's certainly not working in Thomas Cook.'

'You do get us the best holiday deals, though.'

'True.'

'So, come on then, make me sick with jealousy.' She nods towards the stage. 'Is the sex still "out of this world"?'

I smile. 'Never tell him I said that. His ego's big enough as it is.'

'Oh, to be back in those heady early days again.'

'We're only twenty-two,' I laugh. 'You sound like an old married woman.'

'Well, Tom and I *have* been together since we were fourteen. It does feel like a lifetime. We're certainly not at the "at it like rabbits" stage any more. More the "leaving the toilet door open whilst he has a crap" stage.'

'You know you wouldn't change it really.'

Sarah shrugs and I can tell she's trying not to smile. Her and Tom are perfect together. I've been jealous of their connection since the moment they met. But, at the same time, he's the only bloke I know who does actually pass the "good enough for my best friend" test.

There's a sudden cheer as the band come out from backstage and start to mingle with the crowd. Within seconds, Luke is surrounded, and he starts chatting animatedly to a stunning blonde wearing a skin-tight glittery jumper, with boobs so full and round they make mine feel like cushions where the stuffing's fallen out. Luke keeps putting his hand on his stomach, his (almost stylish) reindeer Fair Isle jumper creeping up, the girls he's with practically fainting at the sight of his washboard abs. Perfect Boobs whispers something in his ear and he laughs and whispers something back in hers. And then she lifts up her top and hands him a pen. Obligingly, he removes the lid with his teeth and then signs her equally toned stomach (I bet she's tensing it).

'You OK?' Sarah asks and I jolt myself back to our conversation. 'You know you're the one he's going home with?'

'I know.'

A couple of Luke's band mates come over to join us, but Luke is still stuck signing autographs.

'What did you think?' Cody asks, gazing at Sarah as if his wellbeing rests solely on her answer. He's clearly got a huge crush on her, even though Sarah is totally oblivious to it. She's never had any idea how stunning she is. She has the most gorgeous long blonde hair, currently held back with a sparkly headband covered in stars, and totally straight, whereas mine has always been mousy brown and has this annoying kink to it that means it never sits quite right in any style I attempt. I've dyed it red now, mainly just to annoy my mum and dad, but I'd give anything to have hair like Sarah's.

'It was amazing,' Sarah says with total sincerity. 'That regrets song . . .' She places her hands on her heart.

'Did it work out OK?'

'Perfect. That bit you added the other day lifted it to a whole new level.'

'Ah, thanks, Sar.' Cody flashes his adorable dimples, pushing his long dark hair off his face.

'How about you, Laura? Did you enjoy it?' Rich, the guitarist, this time. He's the joker of the group, always pratting around.

'Yeah, it was good.'

'Only good, hey?' Luke comes up behind me, putting

his arms around my waist, and I can't help the thrill I feel. I'm not getting ahead of myself – we've only slept together a handful of times. But it beats my usual Thursday night sitting on the sofa with Mum and Dad watching *EastEnders*, our tea on trays on our laps.

'I've seen better,' I tease.

'Ooh, hit me where it hurts, why don't you?' Luke leans over, manoeuvring my straw into his mouth and taking a long sip. 'But did you like it, really?' he asks when he's finished drinking, an almost childlike look in his eyes.

'I really enjoyed it.'

'I guess that's as good as I'm going to get.' He laughs and leans towards me, his mouth so close to my neck I can feel my hairs standing on end. 'You look amazing by the way.'

'Thanks. You look *reasonable*.'

In truth, he looks like a god; his jeans hanging beneath the waistband of his boxers, his pale jumper highlighting his gorgeous mocha skin.

'Reasonable enough to tempt you to stay at mine tonight?'

Before I can respond, two girls come over clutching beer mats, putting their bodies between mine and Luke's to make it clear they don't want me around.

'Can we have your autograph? You were amazing,' one of the girls swoons.

Luke gives me a sly wink and I smile back at him and then he starts chatting to the girls whilst signing their beer mats, and I join in with the others' conversation.

'But would you really want to erase them from your mind forever?' Rich says.

'Yep,' Sarah replies without hesitation.

'Isn't it better to have loved and lost than never to have loved at all?' Cody chips in.

'Well, yeah, but I don't want to have to remember it. I'd be right there with Kate Winslet, getting old Jim wiped from my mind in a flash.'

Both blokes laugh. They're talking about *Eternal Sunshine of the Spotless Mind*. Sarah and I watched it a couple of weeks ago and we've already had this debate several times.

'I'm with Sarah,' I say, taking a sip of my cocktail before adding, 'Why would you want to experience all that heartache and regret? Mind wiped, move on.'

'But surely there'd be good memories too?' Cody argues.

'Like the sex,' Rich chips in. 'That's useful for the wank bank.'

Cody punches him in the arm. 'I was meaning more the memories of the nice times you shared together.'

'It's easier for men,' Sarah says, shaking her head. 'It's not real heartache.'

Rich looks mock-offended and puts his hands to his chest. 'You're breaking *my* heart right now, you realize?'

Sarah laughs, and the conversation drifts on to some band that they all went to see last week. As they chat, I find myself turning my body slightly so that I can watch Luke. One of the girls he's with poses for a photo with him, planting a lingering kiss on his neck as her friend takes several shots.

'Doesn't it make you feel amazing?' Sarah asks, holding on to my arm and leaning her head against my shoulder. 'Sleeping with the guy all these girls want to be sleeping with?'

I shrug.

'Imagine if they get really famous and you get to go on tour with him and stuff?' Sarah continues.

I feel a flutter in my chest at the thought. 'We both know he'll have moved on in a couple of weeks. But what are you always saying to me? "Live in the moment"? It's about time I had some fun.'

Sarah nestles into my shoulder. 'Good for you.'

And then suddenly Luke appears beside us. 'Can I borrow her?' he asks Sarah and then he holds his hand out to me. 'Want to dance?'

'All I Want for Christmas' has just started playing. I normally turn the stereo off the second I hear Mariah's dulcet tones but, holding on to Luke's hand, it sounds different.

'You do know she hates Christmas, don't you?' Sarah says.

Luke looks me up and down and then he slowly shakes his head. 'Well, we're going to have to do something about that.'

'Good luck. I've been trying to convert her for many, many years.'

'Who do you think made them put "Christmas jumper required" on the tickets? You're not going to get away with that nonsense with me.'

With that, Luke pulls me into the centre of the dance floor and kisses me right then and there. And we're still kissing when the song comes to an end.

As soon as we walk through the door to Luke's flat, I push him up against the wall and he pulls at my clothes, removing my jacket, lifting up my jumper and pulling down my bra, mouthing each one of my breasts before putting his hands under my skirt and moving my knickers to the side. I kiss his neck, my hands squeezing his bum and tugging at his belt until it releases, then he helps me remove his jeans and boxers. It's so intense it makes me feel lightheaded.

'You're so fucking sexy,' he whispers into my ear when we're finished, before pulling up his boxers. 'However many times I have sex with you, it's never enough.'

I know exactly what he means. Before Luke, I'd only ever slept with two blokes: my childhood sweetheart, Toby, who I lost my virginity to, and Oliver, who worked at Thomas Cook with me for a while. My first time was really sweet. We'd planned it for months. Toby had clearly put fresh bedding on because there was an overwhelming scent of Lenor and he'd put a red rose on the pillow and some romantic music on the stereo. He was gentle and kind but it wasn't exactly *passionate*. And with Oliver, I didn't even fancy him. I just sort of fell into it. So the few times I had sex with him, I was willing it to end and, irritatingly, he wore the fact that he could last for ages like some kind of medal.

But with *Luke* . . . With Luke, it feels like every part of me is on fire and I *never* want it to end.

'So what do you want to do now? Watch a film or something? Do you want a drink? I've got lager.'

'OK, go on then, thanks. I'll try and find a film to watch in your awful collection.'

'Careful or I'll make you watch *It's a Wonderful Life*.'

As Luke gets our drinks, I survey the DVD shelf in the alcove of his cosy lounge, a Christmas tree twinkling in the corner. It still seems amazing that he has his own place. I haven't told him I still live with my parents – that my dad comes and switches my bedside light out for me when I've fallen asleep reading, that Mum still makes me a packed lunch for work, for God's sake. On his top shelf, he has a row of books, all hardbacks – autobiographies of an eclectic mix of musicians from Anthony Kiedis to Bruce Springsteen and a few classic novels such as *On the Road* and *Catcher in the Rye*. When I first saw them, I thought he'd selected the books to make himself look interesting and cultured, but he can talk about them all in detail. His CD collection is equally impressive. Unlike my embarrassing mishmash of nineties boy bands, R'n'B and *Smash Hits*, his are all artists I've never even heard of. The only one of his DVDs I recognize is *Lost in Translation*, but we watched that the last time I was here so I pull out a couple of others (all art house stuff), select the one that sounds the least terrible and put the others back.

'Great choice,' Luke says, coming in with two bottles of lager in his hands.

'Best of a bad bunch.'

He laughs, lying down on the sofa and putting his arm out. 'Come on then. Get your butt over here.'

As we watch the film, he keeps saying things like, 'isn't that a really cool metaphor?' and 'do you notice how they keep using the same refrain?' Usually, I'd find it pretentious and off-putting, but he's so earnest that it just makes me wish that I had proper opinions on things like art and film and music. I've never really thought deeply about any of that stuff.

As the film draws to a close, Luke starts to run his fingers up and down my arm and I feel the inevitable tingling deep in the pit of my stomach. Within seconds, we're kissing and he's pulling my top over my head and throwing it on the floor. I grab at his top too and he takes it off but then he stops, kneeling up, his legs straddling me.

'What?' I ask, suddenly feeling self-conscious.

'I just want to look at you.'

I pull on his arm to bring him back down closer to me, but he resists and shakes his head. Then he starts to remove my bra and I stop him.

'What's wrong?'

'I just feel weird you staring at me.'

'Why wouldn't I want to stare at you?'

Looking up at him, his arms tensed to hold his weight, his flawless skin, he is, by quite some way, the most beautiful man I've ever seen, and it makes me want to cover myself with a blanket or turn out the lights. I've always worried my boobs are too small, my figure a little bit masculine. I remember when all my friends started wearing bras, so I did too, even though I didn't need one. And I waited and waited for my body to change, for puberty to hit, but my breasts never developed much further. I always hated it when summer came around and we went to the outdoor pool to meet the boys and I was the only one that looked like a little girl when the others all looked like women.

'Your body is perfect,' he says, pulling my skirt down. 'There's not a single part of it I would change.'

Feeling empowered by his words (and the several cocktails), I let him take off my underwear, knickers first and then my bra. There's undeniably something arousing about him surveying me, drinking me in, and when he starts slowly kissing every part of me, I'm no longer aware of any insecurity.

The sex is frantic, and I'm conflicted, as always – half wanting to slow it down, and half wanting to race to the finish line. And afterwards, as we lie there out of breath, I can't help wondering when we can do it again. It's *ridiculous*.

Luke reaches underneath the sofa to get a blanket and pulls it on top of our naked bodies and we just lie there for a while before he opens the conversation.

'So, which one was your favourite song? In our set tonight?'

I know exactly which one. As soon as he started singing it, it made my eyes fill with tears and a lump appear in my throat.

'The one about how he made her cry but she'd never felt as alive as she did when she was with him. Do you know the one I mean?'

Luke smiles and starts to sing the song. In the emptiness of the small room, his voice makes every hair on my body stand to attention and I'm glad that I'm lying on his chest, that he can't see my eyes.

'"Accidental Babies". It's the only one of the set that we didn't write. Oh, other than "Last Christmas", of course.'

'Sorry. The others were great too. It was just the way you sang that one, I think.'

Luke shakes his head. 'It's a beautiful song. I'm the first to admit we're not quite there with our writing yet. I'm not sure any of us have experienced the kind of heartache it requires to write a really amazing song. Or the type of love, for that matter.'

'Too busy having fun?'

Luke shrugs. 'I guess. How about you? You've not told me much about your past relationships. Have you been in love?'

'I don't think so, no.' I sit up and reach down for my unfinished bottle of lager and take a drink. 'So what are you going to do when the masters finishes?'

'We're going to go into the studio. Make an album.'

'Wow, that's great,' I say enthusiastically, despite wondering how he can say it without a trace of irony.

A pipe dream, my parents would call it. If I went home and said I was going into the studio to make an album, they'd look at me like my head wasn't on straight.

'How about you? What is it you really want to do?'

'Well, working at Thomas Cook is actually pretty great. I get loads of cheap travel.'

I purposefully use the word 'travel' rather than 'holidays' to make me sound more cultured.

'Yeah, but what about when you were little? When people asked you what you wanted to be, what did you say?'

'A princess?' I joke. 'I'm just kissing a few frogs until I find my prince.'

'A *few* frogs?'

I don't respond, leaving him to wonder, and then sit up and search for my underwear and T-shirt.

'You're not going, are you?'

'Just to get a glass of water. Unless you want me to get a taxi home?'

'Definitely not.'

The thought comes from nowhere: *I could fall madly in love with you.* But I'm well aware that developing feelings for someone like Luke is like ripping your heart out, trampling on it and then finishing it off with a sledgehammer. So I bury it, as deep as I can, like I'm on the beach and I'm covering it in sand.

'Meet you in bed?'

Luke raises his eyebrows. 'Again so soon?'

'I don't mean like that. I mean to sleep. Meet you in bed to sleep.'

'OK, deal. Bring me a couple of slices of chocolate orange, will you? Cupboard above the kettle by the window. And help yourself to anything.'

'Will do.'

LUKE

Whenever Laura comes over, I wish I'd remembered to hide all my embarrassing teenage memorabilia that I've got scattered around my bedroom. I have no idea why I brought it with me from home. The cringey film posters that I thought were cool at the time (*The Truman Show*, *Fear and Loathing in Las Vegas*), the photo collages of me with an array of awful haircuts or pulling moonies at the camera with my mates like an idiot. Usually, as I enter the bedroom with Laura, we're in the process of ripping each other's clothes off so I can keep the lights low and just steer her into bed, but tonight she's walking around looking at everything.

'Come to bed then, Nosy. Nothing to see here.'

'Scared I might find your stash of hard porn? A drawer of sex toys?'

'No. Nothing like that.'

'Love letters from your other women?'

'Oh yeah, a wardrobe full.'

'I bet fans send you their dirty knickers, don't they?'

I smile. 'Just get into bed, will you?'

'Was Paris as amazing as I imagine?' she asks, pointing to the photograph of me in front of the Eiffel Tower with my classmates.

'It was a school trip when I was fourteen so I'm not sure I really appreciated it, to be honest.'

'Did you have a gap year?'

'Yeah, I had a couple of years out after school. We did South America, but I didn't save enough to get to Thailand or Australia like a lot of my mates. I was a bit irresponsible, spending too much on nights out, impressing girls with fancy meals and expensive gifts.'

'And now you're twenty-five you've decided your sofa is enough of a good time, hey?'

I pick up a pillow and throw it at her. 'I hope I can impress in other ways.'

Laura raises her palms to the sky. 'Questionable.' Then she moves towards my Taekwondo medals, picking one up and reading it. 'Wow. Gold medal featherweight. A man of many talents, I see.'

I have no idea why I've got those on display. As soon as she's gone, that's the first thing that's getting tipped.

'It was a long time ago.'

'Why did you stop?'

'I just stopped enjoying it, I guess.'

Laura nods in a way that suggests she senses there is a little more to it but, thankfully, she doesn't ask any more questions. 'Maybe you could try some of your holds on me some time,' she says, coming over and climbing under the covers.

I pull her close and kiss the back of her neck. 'I'd like that.'

She turns over and puts her hand on my chest. 'But first I need sleep.'

Whenever I'm with Laura, it's like I have a permanent hard-on. I mean, I'm a bloke – I've always loved sex. But with Laura, it's different.

A few months ago, I actually started to wonder if there was something wrong with me. I was having this three-some with two girls I met after one of our gigs and I *yawned*. I just couldn't muster up any enthusiasm – even my anatomy stopped playing ball halfway through. I blamed it on drugs, even though I hadn't touched a thing, just in case word got out that the lead singer of Paradigm was impotent. I followed the experience with multiple one-night stands, just to check everything was still working (to be fair I was freaking the fuck out). And luckily my penis just about did its job, but I was desperate to leave each time.

And then I met Laura on a night out with Sarah and she wasn't like any of the other girls I'd met. She didn't spend every second telling me how amazing I was, and it made me realize how boring it had become – because I knew the attention was only because I was the lead singer in a band. It sounds a bit wet saying I wanted someone to like me for me (and the sudden jump from geeky kid who spent his lunch breaks on his own in the music room to bloke with girls actually *following* him around was of course very welcome), but it all just felt a bit fake sometimes, whereas Laura didn't bat an eyelid when I said I was in a band.

'OK, OK. As long as you promise I can have you again in the morning?' I say, wrapping my arms around her.

'It can possibly be arranged.'

She nestles into me, resting her head on my chest. I love it when she lies on me. The way she sort of melts into me like I'm a memory foam pillow.

'You know, when you stay over, I don't want to fall asleep because then it'll be morning and I know that you'll go.'

It sounds like a line. It would be a great line, but it's actually not.

'You say the sweetest things when you're drunk.'

'I'm not drunk. Well, not that drunk.'

'I'm not going to have sex with you right now no matter how sweet you are.'

'I'm not saying it so that you have sex with me again.'

'Invisibility or the ability to fly?'

She always changes the subject when we get anywhere in the vicinity of talking about emotions, but I go along with it.

'Invisibility definitely. Then I could spy on people. See what they say about me behind my back.'

Laura shakes her head. 'I wouldn't want to know.'

'Really? Why not?'

'Because what if someone you really liked said something horrible about you?'

'Then you'd tell them to sod off. Cut them out your life.'

'It's that simple, is it?'

'Of course. Why wouldn't it be? If someone's slating you behind your back and acting like you're their mate to your face, then they need sacking off.'

'I'd definitely fly. Then whenever you'd had enough of a situation you could just take off.'

'Where would you fly to?'

'I don't know. Somewhere hot. Somewhere quiet. A nice beach somewhere. A hammock swinging from the trees.'

'I'd fly on to the stage at Glastonbury, play a set to a sold-out crowd.'

'I'm sure you will one day.'

'I hope so.'

'I'll be able to watch you on TV and say, "I saw his willy once".'

'You did more than just see it. Anyway, who says we won't still be together?'

Laura laughs.

'I'm glad the thought of being in a lasting relationship with me is amusing to you.'

'I'm sorry. It's not that. It's just . . .'

'It's fine. I get it. You're just using me for my body until someone better comes along.'

'You poor, hard done by soul.'

'Sometimes I cry myself to sleep about it.'

'I bet you do.' Laura twiddles her hair, staring at the ceiling. 'So, is that the dream? Main stage at Glastonbury?'

'Oh, I want it all. Sell-out tours. Number one albums. Music is the only thing I've ever felt passionate about.'

'What about the Taekwondo?'

'Sometimes I think I just did that because Dad wanted me to. His dad hadn't let him do it so I think he was just living vicariously through me.'

'Yeah, I know what you mean. Sometimes it feels like Mum sees me as herself reincarnated. Like, through me, she can go back in time and erase her mistakes.'

'What mistakes are those?'

'Oh, she flunked out of school, got pregnant with me aged seventeen so she never really had a career and we always struggled for money. So to make sure I turned out differently, she forced me to go to grammar school, made me dress like a Mormon when I was a teenager.'

I laugh. 'I bet you still looked hot. So, are your parents still together?'

'Yep, since they were fifteen.'

'That's sweet.'

'Yours?'

I shake my head. 'Dad left when I was fourteen. Couldn't keep his dick in his pants.'

'Seems to be a common affliction for men.'

'Not for me.'

Laura nods but I get the sense she doesn't believe me.

'So will I get to meet them sometime?' I ask.

'My parents? God, no.'

'Oh, thanks.'

'I just mean, the whole being in a band thing. I think . . .'

'I wouldn't be good enough for them?'

'No, not that. They'd just think you were going to break my heart.'

'And what do you think?'

'As we established, I'm just using you for your body so, no, I think my heart is pretty safe.'

'Good to know. For what it's worth, I think my mum would really like you. Obviously, unless she knew you were just using me for sex.'

'Do you think?'

'I do. And she's very fussy.'

'But clearly a woman of taste.' Laura pulls the cover up over her shoulder. 'Anyway, I might have to call it a night. I'm exhausted.'

It's true what I said earlier. I *do* hate it when she goes to sleep because I know that she won't hang around in the morning (she never does) and I don't know when I'll see her next. And there's so much more I want to find out about her. I don't want this to just be a thing where we go home together after a night out. And yet I'm not sure how to make it something more – or if she even wants to.

I sit up in bed, knowing that I have to seize the moment. We only have one life, right, and I plan on living every ounce of mine.

'No, we're going out.'

Laura rolls on to her back, a bemused expression on her face. 'What do you mean, we're going out?'

'I mean we're going out.' I grab my jeans and jumper off the floor and start getting dressed.

Laura sits up, leaning against the headboard. 'It's the early hours of the morning. It's December. It's freezing! Where are we going?'

I find her clothes and pass them to her. 'We're going on our first date.'

'You do realize we've been seeing each other for nearly three months?'

'I know. But I've never taken you out, not properly, and I need to rectify that.'

'In the middle of the night?' she asks, getting dressed albeit with a sceptical look on her face.

'No time like the present. You finish getting ready. I'll be back in a second.'

I quickly rush into the kitchen, grabbing some more lagers out the fridge (in lieu of champagne) and a half-eaten pack of mince pies. Then I pull the throw off the sofa, get some candles and a lighter, and shove it all in a rucksack. When I get back to the bedroom Laura is fully dressed, so I take her hand and, on the way out, I help her into my parka. It's ridiculously long on her. She puts the hood up, her face looking tiny amongst the fur.

I grab a torch and we walk for about fifteen minutes, Laura asking where we're going the whole way, until we reach a stile.

'We're going over there.'

Laura raises an eyebrow but climbs over the stile. 'Good job I'm wearing my Uggs and not heels, although you're going to be in trouble if they get muddy.'

We walk through the field – luckily it's frozen rather than squelchy – until we are well away from all the lights of the town.

'Right. Stop here.' I take the throw out of my rucksack and spread it out on the grass and then shine my torch on it. 'Lie down, please.'

'You do realize I'm not going to have sex with you out here?'

I laugh, lighting the candles I brought and putting them around the edge and then lying down on the throw on my back and, with definite hesitation, Laura follows. I wrap my arm around her and pull the leftover edges of the throw around us. 'I thought we could watch the stars.'

It's a clear night and the universe is giving me a huge gift because the sky looks incredible.

I expect Laura to make a sarcastic comment, and as I feel her shivering, I wonder if this is a really stupid idea, but then she says, 'It's beautiful, isn't it?'

We lie there staring up, the stars sparkling like a Christmas decoration.

'It makes you feel really insignificant, doesn't it? Realizing we're just a tiny part of all this.'

'I don't know. I think it makes me feel special.'

Laura turns her head to look at me but doesn't say anything.

'Sometimes I come here when I can't get a song quite right or something. Helps to clear my head.'

'I can't believe I've never done it before.'

'You haven't lived.'

Laura looks pensive for a moment but then she says, 'So this is our first date, is it?'

'It is.'

'Well, it's a good one.'

She rests her head on my chest and I'm glad that she can't see the huge smile that I'm unable to keep from my face. We talk about the band, our school days (I leave out the fact that I was a total loser who got bullied daily). She asks questions about uni and I wonder why she didn't go, because she's clearly super bright. We talk about the planets and constellations and how we can't get our heads around the fact that the starlight we're seeing set off years, decades or even millennia ago.

And then I remember the bottles of lager and half-eaten pack of mince pies and sit up and reach for my rucksack. 'I almost forgot. I brought refreshments.' I lay the items out on the throw between us.

Laura sits up beside me and shakes her head. 'Damn. It was going so well.'

'I know it's not a very impressive spread. Lager and mince pies are a bit of an odd combination, aren't they?'

'It's not the combination. It's just *mince pies*.' She mimes being sick.

I laugh. 'You can't have Christmas without mince pies.'

'You can. I do. And I will for evermore.'

'This could be a deal breaker, you know?' I take a mince pie out of the packet and gobble it messily in front of her.

'This must be how it feels for a vegetarian when they have to sit watching someone else chomping on a hunk of dead animal.'

'I make no apologies.' I open a bottle of lager and hand it to her and then open one for myself. 'What are you doing for Christmas anyway? Are you going away? Staying around here?'

Laura looks at her bottle. 'I'm around.'

'Well, if you wanted to get together, we could go for a drink? Or I'm sure Mum would welcome one more. I don't think I offer her much challenge in the Trivial Pursuit stakes.'

'Steady on, Luke. You're inviting me over for Christmas?'

I glare at her. 'Don't take the piss.'

'You do realize that is basically like proposing.'

'It's fine. You clearly have bigger and better plans.'

Laura snorts. 'We don't really do Christmas. Dad says it's just commercial nonsense. I have tried telling him it's actually something to do with the baby Jesus but he's not buying it, so it's generally a fairly quiet affair.'

'Oh, I always try to make it special for Mum. Dad was a massive Christmas fan, so we'd always have the biggest tree and fancy food and a floor full of presents. He used to do this silly family quiz about all the things we'd done over the year.' I'm surprised that the words get stuck, and I clear my throat. 'Since he left, I've always tried to make a fuss of Mum. We go to midnight mass on Christmas Eve. We're not religious but Mum says she likes the sense of community. Then we go home and open one present each.'

'That's really sweet.'

'Well, if you want to come over for a bit, you're very

welcome. I'll hide the mince pies. I might even buy you a present.'

'I guess I could pop over in the evening if your mum really doesn't mind? I don't want to intrude.'

'Perfect.' It's stupid but, knowing that Laura is coming, I feel the same sort of excitement about Christmas that I used to as a little kid. 'But prior to that, I think we need to squeeze in a second date. Before we progress to meeting the parents and all that.'

Laura smiles.

'I mean, I can't promise a date of this quality again,' I continue. 'But any ideas? What would you like to do?'

'I don't know.' She sighs. 'Just take me out of my comfort zone. I have been stuck there for far too long.'

'You sound like you're forty-two, not twenty-two.'

'Sorry. It's just this town sometimes. Do you ever feel like real life is out there somewhere and we're just wasting our days stuck in Lanmouth where the most exciting event on the social calendar is wreath-making at the town hall?'

'When we first moved from London a couple of years ago, I was a bit like, "what the hell do people *do* around here?" but now I really like it. Especially with the band – I'm hoping we'll get to travel quite a bit with that, so it'll be nice to have somewhere like this to come back to.'

'Well, yeah. I guess it's different for you. For you it's like a quaint little getaway – oh look, what's this strange green stuff? And that cotton wool ball with legs and a head, how cute . . .'

I roll my eyes.

'It's different when you've always lived here,' she continues. 'When you'll probably *always* live here.'

'So move away.'

'I love how simple life is for you.' She shakes her head. 'Anyway, just surprise me.'

'Sky diving?'

'God, no. I'm not all that keen on being *inside* a plane, let alone jumping out of one. I'd love to go up in a hot air balloon one day though, but maybe not in December, hey?'

'By the sounds of things, I better start earning a bit more money.'

Laura laughs and shakes her head. 'It really doesn't have to be anything fancy. I mean, this is great.'

'I think I can do better than this.' I finish my lager and then put the bottle back in my rucksack. 'Right, I'm going to make it my mission. This will be your best Christmas ever. Starting with a mind-blowing second date.'

She looks at me as if she thinks it's bullshit, all just fake charm, so I kiss her under the stars to show her that I'm serious, with a determination in my belly to prove her wrong.

16th December 2005

LUKE

'Will you marry me?'

'You're seriously asking me right now?'

'Uh, yes.'

It's probably not the most romantic time to ask her. I hadn't planned on doing it now, when she's writhing in pain. To be honest, I hadn't really planned to do it anytime in the near future. But then, watching her, I felt this overwhelming awe and the words just popped out.

'I'm huge and sweaty and I keep pulling funny faces and . . . argh.' She stops bouncing on the birthing ball and moves on to all fours again, and I know that there's nothing I can say or do. She seems to travel somewhere else for a few seconds, somewhere unreachable, and then the pain passes and she's back, making jokes and bouncing up and down like a kid on a space hopper.

There's a tap on the door and then the midwife reappears. 'How's it going in here? All still under control? How far apart are the contractions now?'

I check my watch. 'They're still three minutes.'

'OK, great. Feeling like you need to push, Laura?'

'No, not yet.'

'Is it OK if I just have a quick listen in again? Shall we wait for the next one to pass first?'

'Sounds like a plan.' Laura pushes her hair off her face, the strands all stuck to her forehead. 'Luke just asked me to marry him. Is that really romantic or just wrong?'

The midwife smiles. 'I'd say romantic.'

Laura looks at me and then suddenly she's getting off the ball again and puffing like a steam train. When the contraction passes, she lies back on the floor whilst the midwife puts the Doppler to her bump, the reassuring sound of our baby's heartbeat filling the room. However many times I hear it, it still blows my mind. That one day, nine months ago, we had sex and that simple act created a beating *heart*. At the time, Laura was tracking her cycle and it was like clockwork. Except that month it obviously *wasn't* like clockwork and one moment of passion when I uttered the fateful words, 'we won't need a condom this far out, will we?' led us here.

'Yes,' she says, turning her head and looking over at me from her position on the floor.

'Yes what?'

'Yes, I'll marry you.'

'You're sure?'

'If you can look at me right now and still want to marry me, then yes, I'm very sure.'

I go over to kiss her, the midwife subtly moving out of the room to give us some privacy, but just as I reach Laura, she rolls over in pain.

'I want to get in the water. I don't think it will be long. I'm determined to get this baby out before Christmas.'

I force a laugh but my chest feels as tight as a guitar string.

Laura peels off the pads from the TENS machine she's been using to help with the pain and I take it, unravelling the wires and putting it away in its case. It feels good to do something useful for a second. Ever since the contractions started, I've felt so helpless, and Laura being Laura, she's been so stoic that I've felt like a spectator, like she could do just as well without me. Well, obviously not the making the baby bit, but the birthing it.

Once she gets into the water, she seems to enter a trance-like state, sucking on the gas and air at regular intervals and then deep-breathing her way through the gaps.

'It's like a spa. Just with drugs instead of herbal tea,' I joke because I don't know what the hell to do.

If Laura hears me, she doesn't respond. And then suddenly she starts making these low, almost otherworldly sounds and two midwives rush in. I reach out for Laura's hand and am glad when she takes it, squeezing it as if to acknowledge that I'm here.

The next bit passes in a bit of a blur and all I feel is pure terror. Seeing Laura in such pain makes my thoughts race – what if she's not OK? What if the baby's not OK? And then the midwife asks me if I want to see the head and I'm not sure I do considering what it's sticking out of, but curiosity gets the better of me and I lean round to see my baby's face peering up at me from the water.

'Can it breathe?' I ask, panicked.

The midwife smiles. 'Yes, don't worry. Baby is still attached to Mum so he or she breathes through the umbilical cord. Baby is perfectly safe.'

The baby has a fair bit of hair and a little scrunched-up face. I'd like to say it's beautiful but it looks like a gremlin.

When Laura first showed me the pregnancy test, I looked into her eyes expecting to see the panic that felt like it was blocking my throat, but all I saw there was a sparkling light. She sent me out to the shop to get more tests to double-check and when I got to the supermarket I rang Sarah because I thought Laura would have already told her (she tells Sarah most things before me) but she hadn't. The first thing Sarah said was 'Her parents are going to lose their shit' followed by 'Does she want to keep it?'

And it was such a relief to hear her ask the question because Laura seemed so *sure*, and to me it felt like someone had just built a wall across the road in front of me. What the hell was I going to do with a baby? The band was just taking off. If things went to plan, we were going to be touring. Plus I was just a stupid dumb boy. I couldn't be a father.

Sarah said I should tell Laura how I felt, but I knew I had to step up and live with the consequences. So I begged her to never tell Laura about our conversation, took a deep breath and went to find the pregnancy tests, smuggling them through the checkout underneath a box of Weetabix, as if I was trying to get drugs through security. Then I painted on my happiest face and drove home.

And over time, as the shock subsided, I came round to the idea of us having a child together. I've even felt quite excited – decorating the nursery (we decided on a safari theme), buying babygrows and tiny nappies that didn't even look big enough to fit a kitten. But now, as Laura suddenly makes the deep inhuman sound again, I feel like sprinting from the room.

But Laura is still holding me tightly by the hand – and within moments the midwife is reaching down, grabbing our baby and passing it straight to Laura, who turns around and leans against the edge of the pool, the water turning pink. And as soon as its tiny body is in her arms, Laura stares at it with such adoration and awe that it makes me question whether I'm going to feel what I should, whether I'm ready to say goodbye to the ease – the *freedom* – that was life before this.

'Is it a boy or a girl?' Laura asks, her voice shaky as she lifts our baby to the surface of the water so that I can see.

'It's a boy.'

At the twenty-week scan, being the impatient person that I am, I was desperate to find out the sex, but Laura was adamant that she wanted it to be a surprise. And as, in her words, she was the one risking stretch marks, needing to get up for a wee every hour, her boobs turning into 'udders' – it was her that got the final say.

Now, knowing it's a boy, I feel this overwhelming pressure to better myself, to be a decent role model and make sure that he becomes a good man. But what if I'm like my dad and one day I wake up and realize that I can't do it? That I'm a spineless, useless twat who only has room to care about myself? Wasn't my dad once a decent bloke with good intentions?

The midwife helps to put the baby back on to Laura's chest (I'm suddenly incapable of holding a seven-pound object) and she kisses the top of his head. She's a natural. It's like she was destined to become a mother.

After a while, Laura looks up at me, her eyes a little tired. 'Do you want to hold him?'

'Uh . . .'

What if I drop him? Hold him wrongly, not supporting his head well enough, and cause him some sort of irreparable damage?

'Are you sure? I mean, do you want to do more skin-to-skin? I can wait.'

Laura smiles. 'Thank you for clearly listening to my birth plan. But I'm sure that I want you to hold your son and I want to get out of this water and dry off. Then, yes, in a few minutes I will be grabbing him back.'

I lean down and kiss her. 'I'm so proud of you.'

With my heart smashing against the inside of my chest, I take my son in my arms and he looks up at me with these knowing blue eyes and it feels like he's telling me 'time to grow up now, Dad', and it's the strangest feeling; like a new chamber of my heart is opening up, this sudden capacity to love harder and deeper than I even knew was possible. And as my baby boy starts to cry, I realize that I have a choice. To step up or run away. So I bring my son on to my shoulder, kiss the top of his head and stroke his back.

'Welcome to the world, Dylan.'

Laura is being supported by the midwives, a towel wrapped around her, but she looks over and smiles at me with tears in her eyes.

We went back and forth about names for months. We bought books, searched the internet, sifted through our favourite novels in the hope we'd find something. We agreed on a girl's name fairly quickly. Arietti (from *The Borrowers*). But finding a boy's name proved altogether trickier. I suggested Caleb but Laura didn't like it. She liked Aaron but I've never understood the need for the double 'a'. And then one evening I was in the spare room playing my guitar and she walked in, as always with a huge mug of tea cupped in her hands, the cutest baby bump I've ever seen, and just said, 'It's Dylan,' and I understood straight away what she was talking about and said, 'Yes, it is.'

I rock from side to side. And gradually Dylan settles, his whimpering ceasing. And I feel like I've achieved more in this moment than I have in my whole life.

'Baby whisperer,' Laura says, looking up at me from where she is now positioned on the bed with a blanket over her, her knees raised and a midwife at her bottom-half doing something that I'd rather not think about. The fact the midwife is now wearing a Christmas hat makes the whole thing feel slightly surreal.

'I think it's my dancing.'

'Maybe he's got his daddy's sense of rhythm.' Laura gazes at him. 'He's pretty beautiful, isn't he?'

I look at my son's face, which is turned towards me, resting on my shoulder. 'He's the most amazing thing I've ever seen.'

I feel tears rising in my throat again and want to slap myself. *Get a grip, buddy.*

'How are we ever going to get anything done?' Laura asks. 'We're just going to spend all our time staring at him.'

I smile. 'I'll still stare at you a bit too, you know?'

The midwife finishes what she's doing. 'I'll go and make you both a cup of tea. Toast as well?'

We both nod and she leaves us to it, so I sit on the bed next to Laura, lowering myself carefully for fear of dropping our son.

'Do you want him back now?'

Laura stares at him. 'I should probably leave him. He looks happy on you.'

'He'll be even happier on you,' I say, sensing her desperate desire to have him back in her arms. I lower him on to her chest where he continues to sleep peacefully.

Laura nods her head towards the door, which is lined with tinsel. 'December the sixteenth.' She shakes her head. 'I mean, I'm glad it's not Christmas Day, but the poor kid is going to end up with joint presents, never really having a party because everyone's too busy with Christmas stuff . . .'

'I promise we'll make his birthday special every year. Anyway, this date was already significant for another reason. Don't you remember?'

'No, what?'

'It was our first date.'

'The stargazing?'

I nod. I remember the date because it was the night we did the show at the Roundtree. The night the talent scout spotted us, which set the ball rolling to where we are now, recording our first studio album.

'Really? I can't believe that was exactly a year ago. Maybe that's why he was overdue. He was destined to arrive today.'

I smile. 'It was also the day I realized I was in love with you.'

'What? But we'd only been seeing each other for a few months.'

'I know. I still knew. It's OK if you didn't feel the same.'

Dylan snuffles and Laura strokes his back. 'As much as it pains me, I realized I was in love with you on Christmas Day.'

'Christmas Day? The irony! How come?'

'Your mum was showing me that memory book you'd made for her and I remember thinking how thoughtful you were and how beautiful it was that you loved your mum that much.'

'I can't believe I didn't know that.'

'There's lots you don't know about me.' Laura smiles. 'So, how did you know you loved me on our first date?'

'You asked me to take you out of your comfort zone and I realized that I cared as much about making you happy as I did about being happy myself. I'd never felt like that before. Always been a bit of a selfish bastard, truth be told.'

Laura reaches out and grabs my hand. 'Well, you did. Make me happy, I mean.'

After the night with the stars, I booked us a snowboarding lesson for our second date and she spent the whole evening berating me because she could barely sit down her bum was so black and blue from all the falls, but a couple of weeks later she asked me if we could go again so I think she secretly enjoyed it. And I hope I gave her a decent Christmas Day. She came over to Mum's in the evening and I tried to give her some of the things it sounded like she'd missed out on as a kid – I filled a stocking full of silly presents, made her play 'pin the nose on the reindeer' and charades. Mum adored her immediately and they spent the evening ganging up on me during the annual game of Trivial Pursuit.

'I *made* you happy? Past tense?'

Laura kisses the top of Dylan's head. 'Look at me. What do you think?'

'I think you're amazing. I mean, the way you just did all that . . .'

'I didn't have much choice,' Laura jokes.

I shake my head. 'You were so brave. So calm. I would've been a screaming mess. Or I'd have passed out. Or just got them to give me loads of drugs or put me to sleep and cut him out of me.'

Laura laughs. 'It probably *is* a good thing I'm the one that had to give birth.'

'Seriously though, I promise I'm going to do my best to be a good dad. To not totally screw him up.'

'You're going to be an amazing dad.'

'I hope so.'

Because, although it might have taken until meeting Dylan for me to fully realize it, there's nothing in the world I want more.

LAURA

I never imagined I'd be having a baby aged twenty-three and yet, lying here with Dylan on my chest, his little breaths so soft and shallow, the way he snuffles every now and then, the feel of his skin, like paper, I'm certain that this is exactly how my life should be.

Luke and I eat toast from paper plates covered in tiny robins and I regularly wipe the crumbs out of Dylan's soft, downy hair. It's black, like Luke's, and thicker than I expected. I worried that I wouldn't find him beautiful. That the rush of love people talk about wouldn't come. But the reality is it feels like my heart might break with it. That it isn't big enough to contain everything I'm feeling.

Luke's phone keeps making this jingly bells sound whenever a message comes in. His ringtone is even worse – a distorted 'Last Christmas' blaring out whenever someone calls him.

He takes it out of a pocket. 'I expect I've got at least ten messages from Sarah.'

I laugh. 'She did say she wanted to visit as soon as the baby arrived.'

'I'm surprised she didn't battle her way into the birth.' Luke taps on his phone. 'Mum says can she come and see us when we get home. Is that OK?'

'Of course. You don't have to ask. She can come here if she wants.'

'No, it's OK. I'll wait until we're home then you can have a nap whilst Mum and I deal with Dylan.'

I nod, sad that my mum isn't chomping at the bit to visit. My phone's in my bag somewhere but I know she won't have been in touch. She sent a brief message on my due date to wish me luck but she hasn't been in touch since, while Dylan has kept us waiting.

I waited until I was starting to show to tell her and Dad. I was terrified. Sitting in front of the TV, Mum served me up a noticeably smaller portion of shepherd's pie than usual and then mentioned a local gym that was offering three months free.

'I saw a big poster on the wall as I was driving past,' she said. 'No joining fee or anything.'

'I'm not fat. I'm pregnant.'

Mum nearly spat out her mince and potato. 'You're *what*?'

'Pregnant, Mum. I'm sorry.'

I'm still angry with myself for apologizing because I hadn't done anything wrong and I don't regret it. But the look of utter disappointment on their faces made me want to beg for forgiveness. And then Mum said, 'Are you too far gone to get rid of it?' and I ran upstairs in tears and packed as much stuff as I could into all the old rucksacks I could find. Mum came up to say she hadn't meant to upset me but then reeled off a list of reasons why having a baby at that time wasn't a good idea – predominantly that I hadn't yet made anything of my life and that I'd only known Luke a few months and it was likely he was going to break my heart. She didn't use those exact words but it was clear what she was saying.

I told her I was going to move in with Luke. He'd already

asked me to but I'd felt a strange loyalty to Mum and Dad, not yet ready to leave them on their own, but I guess more fool me because they've barely contacted me since I left. A couple of months ago, Mum left a bag of babygrows outside the door of Luke's flat, but that's as close as she's got to showing any sort of acceptance.

Luke puts his phone back in his pocket, stroking my hair and looking into my eyes to show me his attention is firmly back on me.

'I can't believe we're going to take him home,' I say.

It feels impossible. That he'll soon be lying in the bed-side cot we put up a few weeks ago, just in case he came early. The authorities that be are trusting us with a *baby*. We've had such little guidance. It's just like, 'Here's a baby. Now bring it up.' You get more instructions for looking after a pot plant.

'Well, I think he'd be a bit fed up if we left him here.'

With a click, the door opens – the tinsel getting caught and pulling away from the wall – and in walks a ginormous bunch of flowers followed by a beaming Sarah.

'I came straight away. I'm sorry. I'm just so excited.'

Luke gets up, takes the flowers off her and then gives her a big hug. 'We're glad you're here.'

'Oh, I'm so happy for you guys. My two gorgeous friends and their gorgeous new son.' She sits on the bed beside me and strokes Dylan's hair. 'He is just the most perfect little thing I've ever seen. I could eat him.'

'Please don't,' Luke jokes. 'Talking of eating, that toast barely touched the sides. All this giving birth stuff means we missed lunch. I'm going to go and grab something from the hospital café. Do either of you want anything?'

I shake my head.

'No. Just to sit and stare at this one all day long if that's OK?' Sarah says, her eyes fixed firmly on Dylan.

Luke smiles. 'Be back soon.'

'Do you want to hold him?'

Sarah looks at me like I just offered her a rent-free beach house in Malibu and nods, tears dampening her eyes.

I hand Dylan over, a little reluctantly it must be said, and he wriggles around but then settles on to Sarah's shoulder, his face nestling into her neck.

'Sit on that chair if it's more comfortable.'

Sarah stands up as if she's balancing ten plates on her head and then sits down in the chair just as carefully.

'I have to admit, I thought you guys were a bit crazy having this little one, but now I'm just jealous. He is so beautiful.'

'It wasn't exactly planned, was it?'

'I know, but I mean keeping him. It was a brave decision, that's all.'

'You didn't ever think I should get rid of him though, did you? You never mentioned it.'

Sarah focuses her eyes on Dylan and shakes her head. 'Of course I didn't think that. I wanted you to do whatever made you happy.' She looks up at me. 'But it would be OK if you'd considered it. It's a *lot*. And we're still pretty young.'

'We're not that young.'

'You're right. I'm sure I spotted my first grey hair the other day.'

I smile. 'That never even crossed my mind, you know? I know the timing isn't exactly perfect, but to be honest what else would I be doing with my life?'

'There's loads you can do with your life, Laur. Baby or no baby. Don't think like that.'

I wave away her objection. 'I just mean he hasn't interrupted any big plans. I'm really happy.'

Sarah reaches out and holds my hand. 'And I'm really happy for you.'

We sit in silence for a while, both of us entirely focused on Dylan's face.

'He asked me to marry him.'

'What?' Sarah looks up at me. 'Oh, that's amazing. I'm guessing you said yes?'

'I did.'

'So why do I sense some sort of reservation?'

I let out a deep breath. 'Do you think it's just because of Dylan? There's no way he would've asked me if I hadn't got pregnant, would he?'

'He loves you, Laur. Why do you find that so hard to believe?'

I shrug. 'Look at him.'

'Look at *you*.'

'Do you think my parents will come to the wedding?' I ask, changing the subject.

'Yes. I do.'

'I'm not so sure. And what is Luke's mum going to think of them? Talk about coming from different sides of the track.'

'It's like *Notting Hill*.'

'Oh yeah, except Hugh Grant comes from Notting Hill, not Hillview.'

Sarah laughs. '*Pretty Woman* then.'

'I'm not a prostitute.'

45

Our laughter causes Dylan to stir and he starts thrashing his head back and forth on Sarah's shoulder and then crying, a feeble sound at first but soon gaining momentum.

'Wow, he's got a pair of lungs on him,' Sarah says, handing him back.

'Thanks. So you get the good bit and I get the tears?'

'That's what being an "aunty" is all about, isn't it?'

I stroke Dylan's back and sing 'Rock a Bye Baby' softly into his ear and then Sarah joins in. Dylan starts nuzzling into my chest and I lower the cover and move his nose closer to my nipple like the midwife showed me, feeling like when you start a new job and have to keep asking inane questions like where the coffee is kept and how to use the photocopier. Thankfully, within seconds he's latched on and he starts sucking. It's the strangest feeling – being the one to provide the very thing that keeps someone else alive.

'You're a natural.'

'I'm not sure about that.'

Sarah sits back down. 'Are you OK?'

I feel tears forming and wipe them away, careful not to dislodge Dylan. 'It just suddenly feels like I have so much to lose.'

'Oh, Laur. You've just had a baby. Your hormones are going to be all over the shop. It's normal to feel overwhelmed.'

I nod, hopeful that's all it is.

'Do you remember when we were little and you made that amazing science project for that competition at school?' Sarah continues. 'That model of the rainforest showing all the different layers and what lived there?'

Mum and I had worked on it all weekend. I think she

was determined to show all the middle-class parents at school that we could do just as well as them, and we'd had so much fun. Making the trees out of cardboard and tissue paper and then making all the little animals and insects from Fimo. I remember her sending Dad out to get us McDonald's because we were 'far too busy to cook' and he got us strawberry milkshakes as a treat. That was a great weekend.

'Remember how when you showed me I said you were definitely going to win and you said you wouldn't. You weren't just being humble, were you?'

'I just didn't think it was that good.'

'But it was. And that's just you, Laur. You're a winner. You just don't realize it.'

I give her a half-smile. 'Thank you.'

Luke wanders back in, a coffee in one hand, a doughnut in the other, and a cuddly giraffe wearing a tiny Christmas jumper tucked under his arm. He nods his head towards Dylan, who has fallen asleep whilst feeding, every now and again doing these three short sucks and then stopping.

'You better not get too comfy on there, son. I'm having those babies back at some point.'

Sarah uses her cardigan to whip him on the arm. 'Don't be gross, Luke.'

'I'm not. Just want him to know he's only borrowing them.'

Sarah and I both laugh and, as Luke comes nearer, I grab the doughnut out of his hand.

'You said you weren't hungry.'

I take a huge bite. 'Just a tiny bit.'

Luke shakes his head and looks at Sarah. 'She always

does this. "No, I'm not hungry. I don't want anything." Gobble gobble gobble.'

I give him the remains of the doughnut back. 'I *am* feeding another human being here.' I screw up my face. 'Anyway, what's wrong with that doughnut? It tastes odd.'

Luke pauses, his mouth full of the remains of the doughnut he has stuffed in, probably so that I don't have the chance to steal any more. But then he can't stop himself laughing, crumbs escaping his mouth as he does. 'It's a mince-pie-flavoured doughnut.'

'What messed-up nonsense is that?'

Sarah's now laughing as well. 'Oh, you've discovered her aversion to mince pies? Weirdo, isn't she?'

'I'm weird? He bought a mince-pie-flavoured doughnut.'

'Sure to become a classic,' Luke says, rubbing his hands together to brush off the sugar.

'What's that anyway?' I nod my head towards the cuddly toy.

'Oh, it's for Dylan. Geoff the giraffe.'

'Geoff? Did you come up with that?'

'Yes. It's good, isn't it?' Luke holds the giraffe to my lips and makes a loud kissing sound and I smile. 'Do you like his little jumper?'

'Does everything we buy, do and eat have to be Christmas-themed throughout the whole of December?'

'Absolutely,' Luke says. 'I am going to convert you into a Christmas lover even if it kills me.'

'Good luck with that,' Sarah chips in.

'Oh, by the way, the midwife said as long as he is feeding OK then we can go whenever you're ready.'

I'm suddenly terrified. 'Are *you* ready?'

'Yeah, but no rush. You're the one that's just pushed a

seven-pound baby out your bits.' Luke shivers. 'In fact, let's not talk about that.'

Dylan has slipped off the nipple so I hand him to Luke and slowly sit up, feeling sore, and Sarah helps me get dressed. Luke gently lowers Dylan into the car seat, putting Geoff the giraffe with his ridiculous Christmas jumper next to him. Seeing him in there, Dylan looks so tiny, like a doll, especially as the giraffe is bigger than him.

'Do you think the straps are tight enough?'

Luke puts his hand between the strap and Dylan's chest. 'They said in Halfords you should be able to fit a finger in the gap.'

'It's not too tight, is it? It's not hurting him?'

Luke comes over and puts his hands on my shoulders. 'He's going to be fine.'

It takes the three of us about an hour to get the car seat in the car; at first plugging it in too early so that we can't manage to stretch the belt around the back. Then we get the belt all twisted. And then we keep doing it and undoing it because we worry that it's too loose. Eventually, we say our goodbyes to Sarah and then I sit in the back of the car beside Dylan, holding the seat tightly and checking every few seconds that he's still breathing, that Geoff the giraffe isn't smothering him.

Once we get home, Luke helps me on to the sofa, covering me with a blanket, and I drift in and out of consciousness while Luke sits with Dylan. When I'm awoken by a knock on the door, it feels like I've been asleep for a week, but the clock says it's only been about twenty minutes.

'Shall I get it or do you want to just pretend we're not here?' Luke asks.

'I'll get it. You stay there with Dylan.'

I push myself up, everything hurting, and shuffle to the door. When I open it, I immediately feel like I want to cry but manage to stop myself.

'Luke messaged me. I brought you chocolate,' Mum says, her eyes looking like they might fill up too as she hands me three huge bars of Dairy Milk. 'When I gave birth to you, everyone brought flowers or cuddly toys and I remember thinking "What use is that? I'm exhausted and starving".'

I smile. 'Thank you. And you're right. It's exactly what I need.'

'So how are you doing? Sore?'

'Yeah. A bit. But he seems to be doing well.'

Mum nods. 'I'm sure you'll be fine.'

There's a moment of silence where it seems as if neither of us knows what to say. 'I was going to message. We only just got home and I've been dozing.'

'It's fine. I like the name, by the way. Like *The Magic Roundabout*.'

'Thank you. I was thinking more Bob Dylan. Remember Dad used to sing along to "Tambourine Man" in that awful imitation Bob Dylan voice like he had something stuck up his nose?'

Mum smiles but there's a definite sense of sadness to it.

'Do you want to come in and see him?' I continue. 'He's just asleep on Luke but you can have a cuddle if you want?'

Mum looks past me into the room but then shakes her head. 'Don't disturb him. Number one rule: let sleeping babies lie, right? Besides, your dad is waiting in the car.'

'He can come in too, you know.'

'Oh, I don't think he's handling it very well – becoming

a granddad at forty. I think he might be having a mid-life crisis.' Mum laughs. 'He'll probably run off with some teenage girl soon.'

'OK. Well, some other time then.'

Luke comes to the door, Dylan asleep on his shoulder. He turns his body so that Dylan's facing Mum. 'Here he is.'

Mum looks at him and I see her swallow. 'He's lovely. Congratulations.'

'Do you want to come in for a cuppa?' Luke asks.

'No, I just said to Laura, Graham is waiting in the car. Another time. Take care though.'

She pauses and I wonder if she might give me a hug or maybe she's waiting to see if I give her one. When neither of us makes a move, she turns and walks down the path and I have to force myself not to run after her.

'You OK?'

I nod and close the door. 'I think I just need a lie-down.'

'Of course. Mum will be here soon anyway. We'll try to get the place a bit straight.'

There are a couple of cardboard boxes on the floor – one containing Luke's huge collection of reindeers in all materials and sizes and the other half-full of baubles. We were decorating the tree when my contractions started, so it stands there looking expectant.

'I might feed him first then hopefully I'll get a bit of a longer break.'

'Of course. Can I bring you anything? Cup of tea? Snacks?'

I shake my head and hold up the bars of chocolate. 'Think I've got enough supplies here.'

Luke hands me Dylan and I take him upstairs to the

bedroom. I throw the clothes off the nursing chair we bought in preparation and lower myself into it, sitting on the edge of one bum cheek because it feels like I've been stung by a thousand bees between my legs.

I unbutton my blouse and unhook my nursing bra, releasing one of my ginormous breasts. They are so grotesque, I wonder why I ever disliked my small, neat pair. I catch a glimpse of my stomach and it's all squidgy, like a balloon where the air has been released a bit. I didn't mind my pregnant bump because it was firm and smooth, but now the sight of my soft belly fills me with despair.

I hold Dylan's nose to my nipple again, and am relieved when, after a few wiggles of his head, he latches on and begins to suck and I find my eyes beginning to close, my head dropping to my shoulder.

When I wake up, there's a blanket covering me and Dylan's gone.

'Hey, sleepyhead,' Luke calls from our bed, Dylan asleep in the cot beside him.

'I'm sorry. I was feeding and then . . .'

'I think you're entitled to nap whenever you want.'

'Is your mum still here?'

'No, she left hours ago. I had to force her out the door, mind.'

I smile.

'It's late. Do you want to come to bed?'

I force myself up and struggle over to the bed, climbing in and under the covers fully dressed.

'Want me to help you take your clothes off?'

'It's OK. I'm cold. I think I'll keep my top on.' I struggle out of my joggers and pull them out from under the quilt.

'So, here we are. A three,' Luke says. We both gaze at Dylan lying in his cot attached to our bed.

'Here we are.'

'Happy?'

I nod, pushing my hair off my face. It feels slightly crisp after sweating so much earlier.

'Sure?'

Usually I change the subject when Luke tries to probe deeper into my state of mind, but there's something about the exhaustion that encompasses every part of me that makes it easier to open up. I feel almost foetal myself. 'I'm scared as well.'

Luke props his head up on his elbow. 'Oh, God, I'm so glad you said that. I was freaking out back in the hospital and you seemed so calm. I want to get it right, but I feel like I have no idea what I'm doing.'

'Me neither. Can we work it out together?'

'Always.'

I smile. 'He's beautiful though, isn't he?' I stare at Dylan again. It's so hard to take my eyes off him. 'Look at that little nose. I think his might be my new favourite face in the world.'

'Whose was it before?'

I nudge him with my elbow. 'Yours, of course.'

'Bloody hell, you must still have the oxytocin pumping through your veins for you to say something that sweet.'

'Shut up.'

Luke suddenly pushes himself up and heads towards our wardrobe. 'I nearly forgot. I got this the other day.'

He comes back holding a plastic bag, pulling out an item of clothing and handing it to me. I unfold it, unable to stop myself from smiling when I see it.

'A reindeer babygrow?'

Luke takes it off me and lays it down on the mattress beside Dylan. 'Look, it's even got horns on the hood. How cute is he going to look in that?'

I laugh. 'Poor kid. He's going to end up being a Christmas pudding, a snowman, an elf . . .'

'A turkey? Come on, a turkey would be amazing.' Luke reaches back into the bag and hands me something else. 'And this is for you.'

It's a snow globe with a silhouette of a man and woman with a child in between them, all holding hands in the centre of it. I shake it and watch the snow fall on them.

'I know you're not a big fan of Christmas decorations,' Luke says. 'But I thought it looked like us. One day I'll take you both somewhere really snowy and we can have a massive snowball fight.'

'Well, I'd definitely enjoy throwing something cold and hard at your head.'

Luke laughs and climbs back under the covers.

I shake the snow globe again and then put it on the bed-side table. 'I actually really love it.'

'Good.' Luke holds his arm out and I rest my head on his chest, Luke wrapping his arm around me.

'Can we just stay here now until the new year?' I say. 'Just the three of us. And chocolate, lots of chocolate.'

'Sounds perfect.' Luke strokes my hair, the sensation making me sleepy. 'You know, I thought I was happy. In my life before you, I mean. But now, here with you, Dylan beside us, it's like another-level happiness.'

'Cosmic happiness?'

'Exactly.'

I wrap my arm more tightly around his waist. 'Before *you*, life was just . . .' I pause, unable to find the words to describe how I felt before I met Luke. 'Well, it was nothing like this. Thank you. For making life feel like an adventure.'

Luke goes uncharacteristically quiet and then he kisses the top of my head. 'You're welcome.'

And I smile as I watch the last flake of snow drift to the bottom of the snow globe.

16th December 2006

LUKE

'Luke, stop.'

Laura pushes my hand away and rolls on to her side so that she is facing away from me. It feels like the ten thousandth time she's rejected me since Dylan was born but it doesn't get any easier. We've had sex *four times* in a year. Laura says I'm weird for knowing exactly how many times, but when it's only four, it's not like you lose count.

'Come on. He's asleep. A bit of birthday sex.'

'It's not your birthday. It's his. You don't get presents on his birthday.'

'Since when has sex with your fiancée been a present? Surely it's a right?'

'A *right*?' Laura turns over for this and I know I'm about to get an earful.

'Sorry.' I put my arm around her. 'I didn't mean it like that. I just miss feeling close to you.'

'There are other ways to feel close to me, you know?'

'I know. I want all of it. Cuddles, kisses, and, yes, I do want to have sex with you.'

Laura sighs. 'I'm tired. And I just find it hard sometimes – switching from "mum" to "sex goddess". I've tried to explain that to you.'

'I know. But you always look like a sex goddess to me.'

Laura turns on her side and pulls the cover up over her.

'I just want to sleep. He'll be awake any moment and I'm wasting precious seconds talking to you.'

I'm not sure whether to laugh or cry. 'OK, well, I'm going to go for a run.' I get out of bed and search around the hotel room for my shorts and my running top.

'Can't you wait until he wakes up and then take him? You could push him around in the pram.'

'I can't run properly with the pram. I won't be long.'

'Fine. Just be really quiet shutting the door so that you don't wake him.'

It's frosty but the cold air is refreshing as I breathe it in. Running has become my 'thing' – my escape when being an adult feels too much. It's not as peaceful here in Manchester as it is at home, the city streets no match for my usual run past the lake, but I like being out before the city really wakes up. And it gives me the headspace to think more clearly about stuff with Laura. It's tricky when she's lying next to me. I know she thinks it's just about the sex, but it's not only that. I miss the way she used to look at me. I'm not even sure she finds me attractive any more.

As I'm running, my phone buzzes with a message that simply says, 'We're going down to breakfast.' And my heart sinks because I know Laura's going to be angry that *she* was the one that had to get Dylan ready again. I'll have to hear about how *difficult* he was being and, although she won't explicitly say it, the implication will be that, unlike her, I was just focusing on myself as usual.

I turn around and start running back. When I get to the hotel, I'm desperate to have a shower but I don't want to be any later so I head straight to the dining hall where I spot her sitting in the corner next to the garishly decorated

Christmas tree, cutting up a banana and handing slices to Dylan, chatting away animatedly to him. And seeing her lovingly looking after our son – her skin pale, her eyes tired – I feel a sudden wave of guilt.

I grab a bowl and fill it with fruit salad and then pick up a yoghurt and take it over to her.

'Here, you have some breakfast. I can take over with Dylan.'

At first Laura looks like she might snap at me, but instead she takes the bowl and says, 'Thank you. I'm actually starving.'

I kiss Dylan on the head and then sit down beside the highchair and start handing him the slices of banana Laura has cut.

'Good run?'

'Yes, but I'm sorry. I should have taken him. Let you have a lie-in.'

'You should have.' Laura smiles. 'But we had fun, didn't we, Dylan? Had a little birthday shower, played with the shampoo bubbles in Mummy's hair . . .'

'Sounds fun.' I turn to Dylan who is smearing banana goo on his cheeks. 'Well, I suppose I should be saying happy birthday to you.'

'Can you believe he's one? In a way it feels like the longest year ever, but in another way, it feels like only a few weeks ago that he was born.'

'Yeah, time's funny like that, isn't it?'

'A whole year with barely any sleep.'

I wonder if it's a dig at me, Laura doing the majority of the night shifts, but she doesn't look angry, just exhausted. And I *have* got off lightly. Because Laura's feeding him, even when I'm home she takes the brunt of it. I've walked him round a couple of times when he's had a really bad night, but most of the time I barely notice as she grabs him out the bedside cot and shifts up the bed to feed him. Occasionally I'll be disturbed by the night light Laura has attached to her book, but I always go straight back to sleep.

'How about after I've finished practice with the lads, you go back to bed and I'll look after Dylan?' I offer. 'Or you could go for a massage in a spa in the city or something? I'll pay for it. I should be finished by about midday and I don't need to leave to get ready for the gig until about six p.m.'

'I mean, a massage would be nice, but Dylan might . . .'

I reach out and take her hand. 'Dylan will be fine. I promise I won't lose him, or drop him, or let him starve.'

Laura smiles.

'Besides, today's a celebration of you too, you know?' I continue. 'For giving birth to him.'

'And it's the anniversary of our first date.'

It's crazy how long ago that feels now.

'That too. So, I'm going to book you a massage. And then we can go and have a look around the Christmas markets.'

'I knew you'd get Christmas in there somewhere.'

'Well, that's a given.'

'OK. Thank you. But don't let Dylan fall off a slide or run out into the road.' One side of Laura's mouth turns up to show she's (sort of) joking.

'Deal. Now I need to get some food. I'm starving. Full English?'

'Absolutely.'

I get us both breakfast, working my way along the various containers and scooping out eggs, sausages, bacon, beans and the all-important hash browns. When I get back to the table, Dylan starts pointing at the food saying 'yum, yum' and Laura laughs.

'You can share yours, this time.' Laura takes her plate of food out of my hand. 'I'm having all mine to myself.'

Reluctantly, I cut up my sausage, blow it and put it on to a side plate to cool down for Dylan.

'And the hash brown,' Laura says.

I shake my head. 'I don't love him that much.'

'Oh, come on. It's his birthday. Look at that face.'

Dylan is staring at the piece of hash brown on the end of my fork like a puppy who has been told to get away from the table whilst people are eating.

'Seriously. If this is parenthood, I want my money back,' I joke, slicing off some hash brown and giving it to Dylan.

Laura laughs but then she says, 'It's harder, isn't it?'

'What?' I ask, stuffing hash brown into my mouth before Dylan has the chance to badger me for any more.

'Parenthood. Is it harder than you thought it would be?'

'I don't know. I mean, you do bear the brunt of it. I'm sorry about that.'

'It's OK. I know you're trying your best to make a success of the band. And you will. You *are*.'

'Thank you. I promise when you come to stay on the next tour, we'll be put up in somewhere better than a Travelodge.'

'It's fine.'

I shake my head. 'It's not good enough for you.' I check my watch and then down my coffee. 'I better go and wake those lazy bastards so we can have a quick practice. Will you guys be OK on your own for a bit? I'll be back as soon as I can. I'll book that massage for about two p.m., yeah?'

'I thought you said you'd be back about midday?'

'Yeah, I should be. But just to be sure.'

'OK. I'll see you later.'

'See you later, Mister,' I say, ruffling Dylan's hair, and then I kiss Laura on the cheek and head up to the room to shower before I go to wake the lads.

'It's actually sounding pretty good,' Rich says, once we've played the new song a couple of times.

'What do you mean, *actually* sounding pretty good? Was it ever in doubt?'

'Well, it's a bit sappy, isn't it?' Rich says, tuning one of the strings of his guitar. '*You make me see the world with different eyes.*'

I grab one of Cody's drumsticks and throw it at Rich. 'I'm pretty sure you used that exact line on that girl the other night.'

Rich laughs. 'I've got far better lines of my own. I don't need to steal your crappy ones.'

'You do realize they're only sleeping with you because I'm not available.'

'Yeah, you tell yourself that, mate.'

Rich starts strumming on his guitar, practising one of his licks.

'How are things with Laura? Any better?' Cody says quietly, turning away from Rich.

The other night, I drunkenly ended up blurting out to him that mine and Laura's sex life is less than ideal right now, but to be fair to him, I don't think he's mentioned it to Rich. Cody's a decent bloke. And at the time it felt good to offload. But in the cold light of day, I'm embarrassed that the two of them are getting laid on a daily basis whereas Laura just seems to flinch when I touch her.

'Yeah. I mean, we had a good night last night,' I say with a smirk, hoping he can't see straight through it.

'Oh, that's great, mate. I told you you guys would work it out. She's a keeper, that one.'

'Can we go get some food?' Rich interrupts, abruptly putting down his guitar. 'My stomach is eating itself here.'

I check my watch. 'Shit, it's one o'clock. I said I'd get back about midday.'

'Ooh, don't want to upset the old ball and chain.'

I glare at Rich. 'Sod off. It's my son's first birthday. I know you'll probably end up being some deadbeat dad but I'd quite like to do a decent job.'

'Of course you do, mate,' Cody says, tapping me on the back. 'Don't listen to him. Say happy birthday to the little man from us.'

'You staying back here tonight?' Rich asks.

I shake my head. 'Laura's going to stay again tonight. Then she'll go in the morning and we can head off to Liverpool.'

'You're missing out, you know, brother? Honestly, the girls last night were ridiculous.'

'Whatever.'

'Tell him, Code.'

Cody shrugs. 'They were pretty hot, but so is Laura,' he says diplomatically.

'All right, all right. She's *my* missus, you know?' I tease.

Cody laughs.

'Right. I'll see you later, boys. Can you remind Jimmy I need him to have Dylan later?'

'Will do. See you later, bud.'

'Yeah, see you, mate,' Rich chips in and I leave them and sprint back to the Travelodge.

When I enter the hotel room, Laura is storming around shoving unidentifiable items into the nappy bag.

'My massage is in forty minutes. It's going to take me at least half an hour to walk there and I don't want to turn up sweaty and gross from having to sprint.'

'I'm sorry. We needed a little more practice to get the song right. But I think we're there now.'

'Good. Well, I've put his coat and stuff out on the chair for you and packed everything he needs in the bag. Can you just fill his cup up with some water?'

'Of course. Leave it all to me. I've got this.'

'Don't forget his gloves – he finds it really painful when his hands get cold.'

'Not a problem.'

She picks up her handbag and throws it over her shoulder. She looks really cute in a knitted jumper dress and patterned tights, her hair tied up in a loose ponytail. 'Are you sure you're going to be OK?'

I go over and put my arms around her, and then there's a smash from the bathroom. Glancing through, I see Dylan lifting the toilet lid and then slamming it down. Laura instinctively releases herself from my arms to deal with it but I hold her back. 'I've got it. Go. Enjoy yourself.'

Laura takes one more glance towards Dylan and then turns

and leaves. And as she does, I feel like I might be on the verge of a panic attack and realize, with some shame, that I've never been on my own with Dylan before. Well, not for more than about ten minutes when Laura has a shower or is on the phone to Sarah. I've never actually taken him *out*. I guess we could just kill an hour in the hotel room, put CBeebies on, open and close the toilet lid a few hundred times.

Dylan comes tottering out of the bathroom, tripping over a pair of Laura's shoes and then pulling himself straight back up using the bed. *You're a role model, son. You fall down, you get back up.* Plus, he's a *baby*. How hard can it be to take a one-year-old out for a couple of hours? I'll get Dylan a birthday cake, find a little present of some sort for Laura then we'll kill a bit of time in the park and I can turn up to Laura with my head held high.

'Right, kiddo. Let's do this.'

I pick Dylan's coat up off the chair where Laura has laid it out with a woolly hat and gloves, the little snowboots we got him for his birthday tucked underneath.

Dylan starts running away, waddling around on his little chubby legs like a penguin and giggling. When he circles back round in my direction, I grab him and at first he continues to laugh, obviously thinking we're playing a game, but then when I try to put his coat on he starts yelling.

'We're going to go out. Have fun at the park.'

I post one of his arms through the sleeve but there's some sort of resistance as his hand never appears. After pushing a little bit harder and still no luck, I go in the other way, posting my hand through to find his and then grabbing the only finger I can feel that's free and pulling it, him crying as if I'm sawing off his arm.

'I'm not hurting you,' I say, unsure of who the lie is benefiting. 'Come on, hand, just come out.'

All of a sudden, I manage to pop his hand out the cuff, feeling a disproportionate sense of satisfaction as I do. But then I remember I've still got another arm to do and just the thought makes me weary. After nearly dislocating his elbow, I wrestle the other arm in, and then we play a really fun game of me putting his hat on, him taking his hat off, before I somehow manage to manhandle his feet into his boots.

'Awesome. Let's go,' I say, sweat pouring down my back.

But then, with a sinking heart, I spot his gloves. I look over at him, staring forlornly at me like the Michelin man, so padded he's unable to properly move his limbs. And as I try to convince myself that it's not *that* cold outside, I hear Laura's voice in the back of my head, so I pick up the gloves and take them over to Dylan. The poor kid looks at me as if to say, 'Really Dad, do we have to?' and then resignedly holds out his hands. Now, anyone that's ever tried to put gloves on a one-year-old will know that it is practically impossible. Their thumb will not go into the thumb bit and if by some miracle it does then it will take along half the other fingers with it. After several attempts and on the verge of intentionally strangling myself with my scarf, I stuff the gloves into the sleeves of his coat, sling the inconceivably heavy nappy bag over my shoulder and put Dylan into the pushchair.

After bumping, carrying, squeezing and dragging my way through the city to the nearest Tesco, I grab a birthday cake (a caterpillar whose name is apparently Curly) and search the shelves for a '1' candle. Finally finding it, nonsensically in the home baking section rather than next to the birthday cakes, I take one off the shelf and then get into the mile-long queue.

Just as I've paid, I realize I've forgotten a lighter, and from the looks on the faces of the people queueing behind me, there's no way they're going to wait for me to go and get one (festive cheer is not exactly abundant here), so I have to re-enter the shop, get the lighter and queue again. As if in a time warp, when I check my watch it tells me it's a quarter to three, so even though I know that a present from Tesco is shit, when I see a notebook by the till with 'Follow Your Dreams' on the front I manage to convince myself it's inspiring and meaningful, even though really it's trite generic tat.

By the time I get outside, Dylan is screaming like a banshee, not letting up however fast I push him or loudly I sing Christmas songs. I stop in a shop doorway, suddenly the busiest place in the whole of the UK, and bend down so I am at eye level with him, hordes of people with a desperate need to be exactly where I am bashing into my back. As soon as I'm near his bottom end, it's clear why Dylan is screaming, but I'm going to be late for Laura so instead of searching for a baby change, I find a bench, plonk him on the top and search for a nappy and wipes in the Tardis that is the nappy bag. Of course, Laura has dressed him in the most complicated outfit he owns, some dungaree ensemble with cross back straps that are fastened with buttons so small even a borrower would struggle to undo them.

All the people walking past glare at me for daring to change a baby in public, or perhaps it's the fact Dylan's legs are turning purple from the cold, so I work as fast as I can. Then I charge along the pavements, tempted to take out the legs of the three women dawdling in front of me, arriving just in time to spot Laura coming out of the spa looking zen. I'm about to offload a garbled list of all the ways the afternoon has been a nightmare, but then she turns and gives me the biggest smile and I swallow it all down and smile back.

'You look amazing. Good massage?' I say, as I get closer.

She throws her arms around me. 'The best. Thank you so much.' She releases me and then leans into the pram and gives Dylan a big kiss and I notice one of the gloves he had tucked into his sleeve is missing and hope that Laura doesn't notice it too. 'I missed you though. Well, a little bit. Not really during the massage, it has to be said.'

'We had a fantastic time, didn't we, Dylan? It was a piece of cake.'

'Really?'

'Well, no. It would appear Tesco is not Dylan's favourite place. I'm in awe of you actually. I'm so sorry I don't do this more often.'

I feel like flopping to the floor and begging for her forgiveness, but she shakes her head and links her arm through mine. 'Come on. Let's go to the Christmas markets. I'm actually feeling pretty festive.'

LAURA

'Look at these,' Luke says, as we reach a stall, picking up a pair of glasses with mistletoe attached to the frame and putting them on.

'Suit you.'

Luke comes towards me, his face a centimetre from mine. 'It's mistletoe. You know what that means.'

And then he kisses me, a lingering kiss, and I feel the same tingling in the pit of my stomach that I always feel when I'm around him. I'm sure he thinks I've turned into some asexual being, but it's not that I don't fancy him. It's not about him at all.

He takes the glasses off and puts them back on the stall, then picks up an elf's hat to try on Dylan, who looks bemused at the thing being plonked on his head. 'Oh, how cute is that? Look at the little ears. We've got to get him that.'

I shake my head, but he's already got a ten-pound note out of his pocket and is handing it to the stallholder. Spotting a hut selling hot drinks, I go and get us both Baileys' hot chocolates with the works, finding Luke amongst the crowds with a paper bag in his hand.

I hand him his cup.

'Wow, you paid the extra pound for whipped cream,' he says, taking it off me and studying it. '*I could buy a whole can for that.*' He uses a high voice to show he's imitating me.

I slap his arm. 'I can drink them both myself.'

'It's lovely. Thank you.'

He takes a slice of something out of the paper bag and then hands the bag to me.

'What's this?'

'Try it. If I really can't convince you to like mince pies then I think this is going to be the perfect substitution.'

'I'm not sure,' I say, smelling it.

'Just take a bite.' He takes a huge bite of his own slice.

Reluctantly, I do the same and am surprised to discover it's delicious. He can clearly tell I'm enjoying it because a huge smile works its way across his face.

'See?'

'It's not bad. What is it?'

Luke laughs and wraps his arm around me. 'From you that's basically "exquisite". Welcome to the world of stollen – the second-best Christmas delicacy out there.'

We mooch around the market, pointing out all the twinkly lights and decorations to Dylan who seems mesmerized, staring out from the pram. We choose a few wooden decorations for our tree and Luke persuades me to get a giant metal reindeer to put outside the flat even though the front area is shared.

'We won't always be living in that flat, you know? I'm going to get you a proper house with a big garden, I promise. As soon as the band takes off.'

'You know I don't care about the money.'

'I know. But I want to provide you with everything you've ever dreamed of.'

'You have.'

Luke smiles and then we wander past a stall selling

vintage jewellery so I double back, a silver ring with an oval sapphire catching my eye. I slide it on to my ring finger.

'Bit plain for an engagement ring, isn't it?' Luke says, looking at it over my shoulder. Since having Dylan, getting married has fallen by the wayside, and though he's told me numerous times to choose myself a ring, I want it to come from him.

I hold out my hand. 'I don't know. I actually really love it.'

Luke starts to wander off and I'm hopeful that he's playing it cool, that he might pop back tomorrow morning after I've gone.

When I catch up with him, he's looking through the window of a Ladbrokes. I put my hand on his back and he turns to face me with a childlike excitement on his face.

'It's the local races today. Let's put a bet on. December the sixteenth is our lucky day, right?'

'No way,' I say firmly. 'What if we lose?'

'What if we *win*?'

He pushes the pram into the bookies, Dylan now fast asleep, and then grabs my hand and pulls me in too.

'I really don't think this is a good idea.'

'Look, there's one called Santa Claus. *Please* can we bet on that one?'

'It's twenty to one. Doesn't that mean it's almost certainly going to lose?'

'It means we don't have to bet much to win big.'

He goes and puts some money on 'Santa Claus', unwilling to tell me how much, and then we rush to a pub where they're showing the race. We park Dylan at the end of the table, still fast asleep, and Luke goes to the bar, coming back with two glasses of champagne.

'For the celebrations.' He hands me a glass and then clinks his glass on mine.

'Or commiserations?'

Having only had a slice of stollen for lunch, by the time the race starts, I already feel quite drunk. From the outset, Luke is up on his feet cheering – the people around us having a quiet glass of mulled wine staring at him with bemused expressions. As the horses start to hammer down the home straight, I'm stunned to see that 'Santa Claus' is in the lead, and I can't help jumping up and cheering myself. Luke looks at me and laughs and then he holds my hand, our eyes fixed on the TV. But then just before he crosses the finish line, he stumbles, his jockey flying off.

'No,' Luke yells, letting go of my hand and slapping the table. 'We were so close.'

'Bloody Santa Claus. Always been a letdown.'

Luke smiles. 'It's because he wasn't wearing a Christmas hat. It's like Sampson with his hair – Santa's nothing without his hat.'

I laugh. 'I love you.'

'You're not mad at me for losing fifty quid?'

'Fifty quid?'

Luke screws up his face apologetically.

'No, I'm not mad.' I lean over and kiss him on the cheek. 'Shall I get us another glass?'

Luke checks his watch. 'There's nothing I'd love more than to sit here and drink champagne with you, but we need to do the sound check and stuff before the gig, and I got Dylan a cake so I'd like to give him that before I have to go . . .'

I nod, trying to hide the sinking feeling in my chest. 'It's fine. Let's go do cake.'

We leave the pub and walk back to the hotel, my arm looped through Luke's as he pushes the pram, the Christmas lights above the street turning on as the light starts to fade.

Back at the hotel, we put Dylan in front of CBeebies whilst we have a cup of coffee to sober up.

'Why does this fake milk taste so very shit?' Luke says, screwing up his nose.

'Shh,' I say, gesturing towards Dylan.

'He really doesn't get swearing yet, you know. Besides, he's fully immersed in the world of *Charlie and Lola* right now.'

Luke's phone jingles and he takes it out of his pocket, his expression turning serious.

'What is it?'

He shakes his head. 'Nothing.'

'It doesn't look like nothing.'

He holds out his phone so I can read the message.

Happy Birthday to Dylan. I'd give anything to meet him. Please, Luke.

'Your dad again?'

Luke nods. 'I'm not going to have him in Dylan's life so let's not even get started on that.'

I put my hand on his arm. 'OK. Only you can make that decision.'

He grabs the nappy bag from underneath the pram and pulls out a Tesco carrier bag. 'Cake?'

'If you're sure you're OK? That you don't want to talk about it?'

'I'm fine.' Luke takes the caterpillar cake out of its box and pushes in a candle in the shape of a number one. As soon as Dylan sees it, he starts racing towards it.

'Hold up, hold up. You have to blow out your candle first,' I say, holding him back.

Dylan wriggles in my arms until Luke lights the candle. At which point, he stops and stares at the flickering flame. And we sing 'Happy Birthday', Luke's ridiculously beautiful voice making me sound like a dying cat by comparison.

And then when we've done our hip hip hooray, Luke kneels down so his head is level with Dylan's and says, 'Go on then. Blow your candle out.'

Dylan stares at him, his little eyebrows furrowing.

'Like this.' Luke models blowing and Dylan copies, spraying spittle on to his cheeks. 'One more time.'

This time when Dylan blows, Luke does it at the same time. When the candle goes out, we both clap and so Dylan starts clapping too, a huge smile on his face. Then we all sit and stuff our faces, Dylan saying 'yum' as his nose, cheeks and chin get covered in chocolate. 'Yum' was Dylan's first word. His second word was 'cat' (despite neither us nor grandparents nor friends having one). I was a bit put out that it came before 'Mama'.

'Oh, and I got you a little present,' Luke says, pulling a notebook out of the bag and handing it to me. 'I'm sorry it's not wrapped and it's a bit crap, but I just wanted to get you something to say thanks for all you do for us.'

The notebook has 'Follow Your Dreams' on the front in a swirly gold font set against an unpleasant peach colour.

'I thought you could use it to note down all the ways I disappoint you. You could start it now with "buys me shit presents".'

I put my arms around his neck and kiss him. 'I'd rather you and your shit presents than anyone else.'

'Really? You're sure?'

'I'm sure.'

'Right.' Luke pulls away. 'I better get going. Remember I want you to come and see the last song tonight. Jimmy will be here about eight p.m. and I've booked you a taxi to the gig. Just wait in reception.'

'Are you sure Dylan is going to be OK with Jimmy? I can't imagine he knows much about looking after babies.'

'He's got four kids.'

'But did he actually bring any of them up?'

'Yes. All of them. He was happily married for twenty years, you know? Utterly devoted. And then she went off with someone else. Broke his heart.'

'Shut up.'

'Seriously. The only reason he dates a lot of different women now is because he's so hurt. It's all meaningless rebound stuff.'

'Well, that's one way to heal a broken heart; shag anything that moves.'

Luke laughs. 'Honestly, he's amazing with kids. And Dylan will probably be asleep anyway. Please. It's only round the corner. It's really important to me that you come.'

'But what if he wakes up and freaks out that I'm not there?'

'He won't. And if he does, Jimmy will sing to him and rock him back to sleep.'

I let out a deep breath and Luke puts his hands on my shoulders. 'I know you hate leaving him, but if you just do it this once then I promise I'll never ask you to come and see my crappy band again.'

'It's not crappy. And OK.'

'Promise?'

'I promise.'

'Thank you. Today's been really nice.' Luke grabs his bag, stuffs a few things in and then he's gone.

I'm stood in my best stripy dress, my make-up half done, rocking Dylan like a mad woman when my phone rings. It's Mum. I haven't really got time to speak to her but I know she'll only worry if I don't answer.

'Hi, Mum. I'm in a rush to go out. Are you OK?'

'Why is Dylan screaming?'

I move my phone to the other ear, further away from Dylan. 'I don't know. I think he's just overtired.'

'Where are you going?'

'I'm going to see Luke's gig.'

'With Dylan?'

'No, he's staying with Luke's manager.'

Dylan cranks the screaming up to another level.

'You can't leave him like that, can you? And what do you mean, Luke's manager?'

I let out a deep breath. 'Dylan knows him. I wouldn't leave him with a stranger. And I'm trying to settle him first. It's really important to Luke that I go.'

'Well, he needs to realize that the world doesn't revolve around him and that bloody band. Dylan is your priority now.'

'I know.' I continue to rock and stroke, rock and stroke,

but it's clearly not working as Dylan carries on screaming into my ear. Then I hear a knock on the door. 'Look, Mum. I've got to go. I'll call you tomorrow.'

'OK, but make sure you don't leave that boy.'

Considering she didn't want me to have him, it's funny how protective she is of Dylan now he's here.

'I've got it. Bye, Mum.'

I put the phone down and go and open the door to a sympathetic-looking Jimmy.

'Not a happy chap, hey?' he says, squeezing past me into the room.

I give him a look that says, 'tell me about it', and pat Dylan on the back rhythmically as if he's a drum.

'Do you want me to take him? So you can finish getting ready?' Jimmy shouts over the sound of Dylan's crying.

'Do I look that bad?'

'Not at all. It's just one of your eyes is blue and the other not.'

I'd forgotten that Dylan had cranked up the screaming just as I was about to finish my eye make-up.

I give Jimmy a sad smile. 'I don't think I can go. Can you send Luke my apologies? I can't leave Dylan in this state.'

Jimmy screws up his face. 'He was pretty insistent. And Dylan will be fine with me. The taxi will be here any minute.'

I think about handing Dylan over, finishing my make-up and getting in that taxi, but then I look at Dylan's distraught face, hear Mum's voice in my head.

'I'm sorry. Please tell Luke I will come and see him another time.'

Jimmy looks at his feet and I can tell he wants to say something, that he's probably wondering how the hell I expect to keep Luke when he has girls throwing themselves at him every night and I won't even go and see him play this once. But I just can't leave Dylan.

'OK. I'll go and tell Luke. Take care.'

Jimmy leaves, and practically the second he shuts the door, Dylan stops crying and falls asleep on my shoulder and I sit on the bed, picturing Luke up on stage, looking through the faces in the crowd and realizing I'm not there, and I feel like bursting into tears myself.

'So have you had sex with him yet?'

I tuck my phone between my ear and my shoulder whilst I open another pack of Maltesers and start shovelling them into my mouth.

'No,' I say, my mouth full.

'Laura.'

'I thought you were a feminist. You're not seriously telling me I have to have sex with my fiancé to pass some sort of test.'

'No, I'm telling you you need to have sex with your fiancé because you're sprung tighter than a new mattress and it would do you good. Think of it as a release, like having a warm bubble bath.'

I smile, desperately wishing Sarah was here. 'But I'm just so tired. Dylan has slept through the night once since he was born. *Once*.'

'I know.'

'And I just don't *feel* sexy. My boobs are like udders. My once-flat stomach is now like a broken air bed.'

'You're beautiful. And Luke really won't give a shit.'

'But even down there's not right. It's . . . baggier.'

Sarah bursts out laughing. 'You're really selling yourself to me here.'

'Exactly,' I almost shout and then glance at Dylan, who I've placed on the bed beside me, to check I haven't woken him up.

'Look, Laur. Just jump on him like Mr Blobby with your wobbly bits and your baggy frou frou. He'll be blown away.'

I smile. 'I miss you.'

'You too. When's he back anyway?'

'I don't know. Probably late. He wanted me to go and see the last song, but Dylan was crying so I didn't go.'

'Oh, that's a shame.'

'All right, all right. Don't make me feel worse than I already do. I know I'm a terrible person.'

'You're not a terrible person. But that's pretty sweet that he wanted to share it all with you. Who was going to have Dylan though?'

'He sent Jimmy over. Apparently he's super dad to four kids. Organized me a taxi and everything. But Dylan was screaming his head off and it didn't feel right to leave him and . . .' I sigh.

'Jimmy – super dad?'

'*I know*. That's what I said.'

'I thought the only thing he knew how to look after was his penis.'

'Apparently he's nursing a broken heart.'

'Ah, is that what they call it these days? Anyway, I get why you didn't go. It must be hard. The umbilical cord doesn't stretch too far, right?'

'Thanks for understanding.'

I eat another handful of Maltesers and we sit in silence.

It's weird; with anyone else I'd feel like I had to fill it, the empty space, but with Sarah I could stay like this all night, just listening to her breathing.

'I'm scared I'm going to lose him.'

It's really hard to say the words. Even to my best friend in the world.

'You're not going to lose him. He adores you.'

I move the empty wrappers off the bed and put them on the bedside table. 'I think I might have a quick nap now. Then I can be raring to go when he gets back.'

'That's the spirit. And I'll see you tomorrow?'

'Of course. I'll text you when we're nearly home and you can put the kettle on.'

'Will do. Love you.'

'Love you too. Bye.'

I put the phone down, rest my head back on the pillow and just stare at Dylan. His face is so perfect, it almost doesn't feel like he's real sometimes. I want to kiss him, to stroke his soft hair, but I'm terrified of waking him up so I leave him be and just close my eyes too, and within minutes I'm asleep.

When I wake up, Dylan's gone and the sheer panic makes me sit up like the headboard of a sprung chair. I reach for the bedside light and then, just before I turn it on, Luke says, 'Stop, you'll wake him up.'

'Where is he? What time is it?'

'He's asleep in the travel cot. I moved him so that I could get into bed. It's eleven o'clock. You were fast asleep.'

He says it as if he might say 'having sex with another man', fury bubbling beneath his words.

'I was just having a little nap.'

So that I could be full of beans to have sex with you.

'Is he OK now?' he says, nodding towards Dylan.

'What do you mean? I thought you just said he was asleep.'

'I mean he was obviously in a state. For you not to come. Or could you just not be bothered?'

'Oh, come on, Luke. So, I didn't come to see the band play. There'll be other gigs. Dylan needed me.'

'And what about me, Laur? When did *I* stop being a priority?'

I drag my hands through my hair and let out a groan of frustration. 'Why does it always come back to this? You might be used to girls fawning over you, but I have more important things to be doing. Why can't you accept life can't be exactly as it was?'

Luke slumps on to the bed. 'I do accept that. I just want to still be important to you. Tonight meant a lot to me.' He puts his head in his hands and he looks so forlorn that I move over and put my arm around him. I wish he'd show me this side of himself more often. He's always so laid back about everything it makes me feel like I'm the only one who's struggling.

'You *are* important to me. I'm just so tired and sometimes it feels like there's not a lot of me left to give to anyone other than Dylan.'

'Things will get easier. He'll sleep more and you'll feel more like you.'

'I know. But it's not just that. I see you following your dreams and I'm so proud of you, but . . .'

'You'll find yours,' he says, as if reading my mind.

I raise my eyebrows. 'Whilst changing nappies and building yet another tower of bricks for Dylan to knock over?'

Luke puts his hand on my leg and begins stroking my thigh with his thumb. 'You're only twenty-four. You'll find it. And whatever it is, Dylan and I will be cheering you on from the sidelines.'

A sudden wave of guilt fills my chest. 'I'm so sorry I didn't come tonight. I should have left him with Jimmy.'

'It's OK. You're right. He's more important.'

I shake my head. 'But I need to be able to let go a bit. I just find it so hard not to be in control when it comes to Dylan. He probably would've been fine with Jimmy, but I just feel this intense pressure that it has to be me. I know it doesn't make any sense.'

'You love him. You're protective. It's natural.'

'But what is it they say? If you love someone, set them free?'

'Maybe not aged one. I don't think you need to give him the space to find his own path just yet.'

'But I do need to let you help. And your mum. And Jimmy in very, very special circumstances.'

Luke smiles.

'Because I can't do it on my own,' I continue, the words finally forming. 'I feel like I'm breaking.'

Beyond my control, tears fill my eyes and then start sliding down my cheeks and Luke wraps his arms around me and holds me whilst I sob.

'Do you know why I wanted you to come tonight?' he asks, stroking my hair.

I shake my head.

'Because I wrote a song for you. To say thank you for giving me Dylan. For changing my life for the better.'

The regret I feel at not going is overwhelming and I find myself sobbing even harder. 'I know I probably don't deserve it now, but will you sing it for me?'

'Of course.'

I lay my head back on the pillow and Luke grabs his guitar from the corner of the room and then he sits on the bed beside me and sings me the song he has written for me and my sobbing turns to happy tears.

When he's finished, I take his face in my hands and kiss him. *Really* kiss him. Like I used to. And soon we're tearing at each other's clothes and for a short time I don't care about the stretch marks or the wobbly bits. I'm not consumed with thoughts of being a mother. It's just me and Luke. And it's perfect.

16th December 2007

LUKE

We sit by our private pool. It's the perfect temperature. Not a cloud in the sky and a light breeze. Laura was moaning that it's always freezing for Dylan's birthday so I surprised her with a trip to the Maldives. When we first arrived, I have to admit the sight of the giant Christmas tree on the beach – made from discarded coconut husks, painted white with a constellation of fairy lights – although beautiful, gave me a slight longing for a pine tree, a smattering of snow. But lying out on the lounger, the sun on my skin does feel pretty bloody good after the endless dreary rain of the past few months at home.

Dylan is sitting on the ground beside Laura's lounger, turning the pages of his book and 'reading' it aloud. Every time he opens one of the flaps to see whether Spot is there, he says 'no' elongating the 'o' sound, in clear imitation of the way we say it. I smile at Laura, who is looking incredible in her neon-yellow bikini, which accentuates the golden tan she's developed over the week.

'When he has a nap, do you fancy going back to bed?' I squeeze Laura's thigh.

'We've got that boat trip booked, remember?'

I check my watch. 'We've got an hour. How about I take him for a quick walk in the pram and get him to sleep?'

'Look at him. Does he look tired?'

Dylan is now on all fours, like he's performing a

downward dog, looking at us upside down through his legs.

'I'm sure a quick walk would knock him out.'

'Luke, we can't force our child to sleep just so that we can have sex.'

'I'm not suggesting we drug him or anything. Just a nice relaxing stroll.'

Laura reaches over and runs her fingers up and down my thigh. 'Later. I promise it will be worth the wait.'

I quickly cover my shorts with a towel and Laura laughs. Once I've calmed down, I throw the towel off and grab Dylan.

'Right, son, let's have some fun.'

I pop his armbands on, grab a beach ball and then charge into the water, Dylan giggling as it splashes up at us. We play chase the ball and then I try to sink it, wrestling with it like a disobedient sheep, Dylan chanting 'more, more' as it keeps bobbing back up to the surface. I spin him around in the water and he giggles and then he stops and stares at the sky as a helicopter flies over, low and noisy.

'Wa dat?' he asks in a high-pitched squeal.

'It's a helicopter. It flies in the sky like the aeroplane we came on.'

'Wa dat?' he says, again, his eyes looking back up to the sky.

This time it's a bird flying over the pool and he smiles at it and waves as it travels onwards.

'Bye bye, birdy,' he says and I pull him closer to me and kiss his forehead.

'How come you're so adorable, hey?'

People always say when you have a kid, you get to see the world again through their eyes, re-experience the magic, and it's true. I now hear all the things I didn't even notice because he points out every sound; I see the tiny bug on the tarmac, the bee dancing from flower to flower; I laugh when a raindrop lands directly on my nose and am in awe at the sound of thunder or the way the wind can make every leaf in a tree rustle.

'Luke.'

I look up to see Laura at the edge of the pool, her tanned athletic legs and pert bum directly in my eyeline. She points at her watch. 'We've got to get to the boat. Pass him to me and I'll dry him off and get him changed.'

'OK.' I hold Dylan up and Laura grabs him and puts him on her hip, kissing the top of his head.

'I missed you,' she says, blowing raspberries on Dylan's neck as she walks back to the lounger, Dylan in fits of giggles.

I do a couple of lengths and then join them. Laura has the dressing and organizing thing down pat now. She's like a machine. Whereas, even two years in, I *still* forget vital things. The other day I took him to Starbucks and the second we sat down, he did a poo, so I opened the bag only to realize I'd forgotten nappies. *Nappies.* I had to down my coffee, burning my tongue, and shove my brownie into my mouth with eau de shite wafting into my nose.

Once Dylan's ready, we grab a few bits for our boat trip, me sneaking the engagement ring I've bought Laura into my pocket, and then we head along to the beach. I surprised Laura with the excursion this morning. I wanted to do something special to commemorate the date and to give Laura a 'proper' proposal, so I booked us a trip on a yacht, complete with dinner on an uninhabited island. It still gives me a thrill to be able to do things like this for her. Mum and Dad always had enough money – we had villa holidays in Europe, a BMW, a three-bedroom house on the outskirts of London. I never wanted for anything. But this is a different league. Since one of our singles got to number one, it's been insane. Colossal album sales followed and then a sell-out tour. I can provide Laura and Dylan with anything that they want. We no longer have to worry about whether something is good value or whether we really *need* it. Life is just about enjoying ourselves.

We're greeted at the dock by a bloke in shorts and a smart shirt. He kisses Laura on each cheek and then gives me a firm handshake before taking our bags and putting them on the deck. When he returns, he makes a huge fuss of Dylan, telling us how gorgeous he is and tickling Dylan's toes when he acts shy and snuggles into Laura's shoulder.

'Right. Let's get you aboard. Before we leave, sir, can you just check the menu is to your liking? If there is anything I have missed out, I will send someone to get it now before we set off.' He hands me the menu and then helps Laura and Dylan on to the boat, giving them a quick tour before returning to me.

'Looks perfect. Thank you.' I hand the menu back and then I join Laura and Dylan on board.

'Make yourselves comfortable. I want to give you total privacy so I will remain in the cabin, but if there is anything that you would like, please don't hesitate to ask. Let's start with an ice-cold champagne for you both.' Someone from off the boat hands him two glasses, the champagne sparkling in the sun, and he passes them to us and then takes a carton of apple juice and gives it to Dylan. 'We thought a straw would be best, but I can put it in a cup if you'd prefer.'

'This is perfect,' Laura says, helping Dylan to put the straw into his mouth.

'Thank you, Mrs Laura. Well, go and relax and we will start our journey. We should be sailing for about an hour before we moor for a little while, so you can have a dip in the sea if you like, and then we will sail for a further forty minutes or so before we stop on the island for your meal. Does that sound to your satisfaction?'

'It sounds amazing, thank you.'

'Thank you. Enjoy.' He nods his head and then leaves us, and we make our way to the front deck where there are three loungers set out, a mini pool for Dylan and an ice bucket with the bottle of champagne in.

'Wow. This is incredible,' Laura says, kissing me on the cheek. 'Thank you so much.'

'Anything for my two favourites.'

Laura stands at the edge of the deck, Dylan on her hip, taking in the view. 'I remember when I was a kid and we went on our one and only holiday abroad. We rented this pedalo and whilst we pedalled around the harbour past all the fancy boats, Dad started moaning about the bastard rich and how they'd probably never done a hard day's work in their lives.'

'And now you're one of them. And he might be right. Singing doesn't exactly feel like hard work.'

'Well, isn't that what they say – do what you love and you'll never have to work a day in your life.'

'It's true.'

'You're lucky, you know? To be so good at something.'

'Pool,' Dylan says, wriggling to get down out of Laura's arms. It's one of the words he's learnt since he's been here.

'OK. Come on then.'

Laura sits on the lounger and I pass her a swim nappy and Dylan's swimsuit and hat out of the bag. Once he's ready, she places him in the paddling pool and he starts jumping the plastic ducks in and out and then pouring water over them with the little jug provided.

'Well, he seems happy anyway,' I say, lying down on the lounger, Laura lying back on hers too.

'Can you imagine when he goes to school and people ask him what he did for his second birthday? *Oh, I went on a private yacht in the Maldives, darling.* They're going to think he's a right toff.'

I laugh, looking out at the ocean, which is an intense turquoise and as still as a lake. Where it ends, the deep blue of the sky begins, only interrupted by the odd wispy cloud.

'It's stunning, isn't it?' Laura continues. 'I still can't really take it in, can you? The way our lives have changed so much so fast.'

'Actually, about that.' I pull out my phone and locate the details of the new house I've found and then hand my phone to Laura. 'What do you think of this place?'

Laura spends a few minutes scrolling and then looks up at me, her brow furrowed. 'What is this?'

'Our new home, if you like it.'

'What? But we only moved six months ago.'

As soon as we started making a bit of money, I bought a two-bedroomed terrace with a little back garden. I hated seeing Dylan cooped up in the flat with nowhere to kick a ball.

'I know, but you and Dylan deserve better than where we are now.'

'I like where we are now.'

I sigh. Laura is always so sensible with money. I wish she'd just relax and enjoy it. 'So do I. It's fine. But *this* place . . . I went to have a sneaky look last week and it's *amazing*. Honestly, Laur. Imagine living there.'

'I can't.'

'Can't what?'

'Imagine living there. It's beyond anything I've ever seen before.'

'Which is exactly why we should buy it.'

Laura twiddles her hair. 'I don't know. Are you sure we can afford it? What if things go tits up with the band?'

'Thanks for the vote of confidence.'

'I don't mean it like that. I just mean we can't guarantee how long all this will last for. What if we can't afford the mortgage payments in a few years?'

'It won't be a problem.'

'I don't know. It would mean uprooting Dylan again, packing up all our stuff. I feel like I've only just *un*packed.'

I understand why she's cautious, but I wish she'd just get excited, fling her arms around me and jump at the idea of us living somewhere so amazing. It has tennis courts, for God's sake. *Tennis courts*.

'I'll hire someone to do all the packing and the unpacking.' I take Laura's hand in mine. 'Just come and see it. If you don't love it, I'll withdraw my offer.'

'You've already put an offer in?'

'Don't be mad. I explained it was contingent on you seeing it, but I didn't want to lose it. Trust me, when you see it, you'll realize why.'

Laura's face finally softens and she smiles. 'It does look pretty amazing.'

I lift her hand up and kiss it. And then I notice Dylan has gone quiet, his head starting to droop, his eyes glazed.

'I think somebody's tired.'

'Oh, bless him,' Laura says. 'Too much birthday excitement.'

I get up and take him out of the pool and Laura throws me his hooded towel, which I place over his head. As soon as he's in my arms, he rests his head on my shoulder and cuddles in tight and I know that within a few minutes, he'll be asleep. I walk to the front of the boat and sway with him in time with the rhythm of the waves, the perfect view in front of me. Soon, I feel Dylan become heavy and I know that he's fallen asleep, so I lay him on the spare lounger, moving it slightly so that he is in the shade of the parasol, and then join Laura.

'Hey you. Don't squash me.'

'Come here. I want to be close to you.' I manoeuvre Laura so that she is lying between my legs. 'That's better.'

'God, it's beautiful here, isn't it?' She rests her head back on my chest. 'Can we just stay here forever?'

'That'd be nice, wouldn't it?'

'You know, if someone had told me a few years ago I'd be cruising around the ocean on a yacht, a relatively handsome bloke underneath me, my little boy asleep by my side, I would've thought they were crazy.'

I run my fingers up and down Laura's side and she turns to kiss me, her tongue darting in and out of my mouth, my hands cupping her fantastic bum. I look over at Dylan who is fast asleep and then slip my fingers into Laura's bikini bottoms.

'Not here.' She puts her hand on top of mine to still my fingers.

'Why not? Nobody can see us.'

'But it won't be long until we dock,' she says, short of breath. 'What if Hassan comes up?'

'I'll be very subtle. You just lie back.'

Laura turns back over, her bottom pushing into my trunks, and it's hard not to just strip her off and pull her on to me. But instead, I focus all my attention on her, aroused by her arousal as she writhes beneath me. When she climaxes, I can tell she's trying to be silent and I find it so sexy that she doesn't manage it.

We're just in time because the boat starts to slow and then stops, Hassan coming up to drop the anchor.

'Would you like a splash in the sea?'

Laura pulls a towel over herself as if she worries Hassan will be able to see the sexual activity on her skin. 'I better stay with Dylan. You have a swim though.'

'I can watch him if you are OK with that?' Hassan asks. 'Laura?'

Laura glances at Dylan who is out cold on the lounger, his tummy going up and down with each breath. 'Call us if he starts to stir, yes? We'll just have a very quick dip.'

'Of course. No problem.' Hassan stands at the end of Dylan's lounger like a bodyguard.

'Come on then.' I take Laura's hand and we go to the edge of the deck and she begins to climb down the ladder, but I pull her back up. 'Let's jump.'

Laura raises her eyebrows but then she starts to count down from three to zero and we launch into the water holding each other's hands. When we hit the surface, we instinctively let go. But then when we rise back up, I find Laura and put my arms around her and we bob around in the sea. But then she flinches.

'What is it?'

She looks down beside her leg, her face suddenly animated. 'Quick! Look, there's a turtle.'

And sure enough, there's a great big turtle swimming past our legs, along with an array of multi-coloured fish. 'Wow, it's incredible, isn't it?'

'It really is.' We watch the sea life, Laura wrapped around me like a vice. 'You know, I wish we could spend Christmas here. No tinsel, no stupid cracker jokes, no Queen's speech and utterly miserable *EastEnders* episode. Just sun and blue sky and Dylan running in and out of the sea.'

'Then we'll stay on. I'll change the flights, sort the accommodation with the resort. If this is what your perfect Christmas looks like then that's what you'll have.'

'Are you serious?'

'Deadly.'

She leans in to kiss me again but then there's a voice from up on the boat.

'I think he might be stirring,' Hassan calls down. 'I didn't want to disturb you too soon, but I thought you might want to be here when he opens his eyes. I don't want to scare him by being the first face he sees when he wakes up.'

Laura smiles. 'Thank you.'

'We'll come up now,' I add, and we swim over to the edge of the boat and climb up the ladder.

I'm sure that Hassan's trying not to stare as Laura steps up on deck, going straight to check on Dylan before she even gets a towel. He's still asleep but the captain is right – he's fidgeting, which is a sure sign he's going to wake up soon.

'Right, shall we continue? Are you two getting hungry?'

'Definitely,' I say.

'Thank you so much for watching him.' Laura smiles at him and he bows his head and then heads back to the cabin.

When we reach the island, it's amazing – a little table set up ready for us with a large pillar candle in the middle. At the advice of the captain, we take a quick walk whilst our food is set up, along the water's edge so that Dylan can splash in the warm sea.

When we return, the candle is lit and it looks stunning. The food is exceptional – a crab salad followed by sea bass. It tastes so fresh I wouldn't be surprised if they'd caught it whilst we walked. During the meal, Laura's beautiful face opposite me, it dawns on me that this is my life. I made this happen. It's such a total high. And I hope that she feels the same – that I can give her her best Christmas yet.

All at once, the sound of 'Happy Birthday' fills the air and a group of staff come out, all dressed in matching white, carrying a large chocolate cake with two candles glowing on the top.

When they've finished the song, they put the cake in front of Dylan, far enough away that he can't reach out and touch it from his highchair.

'Remember how we blow out the candles, Dylan? Do it with Mummy this time. You can both make a wish then.'

Laura blows gently to show Dylan how and then he

sticks out his lips and makes a puffing sound whilst Laura blows out his candles, her face suddenly thoughtful.

The staff clap and then take the cake off to cut it, bringing us each back a slice and a cake fork and I alternate between a forkful for myself and giving a forkful to Dylan.

'So what did you wish for?'

Laura shakes her head with a smile. 'I can't tell you that, can I? Then it won't come true.'

'Give me a hint.'

Laura dabs under her mouth with a napkin. 'It wasn't for anything new. That's all I'm going to say.'

And I smile, glad that maybe I *have* provided her with everything she ever wanted, that there's nothing more she could ask for. Because I feel exactly the same.

I reach under the table into the side pocket of the bag, suddenly nervous that the ring might have fallen out on the boat, but my hand soon meets it so I pull it out and then get down on one knee on the sand.

'I know I've already done this once, but you deserve a much more romantic proposal and a ring.' I open the box and hold it out to her. 'I know I drive you mad sometimes. That there'll always be sparks flying off at every angle between us – good and bad. But you make me happier than I even thought possible. So will you do me the honour of marrying me?'

She stares at the ring with an expression I can't read and then looks up at me with a shy smile. 'Thank you.'

I take the ring out of the box and push it on to her finger, sitting back down on my chair. 'I'm presuming it's still a yes.'

'Of course it's a yes.'

'And I'm sorry it's taken so long. I wanted to find the perfect ring and the perfect time and I figured when better than in the Maldives on the anniversary of the day I realized I was in love with you, the day of my first amateur proposal.'

'It's perfect. Thank you.'

I sense a slight reservation from Laura, but I can't quite put my finger on it. I wonder if she feels she's heard it all before.

'We will do it this time, I promise. Make sure it's set in stone. We could do it on this day next year. That would be cool, wouldn't it? We could have Christmas songs on the dance floor! What do you think?'

Laura laughs. 'A Christmas wedding? Trust you.'

I take her hand, newly emblazoned with the *very* expensive engagement ring, and bring it to my lips. 'Is that a yes?'

'December the sixteenth, yes. But nothing Christmassy. Deal?'

'One song?' She shoots me a warning look and I smile. 'OK. Deal.'

LAURA

The breeze runs through my hair and across my face as I lie back on the lounger on the deck of the boat. I could easily close my eyes and fall asleep. Dylan's a much better sleeper than he used to be, but motherhood is still utterly exhausting. It's like I'm always on. Even if there are moments of standby, I never totally switch off. I love it. Watching Dylan grow and change is the best experience of my life. It's fascinating. The language acquisition, the way he imitates, the development of empathy. It's like each day he gets closer to being a 'real' human. But the exhaustion is like nothing I've ever known. It's not the sort of exhaustion you can sleep off. It feels like it's in the depth of my bones.

Dylan is sitting on Luke's lap on the lounger next to me, Luke reading him a story. There's something so relaxing about listening to someone read. I guess it's like being a kid again. Mum used to read to me every night. You could tell the teachers were surprised when I started school already able to read. They probably looked at Mum, just a teenager, looked at our address on the register, and thought I'd come in in nappies, barely able to say my own name. But Mum used to spend hours reading to me, her fingers pointing to each word as she said it. And I must have just picked it up from watching and listening to her.

Dylan lifts a flap and then shakes his head. I think they're looking for Spot.

'No,' Dylan says laughing. 'Bear. Honey.'

'Exactly. It's a bear eating honey. Not Spot.'

They turn the page. 'Sssss,' Dylan says.

'Sssss snake,' Luke copies, pretending his finger is a snake and tickling Dylan under the arm with it.

I could watch them all day. There is nothing more appealing than a man being a good father. It's almost *sexy*.

'Rocudile,' Dylan says, pointing at the animal under the bed.

'Yes, that's right. Crocodile. Did you hear that, Laur?' Luke says, turning to me with a look of glee on his face. 'He said "crocodile".'

'Rocudile,' Dylan repeats, beaming at our acknowledgement.

I reach my hand over and ruffle Dylan's hair. 'Amazing new word, gorgeous. Well done.'

When they've finished reading, Dylan automatically reaches over and grabs another book, handing it to Luke, who sighs dramatically but pulls Dylan tighter on to his lap with a huge smile on his face. As I check the time on my watch, I notice the huge diamond nearly blinding me in the sunlight. It practically fills my entire finger. I dread to think how much it cost, to think of all the things we could have bought for Dylan with that money. It's not that I'm not chuffed to finally have a ring. When Luke didn't take my hint and get me the ring I saw at the Christmas market last year, I thought perhaps he'd changed his mind about wanting to marry me. And I'm glad to finally have a date – even if it is in December. But I loved that ring. It was so much less flashy. So much more . . . me.

As soon as we get off the boat, after profuse thank yous

to Hassan, we wander along the water's edge back to the resort bar, chatting about the delicious smells coming from the restaurants we pass, the gorgeous warm evening – and the way we still feel like we're bobbing up and down, like being in a permanent lift. The sea is warm on our feet and the wash of the waves dragging along the sand is the most relaxing sound.

When we reach the pool bar, it's already buzzing, the music loud enough to create an atmosphere but not so loud that it's intrusive. All the tables are occupied – there are one or two families with pre-school aged children, but mainly retired couples and honeymooners.

We spot an empty sofa in the corner and dive on it. The Christmas tree next to us looks totally out of place, like when you find a bauble you accidentally forgot to put away in the middle of summer. Luke goes to the bar, adorned with fairy lights, while I plonk Dylan on the sofa next to me. After his late nap on the boat, there's no chance he's going to sleep anytime soon, so I grab some Duplo figures out of the bag, hoping they might keep him occupied for a little while. He takes them off me and starts jumping them up and down on the sofa, making explosion noises when they fall back down as if they are crashing to their deaths.

'This is for you,' Luke says, handing me a colourful cocktail with a trademark umbrella in it, although this one is covered in reindeers. It's clearly meant in a cool kitsch way, as this place is the epitome of stylish. 'And this is for you, birthday boy.' Luke puts a ginormous ice cream sundae on the table in front of Dylan.

'It's bigger than him, Luke.'

'I thought we could help him with it.'

I roll my eyes and grab a bib out of the bag for Dylan, who is pointing at the sundae and shouting 'Mine, mine, mine.'

'OK, OK, hold your horses.'

Once his bib is on, I start spooning out the sundae and putting it into his mouth, interspersed with spoonfuls for me.

'It's pretty good to be fair,' I say, licking my lips.

'Wait until you try that cocktail.'

I remove the umbrella and take a sip. 'Bloody hell, it's strong. Are you trying to get me shit-faced?'

'Maybe,' Luke smiles. 'I've already ordered another round, so drink up.'

I feel drunk after a few sips. Being a parent seems to have made me a total lightweight. Perhaps it's the permanent energy deficit.

'Beautiful Girls' by Sean Kingston comes on the stereo and half the bar gets up off their seats and starts dancing. Luke picks up Dylan, who has returned to his Duplo figures after gorging himself on sundae, and then grabs my hand. We dance amongst the crowds, Dylan giggling as Luke swings him around, and it's so perfect it stupidly makes me want to cry. The hits keep coming so we spend a good half an hour on the dance floor, people turning to look when they hear Luke's gorgeous voice singing along, until we're hot and sweaty and need a rest.

As soon as we sit down, the waitress appears with more drinks.

'As you requested, sir.'

Luke takes the drinks off her. 'Remember I said you can call me Luke.'

'Oh, OK, Luke.' She swoons. 'Thank you.'

I try to catch Luke's eye to give him a mocking look, but he maintains focus on the waitress. I think it's one of the things that makes Luke so appealing – the way when he's talking to you, he keeps his eyes fixed on you so you feel like he's fascinated by what you have to say, even though now I know he often isn't.

'The drinks were perfect. You did an amazing job,' he says smoothly.

'For you, of course.'

Does she even realize that I am here? The mother of the child who is sitting beside him? However often it happens, it still amazes me. In the beginning, I'd be overwhelmed by jealousy and a fear that I was going to lose him. Now that things are so good between us, I feel more secure. But I still wish it could just be me and him, without the rest of the world getting in the way.

'Do you want me to take that away for you?' She leans across Luke to get the sundae glass, so blatantly putting her breasts in his face that it is almost comical.

'Thank you,' Luke says, a cheeky smile on his face. 'Much appreciated.'

'Anytime,' she says, placing her hand on his shoulder. 'I'm here all night.'

When she walks away, I almost explode. 'What the actual fuck? *I'm here all night.* Is she serious?'

'She's just doing her job.' Luke waves his hand dismissively.

'She was not just doing her job, Luke. She was basically handing herself to you on a plate.'

'Well, can you blame her?' he teases, although there's

a hint of truth in it. He knows how attractive he is. A gorgeous bloke, in a band, with plenty of money – it's a package that's impossible to resist and I know that he's well aware of that. I just have to trust that he means it when he says there's only me.

'I can blame her for trying it on with you when your fiancée and son are sitting right next to you.'

'You like it really,' he whispers in my ear. 'The way she looks at me. It turns you on.'

I roll my eyes, but in a way, he's right. It *is* sexy to be the one he goes home with when everyone else clearly wants it to be them. But I certainly don't want to encourage him.

'Dylan's looking tired. Shall we drink up and go back?' he says with a wiggle of his eyebrows.

I look over at Dylan who is rubbing his eyes with the backs of his hands.

'Come on then.'

We down our cocktails, the strength of the alcohol making me wince, and Luke quickly changes Dylan's nappy in case he falls asleep on the short walk back to our apartment, which he does.

'I'll put him in his cot,' Luke whispers. 'You get your clothes off.'

I'm drunk so I do a wobbly striptease and strut towards the door to our deck stark naked. 'I'll be waiting outside.'

As soon as Luke has put Dylan down, he rushes towards me, following me out on to the deck.

'You need to get naked too,' I say, grabbing his head as his mouth works its way up my thigh.

'Not yet. It's all about you first.'

I put my hands on his shoulders so I can hold him

away from me. 'Uh uh. It was all about me earlier. Now it's your turn.'

Luke looks up at me and then pulls his clothes off, lifts me up and throws me on to the outside bed.

'Promise me we can do this forever,' he says, holding his weight above me.

'Always.'

He lowers his face and kisses me and then I flip him over so that I'm on top, relishing the look of desire on his face and the rare feeling of being completely in control.

Later, we drink champagne in bed, listening to the waves lapping against the deck, the evening still warm enough to lie out with just a thin sheet over our naked bodies. Luke gets his laptop and we look at the house he's found for us to buy in more detail. It looks like something out of a Scandinavian design magazine. So much light that you'd need to constantly wear sunglasses.

'We could use that space for entertaining,' Luke says, pointing to the huge dining area.

'That's a lot of space for Sarah and Tom.'

'There are more people in the world than Sarah and Tom, you know?'

We scroll through the pictures. It's all open plan downstairs and the bedrooms are on a mezzanine level. There's a photograph of what it would be like to be standing and overlooking the ground floor, and it really is magnificent. Then Luke shows me the view from the balcony. The lawn is like a football pitch. I can just imagine Dylan charging around it. And the view of the lake and the surrounding mountains is stunning. It's the kind of view you could look at all day and still find something new in it. Picturing myself sitting there in the summer, reading a book, enjoying my morning coffee – it's an image of pure bliss. And don't even get me started on the tennis courts. But it isn't my home.

'So what do you think?' Luke says expectantly.

'It's beautiful . . .'

'Isn't it? I told you you'd love it once you had a good look at it. Think of all the different places we can christen when we move in.'

I smile, but then my face falls. It feels like breaking it to someone that they haven't got the job when they clearly thought they'd aced the interview. 'It's not for me.'

'Why the hell not?' It's more confused than angry, like he can't fathom a reason why I'm not jumping at it.

'It's just not me. I don't belong there.'

'Of course you belong there.'

I let out a breath. Sometimes I hate how uptight I am about money. But I grew up with *nothing*. And of course I don't want Dylan to have to live my life – my parents always saying no to everything, having to wear clothes that were five sizes too big so that they had growing room, having wet feet all the time because the soles of my shoes were split completely from the body – I don't want him to feel the constant stress that having no money causes, but I don't want him to be entitled or spoilt either. I want him to grow up in the real world, because who knows how long all this is going to last.

'I like our little home. We've made it "us". It's cosy.'

'We could make this place "us". You can choose the furniture, the art on the walls, the cushions – you can choose it all.'

'But look at it, Luke. How can I ever feel at home there?'

Luke places his laptop on the side table and puts his hands on the tops of my arms. 'I know you might not realize it, but you deserve the absolute best in life. And I want to provide that for you in as many ways as I can. But you have to let me.'

I look back through the glass doors into our apartment. The clean lines. The lack of clutter. The light. The way absolutely everything is set up to make life easier and that bit more pleasant. And I know the new house would feel just like that.

'Are you sure we can afford it?'

Luke smiles, sensing he's close to victory. 'One hundred percent.'

'OK.'

'OK?' Luke cups my cheeks and looks me right in the eyes. 'I show you the perfect house and all I get is OK?'

I smile. 'Yes, then. Let's do this.'

Luke kisses me and then he stands up on the bed and starts doing a stupid dance before sitting back down beside me. 'As soon as we get home, I'll take you there to show you. And we'll look at venues for the wedding too. A rustic barn. Candles and fairy lights everywhere. Not a fleck of tinsel in sight, I promise. What do you think?'

'I think it sounds perfect.'

16th December 2008

LUKE

'Can you please ring the caterers? They still haven't responded to my emails to confirm and they're supposed to be coming in a few hours.'

Laura is flapping around the house, Dylan on her hip, a pile of washing draped over her arm.

'It'll be fine. I've paid them so they'll be coming.'

'But what if they've forgotten?'

'They won't have forgotten. Chill.' I continue to strum my guitar. I'm working on a new song that's been going round and round in my head recently. I'm hoping it's going to be our biggest hit yet.

Laura storms over and pulls the wire out of the amp.

'What did you do that for?'

'I can't do everything by myself. It was your idea to throw this stupid party and then, just as you always do, you leave me to actually organize everything.'

I get up and plug the amp back in. 'What have you got to organize? I've paid a caterer so you don't have to worry about the food or drink. I've turned the playroom into a soft play centre to keep all the kids busy; I pay for a cleaner each week because apparently the house is too big for you to manage even though you're here all day every day . . .'

I know when I say it that it's the equivalent of lighting a match next to a highly flammable substance, but I don't expect the huge plastic digger that Laura snatches out of Dylan's hand to come hurtling towards my head.

'What the fuck are you doing?'

Laura covers Dylan's ears and then puts him down and he runs off, probably to find more vehicles now his mother has used the one he was playing with as a lethal weapon.

'Will you stop swearing?' she says through gritted teeth. She looks so furious it wouldn't surprise me to see smoke coming out of her ears.

'You just threw a truck at my head. I'm entitled to swear.'

'I threw a truck at your head because you're being so effing annoying.'

I put down my guitar and go up to Laura, putting my arms around her and kissing her neck. She holds her head away from me but doesn't totally push me off, which I take as a good sign.

'Now look who's swearing?' I tease.

'I didn't actually swear. We have to be careful or Dylan will start using those sorts of words and I'll be revealed as the chav I really am.'

'You worry too much what people think of you.'

'Easy to say when the world worships you.'

'Not the *whole* world.'

There's a glimmer of a smile on Laura's lips so I kiss her neck again and put my hands down the back of her jeans.

'Luke.'

'What?'

This time she *does* remove my arms. 'Stop.'

'But you're sexy when you're angry.'

She moves away and starts grabbing Dylan's toys from the various surfaces he's left them on. 'A cleaner doesn't do all this, Luke. A cleaner doesn't bring up our child. You can't just throw money at everything. You actually have to take part.'

'I'm here, aren't I?'

Laura claps slowly. She can be such a patronizing pain in the arse sometimes.

I pick up my guitar and play the heaviest song off the album because I know how much Laura hates it. 'I prefer the ones that have some sort of melody,' she said when she first heard it, not realizing (or at least I don't think she realized) how offensive that was.

Laura stands there for a moment. I reckon she thinks if she stares at me long enough I might do the right thing and stop playing, but I don't.

'I can't be bothered with this,' I think she says from the movement of her lips.

'What?' I shout over my guitar, just to be a dick. She starts to storm off so I stop playing. 'What?'

'Do you seriously expect a medal for showing up to your son's birthday party? It's easy to show up for all the fun stuff, to turn up and be the hero.'

'So would you rather I wasn't here? That I didn't show up? Because right now I'm a bit confused about how to get things right with you.'

Laura sighs, throws herself on the sofa and rests her head on the back. 'Of course I wouldn't rather you weren't here.'

I grab her legs, pulling her towards me, and then manoeuvre her on to my lap, her legs automatically wrapping themselves around my back.

'You drive me mad. You know that, don't you?' she says, narrowing her eyes at me.

I smile and then lean towards her and kiss her. 'You wouldn't change me really.'

'Seriously, Luke. I would.'

'Think how boring life would be if you didn't have me to get mad at all the time.'

Laura rolls her eyes. 'I need to get on. Despite the fact you clearly think I do bugger all, I need to get the house straight and wrap Dylan's present.'

'I don't think you do bugger all. And you do realize no one is going to care if there are a few toys out and about.'

'But *I* care.'

'Well, you shouldn't.' I push my hands under her top and massage her lower back and she closes her eyes. 'Ooh, there's some tension in there.'

'It's caused by living with you.'

I move my hands round to her stomach and then run my thumbs along the bottom of her bra. 'I know a way to relax you.'

She mirrors me, running her hands under my jumper, over my abdominals and up to my chest. 'Our son is upstairs.'

I put my hands over her breasts and then push my thumbs under the material to caress her nipples. 'Later, then.'

She lets out a deep breath and I can tell she doesn't want me to stop, but then she pulls away, clambering down off my lap.

'I'm going to wrap Dylan's present. We got him a bike, by the way. Just in case you're wondering.'

'I knew that.'

'Yeah, right.'

She goes upstairs and I go back to tinkering with the song I was working on. Maybe I *should* know what we've bought our son for his birthday. But I've been so busy with the band. And she's better at all that stuff – choosing things he'll like and checking the reviews. I'd probably get something useless and she'd moan that it was a total waste of money.

There's a knock at the door so I put down my guitar and go and open it.

'Parcel for Dylan Jenkins.' The bloke hands me a large box.

'Laur, did you order anything else for Dylan?' I shout up.

'No,' she replies, appearing on the mezzanine.

'Package for Dylan.' I hold it up and she comes down to see. I take it to the sofa and we open it, finding a Happyland farm and a card inside. Laura reads it first and then hands it to me. When she puts her hand on my thigh in a comforting way, I know who it's from.

'To Dylan, HAPPY BIRTHDAY!! Hope you enjoy playing with your new farm. Love Granddad.'

'Are you going to give it to him?' Laura asks.

I shake my head. 'We can wrap up the present as an extra thing from us. I'm not giving him the card.'

Laura nods slowly but I can tell she wants to say more. She was the same last year when we got back from the Maldives to find a man-sized teddy bear on the doorstep. *Maybe you should give him a chance. Dylan is a part of him, Luke.* But I don't want to see him. I can't.

Laura kisses me on the cheek and then stands up. 'I'll go and wrap it up.'

'Thank you.'

I rip up the card and throw it in the kitchen bin. Then I go upstairs to find Dylan, who is sitting on his bedroom floor zooming his trains around the track he's built.

'Can *I* play, please?'

Dylan looks up at me. 'You have the blue train.'

I smile. I'm only ever allowed the blue train, rather than his favourite green one. 'Sounds good to me.'

I add a crossing and station to his track and then we push our trains around, me chasing his with mine. 'Go, go, go. It's going to catch up.'

Dylan giggles, pushing his train as fast as he can manage, but the tail of it keeps slipping off the track.

I change direction so that eventually the trains are going to meet in the middle. 'Oh, no. There's going to be a crash.'

Laura puts her head around the door. 'Is that productive play?' she asks, raising an eyebrow.

'It's fun, isn't it, Dylan?' I hurtle my train towards his and they crash head on. 'Aaaaah.'

Dylan laughs. 'Do it again, Daddy. Do it again.'

'Want to join us?' I grab another train out the box and hold it out to Laura. 'It's actually quite cathartic.'

Laura smiles and takes the train and then she kneels down beside us and starts smashing her train into mine, making Dylan laugh again.

'See?'

'Surprisingly satisfying.'

After numerous head-on collisions, Laura stands up. 'Right, I'm just going to go and put those last few decorations out that we got.'

'Laura Baker choosing to put up Christmas decorations? Have I entered an alternative universe?'

'It's a waste, them just sitting in their boxes.'

I smile and then as she turns to leave, I grab her hand. 'I'm sorry. That we're not . . . well, you know . . . that I lost the venue.'

Laura looks at her feet. 'It's OK. It probably wouldn't have been the best having it on Dylan's birthday anyway. The focus should be on him, shouldn't it?'

I wonder if she's just putting on a brave face or whether she's having second thoughts about marrying me at all. 'I guess you're right.'

'Anyway, do you mind getting him dressed for the party? I've put the clothes out on his bed. You just need to put them on.'

'No problem. We can manage that, can't we, Dyls? Let's get party ready.'

Laura's parents arrive first. They've not seen the house yet as we only moved in just over a month ago so I'm looking forward to showing it off – proving to them that I've done all right by Laura despite getting her pregnant so soon into our relationship.

'Wow,' Angie says, her mouth dropping open.

'Come in.' I wave them in and the waitress that I've hired brings over a tray with glasses of champagne on it. 'Would you like a drink, Angie? Graham?'

'Not unless you've got a beer,' Graham says, turning his nose up.

'I'll have one.' Angie helps herself to a glass. 'Thank you, love,' she says to the waitress who smiles sweetly in return. She's probably only about sixteen. I keep catching her taking a second look at me and then turning away as if she's been caught breaking the rules. I expect she can't believe her luck that she got given this gig.

'I'll get you a beer, Dad,' Laura calls, as she comes down the staircase with Dylan in her arms. He's wearing his navy shirt with little Christmas puddings dotted across it and Laura has added a red bow tie.

'Oh, look at you,' Angie says. 'So smart.'

When Laura reaches the bottom of the stairs, she puts Dylan down and he clings on to her leg, hiding behind it. Shuffling, Laura makes her way over with Dylan attached. 'It's Nana and Granddad, silly. You're not shy.'

Angie holds out a present and Dylan reaches out from behind Laura's leg to take it, like a frog sneakily whipping out its tongue to catch a fly.

'Thanks, Mum. You didn't have to.'

'Of course I did. It's my grandson's third birthday.'

'Well, thank you. Let me get that beer and we'll sit down and open it.'

Suddenly, the front door swings open and my mum comes in, a huge bag of presents in her hand. 'Where's the birthday boy?' she announces.

Dylan runs straight up to her and wraps himself around her legs. 'Nono.'

'Hi Mum.' I give her a hug. 'Come on in.' I look over at Laura's parents who are standing in the lounge watching us. 'Shall we all go and sit on the sofas and then we can do some present opening?'

'Sure,' Mum says. 'Hi Angie, hi Graham. Nice to see you again.'

'You too,' Angie says and Graham just nods.

'Right, that beer,' Laura says in an overly cheerful voice. 'Do you want anything from the kitchen, Jenny?'

'No, I'll have some of this wonderful-looking champagne. Thank you, Laura.'

Laura goes to the fridge to get her dad a beer and I sit amongst the grandparents and down my glass, hoping it might make the whole experience slightly less uncomfortable. When Laura returns, the present opening begins and we all try to pretend that Dylan is as thrilled with his pack of crayons from Laura's parents as he is with his ginormous bag of train set accessories and vehicles that he got from Mum.

'Nono, come, come.' Dylan takes her hand and pulls Mum to the kitchen. 'I want a Nono smoovie.'

I think Laura finds my mum a little easier to be around than her own so she's here a lot. It makes me happy to see how close her and Dylan are, but I can sense that Laura feels bad for her parents that Dylan isn't as close to them.

'He loves his crayons, thank you,' Laura says to her parents, clearly trying to divert their attention from Dylan and Mum happily making his much-loved smoothie. Angie's eyes remain fixed on Mum; Graham stares into the depths of his beer.

'Oh, it's just something little,' Angie says, finally turning to look at Laura. 'I would've liked to be able to get him more, but . . .'

Laura waves her hand. 'It's perfect.'

'Kids don't need all these fancy toys. You were perfectly happy with a cardboard box and some scissors,' Graham says to Laura and she smiles.

'So what do you think?' I ask them. 'Do you like the new house?'

'It's amazing,' Angie says. 'The views. The space. You're very lucky, Laura.'

'It's a bit too open for me. All this glass. I'd feel like I was in a greenhouse,' Graham says.

'Well, I suppose it's not going to be to everyone's taste, but we love it, don't we, Laura?' I prompt.

Laura shrugs. 'It's a little bit big for the three of us, but I like the light.'

It's a subtle dig. I know Laura would like another child. She's not explicitly asked me for one, but she'll often drop little hints about how much she hated being an only child and how people keep asking her when we're going to give Dylan a little brother or sister. But I struggle to find enough time for Dylan right now, let alone another child.

'You can never have too much space. Isn't that right, Angie?' Mum calls, pouring smoothie into a plastic cup for Dylan.

'I'd happily swap if you don't want it, Laura,' Angie says.

'Our place is fine,' Graham snaps. 'It's homely.'

'It *is* fine,' Angie chips in quickly, as if she's aware she's in line for an earful when she gets home.

'I'm proud of you for working so hard, Luke,' Mum says, like only a mum can.

Graham snorts. 'If only real hard work paid this well, hey?'

I force myself not to bite and, thankfully, the tension is broken up by the arrival of Sarah and Tom, who come in full of life and laughter as always, followed by a couple of Laura's friends from toddler group that I forced her to invite, one with a little boy and one with four children of various ages. *Four children.* She must have a screw loose.

'I couldn't get anyone to look after them. Hope that's OK?'

'The more the merrier.' I usher her in, followed by her tribe of children. She looks like she's going to the Costa del Sol for a fortnight, the amount of crap she's brought with her. 'I've hired out a soft play for the playroom so that should keep them all busy.'

'Sounds amazing. The kids are going to love that.' One of her children (second, I'm going to guess by their heights) pushes past the lot of us and darts towards the stairs.

'Jeremiah, don't run,' she calls ineffectually, as the boy starts climbing up the outside of the staircase. She hurries towards him but before she can reach him, he hangs and then drops to the floor.

'These stairs are so cool,' he shouts and goes to climb up again but his mum grabs him, sweating by the time she manages to unhook his Spiderman grip from the banister and pull him off. 'Sorry about that.'

She turns to me and I smile as convincingly as I can muster whilst wondering how long it's going to be until lovely Jeremiah is drawing on the playroom walls.

Laura wanders over to greet them and I can tell that she's nervous – the way she's in no rush to get over to us and doesn't quite know what to say.

'Hi Emily. Hi Katie. Shall I take all the kids to the playroom and then I'll get you both a drink?'

The mum of four, Emily, looks like she's just been saved from drowning as Laura guides all the children to the playroom and I lead the mums to the tray of champagne.

'This place is incredible,' Katie says, looking around. 'Thank you.'

'Although I'd worry my children would break that glass in seconds,' Emily says.

'I think it's fairly childproof.'

'That's before *my* children came along,' she laughs and I rack my brain for any large, heavy objects I might need to quickly hide.

Laura comes back in, looking slightly flustered, and I hold out a glass of champagne for her. Absent-mindedly she takes it, and then she says, 'I wonder if we should take those drinks in there. Just to keep an eye on them all.'

I can see the disappointment on Emily's face that her brief moment of peace has been taken away so soon after being offered, but she nods and they all walk along to the playroom. The grandparents have settled on the sofas with Tom and Sarah, so I grab myself a beer, enjoying a moment of calm.

'Who'd have kids?' I joke to the teenage girl still holding the tray of champagne glasses and she smiles, her cheeks flushing bright red. 'You can put the tray down, you know? Sit down if you want.' I tap the barstool next to me, feeling guilty at the sight of this poor young girl here just to serve us. Shyly, she begins to walk over but then Laura comes storming in from the playroom.

'Everyone's probably getting hungry. Can you get the canapés out? We'll have to have ours in the playroom as we're stuck in there. I'm just going to do a large jug of squash for the kids. They're all sweating, charging around.'

I wave her away. 'I'll sort it all. You go and chat to your friends.'

'I can't exactly chat, can I? I keep having to stop Dylan from pushing Archie down the slide. And Jeremiah's nearly smashed our special snow globe by knocking it off the side.'

'I told you, who'd have kids, hey?' I say to the young girl (how awful that I don't even know her name) and she looks like she doesn't know whether to smile or not.

'Must be nice to just sit here and chat,' Laura says through gritted teeth, moving away from the kitchen area so I go with her. 'I've barely said hi to Sarah and Tom. Or my parents for that matter.'

'I'll go and watch the kids. You bring your mum friends in here with everyone else.'

'It's too late now.'

'How can it be too late? Come on, don't be stubborn.' I move towards Laura and put my arms around her. 'How many years until he's in prison, do you think? Jeremiah, I mean.'

Laura smiles. 'Shh. You can't say things like that.'

'Look, try to relax and enjoy it. I did this so you could start to build more of a social circle. I know how hard you've found it.'

'That's because it's hard to make friends at these places. You don't know what it's like. They're all in these bloody cliques. Emily and Katie are the only two people who have ever actually deigned to speak to me.'

'It wasn't a criticism. I just hate the thought of you being lonely whilst I'm not here.'

'You know you could just be here more often.'

'Oh, come on, Laur. I just thought it might be good for you to have some friends with kids so you can chat about Mummy stuff.'

'Oh yeah, what's that? Potty training, tantrums and school places? Because we couldn't have opinions about interesting things, could we?' Laura says it with a smile so I take the opportunity to kiss her.

'You look very beautiful, you know.'

'Thank you.'

I kiss her again and then force myself to pull away, aware other people are only metres away.

'Right, I better get back before Jeremiah launches something at the glass doors or starts strangling someone with the Christmas lights.'

I laugh. 'They'll be fine for a minute. Go and get your friends, I'll sort the refreshments and then I'll go and sit with the kids.'

'OK, thanks.'

Laura goes to get the other mums and I help the young girl (turns out her name is Daisy) to sort out the canapés and then I grab a jug of squash for the kids and head towards the playroom. But as I do, I pause and survey my home. The banisters all around the mezzanine level are wrapped in greenery and fairy lights. Laura's parents, Mum and Tom are sitting on the two large sofas by the Christmas tree. Laura, Sarah and Laura's two mummy friends are standing by the dining table, under the chandelier, drinking champagne and giggling. And for now, all I can hear coming out of the playroom is the sound of children's laughter.

Suddenly, Mum is beside me. 'Pretty impressive, hey?'

'It's not bad, is it?'

'You should be so proud of yourself, Luke.'

'Thank you. I mean, I'm not sure I really deserve it. I just stand there, strum a guitar and open my mouth.'

126

Back when I was in school, the other lads took the piss out of me because I chose to spend my lunch breaks in the music room rather than playing football, and the teachers told me I'd never achieve anything because I was disorganized and lazy. These days I would probably be given a label and, hopefully, some support, but back then I was just dismissed as one of the kids that would never amount to much. And then Dad buggered off, choosing a pretty face over his wife and child. So it wasn't really until I met Rich and Cody at university that I started to feel like I belonged anywhere, started to believe I could be someone. *Well, fuck the lot of you. Look at me now.*

'Don't play down what you've achieved. Your dad is proud of you too, you know.'

'He sent a present again.'

'For Dylan?'

I nod and Mum goes quiet for a moment.

'You know, you don't have to be mad at him for my sake. I got over everything he did a long time ago. We're almost friends now. And he *is* his granddad. Being a grandparent is a pretty sacred thing.'

I shake my head. 'I don't want it for Dylan. What he did to us.'

Mum puts her hand on my arm. 'He loves you, Luke. And I'm sure he'd dote on Dylan.'

'So why did he stop calling? Would you have given up on me?'

'Of course not. I do understand, and you have to do what you feel comfortable with, but just know you've got nothing to prove to me. You've always been the best, most loyal son.'

'And you the best mum.'

She links her arm through mine. 'Come on, let's go and party like the superstar that you are.'

I smile. 'I need to go and check on the kids, then I'll be back. Go and grab some more canapés before all the best ones go.'

'I will. I love you, Luke.'

I kiss her on the cheek. 'Love you too, Mum.'

LAURA

'So are you pleased?' I ask my dad, standing by the glass wall that overlooks our extensive garden. 'You don't seem very pleased.'

'Pleased that you're living here?' Dad pours his beer into a glass. He refuses to drink it from the bottle (real men don't drink from the bottle, apparently, in the same way that real men don't drink lager, only ale).

'Yeah. Isn't this what you always wanted for me? To be successful?'

'There are lots of ways to measure success, love.'

'You don't have to tell *me* that. But you went on and on at me about getting a good job, making money . . .'

Dad shakes his head, swallowing his mouthful of beer. 'It was never about the money.'

'So what was it about, then?'

'I wanted you to *make* something of yourself. You were always so smart. Your mum and I never understood it – how you came from us – but somehow you did and you had all this potential . . .'

'And then I went and threw it all away by getting pregnant?'

'I'm not saying that.'

'You told me we couldn't afford for me to go to uni.'

'Well, we couldn't really. But you said you didn't want to go anyway.'

'I'm not sure I did, but what I'm saying is I don't know what you wanted me to do differently, how I could . . .'

Please you? Impress you? Make you proud?

'I was just trying to teach you to find a job that fulfils you, that also pays OK. I didn't want you to be stuck in a dull job like me, counting the hours until your shift ends, wishing your life away.'

It makes me really sad to hear him talk about his life in this way. Like he feels that he's wasted it trying to provide the best for me and mum.

'But you're not,' he continues. 'You have all of this.'

'But it's not mine, is it? Not really.'

'I don't know. From what I can see, you're doing the harder job bringing up that boy of yours. Definitely the more *important* job.'

'Thanks, Dad. And you know the offer's still there? It was Luke's idea, so it's not like I pressured him into it.'

'I'm not a charity, Laur.'

'I know that. But you don't have to be so proud either.' I elbow him in the arm. 'At least just take enough to have a few years off work, take Mum to travel the world.'

'It's not really our thing. But thanks anyway.' Dad takes a large gulp of his beer. 'I think me and your mum better get going soon.'

'Somewhere better to be?'

Dad offers a sad smile. 'Something like that.'

'Well, you're welcome here anytime, you know that, right?'

'And you to us, if you can bear to slum it these days.'

'Don't be silly. I just never seem to find the time. I know it sounds like an excuse, but looking after Dylan is a full-time job. I don't know where the hours go.'

It's the truth that life does always feel busy, but I also find going home quite depressing. The broken glass that always seems to be on the road outside. The groups of lads on their bikes, drinking and blaring music from some shitty distorted stereo, who always stare at me like I'm a piece of meat when I walk past, the sounds of people yelling coming from the windows of the houses nearby.

'It's fine. I get it. I wouldn't want to come home either.'

'Stop. It's not that. I'm just really busy.'

'Honestly, Laur. It's fine.' He places a hand lightly on my shoulder and I turn and pull him into a hug.

'I do love you, Dad.'

'I know. Of course.'

But as I let him go, I'm not sure that he does, and that makes me really sad.

After everyone else has gone home, Sarah and I sit up on the balcony in front of the firepit, each of us with a throw draped over our legs and pulled up under our arms. Luke and Tom are downstairs cooking sausages or something, even though the caterers provided more than enough food for twice the amount of guests we had. Surprise, surprise, the blokes have left Dylan with us, but luckily he's exhausted after his day of excitement so is sitting beside me colouring happily with the new crayons Mum got him.

'Well, that was a great party.' Sarah tops up her wine and then passes the bottle to me to do the same.

'Thank you. I think Luke probably just wanted to show off the new place.'

'Understandable. If I had a place like this, I'd be making an excuse for a party every day.'

I smile, but I know Sarah can tell that it's forced.

'You OK?'

'It was supposed to be the wedding today, remember?'

'Oh, yeah. Sorry, I forgot.'

I push out my bottom lip.

'Have you re-booked?'

I shake my head. 'He's never offered to and I'm not going to ask.'

'He *is* really busy, isn't he?'

'Too busy to marry me?'

'Well, maybe he's scared to commit to a date and then let you down again.'

Sometimes Luke and Sarah's friendship makes me jealous – not to share Luke with Sarah but to share Sarah with Luke. I know she'd be on my side if the chips were down, but she does have an annoying habit of being able to see his point of view on numerous occasions.

'So how about just not let me down?'

Sarah gives me a sad smile. 'He wasn't sure when the gig was going to be. As soon as he knew, he tried to book, didn't he? He couldn't help that that other pesky couple pipped you to the post.'

'Oh, come on, Sar. He's not establishing himself any more, is he? He can pick and choose when he does his gigs. Venues are desperate for them to perform there. He didn't make me a priority. That's the truth of the matter.'

'He *did* suggest booking that other place.'

'But I wanted the barn. I wanted to come first.'

Sarah puts her hand on top of mine. 'I know. But he *does* adore you. Just remember that. And the band won't always be this big.'

I let out a pained breath. 'I find it hard not to resent him sometimes. The way he gets to go off and travel the world, to follow his dream, and I'm stuck here with the drudgery.'

'It's a pretty nice place to be stuck.'

I wonder if deep down Sarah thinks I'm being ungrateful. I have a cleaner for God's sake, I don't have to work, whereas she's having to work two jobs she doesn't enjoy because Tom has been made redundant and she's not yet managed to find a career doing something with her music.

'I know. I know I'm really lucky to have all this, but I don't really want any of it. I just want him to be here more often.'

'I get that.'

'And it's like he walks in and Dylan thinks he's some sort of superhero. Luke's so much more fun than me, and Dylan never plays up for him, and it just makes me feel like such a bore . . .'

'You're not a bore.'

'A few weeks ago we were watching something on the laptop in bed. It was about ten o'clock and he said, "Why don't we go and lie on a blanket and see the stars." It was what we did on our first proper date.'

'I remember you telling me.'

'Well, anyway, I said no because Dylan was in bed and he said, "Well, just wake him up and take him with us", and I said, "No, that's irresponsible", and I could tell by the look on his face that he was thinking, who the hell have I ended up with?'

'There's no way he would've been thinking that.'

'In the end he just turned over and went to sleep and

I lay there wanting to go and look at the stars. That's the thing. I *wanted* to go.'

'Well, you were thinking of Dylan.'

'But it wouldn't have hurt him to wake him up. He probably would've loved it. And that wasn't even it. It's just like this negative thing that pops up in me, like I'm so bitter that his life's so much more interesting than mine, that *he's* so much more interesting than *me* . . .'

I stop because I know none of what I'm saying makes sense.

'He's definitely not more interesting than you. Trust me, have you ever sat with him and listened to him talk about guitars?' She mimes a huge yawn. 'And I'm a musician.'

I smile. 'I'm sorry. I'm going on about myself. Tell me what's going on with you.'

'Now that you've *finally* asked,' she teases. 'We're actually trying for a baby.'

'Really?'

Sarah nods and I put my wine glass on the table so that I can give her a proper hug. 'That's amazing. I'm so happy for you.'

'It's ridiculous timing,' she says as I pick my wine glass back up. 'With Tom out of a job and everything, but I said to him, we could wait forever if we wait for the perfect moment.'

'Well, look at us. We made it work. At least you guys are married.'

They had a perfect summer wedding overlooking the lake. It was stunning – wildflowers and greenery everywhere. Dylan was the ring bearer so I bought him this adorable matching waistcoat and trousers and he loved tottering down the aisle with the ring cushion in his hand. He walked so carefully, just like I'd taught him, and he didn't drop the rings once.

'It's really bothering you, isn't it? The not being married thing?'

'It's not just that. I never see him, Sar. Other than this ring on my finger, and the fact his name is on some of the letters that fall on the doormat, I don't even feel like I'm in a relationship. He turns up, we have sex and then he's gone again. The only reason I know anything about his life is from the papers.'

Sarah stands up and goes inside, shouting down over the balcony. 'Luke! Get your arse up here a minute.'

'What are you doing?' I ask as she comes back outside.

Sarah smiles. 'Something I should have done a while back.'

'Sarah.'

I hear Luke's footsteps on the stairs and then he appears and Sarah pats the sofa for him to sit on the other side of her.

'What are you two plotting?' Luke asks with narrowed eyes.

'Nothing to do with me,' I say, palms to the sky.

Sarah puts a hand on each of our thighs. 'Now, you both know how much I love you. But from an outsider's point of view – and I might be wrong – I'm not sure you're bringing out the best in each other right now, or that you're communicating properly, and that makes me sad.' Sarah sticks out her bottom lip and we both laugh. 'So I'm going to go and make sure Tom doesn't eat all the sausages and you're going to talk to each other, OK?'

She gives us both a hug and then heads downstairs. We sit in silence for a moment, and then Dylan puts his colouring down and climbs on to my lap, putting his arms around me and resting his head on my shoulder.

'One very tired boy,' I say.

'I think he enjoyed his party.'

'It was great. Thank you.'

'Do you think maybe you'd feel confident enough to invite those mums over again sometime?'

'Yes, I think so.'

'Good.' Luke looks like he might stand up but then he says, 'I know you said it's for the best, but I really do wish I was marrying you today. And I'm sorry the tour starts on Boxing Day – I know it's your favourite part of Christmas.'

'Only because it signals that it's over,' I lie. The truth is it's my favourite part because it's just the three of us. The year before last, we ordered in a curry – my rebellion against turkey – and just spent it on the sofa reading Dylan's new books and watching kids' films (even though Dylan didn't really understand them at the time) and it was bliss. And last year in the Maldives was even better – just the three of us building sandcastles on the beach.

'Dubai will be exciting though, won't it?' I add.

'I'd rather be here with you guys, though.'

'Oh, come off it – adoring fans or a nagging fiancée and a demanding toddler.'

Luke laughs and then looks around at Dylan, who has fallen asleep on my shoulder.

'Can you believe he's three?'

'That's what happens when you're away all the time – he gets older.'

Luke keeps his eyes focused on Dylan. 'I know.'

I put my hand on his leg. 'I'm sorry. I'm being a bitch. Look, I'll quickly put Dylan to bed then I'll come and join you guys. Save me a sausage, OK?'

'I thought you said you weren't hungry.'

'You know me. Always room for a sausage.'

'Indeed,' Luke says, wiggling his eyebrows playfully.

'Shut up.' I whack him with the throw and then try to stand up with Dylan in my arms, Luke pushing me by the bum as assistance. 'Talk later, yeah?'

Luke nods and I carry Dylan into the house to his bedroom, turning on his night light and gently placing him into his bed. I remove his coat but keep him in his shirt and jeans. It's not worth waking him to put his pyjamas on.

Once I've put him down, I sit by his bed and watch him for a moment just to check he doesn't stir and then get scared that I'm not there. Looking at him in the half-light, it still feels like a miracle that he's mine. When you're swept up in the nitty gritty of parenthood, the draining everyday, it's easy to forget this feeling. The overwhelming love. The way you just want to hold them forever. But I want to remember, even in the midst of the busy days, before it's too late. He's already three. I kiss his soft cheek, pull the quilt up over his shoulders and tear myself away to join the others.

When I get downstairs, they're not there so I go outside and find them next to the outdoor fire. Tom and Luke are munching away on their hot dogs and Sarah is putting ketchup on one, which she hands to me as soon as she spots me.

'Perfect timing. Here you go.' She then puts ketchup on one for herself and we get comfortable in the line of deck chairs set up in front of the fire.

'Well, this is the life,' Sarah says, resting her head back, a hot dog in one hand and a glass of wine in the other.

'You're making it hard for a man, you know, Luke?' Tom says.

Luke laughs. 'Sorry, mate.'

'He's still the same boring bastard underneath all this, don't worry, Tom.' I wink at Luke so he knows it's just banter. 'Crap in bed, too,' I add, and then realize that I must be quite drunk.

'Well, we've got that in common then, mate,' Tom says, nudging Luke's arm.

'We're almost like proper adults now, aren't we?' Sarah says once she's finished her hot dog. 'It's terrifying.'

'Do you think we're going to start having conversations about taxes and how irresponsible the youth of today are soon?' Luke adds, and I look at him to see he has a dollop of ketchup on his nose.

'I think you've got a while before you become a proper adult, darling.' I point at my nose and he gives me a confused expression. 'Ketchup. Nose.'

He rubs his face with the back of his hand. 'Better?'

'Perfect.'

He smiles at me and I want to tell him how much I love him, because I do, however much he infuriates me. I vow to make sure he knows before the end of the night.

'Look at the stars,' Sarah says, and we all turn to look. It's a clear night and the sky looks beautiful, the stars twinkling against the black.

'To a beautiful evening with beautiful people.' Luke raises his glass and we all do the same.

As the temperature drops even further, Luke collects some logs from the wood store and throws them on the fire, making it roar. We move our deck chairs closer to it, all holding out our hands to warm them.

'Well, happy birthday to Dylan: the most gorgeous boy in the world,' Sarah says, and I pick up the video monitor that I've put under my chair to check he is still sleeping soundly.

We all raise our glasses again. 'To Dylan.'

'May every one of his birthdays be as perfect as this.'

Once the fire has begun to fade, we come inside to say our goodbyes to each other. As I give Tom a hug, I notice Sarah whisper something in Luke's ear and he nods and whispers something back in hers. And then we swap places and Sarah wraps her arms around me.

'Let him in, OK?' she says into my ear. 'Because that boy loves you more than you could ever imagine.'

'I love you.'

'You too. Sleep tight.'

We see them out and I gather glasses and plates from various surfaces and put them on the worktop near the sink then start to run a bowl of water.

Luke comes over, stands behind me and puts his arms around my waist. 'I'll do it in the morning. Come to bed.'

'I don't mind. I'll get it done now.'

Luke puts his face on my shoulder. 'Please come to bed.'

I turn the tap off.

'Thank you.'

I turn around and Luke kisses me and then wraps his arms around me, and we stand there for a while and it's so nice just to be held. Normally, we seem to flit between tearing each other apart and tearing each other's clothes off. There's very little in between.

Luke takes my hand and leads me to our bedroom where he slowly takes off my clothes and throws them on the floor and then removes his own but keeps his boxers on, his toned physique still giving me butterflies.

'Massage?'

'Really? Not too tired? Isn't that your normal excuse?'

'Shut up and lie on your tummy.'

I lie on top of the quilt and Luke straddles me and then begins massaging my shoulders and it's not until he starts to release it that I realize how much tension has built up in them.

'She's right, you know,' he says.

'Who?'

'Sarah. We've not been bringing out the best in each other.' Luke runs his fingers down my spine.

'I know. I'm sorry.'

'Me too.' Luke presses the heel of his hand around my shoulder blade. 'You used to make me feel like I could achieve anything. That you were proud of me.'

'You used to make me feel like I was the only thing that mattered.' I feel my voice start to catch in my throat.

Luke turns me over, still straddling me. 'Let's try to be better, yeah? Because I really do love you.'

'I love you too.'

He leans down and kisses me, but it's not full of the usual passion, just tender and soft. And I feel a tear fall down my cheek. And then I run my hands over his chest and down to his stomach and this time I lean up and kiss him. And gradually, slowly, we make love and afterwards he lies behind me and holds me and I hope that we can stay like this forever; that life won't find a way back in.

16th December 2009

LAURA

'How long is it now?'

'A minute less than you asked before.'

'So when is *that*?'

I push Dylan's fringe off his face. 'Your party is still over an hour and a half away, gorgeous. But first we're going to meet Nana and Granddad at the café. They might even treat you to a cake as it's your birthday.'

Milk dribbles down Dylan's chin as he shovels his Rice Krispies into his mouth at lightning speed. I reckon he thinks if he eats his breakfast quickly the time will go faster. 'I've finished my breakfast now.'

'Come on then. Let's go and get you ready.'

We go upstairs to Dylan's room and I help him to take off his elf pyjamas. He's still got some of his baby chubbiness, but each day his body seems to be changing, becoming more streamlined. I wasn't prepared for this bit of parenthood. The way you ache for every change, the way you experience every development as a loss – the words that are no longer mispronounced, the rejection of a once loved toy, the now too-small shoes that need to be sent to the charity shop. And in less than a year, Dylan will start school. For so long it seemed like a distant occurrence. In fact, sometimes I even wished for it. A *break*. But now, all of a sudden, it's come upon me and it feels like there's a ticking clock above my head, this sudden need to treasure each and every moment.

I thread his arms into his red Santa shirt and then do the buttons for him.

'I'm going to look really smart, aren't I?' he says.

'You are.'

'Shall we send a photo to Daddy? Will he think I look smart?'

'Very.'

Dylan smiles and his pride makes me want to cry.

We put on his matching Santa joggers and then he poses for a photograph, as always putting on his awkward face as soon as the camera is in front of him.

'Let me see.'

I hold the phone up for him to see the photo I've taken.

'Can I write the message for Daddy?'

'Of course.'

I hand him my phone and he types in a message, taking an age to locate each letter, and then he clearly gets bored as he hands it back to me. It reads 'luf yoo' with a kiss, and it simultaneously warms my heart and makes me really angry. I send it with the photo of Dylan and then leave my phone on the side so that I don't have to know that it takes Luke forever to reply, don't have to sit there waiting for my phone to beep like some kind of sad idiot.

'Let's go and open your present from Mummy and Daddy,' I say, taking Dylan's hand, and he excitedly pulls me down the stairs to the lounge where his present is waiting, ginormous and wrapped in multi-coloured spotty paper.

'Can I open it?' He stares up at his gift, waiting patiently for my response.

'Go for it.'

'Should I wait for Daddy?'

It's a rule we've always had – before he opens any of his presents, he has to wait until Luke and I are both in the room to share it with him.

'Remember Daddy isn't coming home today, but he'll be here tomorrow afternoon and you can show him all your presents then, OK?'

He doesn't need telling twice and rips at the wrapping paper to reveal a giant wooden castle. I had it specially made. At first, I wasn't sure I could warrant the several thousand-pound price tag, but when I saw the other things the artist had made, they were so stunningly beautiful that I saw it as an investment. Something Dylan can hand down to his children if he ever has them. Besides, there may as well be something positive to come out of Luke forever putting the band first.

'Can I play with it?'

'Of course. That's what it's for.'

I hand him another wrapped box. 'Thought you might need some more knights. And possibly another dragon.'

I say 'dragon' with a roar and Dylan rips off the paper and opens the box, going through all his new figures and especially his new dragon, as if he's handling gold.

'I love them, Mummy.' He envelops me in such a forceful hug it nearly knocks me over.

'Good, I'm glad. Happy birthday, darling.'

He lets me go and starts putting his knights into various positions around his castle and then flying his dragon around the whole thing, skipping and roaring. It's a dreary day – the rain hasn't stopped since we woke up. Up until today, Dylan's birthdays have been bright and crisp – bloody freezing sometimes but always bright. Maybe the sun only shines when Luke's here.

'Mummy's just grabbing something from upstairs,' I say as I run up to get my phone. When I check it, it's a relief to see there's a message from Luke.

> To Dylan, happy birthday. You look very smart. Have you
> opened your present yet? I'm so sorry not to be there
> but can't wait to see it tomorrow. I might even bring you
> something extra. Love Daddy x.

And then he's sent another message. To Mummy, I love you x and then a photo of him, guitar strap around his neck, pulling a funny face with Rich and Cody.

Mum and Dad have already bought Dylan a piece of cake by the time we arrive at the café.

'You're late,' Mum says, as I plonk Dylan down on the chair across the table from them.

'Sorry, I struggled to tear him away from his new castle. I'm just going to grab a coffee.'

'And a hot chocolate for me,' Dylan says.

'Please,' I prompt.

'Please,' Dylan parrots.

I leave Dylan with Mum and Dad and queue for our drinks. I opt for a gingerbread latte (it's one of the only good things about Christmas) and get Dylan a hot chocolate overflowing with whipped cream and marshmallows. I can see him chattering away animatedly to Mum and Dad, and then Dad deliberately puts the foam from his coffee on his nose and tries to lick it off with his tongue, Dylan giggling. It's nice to see the playful side of Dad. He can be a grumpy bastard sometimes, but I always remember his fun side too – playing 'Daddy monster' where he'd turn out the lights and then chase me around the room, tickling me until I screamed once he'd caught up with me, sneaking me extra cookies when Mum wasn't looking.

When I get back to the table, Dylan is telling them about Luke's message and his promise to bring him an extra present.

'Would be better if he was just here really, wouldn't it?' Mum says through gritted teeth.

'Mum,' I say, nodding towards Dylan.

'I just mean presents aren't everything, are they?'

'No, I'm having a party too,' Dylan says. 'We're going to play pass the parcel, aren't we, Mummy?'

'We are.'

'Sounds brilliant,' Dad says.

'You were invited too, you know?'

'Oh, we didn't want to intrude with his friends,' Mum says.

'He's four, Mum, not fourteen. He'd love to have you there.'

'Well, I didn't want to intrude with *your* friends. Last year I felt like a bit of a spare part.'

'I'm sorry. I didn't mean for you to feel like that.'

Mum waves away my concern. 'It's how it should be. Don't apologize.'

Dylan licks his finger and uses it to pick up the crumbs left over from his cake.

'So, when's he back anyway?' Mum says.

'Tomorrow.'

'And then when does he go away again?'

'Not until January.'

'Must be nice, mustn't it?'

'He is working, Mum.'

'Did you see that photo he was tagged in on Facebook the other day?'

'Check you out, Mum. Facebook!'

'I'm not a total dinosaur.' Mum rolls her eyes. 'It's quite good, actually. Some of my old school friends are on there. Blimey, they've aged, mind. Although they probably say the same about me. Anyway, did you see it? Them all in that club.'

'I saw it.'

'He didn't look very hard at work, did he? Why couldn't he come home after the gig?'

'He had another gig the following day. There was no point in him coming home.'

'Daddy is coming home tomorrow, isn't he?' Dylan says, his face full of concern.

'Of course he is. Don't you worry about that.'

'Come on, son. I spotted a carousel outside,' Dad says, clearly sensing the conversation is upsetting Dylan. 'Fancy a ride? There might even be a dragon.'

Dylan jumps straight up and takes Dad's hand and I thank him with my eyes.

Once they've left, Mum reaches out and puts her hands on mine, which are cupped around my mug. 'I just worry about you, that's all. You know what men are like and all those girls throwing themselves at him.'

I feel my eyes filling with tears. 'He does love me, Mum.'

'I know. OK. I'm sorry. I didn't mean to upset you.'

'It's fine. Let's go and see Dylan on the carousel?'

'Yes. Good idea. Let's go.'

*

After a manic afternoon of party games, one child being sick all over the floor after too much cake and being chased around by a bloke dressed as a dragon, Sarah and I are sitting on the sofa whilst Dylan watches a *Postman Pat* DVD.

'Vintage, this is.' Sarah nods her head towards the television. 'Old Jess the cat has put in a good paper round, so to speak. She's got to be at least thirty, hasn't she?'

'Pat's not aged a day, to be fair. Still a prime hunk of meat.'

'You'd worry about him passing that nose on though, wouldn't you?'

I laugh and then get up and go to the fridge to get us more drinks, noticing the bowls of unfinished jelly and ice-cream on the side.

'Want to make alcoholic jelly and ice-cream?' I hold up a bottle of vodka and a packet of jelly.

'Will it set?'

'Only one way to find out.'

I grab a jug and pour in the vodka, Sarah peering over my shoulder with a sceptical look on her face.

'Surely we still need some hot water to melt the gelatin?' she says.

'Hmm. I probably should've paid more attention in our science lessons.'

'Rather than eyeing up that dreamboat Mr Terrence, you mean?'

Mr Terrence was possibly the most unattractive man I've ever seen. He smelt of overcooked vegetables, his stomach protruded over his belt, and he had grey hair sprouting from every orifice.

I hand Sarah the jug. Dylan is rubbing his eyes and

yawning. 'I'll go and put Dylan to bed. You work your magic.'

'I'll try my best.' Sarah goes over to Dylan and kisses him on the head. 'Night, night, birthday boy. Thank you for letting me share your birthday with you.'

'Night, night.'

'Love you, Munchkin.'

'Love you too, Aunty Sarah.'

I pick Dylan up. He's so heavy now, but he grips on and I carry him upstairs to his bedroom, where he gets into his pyjamas and climbs into bed.

'Do you think Daddy will get back tonight? He said on the phone he'd try.'

Luke is constantly making promises he can't keep. It drives me mad. For some reason, he thinks it's better to over-promise, as if Dylan won't notice when he under-delivers. But Dylan hangs on to his every word.

I climb into Dylan's bed beside him. He's still in his toddler bed so it's tiny, but I can just about squeeze in with my arm around him and him lying on my chest.

'Look, I know it's a bit rubbish that Daddy isn't here for your birthday, but I know that he will have been thinking of you every single minute of the day, so in a way, you were together because you were in his thoughts.'

I'm not sure it's the truth but it's a lie worth telling.

'Will he be here for my birthday when I'm five?'

'I can't see why not. And do you know what? I'll make you a promise. I will be there for every single one of your birthdays, even if something else really important comes up, even if it means flying around the whole world to get back in time. OK?'

'Even when I'm a hundred?'

'Even when you're a hundred. Now get some sleep, OK? And tomorrow you can spend all afternoon playing knights with Daddy. And how about I make you another birthday cake?'

'So I have two birthdays?'

'Well, yes, sort of.'

'Cooool.'

I smile. 'I love you, Dylan. More than anything in the whole world.'

'Love you too, Mummy.'

I give him a kiss on the forehead and then shuffle out of the bed and tuck his duvet cover back over him. Luke got him this really cute one with little gingerbread men on and sometimes I find him telling them about his day or giving them a goodnight kiss. He leans down and grabs Geoff the giraffe from the end of his bed and pulls it in close to him.

I turn on his night light and it projects stars on to the ceiling. 'Remember to say night night to Geoff.' He holds up his giraffe.

'Night, night, Geoff. Look after Dylan for me on your nighttime adventures.'

I close his door, leaving it a slit open as he likes to be able to see the light from downstairs, and then head back to Sarah, who has done all the washing-up and is spooning out our jelly into a bowl and adding ice-cream. I say jelly – it's basically vodka poured on ice-cream, but I'm exhausted and starving so I'll take it.

We take our bowls to the sofa, both sitting back with our feet on the coffee table.

'Do you reckon we can get drunk on this?' I say, spooning in a mouthful.

'Not sure. It's worth a go.'

'We might have to eat our body weight in jelly and ice-cream though.'

'There are worse things in life.' She scoops up a heaped spoonful. 'Nice tree.' She nods in the direction of our obscene Christmas tree. Luke came home with it a couple of weeks ago and could barely get it through the door. He had to buy three packs of lights just to get close to filling it, and don't even get me started on the number of baubles.

'It looks like it belongs at Rockefeller Plaza or something, doesn't it? It took an entire day to decorate.'

'I can imagine. Luke's idea, I'm guessing.'

'Can you imagine me buying that monstrosity?'

Sarah laughs. 'So, have you spoken to him?'

I shake my head, turning over my spoon so I can lick it clean.

'Do you want me to go so you can ring him?'

'He'll be at the gig. And no, he can ring me. He's the one missing his son's birthday.'

'I'm sure he feels bad about it.'

'Why do you always stick up for him?' It comes out a little more forcefully than I intend it to. 'We were friends first, you know? Don't forget that.'

Sarah puts her hand on my leg. 'You know you're my number one. But I didn't realize there were sides to take. You guys are OK, aren't you?'

I rock my head from side to side. 'This feels pretty unforgivable to me.'

'What was his explanation for agreeing to do the gig today?'

'He said he wasn't thinking when they were sorting the dates and he just forgot. He *forgot* it was his son's birthday. *Forgot*, Sar.'

'Yeah, that's a bit shit. But he's a bloke. They're useless with dates and stuff. Tom always forgets our wedding anniversary.'

'Dylan's little face though. Asking if he was going to make it back. Wanting to share it all with him. Your son is only four once and if you miss it, you don't get it back.'

'I know.'

'*You* booked the day off and he's not even your son.'

'That's because I hate my job and welcome any excuse to book a day off.'

'No, it's not.'

Sarah smiles. 'OK, you're right. That's not the reason.'

'Remember when I first got with him and him being in a band seemed so glamorous and exciting? But now I wish he just worked in a building society or something. I didn't sign up for this. It's not what I want.'

'So what are you going to do?'

'Sit on the sofa with you eating some weird half-cooked gelatin substance and bitch and moan?'

'Sounds like a plan. But seriously, you're not going to split up, are you?'

I shrug. 'Mum basically implied earlier that she thinks he's having an affair.'

'No way. Luke would never do that.'

'Wouldn't he?' Sarah scrapes the last of her bowl. 'Anyway, I'm guessing from your enthusiasm for the vodka tonight that you've not had any success this month?'

Sarah stacks our bowls and then puts them both on the end of the coffee table. 'We've got an appointment with the doctor again next week. Still not found an explanation. I just feel so stupid that I didn't even consider this as a possibility. I just thought we'd stop using contraception and, hey presto, we'd get a baby.'

'I'm sorry. I'm here moaning about Luke being away and you're going through all this.'

'Don't be silly. People go through this every day.'

'Still, doesn't make it any easier. I do believe it's going to happen when you least expect it though.'

'Yeah, I know.' Sarah paints on a brave face. It's something she's always done. Or maybe she just always manages to see the positive. 'I just worry Tom's willy might fall off in the process, poor bloke. At first I think he thought all his Christmases had come at once, but now whenever I tell him I'm ovulating he gives me this woeful expression, like an old dog when you wave a lead in its face.'

'I feel so sorry for him.'

'I know. The hardship. Have you mentioned to Luke yet about you wanting another?'

I shake my head. 'I'm just not sure how he'd react.'

'What, because of how he was when he found out you were pregnant with Dylan?'

'What do you mean?'

'Nothing . . .' She pauses and I know she's keeping something from me because her face has gone bright red and she won't look me in the eye.

'Sarah.'

'I just mean it was a shock. You guys were really young and you'd only been together a few months.'

I feel like someone is standing on my chest. 'He didn't want Dylan, did he?'

Suddenly my phone starts buzzing, making the glass on the coffee table vibrate. We both look at the screen and see Luke's name flash up.

'I'm going to leave you to it.' Sarah drops her feet to the floor and stands up.

'I'll call him back later.'

'I'm exhausted anyway, lovely. The endless sex is obviously taking its toll. I'm not sure how you guys have managed it all this time.' She gives me a wry smile.

'Just tell me if I'm right.'

She puts her hands on the tops of my arms. 'Please talk to Luke and remember I've only ever wanted the best for you. It wasn't my place to say anything.'

I nod, we exchange a quick hug and then Sarah lets herself out. I pick up my phone, letting it ring off, but then it starts up almost immediately so I take a deep breath and answer it.

'Is he still awake?' Luke says as soon as I pick up. 'I don't want to miss his birthday.'

'You *have* missed his birthday, Luke.' I check my watch. 'It's gone nine o'clock. He's been in bed for ages.'

'I thought you might let him stay up late on his birthday.'

'So, it's my fault?'

'You know that's not what I'm saying. I just didn't think he'd be in bed so early.'

Luke has a way of always making me feel like some middle-aged bore, ruining everyone else's fun.

'He was exhausted after his party. It's been a busy day.'

'Yeah, I get that. I'm just gutted to have missed it.'

'You know who else is gutted that you missed it?'

'Oh, come on, Laura. Don't start this again. He's four. As soon as I come home tomorrow and shower him with more gifts, he'll totally forget about it. He'll probably be pleased to drag his birthday out for another day.'

'He doesn't need more gifts. He had his present from us.'

'I know. But I can't come home empty-handed, can I?'

'Why not exactly? You do realize if you were actually here more you wouldn't feel such a need to buy his affection. Plus, he's got tons of presents from his friends. Oh, and your dad.'

'For fuck's sake, has he not given up yet? I hope you didn't tell Dylan who it was from. What did he get him anyway?'

'Of course I didn't tell him. He got him this really lovely book about things for adventurous boys to do – camp-fires and whittling sticks and stuff. It was actually really thoughtful.'

'Unlike me, right?'

I can suddenly hear voices in the background, a bloke's booming laugh followed by a woman's giggle.

'Where are you?'

'I'm outside the pub. We're just having a quick drink before we go back to the hotel.'

'How come the gig finished so early?'

'It was one of those intimate things – small venue, small audience. We tend to do a much shorter set for those.'

'Right.'

'Yes, it went well, thanks for asking. Oh wait, of course, it's not one of your priorities.'

His attempt to guilt-trip me makes me so angry I'm

not sure whether to scream at him and make him see how utterly unfair he's being or burst into tears and let him see how he's breaking my heart. And I can't stop Sarah's words going round and round my head. *Because of how he was when you found out you were pregnant with Dylan.*

'Did you want an abortion?' I blurt out.

'What are you on about?'

'Just tell me the truth, Luke.'

'Has Sarah said something to you?'

'So, it's true.'

I run my hand through my hair. I'm not sure what hurts the most – that he considered getting rid of Dylan or that he decided to talk to Sarah about it and not me. Or maybe even that Sarah didn't tell me.

'I haven't got time to talk about this now.'

'Of course you haven't. There are far more important things to do than have a conversation about how you wanted to destroy our son.'

I can hear Luke's sigh down the phone. How does he always make me feel like I'm the one being unreasonable?

'I was twenty-five. I was in shock. Don't try to make me out to be a bad person for this too, Laur.'

There's so much I want to say to him but instead I put the phone down, go into our bedroom and cry alone into my pillow so that Dylan doesn't wake up and hear me.

LUKE

'Your son is very cute.'

I look up from my phone and see the very attractive girl who has been talking to Cody since the gig finished. She's smiling at me and pointing at the photos of Dylan I've been scrolling through.

'Thank you. It's his birthday today.'

'Oh wow, how old is he?'

'He's four.'

'My little brother is six. He's totally crazy.'

I wonder how young she must be to have a six-year-old brother. I turned thirty this year. *Thirty*. Laura threw me a big surprise party, which was really nice of her, but I had to get wasted because, well, *thirty*. Fuck.

'My parents had me really young,' she explains as if reading my mind. 'Then Mum hit thirty and she suddenly decided she wanted another. There's a fourteen-year age gap.'

'Ah, I see.'

'In case you were thinking I was underage?' She must sense my concern because she adds, 'To be drinking, I mean.'

'It's OK. I wasn't about to report you.'

'Talking of drinks, can I get you one?'

'It's OK. We get ours free. I'll get you one though. What do you want?'

'Oh, thanks. Is prosecco OK?'

'Sure.'

I raise my hand and the barmaid comes over. 'Another whisky?'

'Yes. And a prosecco for . . .?'

'Rosie, thank you.'

'Of course.' The barmaid collects some of the empty glasses from the table.

We end up drinking another three rounds. I can't stop thinking about the disgust in Laura's voice, how there's no way in hell she's ever going to forgive me. Now that Dylan's here, the thought that I wasn't sure about keeping him feels criminal, but at the time – when I felt like just a kid myself – was it really that unexpected? Somehow I end up back in my hotel room, the others joining me uninvited. Rich passes round a bottle of whisky and I take a swig and then pass it on.

When Rosie has her sip, she winces. 'Not sure I can drink this straight.'

'Code, get a can of Coke out the mini bar, will you? And a glass from the top.'

Cody holds up a can of Coke and a can of Diet Coke. 'Which would you like, madam?'

Predictably, Rosie chooses the Diet Coke (she probably weighs less than seven stone soaking wet) and I hold the glass for her whilst she pours in a very generous measure of whisky and then tops it up with Diet Coke.

We're all sitting on the bed. It's a bit of a squash but no one seems to care. Soon Rich is making out with some girl and the rest of us look over at them and laugh.

'Get a room,' Cody teases and then, as the kissing gets more heated, Cody pushes Rich in the back.

'All right, all right. We're going.' Rich takes the girl's hand and leads her out.

'Shall we play a drinking game?' the girl with Cody suggests.

'Ah, I dunno,' I say. 'I'm pretty wasted as it is.'

'How about truth or dare?' Rosie says.

I shrug and Cody slaps me on the back. 'Yeah, he's game. Aren't you, mate?'

'Go on then. I'm not starting though.'

'You start, Shayna. You suggested it.'

'OK. I'll go dare.'

'Snog the person in this room that you fancy the most,' Cody dares her.

Shayna looks around, pauses, and then leans into Rosie and kisses her passionately and I feel like I should look away but at the same time I can't force myself to.

'Your turn then, Rosie,' Shayna says, sitting back down next to Cody, who is looking totally stunned.

'I'll go dare too.'

'Strip down to your underwear,' Shayna says.

'You don't have to do that,' I say quietly. 'It's just a stupid game.'

But Rosie ignores me, lifting up her dress to reveal a set of skimpy black underwear underneath. I can't deny it; she's got an amazing body.

'Bloody hell, Luke. Close your mouth, will you? You're practically drooling.'

'Sod off, you twat,' I say good-naturedly.

'Your turn,' Rosie says and I feel uncomfortable even having a conversation with her whilst she is wearing so little.

'I'll go truth.'

It's probably the safest option but I'm still nervous about what they're going to ask. I guess I could just lie.

'If you weren't practically wifed off, would you want to sleep with Rosie?' It's not the type of thing Cody would usually ask so I know he must be very drunk.

'Of course I would.'

At first I think I just say it so as not to hurt her feelings, but then I realize that it's true. If I wasn't with Laura and I was sitting here right now with Rosie in her underwear, of course the first thing on my mind would be whether I could have sex with her. I'm only human after all. But I *am* with Laura, however much she might hate me right now.

'Your turn now, mate.'

'Hit me with a dare,' Cody says, puffing out his chest.

'Get naked and run down to the bar,' Shayna dares him.

'OK.'

Cody begins to take off his clothes, but I go over and hold his arms down. 'Come on, Code. You know we can't do that kind of thing.'

'It'll be fine. There aren't any press around. I can wear a Christmas hat over my winky.'

'Mate, you're drunk. You really can't do that.'

'Spoilsport.' Cody starts putting his top back on. 'More whisky?' He holds out the empty bottle.

I hold up my hand. 'I'm good, thanks. Maybe you should leave it now too?'

'Want to get another bottle in my room?' he asks the two girls.

Shayna nods and links her arm through his but Rosie stays sitting on the bed beside me.

'I think I'll stay here. See you tomorrow, yeah, Shay?'

Shayna raises her eyebrows. 'See you in the morning, I expect.'

They leave and I try to work out how I'm going to ask Rosie to leave without hurting her feelings, but then she starts massaging my shoulders and it feels so good that I don't want her to stop.

'Blimey, there are a few knots in here.'

'I know. It's been a stressful few months.'

'The band?'

'Sort of. Stuff at home too.'

'Want to talk about it?'

And, to my surprise, I find I do. So I tell her about my phone call with Laura earlier, how she was mad at me for missing Dylan's birthday, how she always seems to be angry at me. And then I tell her about the doubts I had about Dylan at the beginning. And with every word I say, I feel a mixture of guilt and relief flooding through me, arguing with each other as to which will win out.

As I talk, Rosie just listens, her hands kneading away at the tension that has built up in all the muscles in my back.

'Who wouldn't at least *consider* an abortion? It's not like you forced her to go through with it or something.'

'Exactly. But she doesn't see it like that. To her, it makes me evil.'

'She should be grateful that you're such a good dad.'

'Well, I'm not sure I am. But I try. And I love him more than anything.'

She runs her thumbs along the edge of my shoulder blades. 'I'd understand that you had to put the band first. It's obviously going to be hugely important to you.'

'It doesn't come first. She just thinks it does.'

'Well, it sounds like she doesn't appreciate what she's got.'

Hearing Rosie criticize Laura weirdly makes me want to stick up for her. 'I don't think it's like that. I think she just finds it hard.'

'And it's not hard for you? You're working really hard too.'

I look around the hotel room – glasses, bottles and cans strewn across all the surfaces. 'Am I?'

Rosie runs her hand down my back and across my side on to my thigh. 'If you were mine, I'd make sure you knew how wonderful you are. I'd fulfil your every need.' She inches her hand closer to my crotch and kisses my neck and for a second I let her, closing my eyes and trying to force my body to push her away when it feels so good. But then I take her hand to stop her, shuffling away from her and standing up.

'I need to go home.'

'You're throwing me out late at night on my own?'

'No. Stay here. The room's paid for anyway. There's breakfast too if you want it in the morning.'

'Oh yeah, embarrass myself in front of the others when they see you buggered off and left me.'

'I'm sorry. I really am. But I need to see my son on his birthday.'

'Shame you didn't think about that earlier.'

'You're right. It is. Just trust me – you could do so much better than me.'

'Oh, don't patronize me.' Rosie finds her dress and pulls

it over her head. 'I'm sure your girlfriend would love to know you've spent the evening in a hotel room with a scantily clad girl massaging you.'

I give her a pleading look. 'What do you want? Money? Give me your account details and I'll put money in there right now.'

She shakes her head, a look of total disgust on her face, and I know that I've said the wrong thing. 'I'm not a bloody prostitute.'

'I'm not saying you are. I'm sorry. I just don't want her finding out, not reading about it somewhere anyway. Think of my son. I don't want him to grow up and think I'm a prick because of stuff he's read in the archives.'

'I'm sure he won't need to read stuff to realize that.'

I want to slap myself for trusting her, for thinking she was different, that she really just wanted to listen and be there for me. I'm such a fucking idiot.

'I'll tell her myself. Whatever.'

'Bye, Luke.'

I grab my bag, which luckily I hadn't unpacked, and hook it on to my shoulder. 'I'm sorry again. Take care.'

Then I slam the door and run down to the lobby where some of the management are sitting, playing a game of cards.

'All right?' Jimmy says, as he sees me charging towards him. 'You haven't done anything stupid, have you? Need some money to give her?'

I shake my head. 'I just need a lift home. Can you sort me a car, please?'

'Sure. Sit down. I'll sort it.'

*

When I open our front door all is quiet and dark inside so I creep in, take off my shoes and pad straight up the stairs. Dylan's door is slightly ajar, as it always is at bedtime, so I peek through to see him sleeping soundly.

'Luke? Luke, is that you?'

I go through to our bedroom and Laura switches on the bedside lamp.

'I'm sorry it's late.'

Laura's eyes are half-shut in the bright light. 'I thought you were coming home tomorrow. Why have you travelled over a hundred miles across the country in the middle of the night?'

'I wanted to see Dylan. Can I wake him up and just say happy birthday?'

'Are you serious? You know he'll be up all night then.' She peers at the clock on the bedside table. 'Plus, it's technically not his birthday any more.'

'Oh, come on, Laur. I'll sit with him if he won't go straight back to sleep.'

Laura shakes her head. 'No. I'm sorry, Luke, but it's too late. You're too late. I'm not going to let you wake him up because then he'll be a misery in the morning and he's really looking forward to his day with you. Mum and Dad got him swords. He wants to play knights with you.'

Unexpectedly, I feel my eyes fill with tears. 'I came back especially.'

'Don't do that, Luke. Don't make me out to be the bad person in this. I'm far too drained for that right now.'

'I'm not, but I only want to wake him up for a second . . .'

'I'm going to sleep, Luke. Please don't disturb him. And can you sleep on the sofa, please, so that you don't wake me when you come to bed? I'll see you in the morning.'

I don't want her to go to sleep. I want to tell her about tonight, to explain before she hears it from someone else. I want to tell her how in many ways Rosie made me realize that she's right – I could do better. I shouldn't have missed Dylan's birthday. But I know if I tell her right now what happened, things will blow up and she might never let me back in. Now is not the time.

Laura turns the light off so I walk out and tiptoe into Dylan's room and sit by his bed, my hand on top of his cover, feeling how it moves up and down with each of his breaths.

I rest my head back against his wall and look up at the stars on his ceiling. And very quietly, so as not to wake him, I sing him 'Happy Birthday' and then I kiss his forehead. He flinches and for a second I think he might wake up, and I'm both excited for him to know that I'm here, I made it back, and yet nervous that Laura might walk in. But he doesn't wake. He just turns on to his side and falls back into his slow, rhythmic breath.

I lay my face on his bed so that it is facing his. It's funny. When he's asleep he looks like me – the shape of his jaw, the width of his nose, his dark skin. But as soon as he's awake, he looks like Laura – his large, expressive eyes, his serious expression, like he's always a little bit concerned about something, but also when he smiles, it fills his whole face just like Laura's does. Sometimes I wonder how it's possible to love someone as much as I love him. To think that before he existed, I didn't have this capability, my heart wasn't this big. And yet it feels like I keep letting him down. And the fear strikes me as it regularly does. That I am my father's son however much I may want to think I'm better than him. And to think for a second that I considered not having him . . . it's abhorrent. And I totally get it if Laura hates me for it, but the thought of losing her love forever feels like the worst possible thing.

There's a sound outside the door and when I sit up, I see Laura standing there, looking cute in the Christmas pyjamas that I bought for her a couple of weeks ago, matching ones to Dylan's.

'I haven't woken him up, I promise.'

'Come to bed.'

'I don't have to sleep on the sofa?'

Laura shakes her head. 'As long as you don't snore.'

'You know that's your remit.'

'Shut up.' Laura comes into Dylan's room and grabs my hand, pulling me up. I follow her into our room and she removes my clothes for me like I'm injured. Then we climb into bed and instead of me spooning her, she spoons me. And I feel like a child, the comfort I used to get when Mum lay beside me when I had a bad dream or Dad put his big bear arms around me. That's the thing – when he was there he was actually the best dad in the world. He just didn't love me enough to stay.

'I'm sorry I missed Dylan's birthday.'

'I know you are. And you didn't miss it. Not entirely.'

I sit up suddenly, panic filling my chest. 'Do you think he'll grow up to hate me?'

'No. He worships you.'

'But when he understands? When I can't fix it with a bag of sweets or a cuddly toy?'

'No. I don't think he'll hate you.'

I put my hand on Laura's cheek. 'I love you. You do know that, don't you?'

'Yes.'

'I *really* love you.'

'You smell of whisky. You're going to have a headache in the morning.'

'I didn't drink that much.'

Laura raises an eyebrow. 'Having a hangover doesn't mean you get out of bringing me coffee in the morning, you realize?'

'Coffee and breakfast in bed, I promise.'

We lie in silence for a while but I can tell that there's something on Laura's mind. When you've been with someone a long time, you pick up on stuff like that. Even with her facing the back of my head, I can imagine her eyes flitting around, the way they do when she can't quite get comfortable. I turn around to face her.

'I was going to ask you today if you wanted to have another child,' she says. 'Before you told me you were going to miss his birthday. I was going to cook you a candlelit dinner and ask you.'

I don't know what to say. As much as I adore Dylan, I'm so far from wanting another child right now.

'But then you realized I'm a selfish idiot and thought why the hell would I ever even consider having another child with someone like that?'

'No.' Laura moves her head back and forth. 'Maybe.'

'Fair enough.'

'So what would you have said? If I'd asked you.'

I take a deep breath, wondering whether to lie and hope she really has changed her mind and thought better of it, or whether to hurt her by telling her the truth.

'Have you forgotten how bloody hard it was, Laur? How miserable you were at the start?'

'Don't use me as an excuse, Luke.'

'I'm not. I just feel like we should focus on Dylan. On us. You're on the verge of getting your freedom back with him starting school soon.'

'What if I don't want my freedom back?'

'I know you're probably worried about adjusting without him here in the day, but it'll be great, you'll see. You won't be as exhausted and we'll have more time to focus on being a couple again . . .'

'I'll be more fun again, you mean,' Laura interrupts.

'I'm not saying that.'

She turns so that she's facing the ceiling.

'I'm not saying I never want another child,' I continue, trying to make amends. 'I mean, possibly one day, but I'm looking forward to having you back . . .'

Laura sits up. 'Because where exactly have I been, Luke? What if this person you see before you is just me now? I'm not twenty-two any more. I'm sorry if the person I've become is not good enough for you.'

'Stop twisting my words, Laur. You know I don't mean that. I just mean there will be more time for us. You and me. I don't want you to be different. I just want us to spend more time together.'

It's not entirely true. I do miss the person she used to be. No, I miss the way she used to look at me. The way she used to love me.

'That's what I've always wanted. I'm not the reason we barely see each other, Luke. And nor is Dylan.'

I'm so tired of trying to explain to her why the band is so important to me. That I love my job. I'm surely not the only man in the world who has to work away a lot. Do they all really have to deal with this grief?

'I know. What I'm saying is when we do see each other, it will be quality time. Not bitching at each other because one of us forgot to put his bike away before it poured with rain or arguing over whose turn it is to play Dotty Dinosaurs. We'll have more time for us.'

Laura nods. 'I guess. Perhaps you're right.'

'I'm always right,' I joke and Laura smiles, but I can see that it's only pretence.

Then she lies back down, turning away from me and pulling the cover up over her shoulder.

I move towards her in the hope that this time I can spoon *her* but she shuffles a little further away. 'Thank you for letting me sleep in the bed.'

'It's OK. Night, Luke.'

I stare at her back, feeling like there's a galaxy between us, knowing I need to do or say something to make it better. I sit up and turn on the light. 'Let's get married. We'll really do it this time, I promise. We'll find some-where far better than that little barn. Fly everyone out to the Maldives again or something. You loved it there, didn't you? We could hire a huge ship with a waterpark on the deck. Dylan would love it.'

Laura looks at me and I notice how dull her eyes are and wonder whether it's me that's caused the sparkle to dis-appear from them. 'I don't know. I don't think so.'

'You don't want to marry me?' I sound like a little boy. The way I sounded when Dad told me he was leaving.

'In the way it's not the right time for you to have another child, it's not the right time for me to get married.'

I nod, the sadness blocking my throat, and then she leans over and switches my bedside light off and turns away from me. And as I'm lying there, wired and unable to sleep, my phone buzzes, and when I read the text it feels like the whole bottom of my world falls away.

I'm so sorry, mate, I tried to get Shayna to stop her. But she says that Rosie's emailed the papers.

16th December 2010

LAURA

'You nearly lost your trunks on that one.'

Luke refastens the Velcro on his trunks as we walk to the next ride and get in the queue. 'I know. Must have been a treat for you coming down behind me.'

'Not really.' I smile, and Luke gives me a sad smile back.

Occasionally we have moments like this, where we forget, before we remember again and the sadness comes in another fresh wave.

'Is this one even higher?' Dylan jiggles around on the spot like he needs a wee, his body clearly unable to contain his excitement.

'Certainly is,' Luke says, pointing up to the top of the slide, which seems so far away even I'm a little nervous.

A little way up the steps there is one of those height checker things so Dylan goes and stands facing it, running his hand over his head and then moving away and checking whether he reaches the line.

'I'm much taller than you need to be,' he says proudly, even though his hand is far higher than where the top of his head came to.

'You are. Now come on. We'll lose our place in the queue.'

We hurry back to the line and work our way to the top of the steps very slowly, Dylan checking every few seconds whether we're there yet, even though it's obvious we are not sitting at the top of a slide.

When we finally reach the dinghy we need to get into, the teenage lad working there says, 'Right, little one in the front, you two squeeze in behind.'

'It's OK, I can go in my own one,' I say.

'No, you go with him. I'll wait.'

'I just said you guys can go in together.' The boy looks at us as if he thinks we're simple. 'Hurry up though. There's a pretty long queue behind and we get in trouble if we don't stick to the schedule.' He points at the green light above the tube we're about to hurtle through.

'Let's just go together,' I say, and I lift Dylan into the dinghy, sitting as closely behind him as I can, and Luke clambers in behind me.

As soon as we set off, I fly backwards, smashing into Luke, and it's so fast and twisty that I have no choice but to stay there. Dylan giggles the whole way and once we crash out into the pool at the bottom, he shouts, 'Want to go again, want to go again.'

With absolutely no elegance, I clamber out of the dinghy on to the steps at the edge of the pool, Luke leaping over the side into the water and then popping up to the surface.

'What about me?' Dylan asks, his arms outstretched.

'Oh, we're leaving you in there for the day,' Luke teases, and then as Dylan starts to protest, he grabs him and hauls him over the side on to the pool steps.

'That was so fun. Can we go again?' Dylan pulls on my arm.

'You go with Daddy. I'll wait at the bottom.'

'You can go with him if you want,' Luke offers. 'I don't mind waiting.'

178

'Let's all go together again.' Dylan takes hold of both of our hands.

'It was a bit fast for me. I'm going to sit on that bench and wait for you two at the bottom.'

'OK.' Dylan drags out the 'ay' but then sets off to the queue with Luke. I can tell by Luke's face he's hurt that I don't want to go with them, but I just can't face it.

I sit on the bench and wait. It's got to be forty degrees in here but I'm still shivering and wish I'd brought my towel out of the changing rooms. Dylan's been hassling us to take him to a waterpark for ages, so we've given him a cheeky day off school (how much are they really going to learn in a day in reception?). I thought it would be quieter, but by the looks of things we're not the only ones with a disregard for authority. There are a load of fake palm trees dotted around so I lay my head back and try to imagine I'm somewhere tropical and forget that it's freezing and grey outside. For a moment it takes me back to Dylan's second birthday – that gorgeous dinner on the beach when Luke proposed for the second time. We ended up staying on for Christmas that year. Luke changed our flights home, and the resort manager let us stay in the water villa for another ten days. It was the best Christmas I've ever had. Just the three of us. No awkward politics about who we were going to spend it with, no sitting around the table painting on smiles, wearing Christmas hats and pulling crackers, no overcooked turkey. The chef brought us this incredible fish stew and we ate it on the decking, the sea lapping against the stilts, Dylan sitting on the top step happily filling his little watering can and pouring it out.

After what feels like a long time, I feel someone

tapping my arm and open my eyes to see Dylan dripping beside me.

'Ice-cream time,' he says, a huge grin plastered across his face. 'Come on, Mummy. I'm never allowed ice-cream on my birthday.'

'You had ice-cream at your party last year.'

'But not proper ice-cream in a cone with a flake.'

'To be fair, your birthday *is* in December. It's not exactly ice-cream season.'

'It is today.' He races off towards the ice-cream hut as Luke walks in time with me.

'He's funny, isn't he?' Luke says, looking over at him.

'He is. He's wonderful.' We walk in silence for a bit and then I add, 'We're going to have to tell him soon, you know?'

'I know. But not today. Not on his birthday.'

'I agree. But tomorrow maybe? We won't make it sound traumatic.'

'So, what, we'll lie?'

Before I can respond, Dylan runs back towards us. 'They've got a double Mr Whippy with a flake and sprinkles. Can I have that one?'

'Of course,' Luke says as I say, 'What's the magic word?'

'Please.'

'Of course you can, then, birthday boy.' I get a five-pound note out of the waterproof pouch around my neck and hand it to Dylan.

Luke takes the money out of Dylan's hand and gives it back to me. 'My treat.'

I start to protest but Luke holds up his hands. Since Dylan started school, I've been working part-time in

Thomas Cook again. It felt a bit like regressing, walking back through the doors, everything looking exactly the same as it did when I used to work there, but it's been nice to have a bit of my own money. Besides, I can't expect Luke to pay for everything any more.

'Come on, Dylan. How about chocolate sauce as well?' Luke puts his arm around Dylan. 'Do you want one too?'

I shake my head and Luke goes to join the queue with Dylan whilst I find us a table to sit at. After queuing for a good fifteen minutes, Luke and Dylan come over, ice-creams in hand, Dylan already with half of his on his nose.

'How come you got two flakes?' I ask Dylan.

'Daddy told them it was my birthday and they said that I *must* have two flakes then.'

I peer down to the hut and notice it's two young girls behind the counter. That explains the extra flake then. Wherever we go there are people looking at us and whispering to each other. If I studied the people at the tables around us, I'm sure there would be some slyly trying to take a photo, but it's like I've become immune to it because I don't really notice any more.

'Lucky you.'

'You can share my second one if you want, Mummy?'

I put my hand on top of his. 'No, it's OK. You have it. Thank you for being such a kind sharer, though.'

Dylan has to be the most generous child I've ever known. If we're playing at the park, he'll happily let other children have a go on his bike. He lets others go first on the slide and gets off the swing if someone is waiting. He'll always let me have a bite of his cake when we go to a café. I'm not sure how we got so lucky, but he really is one of a kind.

'Can we go and jump the waves now?' Dylan says once he's finished his ice-cream.

'I think we'd better clean you up first,' I say. 'And are you sure you won't be sick bouncing around with all that in your stomach?'

'No, I'll be fine, Mummy.' Suddenly I can picture him as a teenager, me worrying about him going out to some party or other and him dismissing my fears with an arm around my shoulder.

I wipe his face and his hands. 'OK, come on then.'

We head over to the wave pool and Dylan takes each of our hands and pulls us in. We wade through the water until we are as deep as we can go and wait for the siren. As soon as it sounds, Dylan screams and we wait for the waves to appear. They're not exactly huge but Dylan has a great time jumping over them, and then him and Luke start diving into them face first. He's so full of absolute joy, so carefree, it makes my chest ache. Sometimes it would be nice to press pause on life, especially when you know what's coming, but you can't. So I force myself to just enjoy the moment, diving face first into the waves with them, and as they get deeper Luke holds Dylan up and we all bob along with the water, allowing it to take us with it, up and down like boats on the sea.

'Is that the last of it?' I ask, entering the bedroom to see Luke loading stuff into a suitcase.

'I think so. I might take a few of the plates and glasses from the kitchen. Cody and Rich have some, but I don't trust them to have much. Can I have a duvet cover and pillow too? You should have plenty left.'

'Of course. You bought it all, Luke. You don't have to ask.'

'I don't want to deprive you or Dylan of anything you need, though.'

'Trust me. We have far more than we could ever need. I really think we should be the ones moving out. I could move in with Mum and Dad for a bit. I might go slightly insane but we'd manage.'

I smile but Luke just looks sad. 'There's no way I'm making you move out. This is my fault. I caused this.'

'It's not all your fault.'

Reading about the semi-naked girl he had in his hotel room last year was the final straw, but it wasn't the only reason I decided to call it quits. I wasn't making him happy either. Like it said in the newspaper story, he apparently told her all our problems, all the ways I made him feel shit and guilty and not enough. And in many ways he was right. I *was* horrible to him at times. I took all of my frustrations out on him. I *wasn't* supportive of the band. And I realized I'm not cut out for this life. All the time away, all the attention being on him, always feeling inferior. It just made me so miserable that I became an awful person – bitter and twisted and forever trying to score points against him. And I hate that person.

But the thought of telling Dylan breaks my heart. I'm so scared of us changing him from the open, kind-hearted, easy-going boy he is today into someone angrier, far less secure. But we've promised to keep things amicable. To remain a team. I'm hoping that will be enough.

'You know if I could go back and do things differently, I would,' Luke says.

'Me too. But we can't. So we have to look forward, right?

To being the best parents we can possibly be and making this work for Dylan.'

Luke nods and I get the sense he wants to say something more, but instead he turns to the wardrobe and starts checking the top shelf for any more of his belongings.

I slide my engagement ring off my finger. I must have lost weight recently because it slips off easily. When he looks at me, I hold it out, nervous at what his reaction is going to be.

He shakes his head. 'Keep it.'

'I can't. It doesn't feel right. Sell it. It must have cost a fortune. You can buy some bedding and cutlery,' I say, trying to lighten the mood, even though I know that's an impossible task.

'You never liked it, did you?'

'What makes you think that?'

Luke shrugs. 'Your face. I catch you looking at it sometimes and I can tell that you're disappointed.'

'It's beautiful, it's just . . . it was nothing like the one I showed you that day, on Dylan's first birthday at the Christmas market. You probably don't remember.'

'Of course I remember. I thought you were just being your typical cautious self, choosing something cheap because you didn't want me to waste money on you. I just wanted to spoil you. To show you how special you are. But I couldn't even get that right, could I?'

'Don't be silly. It's a stunning ring.'

'But it made you feel like I didn't listen to you, and that wasn't it at all. I just thought that bigger and shinier was better, but it wasn't, was it? Because it wasn't what you wanted. I'm sorry.'

'Please don't apologize.'

Luke pulls an envelope out of his pocket. 'Look, I've probably got this wrong too but I organized something. For us to do this afternoon.' He shuffles from foot to foot. 'I planned it ages ago. Before . . . well, all this, and I didn't know whether to cancel or not but . . . look, Mum says she'll babysit if you want to do it. I'll totally understand if you don't.'

'What is it?'

Luke hands me the envelope. 'I'm going to go and see Dylan for a bit. You have a think about it and let me know what you want to do. We'd need to leave in about forty-five minutes if you decide you want to go.'

Once Luke has left the room, I sit on the bed and open it. When I see the makeshift tickets, it hits me right in the stomach that he remembered.

I start to descend the stairs but then I stop and sit on the middle one, watching Luke and Dylan on the sofa with their backs to me, Luke reading Dylan his favourite book.

'I'd give a fox my socks to sleep in,' Dylan says as they turn the page. I know the book so well that I can visualize the pictures in my head.

'I know you would. And you'd give your tie to a giraffe to use as a scarf.'

'I don't have a tie, silly.'

'That's true, you don't.' They turn the page. 'Oh, you'd definitely give your shoe as a house for a mouse, wouldn't you?'

Dylan smiles. 'Yes!'

'See, he's the kindest giant in town and you're the kindest boy in town, well, in the whole world.'

'In the whole universe?'

'The whole universe.'

There's a crack in Luke's voice that I find hard to hear so I get up and continue to walk down the stairs as if I haven't been listening.

'Good news, Dylan,' I announce. 'Nono will be here soon. She's going to come and look after you.'

Luke looks up at me. 'Are you sure you want to go?'

I nod. 'I have no idea how you managed to wangle this in December but, yes, I'd love to go.'

Luke smiles. 'It's not what you know, it's who you know, right?'

'Where are you going?' Dylan says.

I pick him up in my arms. He's heavy but I can still manage it. I wonder how long it will be until I can't.

'We're going to fly.'

LUKE

'It's really big, isn't it?'

I stopped trying to pretend I wasn't shitting myself about twenty minutes ago.

'The balloon or the basket?'

'Both. Doesn't that basket look a bit heavy to be lifted into the air simply by hot air?'

Laura laughs. 'I'm guessing they've worked out the physics of it all, done the calculations. Air balloons have been flying for quite some time. Think how heavy aeroplanes are, plus all the people and their mountains of luggage, and they don't fall to the ground, do they?'

'There's an *engine* on an aeroplane. Not a little flame and a piece of fabric with a hole in it and some bloody strings on the side.'

'You do realize *you* organized this, don't you?'

'Because you said you've always wanted to do it. *Take me out my comfort zone.* Wasn't that what you said to me?'

Laura looks sad and I feel bad for bringing up happier times, before I cocked everything up.

'Well, maybe it's good for you to be pushed outside your comfort zone too. You're never scared of anything.'

'That's not true.'

'Come on then. Tell me one thing other than hot air balloons.'

I'm scared of being without you.

'Frogs.'

'You are *not* scared of frogs.'

'I am. Seriously. They're all jumpy and erratic and their fingers are too long and their eyes are too big for the size of their heads.'

Laura pulls a face and nods slowly. 'Wow, you've really thought about this a lot, haven't you? I can't believe we've been together over six years and I didn't know this about you.'

We both move around so that we can get a better shot of the balloon now that it has been fully rolled out on the ground.

'I think maybe we spent too much time having sex and not enough time talking,' I say, taking a few photos of the balloon.

I have no idea where it comes from, but I think perhaps it's true. There is so much we don't really know about each other. So much stuff we didn't fully explore.

'I think you're probably right.'

'Not that I didn't really enjoy the sex.' I elbow her playfully and she smiles but I can tell it makes her feel uncomfortable. Ever since she told me that she wanted out of our relationship, she always flinches when we touch, as if my body is covered in spikes that she is trying her best to avoid. Whereas whenever I'm near her, it still feels like the most natural thing in the world to reach out and touch her. I guess in many ways her leaving still doesn't feel real. I feel like I'm going to wake up.

When she first told me, I laughed. I don't know why, because I didn't find it in the least bit funny, but I just didn't know what else to do. We tried to make it work after the newspaper article about Rosie. I explained that nothing really happened and that Rosie was just hurt because I'd rejected her and trying to get back at me. I spoilt Laura with dinners out and weekends away without Dylan, getting Mum to look after him. And we had some nice times. We still had sex regularly. But I could sense that she wasn't really there. She'd go through the motions but there was no passion from her side, so much so that I'd often ask her if she wanted me to stop but she'd always say no. I think that's when I knew that I'd lost her. In the past, even when she was furious with me, she'd grab me, pull at my hair as I entered her, kiss me so intensely that it was as if it was her last day on earth and she wanted to experience everything it had to offer. But after Rosie, it was like she was dead inside. Like I'd killed her.

But, ridiculously, I still didn't expect her to leave. So maybe me laughing was partly disbelief. It was at the end of one of my 'make up for being a total shit' long weekends away. We'd gone for a pub lunch and then a walk at a country park. When we walked past the play park, I could tell that she missed Dylan, that really she would've rather been with him, but she put on a brave face and kept walking. We chatted. I can't remember what about, but things felt fairly normal, well, as normal as they'd felt since she found out about Rosie. The weather was fine but you could feel the coldness starting to enter the air, the leaves starting to fall from the trees. And then we sat down on a bench and this group of girls came over asking for a photograph with me. When I finally got rid of them, Laura wouldn't speak. I thought she was annoyed about us being disturbed, but when I asked her what was wrong, she just came out with it.

'I don't want to be in this relationship any more.'

Just like that. Obviously my laughter didn't go down particularly well. And after the laughter, I started being defensive and trying to guilt-trip her into changing her mind. *What about Dylan? You said you'd forgiven me. I was just hurting. How many times do I have to tell you nothing happened?*

She stayed really calm, which made the whole thing even worse because it made me sure that she was serious. That she'd thought it all through and wasn't just being reactive.

'I'm not who I want to be.' That was how she phrased it. 'I can't be who I want to be when I'm with you.'

It made it hard to argue with. So after my initial defensive crap, I didn't argue and I've spent every day since wishing that I had. Because once the wheels were in motion, once it had been decided, there didn't seem to be any going back. Once we got home, the conversations turned to the practicalities – which one of us would move out (me), how we would split custody of Dylan (he would live with Laura and I would visit all the time and have him stay with me whenever he wanted to), how Laura would cope financially (I would continue to pay the bills, anything to do with Dylan, and she would just pay for things for herself). So once we'd started talking about all that stuff, I couldn't exactly put my hand in the air like a school kid and say, 'Excuse me, but actually I don't want any of this and can we just go back to that conversation by the lake and pretend it didn't happen please, miss?'

The 'pilot' calls us over for our briefing. I'm not quite sure how you can pilot an object that simply follows the direction of the wind, but my mate who pulled the strings to organize this for me said he's really experienced so I'm trying to hold on to that.

We're given our instructions – basically do what you're told as soon as you're told to – and then we wait patiently (nervously) as the inflation process begins. First, they use a giant fan to basically blow the balloon up, and then once it is largely inflated, they begin the process of turning the flame on to heat the air up. Every time the pilot presses whatever it is he presses to make the burner flame, it makes me jump out of my skin.

Suddenly, the balloon rises into the air and it's actually quite an awe-inspiring sight, but before we have time to really appreciate it, the pilot is shouting 'Board, board,' and we have to run over and climb into the basket. Once in, we follow instructions and sit down, holding on to the loops in front of us. The pilot's put some heavy crates in the other sections of the basket, which I'm guessing are to balance us out, but I worry they're going to make it too heavy.

'Are you OK?' Laura asks me, a mocking look on her face, as the pilot periodically turns on the burner and plays with various strings. At least when he turns it on, it's slightly warmer for a while. It's reaching the point where I'm struggling to feel my fingers and my cheeks feel numb. I did ring up and ask whether it was safe to fly in the biting wind, but he assured me it's only six miles per hour, which is apparently perfect for flying.

'I'm OK whilst we're still on the ground.'

Laura smiles. 'I actually like this side of you, you know?'

'You like me being terrified? Do you think you need to see a therapist about that?'

Laura reaches over and hits me on the arm. 'Your vulnerability.'

'Well, *I* don't like it.'

All of a sudden, I think of my dad on the day he told me he was leaving, me begging him to stay like some kind of sap. *Oh God, what if Dylan begs me to stay? What will I say?*

The basket lifts and then it feels like we're rising at speed, like we're suddenly weightless. I grip on to the loops until my knuckles go white and then the pilot says we can stand up. *Stand up?*

The look on Laura's face when she looks out and observes the view momentarily makes me feel great. She looks so content, so wowed – it's why I booked it in the first place. But then I try to stand up and my legs are like jelly and I remain in this kind of half sitting, half standing position with both hands gripping on to the edge of the basket.

'You look like you're squatting down to do a poo,' Laura giggles and then her giggles turn into hysterics, tears streaming down her face. 'Can you take . . .?' She pauses, trying to compose herself enough to get the words out. 'Can you take a . . .?'

She holds out her camera and I infer that she's trying to ask me to take a photograph of her, but I can't manage to take my hands off the edge of the basket.

I also seem to have lost the power of speech but for a vastly different reason to Laura, so I just shake my head and then nod towards my hands.

She finally regains composure and wipes the tears from her face with her scarf. 'I'm sorry. I just couldn't get the words out.'

'I could see that.'

'Do you want me to take a photo of you?'

'Not right now, no. I look like an idiot.'

'You don't look like an idiot, but you don't look particularly well. This is probably the palest I've ever seen you.'

Laura leans over the edge of the basket – *how?* – and starts pointing out landmarks. 'Look at the lakes. Doesn't it look amazing from the sky? It's like something out of *Lord of the Rings.*'

I force myself to look at the landscape (from where I am; not leaning out of the basket. I'm not *insane*). And it is stunning – the frosty fields like a patchwork blanket, the glistening lakes, the snow-topped mountains. But now that I've seen it, I want to be back on the ground. And when I check my watch, we've only done ten minutes of our estimated one-hour flight.

'Would it be really awful if I sat down for a bit?'

Laura looks back at me. 'No, of course not. Sit down if you'll feel better.'

It's such a relief when my bum hits the bench and I can no longer see that we are thousands of feet above the ground in a wicker basket like the one my mum stores her magazines in.

Laura puts her arms on the edge of the basket and rests her chin on her hands, her cute bobble hat pulled down over her ears. I'm so glad that she's enjoying it. When things went sour between us, I very nearly cancelled, but I decided that I still wanted to thank her for giving me Dylan. That hadn't changed. And I'm really glad that we're here. If this has to be our ending then I at least want things to end on a high (quite literally). And maybe it doesn't have to be our ending? Maybe this is the turning point where we start to find a way to piece things back together.

After what feels like a longer period of time than my

entire life up to this point, we start our descent and I manage to stand again. Laura gasps when we look as if we're about to hit the upcoming trees, making the pilot laugh, but I love this bit. The view of the world from this elevation is incredible. We float over the tops of the trees, so close to them it feels like we could reach down and touch the branches, and now I don't want the flight to end.

'This is amazing,' I say, the adrenaline hit of surviving the heady heights we were at before flooding through my veins.

'So now we're going down, you want to stay up?'

'I do. I could stay right here forever.'

We both lean on the edge of the basket, looking out at the spiky fields and skeletal trees and a handful of cows charging through a gate. And then Laura puts her hand on top of mine, her skin icy cold, and I want to savour it because I've missed her touch so much and I know it won't be long before she removes it.

'Thank you so much for this. I really do appreciate it.'

'It's the least I could do. You gave me our son.'

'*You* gave me our son too.'

'Well, yes, technically I did. But I'll always remember you on the day you gave birth to him. I was in awe of you.'

'So you don't regret having him?'

'You're seriously asking me that question?'

Laura nods.

I know that's part of the reason things are where they are between us. That, whatever she might say, she'll never understand why I even considered an abortion.

'Of course I don't regret having him.'

'I just think your life could've been so much easier. You could've just got on with all the band stuff without us holding you back. I bet it felt like a noose sometimes.'

I put my other hand on top of hers. 'No. Never.'

I'm not sure it's entirely true. There are times when it has felt, well, not like a noose, but like something around my ankle, holding me back from really experiencing everything with the band the way I would've done if I didn't have Laura or Dylan. But now I'm desperate for them to hold me back. *Wrap yourselves around me and don't let go. Please.*

'I guess it's all water under the bridge now anyway,' Laura says, removing her hand from between mine. 'I think we should tell Dylan tomorrow. There's never going to be a good time.'

The finality of telling Dylan terrifies me, but I know it's only a matter of time before he notices that Mummy and Daddy don't sleep in the same bed any more, or even the same house. That Daddy leaves late at night and comes back in the morning. I mean, he's used to me coming and going a fair bit, but I'm sure he's going to twig soon that things aren't as they should be. And sooner or later, if Laura is really serious about this, I'm going to have to buy my own place where he can have his own room. I'm sure Laura doesn't understand me moving in with Cody and Rich – she probably thinks I want to experience a 'lads' pad' – but the truth is I just don't want to live on my own. Not yet anyway. I'm not ready.

'OK.'

It's as much agreement as I can give.

'We'll make sure he knows it's not his fault, that we're still going to be great friends, that we'll still all get together for his birthday and Christmas and you'll see him all the time.'

'We will still do that, won't we?'

'Of course,' Laura says. 'It's not like we hate each other, is it?'

Far from it, I think, but I just shake my head.

'Right, into your landing positions please, folks,' the pilot says, so I take one last look over the basket and then sit down, holding on to the hooks, wishing this wasn't it.

Laura sits down beside me and we look at each other and smile and I know that this is my last chance to say something, to stop this madness before it's too late.

'This isn't what I want.'

Laura looks to the floor of the basket and my heart sinks with the balloon as I realize that she definitely doesn't feel the same: she's not going to change her mind. And then all too soon we hit the ground.

16th December 2011

LAURA

'He said he'd help carry stuff. This box of juice cartons is far too heavy for us.'

'It's OK, love. We'll sort it,' Mum says, buttering slices of bread like she's on a production line. The radio is on – bloody Christmas songs on a loop.

'And he said he'd help with the sandwiches. It's not fair that we have to do it all.'

'He'll be here.' However much Luke proves her wrong, Jenny seems determined to see the best in him. I suppose it's the natural mother and son thing. I'll probably be the same with Dylan. But I like to think that if he was being a total waste of space like Luke is, I'd pull him up on it, make him realize it's not OK. But maybe in private she does speak to him and he just doesn't listen. *Who knows?* As close as we've got over the years, I don't feel I can broach it with her.

I check my watch. 'Well, he's forty-five minutes late. It'll be the end of school soon. I had to take a day off work for this. What's his excuse?'

'We did say we could've done it ourselves, didn't we, Jenny?' Mum says. 'We are here to help you, you know.'

I shake my head. 'I couldn't have got back for his party if I'd worked today anyway.'

'I'm sure Dylan wouldn't mind if you missed one of his parties, love.' Mum puts the knife down and stops buttering long enough to put her hand on my arm.

'No way. I'd never do that.'

Jenny moves the box she's loaded up with packets of crisps on to the table. 'Right. What's my next job?'

I squish past her to check my list, which I've pinned on the fridge. My new kitchen isn't really big enough for the three of us, but we shuffle around each other the best we can.

'Shall we cut up some fruit or just do that when we get there? It might go a bit brown and yucky if we do it now, I suppose.'

'Let's take a knife and do that there,' Jenny says. 'Have you got a candle?'

'Oh, shit. I can't believe I forgot a candle. I'll nip out and get one.'

Jenny puts her hand on my back. I can tell she thinks I'm flapping unnecessarily. But I just want to show the world (and Luke in particular, I guess) that I'm on top of everything even though I'm on my own.

'You stay here. I'll go and get a candle. Anything else we need whilst I'm there? A few balloons to put on the gate of the park so people know where to find us?'

'Thanks, Jenny. That would be amazing. I'm still not all that savvy with this kids' party stuff. Not for this many people anyway.'

'Don't be silly. I had years of all this, didn't I? Make the most of it. When they go to secondary school, they barely want to look at you, let alone have some lame party organized by their mum.'

Jenny laughs, grabbing her car keys and running out the door, but the thought makes my breath feel tight. Dylan is six today. What if I only have a handful of birthdays left where he wants to share it with me? *I will happily cut up thirty apples, ninety strawberries and one hundred and twenty grapes. Just please don't take my son away from me.*

I get Dylan's birthday cake out of the fridge and put it on the worktop. It's my first attempt at making a 'proper' cake and I'm worried people are going to think it looks crap: my icing is baggy and the dragon I painted on the top isn't exactly going to give Quentin Blake a run for his money.

'Wow, it's brilliant,' Mum says. 'Did you make it?'

'Thanks for your pretence, but I think it's fairly obvious that I made it. I think Tesco would have done a slightly better job.'

'No way. Dylan will love it. Of course it had to be a dragon cake.'

I thought Dylan's knights and dragons obsession might have eased off by now but it's still going strong, and I find a strange comfort in that – a constant in what feels like a rapidly changing landscape.

Mum starts filling the sandwiches. 'Do you really think jam and butter?' She pulls a face.

'Apparently that's what the kids are eating these days. Crazy, aren't they?'

Mum laughs. 'Did you really have to invite the whole class?'

'It seems to be the done thing, unfortunately.'

'We used to say choose three friends.'

'I know. The good old times, hey?'

Mum smiles but then she looks unfittingly serious. 'Sometimes when I look at Dylan, I feel like I wasted your childhood. I was always so worried about money, about you having what you needed, about your education. I wish I'd enjoyed it more.'

'You only wanted the best for me.'

'I know, but . . .'

Jenny comes back through the door, unknowingly cutting off our conversation as she starts unloading what she's bought. 'A six candle, balloons, a Happy Birthday banner, some snowman lollies to give the children when they leave . . .' She looks in the bottom of the bag. 'Oh, and Matchmakers. They're for us.'

'Thanks, Jenny. You're a lifesaver.'

'Trying to make up for that son of mine.' She gives me a knowing look and I offer her a sad smile. 'I called him. He says he's running a bit behind and he'll meet us at the park. I told him if he's not there I'm going to cut him out of my will. I'm not sure he's that fussed about missing out on my silver jewellery and my mum's fine china, but I wasn't sure what other threat to use.'

'He shouldn't need a threat.'

'I know, darling. I'm sorry. If it's any consolation, I think he's probably struggling with everything. He's been a total lost soul since you split up. I know that's no excuse.'

'He always seems full of the joys of spring when he comes to get Dylan.'

'Men are a proud bunch.' Jenny looks up at the clock. 'Right, you go and get the birthday boy from school. We'll get all of this stuff to the park and meet you there.'

When we arrive at the park, the first person I look for is Luke but he's still not there. Mum and Jenny have found a table and put the cake and jugs of squash on top and the boxes of food and numerous flasks of hot chocolate underneath. They've put balloons on the park gate and the banner along the edge of the table, and when Dylan sees them, his face lights up. Thankfully there are no other families here (to be fair it's bloody freezing), so at least it feels a bit more exclusive.

'Do you think it's too cold to have a party in the park?' I ask Mum, rubbing my hands together. 'Maybe I should've just let Luke pay for the hall.'

One of the problems with Dylan going to a private school is that it always accentuates how little I have and I always end up feeling inferior.

'It's fine. The kids don't feel the cold,' Mum says, her breath visible in the bitter December air.

Jenny puts her hand on my arm. 'I'll go and buy us coffees if we start to get cold. The kids will be fine. It's lovely. Outside: it's where kids should be.'

'Thanks, Jenny.'

A few of the children we've invited have managed to get across town before us, so Dylan runs up to them and they all start happily playing tag and I'm hopeful that the party is going to be OK. But then Luke arrives. And with a sharp intake of breath, I notice that he's not on his own.

She's blonde, of course. Hair perfectly straightened and down to her bum. Even wearing a stupid paper Christmas hat, she looks like a model. Or perhaps she's *too* perfectly beautiful. Not quirky enough to be a model. She's wearing a long, dark green wool coat and knee-high leather boots. Luke looks smart too in a navy peacoat and chinos. And I wish I'd worn something more impressive than my muddy oversized duffel coat or at least done my hair instead of hiding it under a beanie. She bounces along next to Luke, full of faux enthusiasm for everything and everyone she meets. Or maybe it's not faux. Maybe life just hasn't beaten it out of her yet. Either way, she makes me feel frumpy and miserable in comparison.

They greet Jenny, Mum and a few of the parents who have decided to stick around (most leave – is that a *thing* now they're six?), leaving me until last. And then just as they're heading in my direction, Dylan appears from his 'hide-and-seek' hiding place and runs up to Luke, jumping into his arms and causing Luke's paper hat to blow off on to the ground.

'Daddy.' It still hurts when I see how excited he is to see Luke. I get it. He misses him so when he sees him it's a celebration. But it still smarts that I never get the bounding excitement, the huge glee at the sight of my face.

'Hey there, soldier.' Luke twirls him around until he's dizzy and then he puts him down and Dylan stumbles like a drunk and dramatically falls to the floor and Luke copies him and falls down beside him until they're both lying on the frosty grass looking up at the sky.

Luke's blonde companion laughs as if it's a stupid sketch and then, a stab to the chest, she bends down and ruffles Dylan's hair. 'Happy birthday, Dylan. I'm Nathalia.'

Even my name pales in comparison to hers.

'Dylan, this is my special friend, Nathalia. Say hi.'

'Hi,' Dylan says casually, having utterly no awareness of the significance of this moment.

Special friend? Is that better or worse than girlfriend? Maybe that's what the youth of today call having lots of wild sex.

'Can I go and play now?'

'Of course,' Nathalia says, as if she has any say in what my son does.

'Yes, go and play,' I step in, re-wrapping Dylan's scarf around his neck and then sending him back to his friends. Then I turn to Nathalia with a confidence I definitely do not feel and hold out my hand. 'I'm Laura, uh . . .' I pause, wondering how exactly to describe myself. Luke's ex? I settle on 'Dylan's mum'.

Nathalia stares at my hand like she has no idea what to do with it. What is she expecting – a fist bump? Then, to my utter surprise and discomfort, she pulls me into a hug and then kisses both of my cheeks like she's Parisian. Not even air kisses – her lips actually touch my skin and I have a distinct desire to get a wipe out of the nappy bag (still named 'nappy bag' despite the absence of nappies for some years) and wash my face. I force a smile that makes my cheeks ache.

'Lovely to meet you, Laura.'

'You too,' I lie.

'Dylan is a wonderful boy.'

You've said a handful of words to him. For all she knows, he's a spoilt brat who has an hour-long tantrum if he doesn't get his own way or a violent little shit who beats up all the other children in his class.

'Thank you,' I force. '*We* think so, don't we, Luke?'

I sense him baulk at the 'we' but he smiles. 'We do.'

'I've heard so much about him,' she continues and I wonder when. Between mammoth sex sessions? I can't imagine Luke and this girl doing much talking. I expect it's even a challenge for him to keep it PG in front of the children.

'I see.'

Jenny wanders over and I try to gauge if she knew Luke was seeing someone but I sense in her eyes that she didn't. And I find a solace in that. I've grown fond of Jenny over the years and I like to think she's on my side. The day she really likes one of Luke's girlfriends it will feel like I'm being replaced.

'Go and get a drink,' Jenny says to Luke and his new lover. 'I'm afraid there's nothing more exciting than squash, but this is a kids' party after all.'

'Oh, it's OK. We've just been for Christmas dinner at Charlie's. Can you believe my cracker had a little bottle of gin in it? What was yours, Luke? Whisky? We could probably do with something soft, couldn't we?'

I clench my jaw to stop myself from screaming, as Nathalia takes Luke's hand and drags him over to the table.

'I apologize for my son,' Jenny says, hanging back with me.

'Please don't. It's fine,' I lie.

'It is not fine to turn up late because he was having a boozy lunch and to show up with her with no warning at his son's birthday party – honestly, Laura, wait until I get him on his own. You will be getting a very serious apology.'

I shake my head. 'I don't want an apology that has to be forced out of him. I've had far too many of those.'

'I'm sorry. He always made out that you were being unreasonable.'

It hurts to hear how he's framed our relationship.

'I probably was sometimes. We clearly just weren't meant to be.'

We go back to the picnic table and I busy myself with uncovering sandwiches and cutting up fruit to avoid being drawn into any polite conversations. I feel like if I speak, I might break down, so I'd rather just focus on doing. However hard I try though, it's impossible to ignore Nathalia's hand around Luke's waist as they chat to one of the mums who is clearly ecstatic that the father of the birthday boy just happens to be the lead singer of Paradigm. I've not noticed her before. But then a lot of grandparents and nannies seem to do the drop-offs and pick-ups, so you don't always get to meet the actual parents.

'So where do you live?' the mum asks Luke, clearly desperate to impart the juicy gossip to her friends over WhatsApp later.

'Oh, you know that *huge* house up on the hill?' Nathalia says. 'You can just about spot it from town. He lives *there*. It's *amazing*.'

So not only has she been to our house, *Luke's* house, she clearly waxes lyrical about it in a way I could never bring myself to. And I don't even know why I couldn't. Sometimes when I'm sitting in my small back garden, fences either side, the neighbours' kids shouting at each other on one side and the other neighbours' dog barking day and night on the other, I physically ache for that terrace. Luke wanted me to stay there with Dylan, but it didn't feel right, and rather than make him sell it when he loves it so much, I told him to move back in and he kindly put a deposit down on a little terraced house in town for me. He said I could have anywhere I wanted, but I didn't want a huge contribution from Luke and I wanted somewhere with mortgage payments that I could afford.

'The one with the completely glass frontage?'

Luke nods, looking a little uncomfortable.

'Wow. We always talk about that place. It looks incredible.'

'You should see inside,' Nathalia prattles on and I'm tempted to get the jug of squash and pour it all over her head.

'Right, kids,' I shout, walking into the middle of the playground. 'Food time.'

They all rush over from their various hiding points around the park and it's like a stampede as they fight to get to the food first. The only enjoyable bit is when they nearly knock Nathalia off the bench.

'Hold up, hold up,' Luke says, putting his body in the way of the table. 'Are we a herd of wildebeests, or tigers, or are we children?'

'Wildebeests,' one child shouts.

'Lions,' another one joins in.

'Well, the person at the back of the line gets the biggest slice of cake later,' Luke says, clearly trying another approach as his first one failed.

This time, all the children start rushing in the opposite direction and fighting for the back of the line instead of the front.

'Well, that wasn't very successful,' Luke says, performing for the small audience of mums who giggle like schoolgirls. 'Right, sit in a circle and we'll bring the food to you, OK?'

The children do as they're asked and form a circle on the picnic mats we've put out, and the adults help to give out sandwiches, packets of crisps and fruit. Then we give them all plastic cups and go round pouring in hot chocolate. Noticeably Nathalia doesn't get involved, probably not wanting to break a nail, but with the rest of us on the job, the children soon have everything they need and settle down to a quiet chatter as they stuff their faces with food and give themselves hot chocolate moustaches.

For a moment, I end up standing on my own next to Luke.

'I'm sorry I didn't make it to yours to help out. I totally forgot that's what we'd arranged. I thought I was meeting you at the park.'

'It's OK. We managed.'

'I did buy thirty Lego sets to make up for it though. They're mini Santas. They're pretty cool. I thought you could give them out instead of a party bag.'

'Your mum got snowman lollies.'

'Well, now they get lollies and Lego.'

'I think a Lego set each is a bit . . .'

'Before you say it's extravagant, remember one of the kid's parties was at Lego*land*. A tiny Lego set is probably the equivalent to a measly pencil and rubber for most of these kids.'

I don't want to argue with him so I just let it go. And maybe he's right. Maybe it's me that's out of touch.

'Talking of presents, are you in contact with your dad now?'

'No. Why do you say that?'

'He sent the present to my house. I figured you must have told him what had happened between us, but I guess it must've been your mum.'

Luke nods, suddenly thoughtful.

'So how long have you been together?' I try to sound as nonchalant as possible, as if I'm asking him what the time is.

'Oh, we've just been seeing each other for a month or so. It's nothing serious.'

'But you brought her to your son's birthday party?'

'I told him she's my friend. He's not to know we're . . .' Luke trails off. 'You know what I mean. I'm certainly not bringing her home to meet the family or anything. We're just having some fun.'

Unlike I had with you. He doesn't need to say it but it's there in the air between us.

'Well, I'm very happy for you. She's very beautiful.'

'She is.'

My throat constricts and I know I need to walk away before I burst into tears. What did I expect him to say? No, she's not? He's not *blind*. What was I angling for? *Not as beautiful as you?*

'I'm going to go and light the candle. You can lead the singing.'

'Of course. Will do.'

I bring over the cake I've made, trying to ignore Nathalia's 'how cute' comments, and Luke starts up the singing.

'A dragon,' Dylan says over the singing, a look of glee on his face, and I blow him a kiss.

The singing ends and we do six cheers and one for luck and then Dylan blows out his candle.

'Make a wish,' Luke and I say in unison and then we look at each other and laugh and for a moment it's like the old days, but then his new model girlfriend comes over and puts her arm around him, and I realize that it's nothing like the old days.

After gobbling down the cake (I probably should have made it twice the size), the children run off for one last play. I linger near the slide, stamping my feet to keep warm, while Luke and Nathalia greet all the parents as they arrive to collect their children – the women fawning over Luke and the men drooling over Nathalia and then giving Luke looks of congratulations on the upgrade. Luke's right – the kids don't bat an eyelid at the ridiculously extravagant party bag offering and it just confirms for me that I don't really belong in this world.

When everyone else has gone, Dylan runs up to me and gives me a big hug. 'Thank you for my party.'

'That's OK. And thank Nana and Nono for helping,' I add.

'Thank you,' he says and then Luke comes over with a huge gift. I'm irritated before I even see what it is because I know it's going to overshadow the hand-painted wooden shield I gave Dylan this morning.

'Happy birthday,' Luke says, handing the gift to Dylan.

When he rips off the paper, I can see it's a giant Lego castle. Dylan doesn't even play with Lego yet, so buying him a set aimed at advanced builders feels like it's all just for show.

Dylan's clearly impressed, though, as he exclaims 'Wow,' his eyes wide.

'It's really cool, isn't it?' Nathalia chips in. 'Daddy spent ages choosing you the best one.'

God, she's unbearable. I bet she even tells Luke his farts smell like lavender.

'Thank you, Daddy.'

Dylan and Luke embrace and I can tell from Luke's face that he finds it hard to let Dylan go. At first, he asked if Dylan could sleep at his tonight, but I think he could tell from my lacklustre response that it was too much for me so, to his credit, he didn't push it. But then maybe he was just relieved that he could spend all night swinging from the chandeliers with Nathalia guilt-free.

'Right. Let's go home and open all these presents from your friends.'

I hold out my hand for Dylan and he takes it, and Jenny and Mum load themselves up with empty boxes, the now empty jugs and the bags of presents.

'I can help you take the stuff to the car,' Luke says.

'It's OK,' Mum says. 'I think Nana and Nono have got it covered, haven't they, Dylan? We're superwomen, aren't we?'

Jenny tenses her free arm. 'Certainly are.'

Luke goes over and kisses his mum on the cheek.

'Come and see me soon, won't you?' she says.

'Of course I will. Remember we're having dinner on Christmas Eve. I've booked somewhere nice.'

'You don't have to do that, you know. Seeing you is enough.'

'I know, but I want to treat my old mum, don't I?'

'Hey you, less of the old,' Jenny says, elbowing him in the side.

'I guess I'll see you on Christmas Day,' I say to Luke, trying to make it clear the invitation doesn't extend to Nathalia.

'About that . . .' Luke looks at Nathalia and then back at me. 'I wasn't sure what we were doing. I wondered if you had him on Christmas Day this year and then I'll have him on Boxing Day. Then maybe we could swap and do it the other way around next year.'

I'm not sure if Mum senses it on my face – the pain filtering its way into my eyes – but she takes Dylan's hand and guides him towards the car and then Jenny asks Nathalia to help carry things and takes her off too, leaving Luke and me alone.

'I presumed we were spending Christmas Day together like we did last year.' I try to sound as matter-of-fact as I can.

'We've barely spoken for months. I just thought you wouldn't want to do that any more.'

'Are you spending it with her?'

Luke shrugs. 'She invited me to have Christmas dinner with some of her friends. They've booked a restaurant and there's space for me, but I said I needed to check with you first.'

'You've paid a deposit.' It's not really a question.

'Well yeah, but I don't care if I lose it. I just thought you'd prefer it this way. I'm giving you Christmas Day with him, Laura. It's not like I'm being unreasonable about it.'

'You're right. It's fine. It will be better. I'll let you explain it to Dylan though.'

'I can come if you want me to.'

I shake my head. 'But your mum will still be invited.'

'Of course. She'll get two Christmas Days with him. She'll love it.'

'Right. Well, have a wonderful Christmas, Luke. I'll get your mum to drop Dylan round on Boxing Day.'

I turn and head towards the car.

'Laura,' Luke calls and I paint on my most impressive 'I'm totally fine' expression and turn around.

'I don't want . . . it's not,' Luke stumbles.

'It's fine. You're right – it will be better.'

Luke sighs, his head dropping, and I force myself to

walk away. And as I do, Nathalia walks towards me, back to Luke, so I force a brief smile as she passes.

'You OK?' Mum asks as I reach the car. They've packed everything in the boot and put Dylan in the back.

'Fine,' I say, giving her a hug.

As I hug Jenny, she whispers, 'He's not thinking straight' into my ear and because I can't find the words to reply I just squeeze her a bit tighter.

As Mum and Jenny walk back to their cars, I start the engine and as soon as I'm out of view, the tears come like a flood, silently pouring down my cheeks. I'm surprised I can see the road well enough to make it to Sarah's, but somehow I do. And when I pull up on her drive, I lift up my jumper and wipe my face, painting on a happy face for Dylan as I open the back door of the car and let him out. He runs down the path to Sarah's like it's his second home and knocks on her door.

'This is a nice surprise,' she says, lifting Dylan up and giving him a kiss on the forehead. 'I didn't think I was going to see you on your actual birthday this year.'

'I'm sorry.' I come up behind Dylan and as soon as I see Sarah's face, I feel my eyes filling with tears again.

'Dylan, you run inside. Tom's around somewhere. I'm sure he'll play hide and seek with you.'

Dylan does as he's told and runs into Sarah's house and then she opens her arms wide and I run into them and allow myself to fall apart.

LUKE

'God, kids are awful.' Nathalia is holding court with her friends, the way she always does. There's a guy in the corner of the restaurant playing the piano who clearly thinks he's Michael Bublé as he croons out the Christmas classics.

'You do realize I'm sat beside you?'

'Oh, I don't mean Dylan. He's the exception, of course.' She puts her hand on my thigh. 'It was just the others pushing to get food first, moaning they didn't have enough cake, grabbing the party bag without a thank you.'

'I just think kids are inherently self-obsessed,' I say.

'We don't change much, do we?' Lauren, one of Nathalia's friends, laughs.

'True,' Nathalia agrees. 'Talking of which, where's my bloody bottle of champagne?'

She shouts it so loud that the waitress hears and scuttles off, quickly coming back with our drinks.

'I'm sorry. I don't know how this got missed. Have this one on the house as an apology,' the waitress says, looking flustered. It's absolutely rammed – groups of people on their office Christmas do, all overly loud and flirtatious in a way they're going to regret when they see each other at work tomorrow morning.

'I should think so,' Nathalia says with a disappointed teacher expression and then she and her friends giggle when the waitress leaves the table.

'Top up our drinks then,' she says to me, pulling her black sparkly dress down further. She always does this in front of her friends – pretends I'm slightly subservient to her. It's odd because whenever we're on our own, she treats me like I'm a king. Later, she'll apologize profusely, probably offer me a blowjob or something in compensation.

'Here you are, ladies.' I stand up and pour the champagne into their glasses and then feel my phone buzzing in my pocket. Taking it out, I see it's Sarah. She hasn't called me for ages.

'I just need to take this phone call. I'll be back to serve you all shortly.' I bow and they all laugh.

'Oh, you're here mainly as eye candy,' Hetty says. She's a total flirt. On more than one occasion, when she's caught me on my own, she's made very suggestive comments and I have no doubt she would betray Nathalia and sleep with me in a second if I asked her to, but then I'm pretty sure Nathalia shares an ex with one of the other girls, so I'm not sure loyalty is a huge value amongst them.

I leave the table, manoeuvring through the packed restaurant, nearly crashing into a group of blokes in suits doing the conga, and answer my phone quickly before Sarah rings off. 'Hello?'

'Hey, you. It's very noisy. Where are you?'

'I'm at Luccio's. Hold on a second, I'm going somewhere quieter.' I exit the restaurant and head down the road, the cold hitting me as soon as I get outside.

'Luccio's, hey? Very fancy.'

'Oh, you know me.'

'I do.'

Once it's quieter, I stop. 'So, what's up?'

'Does something have to be up for me to call you?'

'Well, no. But I haven't spoken to you in a while. Have you reconsidered my offer? I hope that's what you're ringing me about.'

'No. Our answer remains the same to that.'

'But why?' I find myself pacing up and down the street, strangely unable to stay still and talk on the phone. I'm surrounded by twinkly lights, Christmas songs blaring out of all the pubs, groups of people in Santa hats laughing as they stumble down the street, but I'm struggling to feel in the slightest bit festive. 'That money is nothing to me. Seriously. It would make me happy for it to go to a good cause instead of being wasted on booze and fancy restaurants.'

'It's not just about the money, Luke. I'm so very grateful for the offer, I really am. You are a total sweetheart. But I just can't go through it again.' I can hear Sarah tearing up and it breaks me because she's always so strong.

'But maybe it'll work this time. It's got to be worth another go, right?'

'No. I don't want to be injected with hormones any more and have someone poking things up my fajeeba to retrieve eggs or insert sperm or whatever the hell it is they're sticking things up there for.'

'I get that. But please let me know if you change your mind, OK? Don't be embarrassed to ask for the money.'

'OK. But that's not what I was ringing you about. I'm ringing to give you a telling off.'

'Oh, God. What have I done this time?'

'Come on, Luke. Turning up with Nathalia. That's a dick move and you know it.'

I sigh. 'She split up with me. You do remember that, don't you?'

'You know it's not as straightforward as that.'

'Did she tell you about all the times I turned up at her place literally begging for her to reconsider and she just closed the door in my face? Do you have any idea how stupid that made me feel?'

'You broke her heart, Luke.'

'She broke *mine*.' I hear the exasperation in my voice and take a deep breath, my feet pummelling the pavement. 'I can't feel guilty for the rest of my life, Sar. And I didn't actually do anything wrong. There's not many men in my position who would've resisted temptation as many times as I did.'

'No, Luke. Don't try that with me. I am not going to give you a medal for not sleeping with your many groupies when you were lucky enough to have someone as wonderful as Laura at home.'

'OK, fine. I don't want a medal, but I didn't do anything with Rosie.'

'But it wasn't just about Rosie, was it? That was just the straw that broke the camel's back.'

'No, it wasn't about Rosie. It was about the fact Laura just didn't like me very much. You're right – she was too good for me. So she's lucky to be out of it. But I should be allowed to try to move on with my life now.'

Try is definitely the optimum word. If only she knew how much I wanted to wrap my arms around Laura when I saw her earlier, how I wanted to fall to the ground and beg her to make this *stop*.

'She's not preventing you from moving on. But to turn

up to your son's birthday party with her. No warning. Come on, Luke. You're better than that.'

'Clearly not.'

'Well, be better then. And Christmas? You agreed to always spend it together, didn't you, for better or worse?'

I drag my hand through my hair. 'That was when we *spoke* to each other, Sar. She promised it was going to be this amicable thing where we still saw each other all the time and did things as a family, but she barely even looks at me when I go to get Dylan. She never invites me in. It's nothing like what we agreed, so why would I think she wanted to spend Christmas with me? Do you genuinely think I don't want to spend Christmas Day with my son?'

Sarah goes quiet.

'Look, Nathalia and her friends will be waiting for me. I have to go.'

'OK. Enjoy your evening. And I do still love you.'

I start my walk back towards the restaurant. 'Just tell her that I'm sorry, will you?'

'No. You tell her.'

'You're a pain in the arse, you know?'

'You love me really. Bye, Luke.'

'Bye.'

I put my phone back in my pocket and try to stop thoughts of Laura infiltrating my evening as I go back to my supermodel date and her friends.

Somehow, we've ended up in a club. Some of Nathalia's male friends have joined us and we're all doing shots off the bar. The music is blaring and all the girls are dancing together, men gawping at them, which just makes them dance even more provocatively.

'Hetty's the best in bed.' Callum, the model of the group but actually one of the least attractive, says as he eyes the girls. I'm guessing that means he's slept with all of them, which is a bit odd, but maybe that's how things work these days. God, I sound *eighty*-two rather than thirty-two.

'Well, I've not slept with them all, but Nathalia's hard to beat,' Liam joins in. Then he slaps me on the arm. 'Sorry, mate. Hope you don't mind me saying.'

'Not a problem, mate. You're right. She is.'

'You should have seen the things Lauren was getting up to last night. That girl is a freak. You'd be surprised.'

'It's always the quiet ones that are the dirtiest. Maybe to make up for their lack of personality.'

'Shut up.' James (Lauren's boyfriend/fuck buddy) punches Liam in the side, not entirely playfully. 'She's actually got a really good personality.'

'Not going soft on her, are you mate? You know these girls are only here to use and abuse us. There's no commitment.'

Callum leans in to speak quietly into my ear. 'I think Thalia really likes you.'

'Oh, I don't know. I think it's just a bit of fun, which is cool.'

'I dunno. I was with her for quite a long time. It was a couple of years ago now,' he adds quickly as if he's worried I might be jealous, which I realize I'm not in the slightest. 'I can tell when she likes someone. She used to look at me the same way.' He winks.

'So how come you split up?'

'I wanted to spread my seed, so to speak. Thalia's a great

girl, don't get me wrong, but we're only young once, right? I want to experience everything, you know? And that means exploring different connections.'

'Connections' being a code word for sleeping with all her friends by the sounds of it.

'She said you've got a kid,' he continues. 'That's pretty heavy.'

'It wasn't planned.'

'I've had a couple of scares myself but thank God they were false alarms. No offence, mate.'

'None taken. It's a lot. I get that. Being a dad is pretty cool though.'

'Oh yeah, I definitely want all that one day. Maybe when I'm in my thirties or something.'

He says it like he's saying 'when robots rule the earth'. *It'll be here sooner than you think, mate. Just you wait and see.*

'You definitely make it look much less scary. I mean, I kind of felt like when I had a kid that'd be the end of all my fun, but you're here, aren't you? And you're going home with Thalia.'

'I'm a lucky man.'

'So was it a one-night stand or something?'

'What?'

'Your kid's mum.'

I shake my head. 'We were in a relationship until just over a year ago. It didn't work out.'

'Well, to be fair, you must have girls throwing themselves at you.'

I shrug.

'I'm jealous, mate. Being a model's pretty good, but being in a band, you're next level. Seriously.'

I laugh and then Liam hands us both another shot and we all do them in unison, slamming our glasses on the bar when we finish.

And then I feel arms around my waist and look over my shoulder to see Nathalia.

'Come dance with me,' she says in my ear.

I turn around and she kisses me. 'OK.'

She leads me to the dance floor and we dance for hours, the others joining us, all throwing our arms in the air and singing along to the tunes at the tops of our voices, and it irritates the shit out of me that even that doesn't make me feel better. Even when I should be having the time of my life, I feel like I'm drowning.

'Shall I try it like this?' Nathalia changes position so that she's on top of me, her weight on her arms, her breasts pushed up.

She tries her best but there's no improvement, so I gently manoeuvre her off and lie beside her. It started OK. We were kissing the whole time in the taxi, started undressing each other the moment we came through the door. But as we started to actually have sex, I quickly felt my erection fading – that awful deflating feeling of going flaccid – and I know from experience that once that's happened, there's no turning back.

'I think I've just had too much to drink. Shall we try again in the morning?'

'I'm horny now. Let me try something else.' She moves down the bed but I take her head and gently move it away.

'Look, I'll sort you out. I'm OK for now.'

Nathalia looks up at me as if she's considering my offer

and then comes up the bed and lies on her back like a starfish.

I put in the best performance I can muster and she writhes and moans beneath my fingers. She's so *loud* you could hear her from the middle of town. At first it turned me on that she seemed so into me, but sometimes it feels a bit performative.

When I've achieved my goal, she leans up and kisses me, her hands around my neck, and then she shouts, 'You. Are. So. Amazing.' And laughs excessively.

I'm about to say, 'Sorry about before,' but then I decide not to draw attention to my embarrassing earlier failings. I just hope it's not the topic of conversation when she next meets up with her friends.

We lie back on the bed, naked, covers off and then she blurts out, 'I think I might be in love with you. I know it hasn't been long, but . . .'

She trails off. She does this a lot, not finishing her sentences and expecting you to fill in the blanks.

I kiss her so that I don't have to respond, making it long and passionate so that she doesn't expect the conversation to continue afterwards. When I pull away, she's smiling, so I think she takes the kiss to mean that I feel the same.

Then she puts her hand on my penis. 'Want to go again?'

Thankfully, she seems to have forgotten that we didn't really 'go' the first time, but I gently hold her wrist.

'I'm wasted. In the morning?'

'Only if you make me your amazing pancakes first?'

'Deal.'

She kisses me on the cheek and then turns over. And I hope that she's going to go to sleep because I'm exhausted.

After a few minutes, she pulls the cover up over her shoulder. And then, thank the Lord, I hear her breathing become slower and more rhythmic and then she starts to snore. Yes, the perfect supermodel snores like an old man. But I can't quite drift off. It's like I have this permanent slightly unsettled feeling in my stomach. Like when you're worried about something but you can't remember what it is you're worried about.

I go downstairs and grab myself a glass of milk, turning the Christmas tree lights on and sitting on the sofa in the dark, just watching them twinkle. I wasn't going to bother with a tree this year but Dylan insisted we go out and buy one. When we were decorating it, I found myself missing Laura's snarky comments about us taking up all the power for the whole neighbourhood and needing a ten-foot ladder just to put the angel on the top.

I pick up my phone from the bedside table and look on Facebook, scrolling mindlessly through photos of holidays, nights out, friends on jet skis or paragliding. And then a photo of Dylan surrounded by presents and wrapping paper appears. 'Thank you so much to all of Dylan's friends for the amazing gifts. One happy boy,' reads the status. I smile at his joyful face and then feel the familiar ache in my chest at not being there to share it with him. *Looks like you've got some amazing things. Can't wait to see them x* I comment and then I scroll on, but I can't muster any enthusiasm so instead I look through the gallery of photographs on my phone. There's some recent ones of me and the boys, clowning around in the studio, mostly taken for social media. There's one of me and Nathalia that one of her friends took on a recent night out, both looking much more wasted than I remember being. Last Christmas when Laura came here and we tried to make it as normal as possible for Dylan. And then, further back, there are the shots of the hot air balloon and before that one of Laura in a restaurant holding a glass of wine and smiling. I'm pretty sure it was the night before she told me she wanted to call it off. Looking at it now, I can see the sadness in her eyes, the way the smile looks like an effort. But maybe I'm just projecting that on to it now that I know how unhappy she was. I scroll further back, through a load of Dylan's milestones. His first lost tooth – Dylan holding it in his hand whilst he proudly shows off his gap. Dylan fast asleep wearing his school uniform on the night before his first day at school.

I swipe through more photos quickly – days out, Dylan with ice-cream around his mouth, one with him holding an Easter egg the size of his head, one with him face-painted as a dragon – until I get to one of Laura and Dylan on the day we got the keys to the house. It's funny, but once you have children, all the photos are of them. There are so few of your partner. In this one, they're standing by the front door, arms in the air in a cheer, Dylan with the keys in his hand, huge smiles on their faces. I stare at the photo for a while and then put the phone on the sofa cushion, the screen still on, and lie down, falling asleep looking into Laura and Dylan's eyes.

16th December 2012

LAURA

'I feel like a whale.'

'You look beautiful.'

'People always say that but they're just being polite. I look like a potato with a head.'

'A beautiful potato with a head.'

Sarah laughs.

I pick up yet another piece of Lego off the floor before it pierces a hole in the sole of my foot.

'Dylan, please stop leaving your Lego on the floor,' I shout up the stairs.

He's in his bedroom doing something. Probably more Lego. Ever since Luke bought him the Lego castle for his birthday last year, he's been obsessed.

'Sorry, Mummy,' he shouts down.

Sarah sits down at the dining table. I say dining table but that's probably a more extravagant description than the little table I got to fit into the corner of the kitchen warrants. I was just sick of Dylan and I eating on the sofa, him constantly spilling ketchup or chocolate ice-cream on it and me having to frantically wipe it before it stained.

'It's so hot,' Sarah moans, wiping her forehead with the back of her hand.

'It's only five degrees outside.'

'It's forty degrees over here with this little madam on board.' She strokes her tummy affectionately.

They found out they were having a little girl at their twenty-week scan. Sarah came straight over to mine in floods of tears. 'What's wrong?' I said, putting my arm around her and fearing the worst. 'It's a girl,' she managed to splutter. I shook my head, still confused. 'So why aren't we celebrating?' She looked me right in the eyes. 'Because I wanted a baby just like Dylan.' I cried then too, and we just held each other for a really long time. The following day we went out and bought some girlie baby clothes and celebrated properly with waffles and ice-cream. I was so happy for her. After all the heartache – what felt like a thousand negative tests ('I feel like a dog, all I do is pee on sticks'), the endless investigations, the failed IVF attempts, and then, as if by magic, when they had decided to give up, a healthy pregnancy. I'm desperate to finally meet her daughter. But sometimes, in the middle of the night, I envy her. That she has it all to come when Dylan's childhood seems to be flying by so quickly.

'Do you want a drink to cool you down?'

'No. Then I'll just be peeing all bloody day.'

'You could borrow one of her nappies.'

'I might need to.'

I lay out ten party bags on the worktop and start to fill them with plastic tat. At least this year people don't seem to be doing the whole 'invite the entire class' thing. We're doing a laser tag party at the local soft play centre because I've come to realize that the fifteen pounds a head it costs for someone else to do all the work is worth every penny. Activity is organized, food is prepared – all I've had to do is make a cake and sort out the party bags.

'So, how's he doing?' I ask Sarah.

'Who?'

I raise my eyebrows.

'Oh, *him*.' Sarah smiles, but then her face turns more serious. 'The new album's been a total flop. He's taking it hard.'

'It *is* quite a new sound.'

'You've listened to it?'

I shrug. 'Dylan makes me play his music all the time.'

Sarah gives me a knowing smile. I actually love the new album. It's got a rawness and a sophistication that the others didn't. Often, when Dylan's at school, I'll play it full volume and sing along as I do the housework. Sometimes, I put my headphones on and listen to it in bed.

'I think perhaps you're right. It's too different. For some reason, the fans haven't quite grown with them. I do feel sorry for him though. It can't be easy.'

'It was always going to happen one day though, wasn't it? Perhaps they'll be like Take That and reunite when they're nearing their fifties.'

'Maybe don't say that to him.'

I laugh. 'I'll try not to.'

'He still asks about you all the time, you know?'

'Is that before or after he's shagging Sasha?'

Sarah rolls her eyes. 'They split up.'

I pretend to look at the calendar. 'Oh yeah, it's nearing a month. Time to bail.'

'You're a bitch, you know?' Sarah smiles to show there's no malice in it. 'How about you anyway? Still not hooked up with any handsome strangers?'

'I'm not sure the narcissistic seven-year-old that's always tagging along with me is all that appealing.'

'Really? I thought blokes would be eating that shit up.'

'Shocker, isn't it?'

'Well, I think your New Year's resolution should be to try harder. You owe it to your vagina.'

'Is that right?'

'It is. I'm scared it's going to close up like a Venus fly-trap. Plus, you're thirty now. Your beauty's going to start fading soon.'

'Thanks a bunch.'

'I'm joking. You'll always be beautiful. But I'm still worried about your vagina.'

I laugh. 'It would be nice, I guess. *Obviously* we don't need men. We run the world as the legendary Beyoncé repeatedly tells us. But it'd be nice to just have someone *there* sometimes.'

'Totally. As much as Tom irritates me a lot of the time, and he smells, and he brings home brownies and cheese-cake when I'm trying to eat healthily and he's basically just a *man* . . . I still think I'd go insane if I didn't have him to talk to at the end of the day. And when I have a bad dream, I wake him up and he puts his big hairy monkey arms around me and I feel safe, you know?'

'God, I think that's the sweetest thing you've ever said about him. Even with the "he smells" bit.'

'Pregnancy's clearly making me soft.'

I smile. 'So, are you coming to the party or are you just here to eat all the party rings?'

Sarah pauses with a party ring in her hand and surveys the nearly empty packet. 'Sorry.'

'It's OK. I only bought them for me really.' I take two out of the packet and shove one in my mouth. Then I add a balloon to each of the party bags and sit down next to Sarah.

'Would you mind if I didn't come today? I'm not sure I can cope with a sweaty soft play with noisy seven-year-olds charging around.'

'Seven. Blimey. It sounds so old when you say it.'

'I'm guessing from the narcissist comment that he's still going through his difficult phase?'

I nod. 'Tells me he hates me multiple times a day, broke a vase the other day by throwing the TV remote at it.'

'You sure it wasn't an accident?'

I shake my head. 'He's a great aim. Maybe he'll put it to good use one day. Archery in the Olympics?'

'He could join the army.'

'Over my dead body.' I take a bite of my second party ring. 'Sometimes it's hard to like him, you know? And then I feel cripplingly guilty.'

'I'm sure that's normal.'

'The worst thing is the second Luke picks him up, he's all sweetness and light. Saves the little-shit stuff for me.'

'That's probably because he feels safest with you.'

'Great.'

'Talk of the devil.' Sarah holds out her arms as Dylan comes into the room and then she pulls him into a hug.

'I'm hungry,' he says, standing awkwardly by Sarah's side.

'Hi Aunty Sarah, nice to see you,' I prompt.

Dylan looks at Sarah and smiles then he turns back to me. 'I'm hungry. Can I have a biscuit?'

'No, you can have some fruit or a cracker.'

'You're having biscuits.'

I grab the empty packet and throw it into the bin.

'Aunty Sarah's pregnant. When you're pregnant you can eat biscuits.'

'*You're* not having a baby.'

'I haven't been eating any biscuits.' I quickly rub at my face in case there are any rogue crumbs.

'She has,' Sarah whispers to him and Dylan snaps his head to stare at me open-mouthed and I can't help but laugh.

'As it's your birthday then.' I grab the biscuit box out of the cupboard, open it and put it in front of Dylan.

'I want a party ring.'

'Well, unless you want to jump into Aunty Sarah's mouth, travel down her throat and take a masticated biscuit out of her stomach, your options are digestive or custard cream.'

Grumpily, Dylan takes two custard creams from the biscuit box. 'I'm having two then to make up for the fact they're not party rings.'

'Seems fair enough to me,' Sarah says.

'Hey you. He does not need any encouragement. He's already a chief negotiator.'

'What's a negotiator?'

'Someone who always manages to make deals and persuade people to do things they want them to do.'

'Oh yeah, that's me.'

Sarah and I both laugh.

'At least he's self-aware,' Sarah says. 'Anyway, you, somebody told me I had to give you a present because it's your birthday. Have you ever heard of this nonsense before?'

Dylan laughs.

'It's in the lounge. Hope you like it.' She lets Dylan go

and he runs into the lounge and comes back with the opened present. It's the Lego Batcave he's been eyeing up for months.

'That's far too much, Sar. Let me give you some money towards it.'

'Nonsense.' Sarah waves my protests away. 'You're only seven once. Isn't that right, Dylan?'

Dylan nods. 'Thank you, Aunty Sarah.' And then he goes up to her and kisses her on the cheek and then strokes her tummy. 'Thank you, Boo Boo.'

And it's times like this that I adore him so completely that I feel guilty for all the times he drives me up the wall. Although sometimes it feels like I'm living with an obnoxious teenager, really he's still so young. Regulating emotions is difficult when you're an adult, let alone when you've only been on the earth for seven years.

'Come here.' I pull Dylan into a hug and plant a great big sloppy kiss on his cheek as he squirms away.

'Mummy, stop.'

I kiss him all over his face, on his head and his shoulders, and he giggles and tries to get away so I chase him into the lounge until he manages to escape upstairs.

'Beat you, Mummy,' he calls from the landing.

'You did. Twenty minutes until your party, OK?'

'OK. I'm just going to start my Lego.'

I go back into the kitchen. 'Do you want anything else?'

Sarah pushes herself up, moaning like an old lady as she does. 'No. I'm going to get back. Have a wonderful party though.'

'Oh, it'll be a joy.'

'Is Luke going?'

I hold my hands up to the air. 'Supposed to be.'

'Give him my love, won't you?'

'Will do. Not that he deserves it.'

She kisses me on the cheek, her bump grazing my side. 'You know, sometimes I feel utterly terrified about having this baby. But when I look at you and Dylan, all that goes away and I just feel excited.'

I stroke her bump. 'Thank you.'

The party is a dream. Parents wave off their children with a look of relief and then I hand them all over to some spotty teenager to demonstrate how to use their laser guns whilst I sit in the café drinking a cappuccino and eating a piece of (not) well-earned flapjack. Even the Christmas songs blaring out can't ruin it for me. As the children are loaded up with their guns (is it entirely suitable to be putting pretend firearms into the hands of seven-year-olds? This flapjack tastes so good I'm not sure I care), I notice one of the dads has stayed behind and is sitting along the bar from me wrestling with a piece of tinsel that keeps falling on his head.

'You're welcome to leave,' I shout along to him.

He cups his hand around his ear and I shuffle closer to him so I don't have to raise my voice quite as much to compete with Noddy Holder.

'I said you are welcome to leave your child here. Sorry, I don't know which one they are. I'm not sure I've seen you up at school before. Is it usually Mum who does the drop-off?'

I hate the way parents become simplified to 'Mum' or 'Dad' as a name. Even 'Dylan's mum' is a bit of an insult really. As if my identity is solely wrapped up with him.

'No, we're relatively new. Noah and I moved here about two months ago.'

I recognize the name Noah immediately. Dylan's always telling me how he gets up on his chair and dances in the middle of lessons. He sounds like a hoot.

'Oh, I'm sorry I haven't noticed you before.'

'There are a lot of parents in that playground. I don't exactly stand out.'

Actually, he's a very good-looking bloke. I mean, not in a 'shout about it' sort of way. People wouldn't stare at him open-mouthed like they do at Luke. But he has a kind face – hazel eyes with a twinkle of humour in them, stubble, dark messy hair that he clearly doesn't bother to style, a warm smile.

'Well, I'm Dylan's mum, obviously. Laura.' I hold out my hand and Noah's dad shakes it.

'I'm Sam.'

'Nice to meet you.' I take another bite of my flapjack and then wonder if I should offer some to him, but then decide that might just be a bit weird. 'So how come you moved here?'

'Noah's mum and I split up and I just wanted a fresh start, I suppose. She works away a lot of the time and only sees Noah every other weekend, so it didn't really make much difference to her where we decided to settle.'

I nod, taking a sip of my coffee.

'It's really beautiful around here and we're very outdoorsy, so it's great that we can paddleboard and wild swim and hike and stuff. Sorry – outdoorsy – that makes me sound like a twat.'

I nearly spit out my drink. 'Sorry. I wasn't expecting you to say that.'

'Well, it's true, isn't it? It's pretentious. We like being out-doors, that's all I mean.'

'Fair enough.'

'You?'

'Yeah, we like being outdoors, I guess.'

Although the last 'outdoorsy' thing we did was a walk from the supermarket door to the car in the car park.

'I meant more Dylan's dad? I mean, I heard on the grapevine who he is.'

'Oh yeah. He's the talk of the playground.'

Sam smiles.

'You've probably also seen by the amount of time he gets snapped with different women that we are no longer together. In fact, I think the rest of the world knows more about his love life than I do. I stopped reading the papers a long time ago.'

It's not entirely true. I try my best to avoid them. Nothing good can come of seeing Luke with a variety of stunning women ten years younger than him. But some-times I can't help a late-night scroll and then I always end up regretting it.

'I'm not really into celebrity gossip.'

'Very wise.'

'It must be weird for Dylan, everyone knowing who his dad is.'

'To be honest, I think they're still too young for it to be a thing. Watching the other mums with him can be amusing though. I'm sure they all tell their children to befriend Dylan just so they can get invited to his parties and meet Luke.'

Sam laughs. 'I'm surprised I'm the only one hanging around today.'

'Oh, I think they all know by now that Luke never turns up on time. You wait until we near the end of the party. There'll be swarms of them, all dressed up in their finery as if they're going out to a fancy restaurant rather than a kid's party.'

Sam laughs again and it makes me feel good.

'So how come you stayed on? I'm guessing it wasn't to meet Luke?'

'Oh yeah, I'm his biggest fan. I've got a photograph of him in my pocket I want him to sign.'

'I really hope you're not serious.'

'No. The truth is, Noah struggles a bit to control his emotions sometimes so I wanted to stay around to check he doesn't start attacking anyone.'

'To be fair, I think that's the aim of the game today.' I nod my head towards the children, who are running around pointing their laser guns at each other like they're in the army.

'True. I'm just concerned he might use his gun to hit the others over the head. He's a sweet boy deep down. He's just going through a bit of a violent phase.'

'Oh, Dylan's a total pain in the arse at the moment. Apparently they have a rush of testosterone at this age or something. I hope so, because if not then he might just be a knob.'

I notice how Sam's whole face changes when he laughs. With some people, laughter feels performative, but with Sam, all his features light up and it feels genuine.

'I'm so glad you said that. I was giving it the whole "he's a sweet boy deep down" whilst thinking "he's an actual monster".'

'"It's a phase." They're the golden words for all stages of parenting. Stops you from driving your car off a bridge.'

Sam opens the rucksack he's brought with him and pulls out his phone. At first, I think he's looking for a way to exit our conversation, but then his face flushes.

'Do you want to exchange numbers? We could share parenting tips. Or more likely parenting fails – well, from my side anyway.'

'Sure.'

He types in my name and then hands me his phone for me to add my number. I'm chuffed to see he's listed me as Laura rather than 'Dylan's mum'.

'There you go.' I hand him his phone back.

'Thanks.' He presses on my name and rings me and my phone buzzes then he puts it straight down. 'Now you have my number too, in case you're really desperate.'

I add him as a contact and then he points at Dylan who is on the top floor of the soft play, hiding behind a roller, aiming his gun at some poor unsuspecting victim at the bottom of the slide.

'Look, your son is literally annihilating mine.'

'That's Noah?' The poor boy at the bottom is looking around to see why his gun keeps vibrating but he clearly can't work it out.

We both stare at them for a minute and then look at each other and burst into fits of giggles.

LUKE

I'm actually taken aback by the pain I feel in my chest when I see Laura flirting with another bloke. I can tell that she's flirting because she keeps touching him in subtle ways – a hand on his arm, a nudge in the side. And she's making him laugh. Laura uses humour in the same way that some women use red lipstick or a low-cut top.

I stand back and watch for a while. I'm not sure it's a choice. It's like my body is stuck firmly to the spot. A little like the way you can't help but look when you drive past a car accident. You know you don't want to see it but you can't help but gawp. It's been over two years now so I know I shouldn't feel this way, that it's probably not normal, but I can't help it.

He's not all that. He could do with a shave and a proper haircut. He's probably married anyway, getting his thrills from flirting with other mums at a kid's birthday party. It's sad really.

Once I can force my legs to move again, I go over and tap Laura on the shoulder and I can tell by the startled, 'just got caught out' expression on her face that my suspicions were correct and she was indeed flirting. Not that she's technically doing anything wrong.

'Oh, hi, Luke. You made it then.'

'Of course I made it.'

It pisses me off that she's trying to make me out to be

some sort of absent flaky dad in front of this guy who is obviously Mr Helicopter parent, the only one to stay at the party. Unless he just stayed to chat Laura up, playing the saintly dad when he's just trying to get his end away.

'Well, this is Sam, Noah's dad. Sam, this is Luke.'

Sam holds his hand out and I shake it limply. 'Isn't Noah the new kid who's always getting into trouble?'

It's a dick thing to say and Laura glares at me, rightly so, but Sam just laughs. 'Yep, that's the one.'

Laura smiles at him, an irritatingly apologetic smile that just makes me want to be more of an arse.

'So why are you hanging around? Can't trust him not to beat the shit out of the other kids?' I snort, framing it as just banter, but I think he's well aware of the animosity behind it. Us men can soon pick up on it when it's there, like the initiation of a duel – all that's missing is the swords.

'That's exactly it. Noah and a large heavy object doing a combative activity. Not a safe combination.'

For some reason, Sam doesn't seem to be picking up his weapon and it's really bloody annoying.

'Do you want to see the cake?' Laura says and I get the sense she's asking Sam more than me. 'I made it myself. Just call me Nigella.'

'Oh, I don't know about that.' I nod towards her chest and her and Sam both give me a look that makes me feel about two feet tall.

'What I absolutely love about Nigella is her total disregard for any movement towards healthy living,' Sam says. 'Her recipes are like, add a bag of sugar, a whole tub of lard and then in case you think you're finished there, just sprinkle on another generous helping of saturated fat.'

Laura laughs. 'Remember I used to say that to you, Luke? You've got Jamie Oliver on a crusade to make the next generation less likely to die of heart disease and Nigella's just there like, bring it on.'

'No, I don't remember you saying that.'

I do. We laughed about it watching the Christmas special the week before the big day. It reminds me that we used to laugh a lot, in between the arguments, the blame games and the defensiveness.

'Well, I did. You probably weren't listening as usual.' She raises her eyebrows at Sam.

'We can't multitask, can we, us men?' Sam says. 'Watching a TV programme *and* having a discussion about it? Bloody hell. What do you expect of us?'

I'm not sure why he's being nice to me. If I were him, I'd side with Laura and push the lowly ex even deeper into the pit, especially when I've been such a dick to him.

'Anyway, I was going to get the cake, wasn't I? Brace yourself, guys, it's pretty spectacular.'

Laura walks away and for a moment it's just Sam and me. We don't speak at first but then the silence feels awkward and I'm guessing Sam must feel the same because he says, 'It's a great party. I didn't realize they did this here.'

'Yeah, Laura organized it. I mean, we talked about it a lot, of course. We're still really close.'

'That's cool. I wish I was closer to my ex, for Noah's sake.'

So Noah's mum is an ex. *Awesome.*

'Laura seems really great though,' he continues, setting out his stall, and before I can reply Laura walks in holding a cake in the shape of a Lego brick in Dylan's favourite colour – yellow.

'Wow, it's amazing. Seriously,' Sam says and he appears so genuine, it's getting harder not to like him, apart from the fact he clearly wants to sleep with Laura.

'It's really great,' I mutter. 'Well done.'

'Well, to be fair, I used a mould for the cake, but decorating it was a bit of a bastard. A fair bit of icing might have ended up getting thrown across the kitchen.'

'I'm sure he's going to love it. Noah would be ecstatic with a cake like that. Sam always just gets one made. I mean, they're amazing, but it's not the same, is it? Sorry, that makes me sound totally chauvinistic. I'm aware I could make a cake myself. The fact I have a willy doesn't mean I can't decorate a cake.'

'I thought you were talking about yourself in the third person,' Laura says, echoing what I was thinking. 'I wasn't sure which was worse – that or the chauvinism.'

'Oh no. My ex is also Sam – Samantha. Not the best decision, that, really.'

'Well, I think not being with someone because of their name would probably be worse.'

'True.'

I can already see where this is going to end up and I don't like it one bit. I know I don't have a leg to stand on as I've slept with half of Lanmouth since Laura and I split up, but it's different. They weren't nice decent people who might one day care about me, or that I might one day care about. I'm very aware they're with me because of who I am, although I can see that fading pretty soon. Every time I hear the new album, I want to throw something at my former self. Why did I suggest we try something *new*? It was my stupid fucking heartbreak album and young girls aren't interested in that stuff. They want songs that tell them how wonderful they are, how much you adore them. And, I hate to say it, but maybe we're just getting too old. Sometimes in the studio, I look across at Cody and Rich and they just look a bit duller, a bit less fresh. Their skin, around their eyes, around the tummy. I'm sure if I really studied myself in the mirror, I'd see the same thing, but I tend to just give myself a cursory glance, too scared to look for too long.

'I think I might go and ask that lad if I can have a gun. Go and get involved,' I say.

Laura laughs in a patronizing way, like I'm so *childish* and she *despairs* of me, so I just walk away, get myself a laser gun and expel all of my discontent by shooting a bunch of screaming school kids.

'Can you do Mummy's special hot chocolate on Christmas Day?' Dylan asks. 'It's not Christmas without it.'

We're back at Laura's. I managed to persuade her to let me come back to hers under the pretence that I wanted to spend more time with Dylan on his birthday. It's not that I don't want to spend more time with Dylan. But the crux of the matter is I want to spend more time with Laura. The short interactions when I pick Dylan up or drop him off are never enough.

'Of course we can,' I reply. 'You'll have to teach me how to do it, though.'

'Like this,' he says holding up his snowman mug – hot chocolate topped with whipped cream, marshmallows *and* chocolate sprinkles. 'And I'll see you the next day, won't I, Mummy? I'll have two Christmas Days like last year.'

'Exactly,' Laura says, with faux enthusiasm. 'How lucky are you? Not many boys get two Christmas Days.'

'You can join us if you want?' I offer. 'If you don't have other plans?'

Laura seems to consider it for a moment, and I realize how excited I am at the thought that she might accept, but then she says, 'I've promised to help Tom with the Christmas dinner. Sarah says she can't reach the oven with her big bump. But thank you for the invite.'

Dylan slurps the last of his hot chocolate and then runs off upstairs to play.

'Sam seemed nice.'

'He did seem nice,' Laura says, drinking her coffee and not taking the bait.

'Nicer than me?'

'Definitely nicer than you.' She delivers it with a deadpan expression but then her face breaks into a smile.

'Do you think you'll end up sleeping with him?'

'Luke.'

'What? It's a reasonable question.'

'No, it's not.'

'OK, it's not reasonable but I want to know.'

I realize I sound like a child but I can't help myself. It feels like there's so much unexplored emotion there, so much left unsaid. Sometimes it feels like my body is overflowing with it, like I just need to *release* it, like water flooding over the top of a dam.

'Do I ask you about who you're planning on sleeping with? Or who you are in fact sleeping with? There's been so many we'd be having to have this conversation on a weekly basis.'

'That's not fair.'

'Really?'

'I think you could do better.'

'You got that from a ten-minute conversation with him?'

'So, you think he's perfect, do you?'

'Are you drunk?'

'Of course I'm not. I just drove over here.'

'It's just you're acting very strange. Since when have you cared about my love life?'

'Since there's the chance of you having one.'

Laura nearly spits out her coffee, but luckily it's due to laughter and not anger. 'Who says I haven't been sleeping with blokes right, left and centre?'

'I'd know.'

'Really?'

'Yes. You get a look.'

Laura raises an eyebrow. 'Seriously?'

'And you'd tell me, wouldn't you?'

'*You* don't tell *me*. I have to read about it in the paper.'

'Do you want me to tell you?'

'No, not really.' Laura runs her hands through her hair. She's let it go back to her natural light brown colour and, although it's not as striking as the red she had throughout our relationship, she looks really beautiful.

'So have you?'

'Have I what?'

'Slept with anyone else?'

She stands up, wrapping her hands around her mug, and walks further into the kitchen, putting the worktop between us. 'You said you came here to spend time with Dylan. Why don't you go up and see him?'

I move towards her, my arm on the worktop, my body so close to hers it feels like an electrical current is travelling from her body to mine. 'Why are you avoiding the question?'

'Because it's none of your bloody business.'

I know she's pissed off but there's something else there too – a tension that makes it really hard not to just lift her up on the worktop and pull down her jeans.

She pauses for a moment and then pushes past me and walks into the lounge. 'We're not doing this, Luke.'

'Doing what?' I follow her in, standing so close to her I can almost feel her breath on my skin.

'It's not fair on Dylan,' she says in a hushed voice. 'If he were to hear us . . . it's confusing for him. Just go and play with him, OK?'

I don't know what gets into me but I grab her, pulling her towards me to kiss her, but as soon as my lips touch hers, she pushes me away so hard I almost fall over. And then suddenly Dylan is there, staring at us.

'Will you come and build a superhero mech with me?' Dylan asks.

I try to make eye contact with Laura but she busies herself tidying away toys.

I place my hand in the centre of Dylan's back. 'Of course I will. Let's have a competition to see who can build the best one.'

We sit on the floor amongst the boxes of Lego. It makes me a little sad to see all the knights and castles paraphernalia abandoned under the bed or on shelves, getting dusty; pushed aside for Batmobiles and brightly coloured Joker creations. Just another reminder that my boy is growing up and that I'm missing far too much of it.

'Are you staying here tonight, Daddy?' Dylan carefully selects grey, black and yellow Lego pieces from the boxes to make sure his mech stays authentically Batman.

'No, it's Mummy's weekend, isn't it? And anyway, it's Sunday.'

'I know. I just thought because you were kissing Mummy maybe you were going to live here again.'

I stack alternate red and blue blocks on top of each other, hoping that if I focus on my Spiderman mech, Dylan won't see the emotion on my face.

'I wasn't kissing Mummy. I was just whispering something to her.'

'It looked like kissing to me.'

'Does it get confusing sometimes?' I ask, changing the subject. 'Having to stay at different houses?'

Dylan shrugs. 'Not really.'

'Good.'

'But sometimes I want to see Mummy when I'm at yours and sometimes I want to see you when I'm at home.'

He says it completely matter-of-fact, unaware of the guilt it stirs in me. And it also doesn't pass me by that he calls this place 'home' now. I guess home is wherever Laura is, which is probably how it should be, but it still hurts.

'I like it best when we're all together,' he continues, adding some sort of hinge contraption to his mech to increase its superiority.

'I like it best when we're all together too.'

'We could all live together in this house now. I like this house.'

'The thing is, Mummy and Daddy are just friends now and you don't live with your friends, do you?'

'I'd like to live with Noah.'

I laugh. 'But you don't, do you? Because he lives with his family.'

'But you *are* my family.'

I put my hand on the top of his head. 'I know. It's complicated, isn't it?'

He holds up his mech, thankfully distracted from our conversation by the fact he has finished his creation. 'It's a little bit better than yours, isn't it?'

The way he says it makes me laugh, a kid's attempt at being tactful.

'Just a little bit, yeah. I'm giving up on mine.'

'Mummy says you should never give up.'

'If Mummy saw this terrible mech I think she'd make an exception.' I hold up my model and the arm falls straight off.

Dylan puts out his hand. 'I'll sort it out for you.'

I give him my model and he starts removing certain bricks and adding new ones to fix it.

'Mummy says you've been shouting at her a little bit?' I tread carefully so as not to cause an eruption. I don't tend to get the same sort of abuse that I know Dylan inflicts on Laura, but I do get the meltdowns sometimes – the trashing of his Lego or throwing his football at the window.

Dylan shrugs. '*You* shout at her.'

'No, I don't.'

'You do, and she shouts at you.'

I hate that he's heard that and vow, for probably the hundredth time, to do better.

'Well, that doesn't make it OK. She's an amazing mummy to you, OK, and you shouldn't be shouting at her. She only ever wants the best for you.'

'But she's annoying sometimes.'

'Everyone's annoying sometimes. You are seriously lucky to have her. So be nice to her, OK?'

'OK.'

He hands me back my mech, which is significantly better now, and then Laura puts her head around the door. 'I'm sorry to be a bore, guys, but it's time for bed now, Dylan.'

'I'm not going to bed.' Dylan puts his hands on his hips, a scowl on his face that is almost comical.

'Sorry, lovely, but it's school tomorrow,' Laura replies calmly, but I can see in her eyes how tired she is.

'I don't want to go to bed yet.'

'I know. I understand. But the party went on late and you need to be up in the morning.'

'I'm not going.' Dylan (ironically) throws himself on the bed, his face buried into the pillow, his fists pounding the mattress.

'Leave it to me,' I say.

'Sure. Because you're so much better with him than me.' Laura shakes her head. 'Fine.'

She shuts the door and I put my hand on Dylan's back. 'I can read you a story.'

Dylan shakes his head, his face still in the pillow. Then slowly he turns over.

'*You* wouldn't make me go to bed.'

'That's because Mummy is a better parent than me. I know it doesn't feel like it right now and it feels like she's ruining your fun, but it's actually because she cares about you. She's looking after you so that you're not too tired tomorrow and you can go to school and enjoy telling all your friends about your presents.'

Dylan does the most enormous yawn.

'See, you're exhausted.'

'I'm not.'

'Well, I'd really like to do a story.'

'OK, but you can't do our chapter book as Mummy will be sad to miss out on the story, but we could do a picture one.'

I love how, even when he's cross with Laura, he still remains so loyal to her. 'Sounds good to me.'

I pick Dylan's pyjamas up off the floor and hand them to him. 'Glow in the dark snowmen? I haven't seen these before. They're awesome.'

'Mummy got them for me. When we got my old Christmas pyjamas down from the loft, they were too small because I'd got so tall,' he says proudly, and again it hits me, the bittersweet realization that my little boy is growing up.

Once he's in his pyjamas, he grabs Geoff from the end of his bed, climbs under the covers and then draws his favourite soft toy into a tight hug.

'Can we have *The Smartest Giant in Town* please, Daddy?'

'Do you still like that one?'

Dylan nods, but he looks a little bit embarrassed.

'Good job, because I still *love* that one.'

He smiles, seemingly reassured that if a grown man can like it then it's still OK for him to do so at the grand old age of seven.

When we get to the song part, we sing it together and a feeling of warmth radiates around my body and I'm actually sad when we get to the end.

'Time for sleep now.'

Dylan's eyes look heavy. 'Do I have to go to sleep?'

'You do. Night night, birthday boy. Love you.'

'Love you too.'

I kiss Dylan on the head and then venture downstairs where I find Laura tidying frantically with one hand, a glass of wine in the other.

'Spending time with me driven you to drink?'

She looks up and I can see the fury in her eyes. 'You can't do this, Luke.'

'Do what?'

'Interrogate me about who I may or may not one day sleep with. Try to *kiss* me. What were you thinking?'

'I wasn't thinking, Laura. I was *acting* on how I felt at the time, on how I could tell you were feeling too. You should try it sometime.'

'Fuck you.' Laura stands up, slamming her glass on the side with such force I'm surprised the stem doesn't snap.

'That's better. At least show me some emotion.'

Laura lets out a pained breath and shakes her head. 'Where have you *been*, Luke? You haven't given a second thought to me whilst you've been riding high with the band, sleeping with every twenty-something that walks. And then your album flops and, God forbid, someone shows some interest in me and suddenly you come running back. Because there's no way I'm allowed to be happy, is there?'

'That's not fair. And the album didn't *flop*. It just didn't do as well as the others.'

Laura laughs, the sound dripping with bitterness. 'Out of everything I said, that's the bit you care about.'

I should just tell her the truth – that there hasn't been a day that's gone past, an hour, that I haven't thought about her, that I haven't wanted to kiss her, to hold her, to just have her back in my life, but I know there's no point because she doesn't feel the same. She's made that very clear tonight.

'You do remember you split up with me, don't you? You didn't want me. None of this was my choice.'

'Yeah, it's an easy get out, that one, isn't it?' She paces back and forth. 'This has always been our problem, Luke. You never listen. You never understand what *I* need. It's all about *you* and what *you* need.'

I stand up. 'I'm going to go.'

Laura pauses, suddenly totally still. 'Of course you are.'

I should just apologize, admit I was wrong, prove I can do better, but instead I head for the door, even when Laura slumps on to the sofa, her head in her hands, sobbing. And worse, even when I notice Dylan's little feet on the middle step of the stairs, knowing he's probably heard every word.

16th December 2013

LAURA

'So, I've brought chocolate.' I take the giant bar of Dairy Milk out of my bag followed by all the other stuff I've brought. 'Or peanuts in case you fancy something more savoury. I wasn't sure how you'd feel. I've brought trashy magazines. I can read them to you if you don't feel up to reading them yourself. And I've downloaded last night's *Strictly* results show on my iPad. Did you see the Saturday night show? Sorry, you probably didn't.'

Sarah gives me a sad look. 'I haven't turned into someone else, you know? I still watch trash TV and argue with Tom about not putting things in the right place in the dishwasher.'

'Of course you haven't. I'm sorry.'

'Please stop saying sorry, Laur. Can we just be us, please? Normal us, I mean.'

'Of course.' I turn back to my bag. 'I brought brain games if you feel up to them. And this really good book I'm reading. It's . . .' I flip over to the back cover, '". . . funny and heartwarming". What do you think?'

'Right now, I just need to close my eyes because my head feels like it's being stabbed with a thousand ice swords.'

I look at Sarah, the cold cap tight on her head. She looks like a boxer, albeit with none of the strength.

'I'm sorry. You close your eyes. I'll shut up.'

'You're apologizing again.' She smiles and reaches out

for my hand. 'Don't shut up. Just talk to me about normal crap.'

'That Aljaz is a bit of alright, isn't he? He's livened up the show a bit.'

'Best thing about a Saturday night.'

'Who do you think is going this week? I reckon that Patrick is on his last legs, don't you think?'

Sarah winces, her eyes still tight shut. 'Definitely.' Then after a pause she says, 'Actually, can we talk about this later? After the first half-hour or so it gets easier and I'll be able to dissect *Strictly* properly then.'

'Sure. Whatever you need.'

I can't help feeling that I'm getting everything wrong and wish I could do better.

'Thank you for coming.' Sarah opens her eyes a crack. 'I do really appreciate it.'

'You don't need to thank me. I'm just sorry I'm probably not as good as Tom. I feel like I don't know what to say or do to make it easier for you.'

'Just being here is making it easier.'

'How is Thea? Is she feeling any better?'

'Not really. The worst bit is I can't hold her in case I catch whatever it is she's got. Tom insists that I should be in our bedroom and will not allow me to sleep on the sofa, so it means he has to sleep on Thea's floor next to her cot.'

'Oh, bless him.'

'I'm scared she'll become closer to him, especially now I'm no longer feeding her.' Sarah's voice cracks and I'm glad her eyes are closed because then she can't see the tears in mine.

'There's no one like your mum. Don't worry. You'll always hold number one spot in her eyes.'

'I don't know. I feel so distant from her right now and I know these first few years are the critical ones. But sometimes it's just too much. The physicality of it when I'm not feeling one hundred percent. And emotionally – it's a lot to process. There's not always a lot of me left, you know?'

'Of course. Honestly, Sarah. Don't worry another second about that. You two are going to be the best of friends. I'll be super jealous when Dylan buggers off and abandons me and Thea stays loyal. What's the saying? "A son is a son until he finds a wife, a daughter is a daughter for the rest of your life."'

'That's bollocks though. You and Dylan will be besties forever.'

'I hope so. I'm not sure we were besties this morning when I told him he couldn't have five chocolate Weetabix for breakfast.'

The volunteer who fitted Sarah's cold cap brings us over a cup of tea each and holds out a plate of Quality Street. 'Take one quickly before all that's left are the toffee pennies,' she says conspiratorially.

I take an orange cream and Sarah grabs a hazelnut triangle. 'Thank you.'

The lady – I think she said her name is Tina – smiles and then continues on to the next bay.

'See, it's like a spa day,' Sarah jokes. 'Cups of tea, chocolates, time to read magazines and watch trash TV. Being pumped full of poison.'

As much as I'm happy to hear her humour returning, I can't stop the feeling that I need to cry. Not that I could forget, faced with the sight of the strange red liquid dripping down into Sarah's veins, the beeping of the machines and the constant back and forth of the nurses, but hearing Sarah mention the chemotherapy explicitly is a stark reminder of the utterly shit curveball the powers that be have thrown us. Well, thrown her really. I'm just a spectator. To think that just ten months ago, I was sharing the most amazing moment of Sarah's life with her. She opted for a home birth and it all happened so quickly that Tom struggled to get back in time so I held her hand through the contractions, stroked her back, fanned her when she felt overwhelmed. Tom arrived just in time to see Thea's grand entrance and it was magical to watch her enter their lives, to be in that room so full of love and wonder. And now we're here.

'It's amazing how low our standards become when we have kids, isn't it? Having a poo is a treat sometimes.'

'I'm not sure this frozen scalp treatment is quite as good as a hot stone massage though.'

'It's working well though, isn't it? Your hair still looks really good.'

Sarah's face forms a sad smile. 'It's started falling out big time. I'm lucky. I'm keeping the bit at the front so you can't really tell with my scarf on. But I keep finding it all round the house and I'm too terrified to wash it or brush it, so I look a bit like a greasy scarecrow.'

'You look beautiful.'

'I miss my eyebrows. And my eyelashes. Who knew that eyelashes were so important? Why did I never appreciate the joy of putting on mascara and suddenly looking a thousand times better?'

I give her a sympathetic look, suddenly feeling guilty for not appreciating my eyelashes. I feel guilty about everything right now.

'Do I sound really shallow if I say it's the worst bit? Looking in the mirror and not seeing me. Other than the high chance of death, of course. That's obviously slightly worse.'

'Come on, let's find out who's in the bottom two,' I say, quickly changing the subject, holding up my iPad and moving my chair as close to Sarah's as I can get with the various machines in the way. I know perhaps I should see her humour as her desire to open up about her feelings around what's happening, and I know that I'm the shittest friend ever not to be able to go there with her. But I just can't.

'I'd rather be hit by a train or something, you know?' Sarah continues and I press pause on the iPad. 'It's the knowing, isn't it? The realization of all you're going to miss out on – Thea's first steps, the little personality quirks that aren't apparent yet, her first day at school, her wedding day. But it's not just those special days. It's all the days. The ones you don't really appreciate until you realize you might not get them.'

I can't help it. The tears fill my throat and I have to cough to dislodge them. 'You are going to see all of that with Thea. All the boring days when you feel like if you play peek-a-boo one more time, you'll end up in a hospital for the insane. The screaming tantrums because the bowl you chose for her breakfast is not quite the correct blue and the amount of milk on her cereal is either that tiny bit too much or too little depending on her mood. The nights when you are so exhausted and she just blankly refuses to sleep. The un-drunk or stone-cold cups of tea and interrupted meals.' I take Sarah's hand in mine and squeeze it. 'You're going to suffer it all, OK? I've had to go through it these past eight years. There's no way you're getting out of it.'

Sarah smiles but I can see how scared she is and I wish there was more I could say to convince her she's going to be all right. I wish that I could convince myself that she's going to be all right.

'Come on then.' She takes the iPad off me and puts it on her knee. 'Let's find out who goes.'

We sit and watch *Strictly*, chatting all the time, and if it wasn't for the interruptions from the nurse changing the bag of medicine over, it would almost feel like old times, when our opinions on minor celebrities and how capable they are at moving around a dance floor seemed the most pressing thing in our lives.

After three hours, the machine beeps to tell the nurse that Sarah's chemo is finished for this week. I move out the way as the nurse comes in to check the bag is totally empty and to put the one on that helps to wash Sarah's veins so they don't get too badly damaged.

'How are the side effects so far?' the nurse asks.

'Oh, you know, could be worse.'

'Nausea or sickness?'

'I feel nauseous most of the time, just underlying, you know?'

The nurse nods. 'You taking all the anti-sickness meds?'

'Yeah.'

'Ulcers? Sore mouth?'

'Ulcers, but I'm managing to eat, when I don't feel too sick, that is.'

'Constipation?'

'For the first few days, yes, then it eases. I take the Laxido.'

'Good. Pain?'

'Up my arm.' Sarah traces her vein and the nurse starts to rub it.

Whenever I ask Sarah how the chemo is going, she always says it's fine. I'm sad that I didn't know all the side effects she's been dealing with. You'd never know. Except for the odd nap in the afternoon, she carries on as if she's not having any treatment at all, playing with Thea and keeping the house straight. But that's Sarah.

'It doesn't feel too swollen, but if it gets any worse call us, OK?'

Sarah nods.

'We're always here. Twenty-four seven.'

'Thank you.'

'Are you doing the injections yourself?'

'My husband does them. Quite unwillingly, it must be said.'

Sarah has told me about the injections. They're to encourage her bone marrow to create white blood cells to help her fight infection. I only know about them because she joked about how Tom nearly fainted the first time he had to do it.

'You can always pop into your local surgery and get the nurse to do it, but people often find the after-effects are less painful if you do it before you go to bed. Then hopefully the worst of the pain is whilst you're asleep.'

'Yeah, it's fine. He manages.'

'Right, well you've got another half an hour on the cold cap and then I'll take your cannula out and you're free to go.'

'Thank you.'

The nurse goes to deal with someone else and I move back closer to Sarah.

'You're so brave, you know?'

She waves my praise away. 'You'd be exactly the same.'

'I really wouldn't.'

'You would. For Dylan.'

'But you don't have to be with me.'

'I know. But I'm OK. In a way the treatment is the best bit. At least it feels like I'm doing something to get rid of the bastard when I'm here.'

'Absolutely. Blasting the mofo.'

Sarah smiles. 'Will you read me an article or two out of one of those magazines you brought? I'm quite tired.'

'Sure. Close your eyes and rest your head back.'

I help her lower the back of her chair and she lies back and closes her eyes. Getting the chance to look at her, she looks so pale. No. Worse than pale. She looks grey. After seeing her so glowing throughout her pregnancy, it makes the change even more heartbreaking. I turn away and just start reading, hoping she might get lost in the words, even though there's no way that *I* will.

She told me on a Tuesday afternoon. We were sat out in the garden enjoying the last of the autumn sunshine, drinking cups of tea and chatting about Dylan and Thea as we usually did. And then she just came out with it. *I've got breast cancer.* Just like that. No preamble. No, 'I was feeding Thea and I found this lump so I went to the GP thinking it was just mastitis.' She did tell me all that eventually, but that came after. At first she just hit me with it – bam – and my stomach fell through the floor. I struggled to listen to the details. The GP had thought it was just feeding-related but she'd referred her to be on the safe side, and she'd been lucky to get a cancellation the following day where from the ultrasound the specialist had told her she was fairly sure it was cancer. There were two tumours in her right breast. She'd had to wait for the biopsy results for two whole weeks and she hadn't told me. Two weeks with that going round and round in her head and she didn't say a word. I was furious about that. I still am a bit, but I know that makes me a really shitty person. That she was going through all that, trying to protect me because she didn't want me to worry unnecessarily if it turned out to be nothing, and I'm angry with her for keeping it a secret.

Anyway, I said all the right things, of course, or at least the things I perceived to be right. That breast cancer was easily treated, it was one of the best cancers to have, she'd caught it early, et cetera, et cetera. And then she told me that her type of breast cancer was not the easy-to-treat type you read about, that she had the worst type of breast cancer, and that she'd been doing some research and because it was classed as postpartum that lowered her odds even further. I dismissed all her concerns. Told her she was a fighter. That she defied odds, didn't go along with them. That there was no way she was going to be beaten by something as unoriginal as cancer. *You'll be killed by a bolt of lightning when we're ninety-four and sitting on the balcony of our swanky nursing home. That's the kind of unique way you'll go.*

That night, I found myself sitting naked in the lounge, my phone in my hand, googling medical journals like a crazy woman. I'd got out of bed as if somehow I wouldn't feel like I was about to have a heart attack if I was up and about. The words circled around my head – 'dismal prognosis' on repeat – as if I'd kept pressing return on a dying computer and it just kept duplicating the same phrase. Every time I found a negative factor, a down point, Sarah had it. Hormone negative. Multiple tumours. Postpartum. Likely node involvement. The day before I'd not even known any of these things existed. That this menace was just waiting in the shadows ready to take one of us at any time. And the one person that I would usually turn to about something like this, the only person who would truly know the right thing to say to make me feel better, I couldn't say a word to because how could I ever show her the fear? *I think there's a high chance you could die, and I don't know how I'm going to carry on in the world without you.*

I thought about calling Luke but I was scared that he'd disappoint, that he wouldn't step up, and I knew I'd never be able to forgive him if he didn't. So I just crawled in beside Dylan, careful not to wake him, and finally fell asleep breathing in his sweet smell.

My phone buzzes on the side as I'm absent-mindedly putting a stack of DVDs Dylan's left out back into the cupboard before the party. Well, it's not exactly a party. I told Dylan he could invite one friend over for a play and invited Sarah over in some probably misguided attempt to lift her spirits. To make life feel more normal. And then Luke found out and said he couldn't believe I hadn't invited him so now he's coming too. But I'm dreading it. The exhaustion of putting on a brave face.

I'm already tired out from taking Dylan sledging after school. Ironically, it's been a perfect winter day. After a decent covering of snow in the night, it's been bright and crisp. Walking into chemo with Sarah, the snow crunching beneath our feet, the sun making it sparkle, it felt almost insulting in its beauty. And watching Dylan flying down the hill, pure joy on his face, a gorgeous blue sky behind him, it made me so angry that I couldn't enjoy it with him, that my mind was elsewhere.

Running a few minutes late. Sorry. Noah decided it was the perfect time to have a full-blown meltdown. Hope chemo was OK x

Since Dylan's party last year, him and Noah have become best friends so I see Sam quite a bit – dropping off and picking up, and sometimes we take them to the park together so neither of us has to have our house trashed by them charging around and play-fighting. Sam invited me out for a drink about six months ago but I told him I was busy and he hasn't asked since. Sometimes, when the loneliness of being a single mum gets too much, I wish that I'd said yes instead of spending the night on my own binge-watching *Orange is the New Black*. But it just felt too soon. And besides, it would be complicated for Dylan now him and Noah are such good friends.

Even running late, Sam still arrives before everyone else. As soon as I open the door, Noah charges past me and runs upstairs to Dylan's room.

'Hi Noah,' I shout after him but he doesn't respond.

'Sorry about that,' Sam says. 'Basic manners are still a bit of a work in progress.'

'Oh, don't worry. You know Dylan is just the same.'

'I don't know. He usually manages "hi" as he's taking his shoes off and throwing them at the mat.'

I smile.

'Noah was hitting the cat with a wooden spoon just before we left. Should I be concerned?'

'Was the cat being a dick?'

Sam laughs. 'Total.'

'Seems fair enough to me, then. Anyway, Dylan told me I'm the worst mother in the whole of the *universe* this morning because I wouldn't let him have a proper party. So apparently even alien mothers are better than me.'

'This is a great party.'

I shrug. 'It's all I can manage.'

'I get that. How is she? How was today?'

'She's incredible.'

'I promise I've performed a thorough health check on Noah. If he so much as clears his throat feel free to put him out on the doorstep and I'll come and get him.'

I smile. 'Thanks.'

'And you know I'm always here if you want to talk about it.'

'I know. Thank you.'

And I wish I could talk to him about it, because I'm sure he'd say all the right things, but I just can't. I don't know why. All I know is that, ever since Sarah's diagnosis, I've built a wall around me that I'm too terrified to pull down.

*

The boys are riding down the stairs in a cardboard box, re-enacting the sledging from earlier, when Sarah knocks on the door.

'Right, stop. Calm down,' I shout at them. 'Aunty Sarah is here. Remember what I said, Dylan. No cuddling.'

'I know, I know. Don't go too close in case I have any germs.'

I put my arm around him. 'Well, you are a snotty, smelly eight-year-old now. You're probably teeming with them.'

'I am not.' Dylan turns to look at me and screws up his face.

When I open the door, Sarah has painted on a huge smile and is carrying a large gift wrapped in superhero paper. 'Happy birthday, Dylan,' she says, holding it out.

Dylan stays where he is, his hands firmly down by his sides.

'You can take your present,' she says.

He reaches out and takes it. 'Thank you, Aunty Sarah.'

'You're welcome, my favourite eight-year-old. Don't tell Noah,' she whispers. Noah seems to have disappeared, probably to the kitchen to steal biscuits, knowing him.

And it's stupid, but just seeing Sarah with my son on his birthday, the Christmas tree sparkling behind them, makes me want to cry. The scarf on her head, her slightly swollen face, her lack of eyelashes or eyebrows – she suddenly looks like a cancer patient, and I can't help but picture Dylan on his next birthday or the one after that. What if she's not there?

Noah comes out of the kitchen with chocolate around his mouth and then grabs Dylan's birthday present out of his hands and starts hurtling up the stairs, Dylan chasing behind screaming at him, so I say, 'Welcome to the "party",' making air quotes with my fingers. And then I lower my voice, 'I have a horrible feeling Noah might have helped himself to the birthday cake and just to top things off, Luke's decided he wants to come.'

'And now the seriously ill person has just arrived to lighten things up. This year's going to be the birthday party you never forget,' Sarah says, and I take her hand and squeeze it.

LUKE

'You moving in or something?' Tim, the landlord, wipes the bar in front of me and then goes to put another song on the jukebox. '"Fairytale of New York". Now this one's a classic.'

I drink the last of my pint. 'Actually, I need to go.'

'Surely you haven't got somewhere better to be than this?'

'It's my son's birthday. He's eight.'

'Great age. Enjoy it, Luke. It goes in the blink of an eye. See you tomorrow, I expect.'

I pick up my flat cap from the bar, doff it to him and then place it on my head. I can see my breath when I get outside so I put on my coat and as I do, my phone beeps in my pocket.

> Sorry it's so late this year. It's been manic today. But happy birthday to that grandson of mine x

I guess I must be drunk because instead of deleting the message like I normally do, I press on Dad's number, initiating a call. It rings for ages and I nearly chicken out and put the phone down but then he answers.

'Luke?'

'Hi Dad.'

'Bloody hell, son. I can't quite believe it's you. It's so good to hear from you.'

There's a lot of noise in the background, the sounds of a busy family life, and I suddenly feel unable to speak.

'So how are you?' Dad prompts. 'How's Dylan?'

'We're OK. I mean . . .'

I hear a voice, someone saying something to him, and he must cover the mouthpiece to say something back because there's a rustling sound and then he says, 'I'm really sorry, I can't be long.'

'Oh, OK. I was just calling to say . . . well, I was wondering if you wanted to catch up sometime?'

'With Dylan?'

He sounds so excited – I hadn't considered that he would immediately think I was inviting him to meet his grandson. Not that I'd considered anything – I just felt a sudden need for my dad. I've survived without him for twenty years so I don't know why today it suddenly feels like I can't do it for another day.

'No. I mean, maybe at some point, but first I was thinking just us, a beer or something?'

'Oh, OK.' The disappointment in his voice is like a hit to the solar plexus. 'You're not old enough to drink beer though, are you?'

'Sadly, yes.'

'Sorry, stupid joke. I'm well aware of all the years I've missed, Luke. Truth is I don't really know what to say.'

'I know. Me neither.'

'A beer would be great, but I'm so busy at the moment. I'm not sure when I'm going to get the chance. But I'll call you, yeah?'

I've thought about this moment my entire life. Me finally getting in touch: Dad tearful with elation. The dramatic reunion when he looks at me, tells me how proud he is of me and then pulls me into a hug. But he's hardly bothered. And I feel like such an idiot.

'Sure.'

I'm about to hang up when I realize I'm never going to speak to him again, so I might as well lay all my cards on the table. 'Why did you stop calling, Dad?'

'What do you mean?'

'When you left. You just gave up.'

'You made it clear you didn't want anything to do with me, Luke. I was just respecting your wishes.'

'I was fourteen. I didn't bloody know what I wanted. What I needed.' I can hear the strain in my voice and it's humiliating, but I'm too drunk to cover it up.

'I'm sorry. I tried my best. But I also had Sandy to care for and then the boys.'

'It's fine. I get it. I was replaced.'

'That's not how it was.'

'So how was it exactly?'

'I don't know,' he stumbles. 'You know how it is. I wanted to try again but, well, the years just go before you really notice, don't they?'

'Not to me, no.'

I put the phone down and slip it in my pocket, putting my collar up to keep the wind off my face. There's no way I can stand there and listen to how easily the years trickled by for Dad without me in his life when I've felt the loss of him in every single one of mine.

As soon as I get to Laura's, I go straight to the fridge and help myself to a beer.

'Of course you can have a beer. Thanks for asking,' Laura says sarcastically.

'Surely I don't have to ask?' I get a bottle opener from the drawer, crack open the beer and then sit at the table and down almost half of it in one go.

'No, but you could say hi to Sarah and me.'

Although Sarah is sitting across from me, I'd barely noticed her. She's here so often, it's like she's part of the furniture. But now that I do look at her, headscarf wrapped around her head, her skin so pale, it just makes the world seem even darker.

'I was getting to that part. I just wanted to get a drink first. Hello, Sarah.' I look at Laura. 'Hello to you, too.'

'Dylan's upstairs with Noah if you want to go up and see him. Maybe give him his present?'

I put my head in my hands. 'Shit.'

'You have got him a present?' Laura glares at me.

'Of course I got him a present. I just left it in the bloody pub. I'll get it back tomorrow.'

'It's his birthday *today*.'

'It's not going to kill him to wait a day, is it?'

'I'm just going to go and see Dylan and Noah,' Sarah says, clearly sensing an argument brewing.

'No, you don't have to do that.'

'It's fine. I'm missing out on the pillow fight and I can't have that.'

'Go easy, OK? They can get pretty rough.'

'I'm not that weak, you know? Not yet anyway.'

Laura gives Sarah a sad smile and then Sarah gets up from the table and goes out.

'So, you've spent the day in the pub?'

'They've dropped us. The record label. One bad album, a few less than sold-out gigs and it's "see ya fucking later". They wouldn't even listen to all the stuff we've spent months working on. I've written some really amazing stuff, poured my heart and soul into those songs.'

'Modest as always.'

'They're good songs.'

'I'm sure they are, Luke.'

'Oh yeah, course. Can't expect you to believe in me.' I stand up and pick up my beer.

'I always believed in you, Luke. I'm sure they are great songs. I thought the previous album was brilliant too.'

'You never told me.'

'You never asked.'

I sit back down and take another large swig. 'We made millions for those bastards and now they've just washed their hands of us. You can't treat people like that, you know?'

'I know. It's a really fucking shitty world, right?'

'It really is.'

Laura sighs. 'I'm going to go and spend time with our best friend and our son. You're welcome to join us.' She heads towards the door.

'Bored of listening to me, are you?'

She stops, turns around, and the look she gives me makes me feel the size of an ant. 'You know what? After a day of chemo with Sarah, yes, I really am.'

After offloading her guilt trip, Laura storms out. It's not until I stumble over thin air on the way to the toilet that I realize how drunk I am. I have a wee, getting some on the seat and then wipe it off, washing my hands and rubbing some water on my face to try to sober up a bit before I go to see Dylan.

When I leave the bathroom, I notice Sarah, sitting on the piano stool playing Dylan's keyboard. He decided he wanted one after they had a go on them at school, but he barely ever plays it. The most use it gets is him turning on the demo and dancing around the living room to it. The piece of music Sarah is playing is beautiful. It's in D minor and every chord she plays cuts right through me.

'Your own composition?'

Sarah startles, stops playing and looks up at me. 'Sorry, it's a bit melancholy, isn't it? I should be playing "Jingle Bells" or something.'

'You OK?'

'Yeah, I was just having a little rest. It's getting a bit lively between Noah and Dylan. I haven't quite got the stamina to keep up right now.'

She gets off the stool and slumps on the sofa and I sit down beside her, careful to leave a bit of a gap in case I'm harbouring any unknown viruses. 'OK for me to join you?'

'Of course. Although you sound drunk. You're not going to talk drunken crap at me, are you? I don't mind when I'm drinking too but I don't think chemo and alcohol are a great mix.'

The guilt floods through my veins. I know I should've shown up more for her. She called me to tell me a few weeks ago. Apparently, she'd told Laura not to say anything as she wanted to tell me herself. She was so calm, so matter-of-fact. I said the typical trite things about her being a fighter and gave her that empty offer that people do of 'anything I can do to help, just shout'. And then I ended the call and threw my phone at the wall, smashing the screen. I sent her a bunch of flowers and I've messaged Tom a couple of times just to check in, but I've not seen her. Coward that I am, I haven't been able to face it. I haven't even talked to Laura about it. Truth be told, I can't handle her pain. Or my own, I guess.

'I'll try not to talk drunken crap.'

'Why are you drinking so much, anyway?'

'Because my life's not worth living.' I pause, wanting to slap myself around the face. 'Sorry. That was a really insensitive thing to say. I'm a waste of space.'

'Give it a rest.'

'What?'

'The "I'm a worthless piece of crap" thing.'

'Well, I am. That's why the record label no longer wants me. Why Laura no longer wants me. Why my dad gave up on me.'

'You do realize I have cancer, don't you? You're seriously going to try the whole "woe is me" thing with *me*?'

I smile. 'Sorry.'

Sarah shakes her head. 'Actually, it's quite nice to be honest. People have suddenly stopped talking to me about their problems. It's like they feel guilty because they think their difficulties pale in comparison to mine and that I'll think they're moaning about nothing. But I want to hear about other people's stuff. I just want people to treat me like they normally would rather than constantly worrying about offending me.'

'Well, you're lucky that I don't seem to have that sensitivity.'

Sarah laughs. 'I am. I can always count on you for a healthy dose of narcissism.'

I laugh. 'You love me really.'

'I do.'

'I *am* sorry though. For not showing up for you more. For being a bit of a mess when you probably need me to be better. It's not because I don't care about you. I actually think about you all the time.'

'Really?'

I nod. 'Well, when I'm not thinking about myself, of course.'

'I don't need you to be better for me. I have Tom. And Laura. But I need you to be better for her. She needs you. She always puts on a brave face with me, but I know she's scared. She just doesn't want to tell me because it's like she's saying I might die.'

'She doesn't talk to me either. I expect she talks to Sam.'

Sarah crinkles her face. 'Why do you say that?'

'They meet up, don't they? Take the boys to the park together and stuff? It's obvious he fancies her.'

'Of course he bloody does. Look at her.'

'Exactly. So you think something's going on too?'

Sarah shakes her head. 'I keep trying to persuade her, but she says it's too complicated with Dylan being best friends with Noah and everything.'

'But she does like him?'

Sarah laughs. 'You know you're supposed to want the best for her.'

'I think we've just established I'm a selfish arsehole. And besides, I don't think he is the best for her.'

'But you are?'

I roll my eyes. 'OK, I'm not quite saying that. I know I made her cry.'

'A *lot*.'

'All right, all right. But when it was good . . .' I tail off, unable to put into words how happy she made me.

'I know.'

'Do you think she'll ever love me again?'

'She still loves you now, Luke.'

'But I don't mean like an old mangy cat that keeps turning up at the door and you eventually grow *fond* of it. I mean, do you think there's a chance she'll ever be *in* love with me again?'

'I don't know.'

'Of course you know. You know her better than she knows herself.'

'I really don't know. But I *do* know that right now you need to let go of all that stuff. Because while you're still madly in love with her you can't be what she needs. She needs you to be there for her, not to try to sleep with her.'

'That's not fair.'

'You know what I mean. Just be her best friend. And if I'm not here . . .'

'Sar.'

'There's no point in pretending it's not a possibility. Promise me you'll take care of her. If I can't, I mean.'

I let out a deep sigh. 'I worry I'm not good enough. Not up to the job.'

'Well, you'll never be me. That's a given. But if I can spend my weeks being pumped full of poison and still look after a ten-month-old then you can sort out your crap and be a good friend to her.'

'I know. You're right.' I run my hands through my hair.

'I'm so sorry you're having to go through this, by the way. I know I might not have said it, but I'm fucking furious that this is happening to you.'

Sarah shrugs. 'I'm just one of many. Nothing special. Honestly, those places are like production lines.'

'Stop being so bloody stoic.'

Sarah goes quiet and when I turn to look at her, she has tears in her eyes. 'If I'm not, I'm scared I'll fall apart and never mend.'

I wrap my arms around her, the need to comfort her overriding any concerns about keeping a distance. And she doesn't move away so I know that she's glad, that for once I've done the right thing. 'You're not going to die, you know? I won't fucking let you.'

She pulls away enough to look up into my eyes and when she does, I can see hers are full of fear. 'Promise?'

I guide her head to rest on my shoulder and stroke the top of her arm. 'I promise. Laura would be an absolute misery if anything were to happen to you and I'm not going to put up with that for the next however many years.'

Sarah sits up and smiles at me.

'Wanna play and I'll sing?' I nod towards the keyboard.

Sarah shrugs and then gets up and moves on to the stool. And then she plays the opening bars of 'Christmas Lights' by Coldplay and I swallow down the lump in my throat. 'Well, except for the gorgeous weather, it doesn't really feel like Christmas at all, does it?'

I shake my head and then I squeeze on to the stool beside her and sing while she plays. When we finish, she kisses me on the cheek. 'You know, deep down, you're so much better than you realize.'

I pull her in tighter and rest my head on top of hers. 'Thank you.'

After I've sobered up with a coffee, I venture upstairs to see Dylan. When I get nearer, I hear Laura playing a game of Simon Says with the boys, so I stand in the doorway and just watch for a while, both of them laughing when Laura speeds up to catch them out.

'Oh, I didn't realize you were there,' she says, looking up. 'I'm going to go and see Sarah. You have some time with Dylan. I think your dad will be here in a minute, Noah.'

I continue the game of Simon Says with the boys until Noah is called down. I'm tempted to go down to see how Laura interacts with Sam, to see if I can pick up on any sort of spark, but Dylan wants to show me his new remote-control car so I resist the temptation and help him set up a track to race the car around. We play for a while and then he asks if he can watch a film on his tablet so I agree as long as he puts on his pyjamas and gets into bed.

When I get downstairs, Laura is sitting on the sofa on her own staring at the Christmas tree, the radio playing quietly. The room is dark except for a candle on the fireplace and the Christmas tree lights twinkling and reflecting in the black television screen. Her tree is tiny compared to the ones I used to make her get and most of the baubles look homemade, whereas I always insisted we had the most extravagant decorations money could buy. Sometimes I wonder what I was trying to prove. I can tell she's let Dylan help with the decorating as it's a bit of a mess, but there's a charm to it that our tree never had.

'Has Sarah gone?'

Laura looks up at me and nods.

'I let Dylan watch a film on his tablet. Is that OK? I think he'll probably fall asleep watching it anyway. He seems pretty whacked.'

'It's fine.'

'Well, I guess I should leave you to it. Thanks for having me over and I'm sorry for turning up drunk. It's not just the band stuff, it's just been a really shit day, but it's nothing compared to what you've been through today so I'm sorry.'

Laura nods her head towards the kitchen. 'There's a bottle of wine in the cupboard by the fridge. You're welcome to share it with me if you want? Unless you've got somewhere to be.'

'No, nowhere. That'd be nice. I'll go and get it.'

I go into the kitchen and find the bottle of wine in a cupboard with about ten bars of chocolate. I remove the cork and then take the bottle and two glasses into the lounge.

'Enough chocolate?' I pour Laura a glass of wine and hand it to her and then pour myself one before putting the bottle on the side table and sitting on the sofa.

'It's my feeling glum cupboard. I basically live in there at the moment.'

'Want to talk about it?'

'I'm not sure if I can. Want to talk about your stuff?'

'You know, actually, no, I don't. But thanks for asking.'

'Some days I wake up in a cold sweat,' Laura blurts out suddenly. 'Terrified that I'm going to find a lump somewhere and walk into the doctors to find out I've only months to live. And then I wonder if that would be easier – to be the one that's going rather than the one that's left behind.'

'Sarah's going to be OK, you know.'

'But we don't know that, do we? What if she's not? I've read article after article about her odds. They're not exactly great.' She rubs her forehead and then massages her temples. 'I don't think I'd ever feel happy again. If I lost her, I mean. Ever since she told me about her diagnosis, the whole world has felt grey. I can't find any pleasure in anything. Not even in Dylan. And I feel so guilty about that. But everything just feels so pointless.'

I know exactly how she feels because I've felt that way since the day she left.

'I'm sorry,' she says, drinking another large gulp of wine. 'I shouldn't be offloading on to you.'

'Why not?'

'Well, you've obviously got your own stuff going on. Unimportant, trivial stuff it may be, but it's stuff nonetheless.'

'Sod off.' I jab Laura in the side with my elbow and she laughs, and it's the greatest sound.

'God, I even feel guilty for laughing,' she says.

'You shouldn't feel guilty.'

'But I do. Why is it her and not me? Why do I get to keep my hair? My boobs?'

'Come on. Losing your boobs would be a tragedy for the world. I mean, don't get me wrong, Sarah's are a loss, but yours . . .'

Laura bites back a smile. 'Luke, we shouldn't be joking about this. It makes us terrible people, you know.'

'Oh, I already knew I was a terrible person.'

'It feels nice though. To laugh, I mean.'

'Well, anytime you need someone to share inappropriate jokes with, I'm here.'

Laura leans over and grabs the bottle of wine, topping up her glass. 'Want some more?'

Feeling her body so close to me, I feel my chest pull tight and my breath get short, but I manage to nod and she fills up my glass.

'Every time I see someone smoking, eating saturated fat as if it's going out of fashion, drinking like a fish – I want to kill them. Because Sarah did everything right and she's the one with cancer. It should be them.'

'I know.'

'I know there's never a good time for something like this,' she continues. 'But the timing is so fucking cruel. She waited all that time for Thea and now she can't even enjoy it. She should be concentrating on planning for Thea's first Christmas – choosing her stocking, buying a Christmas tree decoration with her name on it, starting all those traditions that are going to become a precious yearly staple. But that's all tainted now because she doesn't know if she'll get to experience any of that with Thea going forward.'

'You have to be positive, Laur. Hope is all we have, right?'

'I guess.'

'Anyway, on the subject of Christmas, I was wondering if we could spend it together again this year?'

'You sure you haven't got some other girl to spend it with?'

I shake my head. 'I'm so sorry I started this whole separate Christmas thing. I've regretted it ever since.'

She pauses and I'm terrified that she's going to say no, but then she says, 'Well, it has been a bit quiet without you and those bloody musical socks of yours.'

They used to drive her mad – every time I moved my

legs it set them off, a high-pitched 'We Wish You a Merry Christmas'.

'Christmas isn't Christmas without them,' I say.

Laura smiles but then her face falls. 'She's going to be there, isn't she? This Christmas? Next Christmas? All the Christmases I have left?'

I put my arm around her, pull her towards me and kiss the top of her head. 'I truly believe she is.'

The familiar introduction of Joni Mitchell's 'River' starts playing on the radio and I sing along quietly, my voice no match for her beautifully haunting tone.

'Now this is what you call a decent Christmas song,' Laura says.

'But it's just so sad. Is this how you've always felt about Christmas? Wanting to skate away?'

Laura shrugs. 'Maybe before Dylan. And definitely last year spending it without him.'

'Remember that Christmas Day when he was three, once everyone had left and Dylan had fallen asleep on the sofa? The light of the moon was shining through the glass and I said it felt like a spotlight on a stage and we danced for ages.'

'I didn't want to go to sleep because you were leaving for that Asia tour in the morning.'

'Is that why you wouldn't go to sleep that night?'

Laura nods. 'I didn't want Christmas to be over, for you to be gone again.'

There's a huge part of me that wishes I'd never started the bloody band, but then it's also brought me so much joy.

I sit up and hold out my hand. 'Want to dance now? For old times' sake?'

Laura stares at my hand for a minute but then she puts her glass on the side and takes it.

And we dance to the saddest Christmas song ever, and when I see the tears in Laura's eyes, glistening in the tree lights, I know that I have to put her first and that to do that, to be better, I need to let her go.

16th December 2014

LAURA

'I was worried he might be a bit old for this. That we might have missed the window,' Luke says, as we sit at a little wooden table drinking hot chocolate whilst one of the 'elves' shows Dylan how to make gingerbread. The weather outside is minus twenty, the snow falling steadily past the window, and the hut is lined with twinkling lights and old-fashioned Christmas decorations, making it feel so magical that even I could almost believe this is Santa's real home.

'Are you kidding me? It's perfect. Thanks for this, Luke, but you really have to let me give you some money towards it.'

Luke holds up his hands. 'It's something I always wanted to treat you guys to but then . . . well, you know, life got in the way. It's my last blowout before I have to start watching the pennies a bit more.'

It feels far too much, paying for us to come to Lapland, but I know Luke won't accept a contribution however hard I try to force him. He surprised me with it a few weeks ago, handing me an envelope when he came to collect Dylan. I couldn't believe my eyes when I saw the plane tickets and the photograph of the lodge he'd rented. The first thing I said was 'But I haven't got any thermal clothes,' and he said, 'I knew you'd say that,' and handed me a bag from behind his back full of winter gear.

'You might have to get a real job soon, you know?' I tease.

'Never.'

'I don't blame you. Real jobs are pretty shit.'

Working in Thomas Cook again for the past few years has been a real blow. It's not that there's anything wrong with the job per se; it's more that it feels like going backward. I never thought I'd be thirty-two and still doing something I don't give a shit about.

Luke takes a sip of his hot chocolate, giving him a liquid moustache. And then an excited smile creeps across his lips. 'I've found a band. They're called Partners in Crime.'

It's stupid but I can't help my stomach falling. It's almost felt like I've had Luke back since the band got dropped. It's been really nice to spend more time together as a family, albeit just as friends, and now it feels like I'm about to lose him again. 'Are you going to be the lead singer?'

'Oh, no. I mean to manage. I think my performing days might be behind me. But I was at the Crown about a month ago and they were playing and I had this brainwave that maybe I could put my experience to good use. I offered to sign them then and there and they said yes.'

I disguise my relief with my enthusiasm for his new venture. 'That's amazing.'

'I'm scared I'm wrong and they're shit. Will you listen to some of their stuff later? See what you think.'

'Of course, but I'm not sure it matters what I think. I haven't got a clue what stuff the kids are listening to these days.'

'It matters to me.'

'Well, OK then.'

Dylan comes over, the gingerbread man he's just cut out resting on the palm of his hand. 'Look. I made it myself. Well, with the help of Santa's elves.'

I look for a trace of irony in the way he says it, a gently mocking tone, but I'm pretty sure there isn't any. That he still believes. And it makes my chest ache. Sometimes when I hear him talking to his mates, peppering his sentences with the latest expressions, or refusing to wear his coat because it's not considered 'cool', it feels like he's growing up so fast, but then moments like this remind me of his innocence and I want to grab on to it, to cherish it before it disappears.

'Well done,' I say. 'Looks delicious.'

'We're going to put it in the oven now and then we can decorate it.'

'And then I can eat it,' Luke teases.

'No way. It's all mine,' Dylan says, walking back over to the lady who was helping him, who is now waiting by the oven.

'You need to find your passion as well,' Luke says, continuing our previous conversation. 'You've spent so long doing stuff for Dylan. It's time you did something for you.'

'He's only nine. I'm not totally redundant as a mother, you know.'

But he's right. Dylan doesn't need me as intensely as he used to and I do feel lost sometimes without the purpose that being a full-time mum gave me.

'You'll never be redundant. But that doesn't mean you can't focus on yourself too.'

'I don't know. I don't even know what I feel passionate about.'

'Oh, come on. When do you feel most alive?'

When I'm with you. The thought hits me right in the stomach. It's a surprise, even though deep down I've always known it.

'I don't know.'

'Then that's your homework. I want you to go away and think about the last time you were doing something that made you excited, where the adrenaline hit you and you just wanted to do it again and again. Because that's what you should be doing.'

Luke races up to the top of the little hill, pulling the sledge, and Dylan follows behind. When Luke first handed me tickets for the 'Santa's home' experience this morning, I thought it might be commercialized crap, trying to sell you ridiculously overpriced souvenirs at every turn. But to be fair to Luke, he did his research and chose the more authentic Santa experience. And when the coach dropped us here, in the middle of nowhere, the sky vast swathes of pink and purple like Monet has taken a brush to it, I couldn't quite believe how beautiful it was.

'Wee hee,' Luke shouts as he and Dylan hurtle past my legs, nearly crashing into me.

'Come on, Mummy. Come with us this time.'

'Oh, I don't know. I'll probably fall out and look stupid.'

'So you look stupid,' Luke says. 'I promise I won't laugh. Well, not too much. Come on.'

He takes my hand and drags me up, pulling the sledge with the other hand, and Dylan runs alongside us, laughing at me being forced into it by Luke.

'You'll enjoy it, Mummy. It's so much faster here. And it doesn't hurt when you fall out like it does at home. It's so soft.' He jumps sideways into the snow to demonstrate and looks like he might keep falling forever. 'Help, I'm stuck,' he shouts.

Luke lets go of my hand and walks across and lifts Dylan up with one arm, carrying him underneath it. When we get to the top, Luke dumps Dylan down and sets up the sledge.

'OK, let's go in order of size,' Luke says, sitting down at the back.

I sit down and then Dylan climbs in in front of me, pure glee flooding his face.

'I'm scared,' I say. 'What if I fall out?'

'Don't worry, I won't let you,' Luke says into my ear and then he wraps his arms around us and pushes off with his feet. And with the weight of all three of us, we fly to the bottom, the snow spraying up at us from the sides, and by the time we're all thrown out at the bottom in a heap, we're in fits of giggles.

'That was so much fun,' Dylan says, struggling up. 'We go so much faster together. Let's do it again.'

'I thought you said you wouldn't let me fall out,' I say to Luke, wiping the snow off my jacket and ski trousers.

'Well, at least I cushioned your landing.'

'True. Come on then. Let's go again.'

'Race you both to the top,' Luke says, running off up the hill.

So Dylan and I chase him, me coming last, and we spend another half-hour just going up and down the hill. And then Luke starts gathering snow in his hands, pressing it together, so I should expect the snowball that comes hurtling towards my face, but it takes me by surprise and nearly knocks me over.

'Hey you,' I shout, and then I gather some snow myself

and chase Luke until I can get a shot right at his head. The snow gets stuck in his hair and he shakes it like a dog coming out of the water.

'Right, the fight is on.'

Dylan joins in too, both of us ganging up on Luke until the cold has eaten into our bones so fully that it feels like we'll never warm up. And then it's our time slot to have our photo with Santa so we head towards the cabin. Whilst we're in the short queue, I get a message from Sarah – a photo of her, Thea and Tom with a very poor Santa impersonator, whose beard is falling off to reveal his five o'clock shadow beneath.

Look, we're meeting Santa too. Happy Birthday to Dylan! Hope you're all having an amazing time. We miss you!xx

Sarah's hair has thickened up a bit now and she's had it cut into a cute little crop that somehow makes her look even more stunning than she did before.

'She does realize it's only one of his helpers?' Dylan says, as I show him the message. 'The real one is right here.'

'I know. I think they're just pretending for Thea. She's a bit young to explain it all to, isn't she?'

'I'll explain it to her when she's a bit bigger.'

I run my hand through his hair. 'She is going to love you so much.'

'She already does,' Dylan says incredulously.

'You're right. Silly me. She does.'

'She looks really well,' Luke says, peering at the photograph over my shoulder.

'She does, doesn't she?'

When Sarah told me that her chemo had been successful,

that her tumors had been almost entirely destroyed, I think I cried every day for a whole week. Because tests had revealed she had the 'breast cancer gene' (*I always knew I had things in common with Angelina Jolie*), she decided to have a double mastectomy. And then radiotherapy followed.

A month or so ago, when all her treatment finished, I threw her a party followed by a spa weekend away. But whilst we were sipping champagne and having our nails done, she said, 'I don't want to sound ungrateful, but I don't feel like celebrating.' And it was such a relief because I'd not enjoyed a second of it. I'd been forcing the jubilance because I thought that's what Sarah would want. But I understood her feelings completely – it felt like tempting fate. Like someone up there might be waiting with a smirk to say, 'Ha ha, fooled you.'

And every time someone says she looks well, it's there. A voice in the back of my head. I wonder if it will ever go.

When it's our turn, we go into 'Santa's workshop' – Santa sitting there in a big rocking chair. And as Luke and I sit down on the bench beside him, Dylan just stops and stares at him, his mouth falling open.

'Hello,' Santa says, his Finnish accent making him sound even more authentic.

'Hi.' Dylan sits on the bench with us, his eyes never leaving Santa, and the 'elves' take my camera and Luke's phone.

'Do you want one with just the two of you and I'll have one with me?' Luke asks and I can't help but feel hurt. Because I've started to see us as a family again and I don't want to think of us as two broken parts, even though of course that's what we are.

'No, I'm OK, but you have one. I'm happy to move out

the way.' I start to stand up but Luke takes my hand and pulls me back down.

'I think I can bear to look at your ugly mug on the wall.'

We look at the camera for a few more shots and then it's our time to move on.

'Wasn't that cool?' I say to Dylan. 'Meeting the real Santa.'

'It was the best,' Dylan says but there's a disappointment in his voice and I wonder, with a sinking heart, if he suspects this is all just make-believe.

'What's up?' I ask, putting my arm around him.

'Nothing. I just thought . . . well, because he's Santa I thought he might give me a present. It doesn't matter though. It was still really cool.'

Luke catches my eye over the top of Dylan's head. 'I just need the toilet. I'll meet you at the reindeers.'

I take Dylan outside and we put our hats and gloves back on and head towards the reindeer enclosure, but then Luke catches us up, a paper bag in his hand.

'I just bumped into Santa. He said he forgot to give you this.' Luke hands Dylan the bag and he pulls out the little reindeer keyring that's inside.

'I knew he'd give me a present. I love it.'

I smile at Luke, wondering why I struggled to appreciate it before – what a brilliant dad he is. What a brilliant *person* he is.

Dylan goes over to the reindeer enclosure, holding up his little cuddly one to show them. 'Hi reindeer. I'm your friend – mini reindeer,' he says in a squeaky voice.

'Sometimes he feels so grown up,' Luke says, 'but he's still just a baby, isn't he?'

'I know.'

'He seems to be loving it, doesn't he?'

'He is. He'll remember this trip forever.'

'I hope so. I feel like I owe it to him.'

I shake my head. 'You're a great dad, Luke. And thank you for letting me tag along and share this with you both.'

'Of course. I'd never have done this without you. You deserve to share all this with him too.'

He walks towards Dylan, who is busy creating a conversation between mini-reindeer and his real-life reindeer friends. 'Shall we go and warm up in the hut with some hot berry juice and toasted marshmallows?'

'Yey,' Dylan says, clapping his hands. And then they walk along, Luke with his arm around Dylan, and I follow.

The hut's empty so we take the bench closest to the fire. Luke helps Dylan to spear marshmallows on to a metal stick and then Dylan holds it just above the flame.

'It's like that time I forced you to go camping,' Luke laughs. 'Remember? I said it wasn't going to rain and you said it would, and you were so grumpy with me because it rained every single day.'

'I'm sorry I was grumpy.'

'I should've believed the weather forecast, to be fair. Always been my problem – blind optimism.'

'There are worse problems to have.'

Luke smiles. 'I'm sure I had quite a few of those too. But I've been working on it. I hope I'm doing better.'

'You're doing great.'

Luke pops a marshmallow in his mouth untoasted and then hands the bag to me. 'So, did I ever achieve my mission of getting you to like Christmas? I mean, you just met *Santa* and you didn't seem to break into hives.'

I put the bag of marshmallows down, take off my gloves and hold my hands out to the fire to warm them up. 'You achieved your mission. Well, the ones we've spent together anyway.'

'Yeah, Christmas Day without Dylan was pretty brutal, wasn't it?'

I stare at the flame so I don't have to look at Luke. 'And the ones without you.' I suddenly feel too exposed so I add, 'I mean, we were a bit lost for what to do without your annual family quiz.'

'Ah, yeah, that classic.'

'And yours and Dylan's ridiculous matching costumes.'

'The Christmas puddings were a strong year.'

'I think last year's turkeys were my favourite.'

Luke laughs. 'I'm not sure your mum was so impressed.'

I laugh too and then Dylan takes his marshmallow away from the flame and starts to remove it from the stick. 'Ow, it's hot.'

'So would you be if you'd just been dangled above a fire for five minutes,' Luke says.

Dylan blows on it and then pops it in his mouth. Once he's finished, he licks the remaining goo off his fingers and puts another marshmallow on the stick.

Luke taps his watch. 'Make this one quick. Nearly time to get back on the coach.'

And I feel this strange sense of panic – that the moment's going to be gone and I'll never have the chance to tell Luke about the feelings I've been trying to deny for so long.

'The thing is, Luke. It's just I . . .'

And then the door to the hut opens and we look up to see the tour guide. 'Time to go, I'm afraid,' she says, and Dylan quickly grabs the marshmallow off his stick and shoves it in his mouth. 'Have you had a good time?'

'Brilliant,' Luke says and Dylan nods excitedly.

'Bet you don't want to leave, do you?' the guide says, holding the door open for us to exit the hut.

And it's true. I really don't.

LUKE

We sit on the back seat of the coach, Dylan between Laura and me. It's pitch black outside now and it's so warm in here that I feel like I could fall asleep at any moment. Dylan must feel the same, because he leans into me and I put my arm around him and it's not long before I feel him drifting.

Laura's phone starts ringing and at first it looks like she's going to ignore it but then she answers.

'Hiya,' Laura says in a hushed voice. 'Yeah. Yeah, it's amazing.'

I'm pretty sure it's a man's voice on the other end of the line – I expect Sam, as I know they speak a lot – and it makes me realize how far I've come because, although there's still more than a twinge of jealousy, it no longer makes me feel like I want to rip my heart out.

Laura looks over at Dylan. 'Yeah, he's asleep. It's been a busy day. Tell Noah I'll pass the message on and we'll see you guys when we get back. He still wants to go and see *How to Train Your Dragon 2* at the weekend.'

So, it is Sam.

'Yeah, I'm in,' Laura says. 'If only for the popcorn and the two hours' peace and quiet.'

They chat for a bit longer and then say their goodbyes, Laura slipping the phone back into her bag.

'Noah wanted to say happy birthday.'

I nod and then we both go quiet, her staring out of the window and me looking straight ahead.

'I'm sorry for how I acted when you were chatting to Sam that first time. It wasn't fair. I should've encouraged you to be happy.'

'It's OK. That was ages ago.'

'I know, but I never apologized. For what it's worth – he seems like a really good bloke. And Dylan and Noah are like brothers. It's a ready-made family. You always said you didn't want Dylan to be an only child.'

'We're just friends, Luke.'

'But it would be OK if it was more than that. I'd be happy for you. That's all I'm saying.'

'Well, it's not like that.' Laura wraps her hair around her finger. 'So how about you? I can't keep tabs on you now that you're no longer in the papers.'

'There hasn't been a lot to keep tabs on.'

It's been nine months since I've slept with anyone. It sounds trite but I've been trying to focus on getting myself sorted – I've ditched the drink, been playing the guitar again, tinkering with some new songs, trying to sort out some early gigs for Partners in Crime.

'Offers dried up, have they?'

'Something like that.'

'I'm sure you'll soon be able to play the hot manager card. Jimmy seemed to do OK out of it.'

I smile. 'Maybe. Actually, I have been asked out on a date.'

'Really?'

'Don't sound so shocked. I'm not *that* unappealing.'

'No, I didn't mean that. It's just . . .'

'A bit out of nowhere, I know. She's the mum of one of the lads in the band I've taken on. I know, I know, I'm a hundred and three.'

Laura smiles, but it feels a bit half-hearted. 'Where are you going to take her?'

'*She's* cooking *me* dinner. She came to one of the lads' gigs and we just got chatting. She seems down to earth. And you'll be glad to know she's our age.'

'You know you're older than me.'

'OK, well, she's *my* age. I don't know if it'll go anywhere but we seem to have quite a lot in common, so I thought it was worth a go.'

Laura nods. 'I'm happy for you.'

'Thanks.'

When the coach pulls up outside the closest hotel to our lodge, I gently nudge Dylan to wake him up and we put on what feels like a hundred accessories to stop us from freezing to death. We walk back, the snow crunching beneath our feet, and then suddenly, as we get to the little lane that leads back to our lodge, Dylan stops.

'Look at the sky.' He points upwards. 'There's a green light dancing across it.'

Before we came, I showed Dylan some YouTube videos of the northern lights so every time he sees the flicker of a light from an aeroplane or the wisp of a cloud moving across the sky, he thinks he's spotted them. But as I look up, I can't believe it, he's right. I glance at Laura who is staring skyward, her mouth open.

'Oh my God,' she says and I'm sure I can hear tears in her voice.

'You're right, Dylan. Those are the northern lights.' I put

my arm around him. 'You know, some people search for a lifetime and never manage to see them.'

'Look at that one,' Dylan says. 'It's like a big swirl.'

We sit on a snowy wall and watch the majestic sky, my arm around Dylan and Laura holding his hand.

'It's magical, isn't it?' Laura says, her eyes not leaving the celestial light show.

'Incredible.'

We sit in silence, all of us too awed to speak. And then after a while, I feel Dylan shivering beneath my arm. 'Back home for hot chocolate and a story?'

Dylan nods and I help him down off the wall and we head back to the lodge, Dylan in the middle and Laura and I holding his hands.

'It's like that snow globe you bought me. Remember, when Dylan was born?'

'Oh yeah. God, I haven't seen that thing for years. I wonder where it got to. I'll have to search the loft.'

'I've got it,' Laura says. 'I put it on my bedside table every Christmas.'

'Oh. Well, now it will remind you of being here.'

'It will.'

Back at the lodge, I make hot chocolate while Laura gets Dylan into his Christmas onesie – penguins and polar bears marching in lines across it.

'Well, that was a pretty amazing day, wasn't it?' Laura says, as she and Dylan climb the stairs to the bedroom they are sharing on a mezzanine level. 'A magical light show, just for your birthday.'

'Best birthday ever,' Dylan says.

'Remember when we sat and gazed at the stars with Sarah and Tom on Dylan's third birthday?' I say to Laura, following her up the stairs.

'Where was I?'

'You were asleep,' Laura says, climbing into bed with Dylan, a book in her hand, and pulling the cover up over them both. 'I remember watching you on the baby monitor.'

'So you basically abandoned me?'

We both laugh, and I hand them each a hot chocolate.

'You were only upstairs. In the old house.'

I had to sell it earlier this year. I almost cried when I handed over the keys.

'The big house,' Dylan says, taking a sip of his drink and giving himself a chocolate moustache.

'Certainly was,' I say. 'The good old days, hey?'

'I like it better now,' Dylan says, jumping his little cuddly reindeer around on the quilt with his free hand.

'Really?' Laura asks.

'Yeah, because you and Daddy are friends.'

Laura looks at me and then says, 'Yes. Daddy is my best friend. Well, except for Aunty Sarah.'

'And not when Mummy steals my brownies. Then she's not my friend.'

Dylan laughs. 'Can we have the story now, Mummy?'

'Of course.' Laura puts her arm around Dylan and opens the book.

'Come and listen, Daddy.' Dylan shuffles along so that I can climb in beside him. 'It's about this boy who gets stuck at school in the snow.'

'Sounds cool.'

Laura reads the story and I rest my head on Dylan's shoulder and listen. And then when the story's finished, I kiss him on the forehead and stand up. 'Time to get some sleep now. We're going snowmobiling tomorrow. Happy birthday, kiddo.'

'Night night, Daddy.'

I go downstairs and put some logs on the fire, and it's not long before Laura comes down and joins me.

'Your best friend?' I say to her as she puts her mug on the side and then sits on the sofa, pulling her legs up and wrapping her arms around them. 'Did you just say that to make Dylan happy?'

She shakes her head. 'You've been in my life for ten years now. We've shared a lot.'

'So, it's just a longevity thing?'

Laura gives me a look. 'Will you stop fishing for compliments, please?'

'I'm sorry. I'm not. It was just nice to hear.' I throw another log on the fire and then lean against the sofa. 'Ten years? Bloody hell.'

'I *know*. People get shorter sentences for murder.'

I smile and Laura stands up and goes to the freezer. 'I'm going to have a Baileys. Want one?'

'I stopped drinking, remember?'

Laura taps the ice cube tray on her glass and a couple of ice cubes clink into it. 'I knew you'd cut down but I didn't realize you were teetotal.'

'Oh, you know me. I've got a bit of an all-or-nothing personality. Maybe after a while I'll be able to have a couple of drinks here and there, but for now I'm better off abstaining altogether.'

'Fair enough.' Laura pours some Baileys into her glass and then comes back over to the sofa.

I rifle through the pile of board games in the cupboard beside the sofa. 'Scrabble?'

'Oh, go on then.'

'With the proviso that all words must be Christmas-themed.'

Laura laughs, getting down on to the rug and putting her glass on the wooden floorboards beside her. 'Well, that's a given. It *is* December, right? And, to be fair, we are in *Lapland*.'

I unfold the board and give Laura a stand for her tiles, then set up my letters on mine. 'You know I'm going to whoop your arse.'

'We both know our son gets his intelligence from me.'

'Ha. Is that right?' I arrange my letters to spell the word 'tree'. It's not the best start, but having chosen a V and an X, I don't have the greatest number of options.

'Ladies first,' I say, hoping Laura will put something down that will help me out.

She lays her letters out across the centre star. 'Twelve points. Not a bad start.'

'Jesus? That's a name. That's not allowed.'

'It's Christmas-themed. Surely we're not following the rules to a T?'

'You still can't have proper nouns.'

Laura gets out her phone and starts typing. 'Ha, Jesus is a valid Scrabble word.' She holds out her phone for me to see. 'A size of paper in France.'

'Oh, come off it.'

'Twelve points it is.'

306

I still can't do better than 'tree', so I add the T, R and E to her letters. Over the course of the game, we lay some Christmas classics like 'tinsel' and 'snow' and some weaker connections like 'dark' and 'smell'. Laura scores a blinder with 'quiz' and we argue over my contribution of 'sex', which there's no way I'm backing down on because I manage to place the X on a triple letter.

'People have more sex at Christmas.'

'Says who?'

'The amount of September birthdays, that's who. I bet you know tons of people born in September.'

'Fine then. I'm going to add "bladder".'

'How is that possibly linked to Christmas?'

'You drink more at Christmas so you wee more.'

'Seriously?'

'If you can have sex, I'm having bladder.'

She wins in the end, 103 to my 97, and we put the tiles back in the drawstring bag and then put our stands back in the box. The fire has all but died out, a few tiny embers still glowing orange in the bottom.

'Well, I think I'm going to call it a night. More exciting adventures tomorrow,' I say, taking the cushions off the sofa before pulling out the legs of the sofa bed.

'Sure. And thank you for today. You know, for the first time I think I might believe in Santa.'

I smile. 'Night, Laura.'

She puts her glass on the worktop and then starts to climb the stairs but pauses. 'Did you mean it earlier when you said you'd be happy for me to move on?'

'Of course,' I lie, feeling sick at the thought of her finding happiness with someone else, especially as it's obvious from her question that she does want to pursue something with Sam. But I know it's only fair to let her do so. 'Like Dylan said – it's better now, isn't it? Us being good friends.'

Laura nods and then carries on up the stairs. 'Night, Luke.'

16th December 2015

LUKE

'I love it.'

'For real?'

'Absolutely. This *has* to be on the album.'

The lads look up at me with beaming smiles and then taper them, because of course it's not cool to look like you give a shit about anything when you're eighteen. But I can tell that my approval means a lot to them and there's definitely something paternal in the way I feel about them, which is *terrifying*. When did I get so bloody old? A few years ago, I would've been out drinking with lads like this and now I find myself giving them advice and feeling like I need to look after them.

They joke among themselves for a bit and then Tris, the guitarist, starts jamming and they all join in, messing around with different licks and trying out new refrains, and I can't help but miss it. Being a manager is brilliant. Taking these guys on was one of the best decisions of my life. But I still miss it. God, I miss it. The feeling of standing on a stage and everyone singing along to a song that you wrote – I don't think I'll ever experience a feeling like it again in my whole life.

'I'm going to leave you guys to it,' I shout over the music and they nod and wave me off.

As I leave the studio, I take my phone out of my pocket and message Rich and Cody. We still have a WhatsApp group, meeting up every couple of months for a beer – or a non-alcoholic cider for me these days – and a catch-up, but we haven't played together since it all fell apart. I don't know why. Maybe it's been too raw. Maybe we've all been busy forming new lives.

At work, Cody replies. *Trying to work out how many hours it is until I retire.* He works in insurance and hates it, but he has a wife and new baby to support now.

Rich is more of a free spirit. He plays in a band doing wedding gigs and does a bit of temp bar work at festivals. But he's never settled down or done a 9 to 5. There's no response from him for a while, but then to my surprise he writes, *Sure. I'll be at yours in ten.* And I notice the huge smile appearing on my face as I drive home.

There's nowhere to park outside my place as usual, so I park down the road and walk up. Once in, I pick up two bar stools from the kitchen and squeeze them into the lounge so we have somewhere to play. I switch on a few lamps because it's always dark in this place regardless of the weather outside. And then I go upstairs and grab my guitar off the hooks on my wall. I always picture it like a teddy bear – that sort of automatic comfort I feel when I'm holding it to my stomach. For quite a long time after the band split, I couldn't play. I couldn't even bear to look at it. But after a while, I started picking it up again. And it always makes me feel better when I do.

There's a knock on the door and I go down to see Rich peering through the window, guitar in hand. When he sees me, he sticks his tongue out and I smile and open the door to let him in.

'Hey mate,' he says, drawing me into a hug with his

spare arm and slapping my back. 'Looking like shit as always.'

'Likewise, mate.'

The years have not been particularly kind to Rich. Whereas I like to think I'm maturing like a fine wine (ha), time seems to have dulled Rich's complexion, drawn deep crevices into his forehead and around his eyes, and added multiple pounds to his middle. He dyes his hair black – I'm fairly sure it went grey very early on although he's never admitted to that, claiming he's just going through his Goth phase.

'So what's brought this on, then? This sudden craving for nostalgia?' Rich sits down, lowering his bar stool, and then starts to tune his guitar.

'I don't know. I was watching those lads I've taken on and I just thought . . .'

'I heard them on Radio One the other day. Congrats, mate,' Rich interrupts.

'They sound all right, don't they?'

'A bit 5 Seconds of Summer, but it beats all the bloody R'n'B on the radio at the moment. If I hear that frigging "Happy" song one more time, I think I might shoot myself.'

'That would be ironic, wouldn't it?'

Rich laughs. 'In all seriousness, though, I definitely think they've got something. Good find.'

'Cheers. Not quite as lucky as Jimmy was to find us, but it beats getting a job in a supermarket.'

'Too right. That's how I feel about the wedding band. I mean, it's a bit soul-destroying when they make me play Shania Twain for the hundredth time, but at least I'm playing, right?'

'Absolutely.'

'Talking of playing, I didn't come here for a chat. Which one are we starting with? And don't say any of the ones off that bloody heartbreak album or I'll throw something at you.'

I smile, glad that it's been long enough that we can laugh about my epic mistake that was pouring all of my misery about losing Laura into an album. 'Shall we do "Enough For You"?'

Rich nods. 'I can handle that one.'

I count us in and then we start and even without Cody, for a while it feels like the old days and just singing and playing together is such a huge release, I wonder why it's taken us until now to do it. We tour through our various hits, the notes coming back to us automatically, like riding a bike. And I love every single second of it.

'Now *that* is a perfect egg.' Abby slides a fried egg on to my plate next to some granary toast covered in baked beans.

She's right. It *is* perfect. The yolk runny, the bottom without a trace of black.

'You're an eggspert.'

Abby rolls her eyes and then laughs.

'You not having one?'

She kisses me on the cheek. 'No, I haven't done my yoga yet. I'll have something after.'

'OK. Miss you.'

'I haven't gone yet.'

'Well, just the thought of you going makes me miss you.'

'You're a soppy bastard.' She fills her water bottle and then goes off to the conservatory where she always does her yoga and her workouts. I make myself a second coffee and then watch her from the dining room whilst reading *NME*.

'Be careful,' I call through. 'If you hold that downward dog for much longer, I'm not going to be able to resist coming in there.'

'You know I take my yoga very seriously,' she says, slightly short of breath. 'No interruptions.'

'Spoilsport.'

She glides into a standing position and smiles at me. '*After* yoga you might be in luck.'

'Sure you won't need to meditate then? Make yourself a spinach and ginseng smoothie?'

'Don't be jealous. Just because my body is a temple and yours is a cesspit.' Abby reaches to the sky, her top riding up to show her impeccably toned stomach. 'Now sod off. I can't concentrate with you watching me.'

'Too much of a temptation?'

'Not at all.'

I take my magazine out to the garden room and sit and read with my coffee. I love Abby's garden room. It's so restful looking out over her impeccable lawn, neatly planted borders, the wind chimes swaying in the tree, the little water feature that trickles away gently. I've become a sad old bastard, but there's nothing I like more than sitting here with my coffee in my hand, the heater on in the corner, the low-level sun coming through the glass, reading a magazine or listening to a podcast.

Once Abby's finished her yoga, she strolls down the garden with her water bottle in her hand and comes and sits on my knee and I wrap my arms around her.

'Want a sip of my coffee?' I say, holding it up.

She shakes her head.

'Too close to poison?'

She slaps the side of my thigh and takes a sip of her water. 'You know, I could get used to this.'

'What?'

'You, here. Waking up with you in my bed, afternoons sitting in here, followed by sex . . .'

'I'm sold. I'm not sure Seb would be too happy about it, though. Me ravaging his mother on the kitchen table.'

'That's our next location, is it?'

'Could be.'

'He'd get used to it though. Not the sex bit, of course. We'd have to be a bit more discreet with that. But you being here. Permanently, I mean.'

I don't speak and she turns her head to look at me. 'Sorry. Too soon?'

'Actually no. I'd really like that.'

We've been dating for less than a year but everything feels so easy with Abby – there's no stress, no drama. With the younger girls I dated, I always felt a bit like I had to put on an act. I mean, I'm only thirty-six, but it still felt like a gulf sometimes. Whereas Abby is more mature, also a divorcee. Well, not that Laura and I ever managed to make it down the aisle, but it felt like a marriage. And losing her has definitely felt like a divorce. Abby gets that I have baggage because she has her own, too. She wants the adventure she feels she missed out on by having children young. When I'm with her, it feels like starting afresh. Like I can be a totally new person.

'Really?'

'My only concern would be how Dylan would take it. Your place is tons nicer than mine but it's still his home. Well, one of his homes anyway. He's had a fair bit of moving around.'

'We could turn the spare bedroom into his room. He could help us decorate to make it feel more like his.'

I kiss her cheek. 'That's really sweet of you, but do you think Seb would be OK with it?'

Abby shrugs. 'He's eighteen. If the band takes off in the way it seems to be doing, he's not going to want to live here much longer. I love that boy with my whole being, but I need to live for me too now. I've not done that for eighteen years.'

'Yeah, I get that. I suppose the problem is I don't feel I've sacrificed *enough* for Dylan over the years. I always feel a little bit in debt.'

'You guys are super close.'

'I hope so. I just feel I didn't put him first enough at the beginning, so I really want to do that now. Can I sound it out with him first? Would that be OK?'

'Of course. You never have to check with me. I get that Dylan comes first. That was always part of the deal when we got together. I know that.'

'I love you,' I say into her ear.

She turns around and kisses me. 'I love you too.'

'Want to go and test out that kitchen table?'

Abby nods. 'I'll run in and shut the blinds.'

Then she scurries off inside and I follow her in.

I spot Laura drowning in the ball pool. Thea's next to her, sunk so low that it looks like there is a disembodied head sitting on top of the balls. I squeeze past a group of children, loudly fighting over who gets to ride on the large mechanical reindeer, until I'm close enough for Laura to hear me.

'Soft play? Really?'

'I know. It's hell on earth,' she shouts through the netted barrier. 'If I hear "I Wish it Could Be Christmas Everyday" one more time I think I might strangle myself with the tinsel that's adorning that tree so beautifully.' She nods towards the Christmas tree at the edge of the room – decorated with a single piece of tinsel, nearly bare, hanging off the side, about five baubles in total, all placed near the bottom, and an angel on top whose halo seems to have bent at a jaunty angle.

'Come on, you wouldn't want to ruin that tree. They've obviously put a great deal of care into decorating it.'

Laura smiles and then Thea starts to squeal as she sinks even further into the coloured balls so Laura pulls her out, posts her through the little gap where you exit the pool and I lift her out and place her next to me on the padded floor. Then Laura clambers out herself, slithering through the hole and landing on the floor on her tummy. 'Sadly it's the only place I can think to go on a rainy Wednesday after school where both a ten-year-old and a nearly three-year-old can be entertained for an hour,' she says, sitting up.

'True. What happened to the weather? It was glorious about an hour ago.'

Laura reties her shoelace, which has come undone. 'Sod's law, hey? I was looking forward to a birthday tea in the park. Instead, it's chicken nuggets in this dump.'

'Have you heard from Tom? Is Sarah OK?'

'She's out of surgery so they're just making sure she can eat and wee and stuff and then he'll bring her home.'

'Oh good. And how is she emotionally?'

'She's been better.' Laura goes over to help Thea get on to the first ledge to climb up to the big slide. Just as she does, Dylan comes charging past with Noah. 'Dylan, go up there with Thea, will you? I'm not sure I can fit.'

'Muuuum. Do I have to?'

'Yes, you do.' I tap Dylan on the back. 'Take her with you.'

Dylan sighs and then takes hold of Thea's hand, much to her delight. She adores Dylan. Whenever they're together, she just wants to follow him around.

Having passed on her duty for a few minutes, Laura comes back and sits beside me on one of the soft squishy blocks.

'She's absolutely gutted that she's not going to have any more children. She could've put it off a bit longer, but every time she feels a bit bloated or has pain or whatever, she's convinced she has ovarian cancer. She says it's ruining the time with the child she does have.'

'That's hard.'

'I think she's scared too. Of it coming back and of having *two* children that she has to leave behind.'

'The world's so fucking unfair, isn't it?'

'Certainly is. But then she's still here, so it's pretty amazing too.'

Dylan comes back, holding Thea out in front of him like she's a bomb that might detonate if he holds it too close to him.

'We want to go on the death slide and she's too little.'

'But she wants to be with you.' Laura takes Thea off Dylan, her bottom lip starting to tremble.

'Please, Mum. It *is* my birthday. I'll play with her again later, I promise.'

Laura lets out a groan. 'Fair enough. Go on then.'

Dylan and Noah run off at speed before Laura has a chance to change her mind and Laura places Thea down on the floor and kneels down so she's at her eyeline. 'Do you want me to go on the slides with you?'

Thea nods, her lip still wobbling.

'Shall we chase those cheeky boys?'

Suddenly Thea's face breaks into a smile. 'Yeah.'

'Come on then. Let's go.' She takes Thea's hand and then looks at me. 'The joys of being a godmother, hey? See you in a bit.'

She runs off with Thea and I wander over to the café and grab a coffee and a mince pie. It looks shop-bought so the three-pound price tag seems a bit excessive, but it *is* Christmas so it's got to be done. Every now and again, I'll spot Laura whizzing down the slide with Thea on her knee or Dylan and Noah running past followed by a giggling Thea with Laura close behind until suddenly they all appear beside me looking red-faced.

'I'm starving,' Dylan says, throwing himself on to a chair behind me, running his hand through his hair and making it stick up with sweat. Noah sits next to him and Thea climbs up and sits on the chair on his other side.

'Pizza?' I ask, getting down off the stool.

'Yes,' the boys cheer, followed by a mini-cheer from Thea.

I order the pizzas and a slushie each and take them over. The table is extremely quiet as the kids stuff their faces, except for the occasional slurping sound as they all try to suck up crushed ice through their straws.

'I reckon those slushies might actually be radioactive, you know? Look at the colour of them.'

Laura's right. They're supposed to be raspberry flavour but I've never seen a raspberry that colour in my life.

'Do you think Sarah might kill me for getting that for Thea?'

'It'll be fine. We just won't tell her,' Laura says, but when Thea takes the straw out of her mouth, I notice her lips are bright blue.

'I'm not sure we're getting away with that one.' I nod at Thea and everyone looks at her and laughs so she laughs too.

When we've taken a few years off the kids' lives by filling them with crap, Dylan and Noah run off for one more slide, but Thea sleepily climbs into Laura's lap and rests her head on her shoulder.

'You tired, gorgeous girl?' Laura gently strokes Thea's back and Thea nods. 'OK, my darling, you rest your head on me. We'll go home and see Mummy soon.'

Laura tucks Thea's hair behind her ear and then continues to stroke her back.

'Would you ever have another?' I ask her. She's such a natural, it seems a loss for her to only have one child, even though the thought of her having another child with someone else still makes me feel strange.

'I don't think so.'

'Sarah says you and Sam are finally dating.'

Laura shakes her head. 'I think Sarah would *like* us to be dating. But we're just going out for a meal. Tonight, actually, as you've got the boys at yours.'

Dylan and Noah charge back, take a sip of their slushies and then run off again.

'How about you and Abby?' she continues.

'Nah, we're happy as we are. We get to go out for dinner when we want, go to gigs, travel. I love having Dylan but I wouldn't want to do it all again.'

My phone keeps buzzing in my pocket and I pull it out to see it's Dad calling so I press cancel. He's called quite a few times since the night he basically told me he was too busy to see me, but I've never answered. Straight away, it starts buzzing again and I put it back in my pocket.

'You can answer it, you know?'

'Oh, it's just the yearly message from Dad.'

'There wasn't a present this year.'

'He sent it to mine. Mum must have told him Dylan was staying with me tonight.'

'That's sweet. You know, I could take Dylan to meet him if you didn't feel up to seeing him?'

'Thanks, but no, it's OK. So, what's going on in your life at the moment anyway?' I ask and I think Laura can tell that I need to change the subject. 'I feel like I haven't spoken to you properly in ages.'

'I guess our lives have sort of gone in different directions.'

'I guess so.'

'I do actually have some news.'

It's odd, but I feel nervous about what she's going to say. 'Oh, yeah?'

'Remember that homework you set me, last year when we were in Lapland – to figure out a career that I'd feel passionate about?'

'Yes. Have you?'

'I remembered how magical it was sharing Thea's birth with Sarah, how fulfilled it made me feel. So I'm going to uni. To train to become a midwife.'

'Wow, that's amazing.'

'Mum isn't too impressed. After all the grief she gave me about not fulfilling my potential, then I finally suggest doing something I thought she'd be pleased about and it's all, "what about Dylan?", "it's such long shifts", et cetera, et cetera. But I need something for me.'

'Of course you do. I can help out with Dylan. Don't let your mum put you off.'

'I'm terrified, but I've played it safe all my life. And with Sarah getting sick and everything . . . well, I just realized I don't want my life to pass me by. And now that Dylan's getting older, he doesn't need me in the same way he used to, so it seemed like the perfect time.'

'Absolutely. When do you start?'

'Next September. So I've got some time to get Dylan sorted. Anyway, talking of careers, I heard Partners in Crime on Radio One the other day. Congratulations. I was jumping up and down in the kitchen, so goodness knows how you must have felt.'

'Thank you. I may have let out a small squeal.'

'I'm sure they're going to be huge.'

'I hope so. They're working really hard, so they deserve it.'

'You sound like a proud dad.'

'I know. What happened to me?' I put my head in my hands dramatically and Laura laughs.

'It'll be Ovaltine and slippers at bedtime soon.'

'I got excited about the purchase of a coffee maker the other day. Sad times.'

'Oh, I'm fully on board with all that. Being in bed by nine with a hot chocolate and a good book is the sign of a great night to me these days.'

'What do you mean, "these days"?' I tease.

'Bugger off. We can't all spend our lives partying like it's 1999.'

'Talking of the old days, I saw Rich this morning. We had a little play together.'

'A little play together?' Laura raises an eyebrow.

'Of our guitars. I would've said a jamming session, but I know you'd only take the piss. Anyway, my point was, it was so much fun.'

'You should start writing again. You're a brilliant songwriter.'

'I don't know. That last album . . .'

'I thought it was beautiful.'

'So did I,' a voice says, and I'm shocked to see Abby. For some strange reason, I feel like I've been caught out.

Abby leans over the table and shakes hands with Laura. 'Nice to finally meet you, Laura. I'm Abby.'

'Nice to meet you too,' Laura says quietly.

'Where's Dylan?' Abby asks.

'Oh, he's chasing around somewhere.'

'And this must be Thea.' Abby gives Thea a warm smile and Thea buries her head even further into Laura's shoulder.

'I think she's tired and probably missing her mummy.' Laura checks her phone. 'In fact, we should probably be going soon. OK for you guys to take over now?'

'Of course. We'll probably get going ourselves in a minute. Give my love to Sarah, yeah?'

'I will do.'

Just as Laura finishes packing her bag, Dylan and Noah come running over. 'Can we have some candyfloss? They only sell it here at Christmas.'

'Hello, Abby. Nice to see you,' I prompt.

'Hello, Abby.' Dylan goes over and gives her a hug and I catch Laura staring at them.

'Hello, you,' Abby says, rubbing her knuckles on his hair. 'I've got a giant cake for you at home.'

'Awesome.'

'And your dad and I have got a Mario Kart tournament lined up. You know I'm never going to let you knock me off the leaderboard.'

Dylan laughs. 'We'll see about that.'

Laura stands up, Thea on her hip, and swings her rucksack on to her back. 'Right, I best be off. Nice to meet you, Abby.' Then she comes round to our side of the table and Dylan wraps his arm around her.

'Love you, Mummy. See you after school tomorrow.'

'Will do. Happy birthday, gorgeous.' Laura kisses Dylan on the top of his head. It won't be long until he's as tall as her.

'Has Luke asked you about Christmas?' Abby asks, just as Laura starts to go, and I wish she hadn't because I would have liked to have spoken to her about it first.

Laura turns back to us and shakes her head.

'We thought we'd have it at mine this year. My house is a bit nicer than Luke's.' Abby laughs. 'Would you like to join us?'

'Um, well, I better check what my parents are doing, but thank you for the invite. It sounds lovely.'

'Well, they are welcome too. The more the merrier.'

I know I should be grateful to Abby for being so welcoming, but I can see how uncomfortable Laura feels.

'I'll ask them. Thank you.'

'No problem.' Abby smiles at Laura and then puts her arm around Dylan. 'Right, did someone say something about candyfloss?'

And all of a sudden, Laura's gone.

LAURA

When we get to Sarah's, Thea charges through the house looking for her.

'Where's Mummy?'

Tom grabs her on her run through the lounge. 'Hey monkey, what about me?'

'Aunty Laura said Mummy is home.' She looks distraught, and I wonder how much the past couple of years have affected her. I know Sarah has tried her best to keep Thea sheltered from it, but I wonder if bits have filtered through.

'She is. But she's very tired and sore, so you can go up and see her but you must be really gentle, OK? No jumping on her, and you might have to save the cuddles for a couple of days.'

'Mummy said just side cuddles.'

'Well, sounds like Mummy has it sorted as usual. You're very lucky to have such a super mummy, aren't you?'

Thea runs off upstairs and when I really look at Tom, I can see he's exhausted.

'How is she?'

'Oh, you know, "I'm in a *little* bit of pain" meaning she's in agony.'

'Yep, that's our Sarah.'

'It makes me so angry I could scream.' It's very rare for Tom to show any emotion so I know Sarah must be in a bad way.

'Watching her in pain,' he continues. 'Plus, not being able to give Thea a brother or sister . . . I know she feels guilty for her decision. I keep telling her it's more important to me that she eliminates some of her worry, but I know she feels she's let me down.'

'I know.'

Tom automatically makes me a cup of tea, adding half a sugar and then handing it to me.

'And the truth is I *am* gutted about Thea being an only child.' He pauses. 'Sorry, I mean Dylan clearly hasn't suffered for it, but it would've been nice to experience it all again, you know?'

I give him a sad smile. 'I think this might be the most you've ever opened up to me. It's only taken you about twenty years.'

'I'm sorry about that. I guess growing up I was taught that you don't complain, you stand strong.' He says it in a haughty voice that I guess is reminiscent of his parents.

I take a sip of my tea. 'I think you have a right to complain right now. I think it would be entirely justified if you totally fell apart.'

Tom shakes his head. 'I can't do that. I think she's worse this time than she was with the cancer, with the mastectomy and everything. Maybe it's all just suddenly hitting her, I don't know. Will you try to get her to open up about it all?'

'Of course I'll try.'

'She wouldn't have survived it without you – emotionally, I mean. Thank you for always holding her. I feel totally useless through it all.'

'Trust me, I feel totally useless too. You are her rock, I promise you that.'

Tom smiles and for the first time ever his eyes look teary, and I'm terrified he's going to start crying because I have no idea what I'd do with that. But then Thea comes running down and Tom immediately paints on a smile and opens his arms wide for her to jump into them. 'Hot chocolate with whipped cream?'

'Yey.'

'I'll go and see her.'

'Thank you,' Tom mouths and then starts spooning hot chocolate into a mug with Thea still under one arm.

When I get into Sarah's bedroom, she's got the blind down and she's propped up in bed, the quilt up to her chin.

'Feeling like shit?'

Sarah winces and then shuffles her position slightly. 'They pump you full of air and it makes your shoulder hurt. Weird, hey?'

I sit down on the side of her bed and take her hand. 'And mentally? Don't just say you're fine.'

'The heady mix of morphine and codeine has removed my filter, you'll be glad to know. Or not, as it may be, when I spew out all my twisted crap.'

'I'm all about the twisted crap. That's what I'm here for.'

'I wish I hadn't done it,' Sarah blurts out. 'That I'd not been so neurotic and listened to the doctors and waited until I was forty.'

'Oh, Sar.'

'I wanted a big family. Three to four kids.'

'Come on. Four kids is a circus, not a family.'

I'm pleased to see a slight smile on Sarah's lips but then her face quickly falls again. 'But then we had those fertility issues so it messed up the timeline. If we'd tried again and then it had taken ages and we'd had to make the nightmare decision of whether to stop trying and have the op, or carry on putting me at risk of ovarian cancer . . .'

'It would have been an impossible dilemma.'

'And now when I think of a newborn, all I can think about is Thea screaming as I had to stop feeding her overnight, Thea lying in our bedside cot whilst I lay there feeling sick from the chemo – I still get the smell of it in my nose sometimes, you know?'

It feels incredibly important that I don't speak, that I just allow Sarah to finally offload.

'I would've felt guilty that I couldn't breastfeed,' she continues. 'And on the other hand I would've felt guilty that the new baby didn't have its first year ruined by cancer in the same way as Thea did. And every day I would've been stressing about fucking malignant cells growing whilst I wasn't paying attention so I wouldn't have enjoyed any of it anyway.'

'From a totally selfish point of view, I'm glad that you've hugely reduced your risk. Forty to sixty percent is too high a chance for my liking.'

Suddenly, Sarah starts to cry. 'Why did I have to have the gene? It feels like a curse. I know lots of people have lots worse to contend with, but . . .'

'Say it, Sarah. It's not fucking fair. I know there are children starving in Africa and war-torn lands. I get that we are fortunate in a lot of ways. But you are absolutely right to feel angry about this. It's not fair and you don't deserve it for a second and it is really shit.'

'Thank you. For not thinking I'm an ungrateful, whining "woe is me" misery.'

'Fucking hell, Sarah. If I were you, I'd hate the entire world. I do hate the world. I hate the world for you.'

'Don't do that.'

'I'm trying not to.'

Sarah shuffles down the bed and rests her head on the pillow. She suddenly looks exhausted.

'Do you want me to leave you to rest?'

'You're going to slate me for being an awful feminist,' Sarah continues as if she didn't hear me. 'But I feel like I'm no longer a woman. First my breasts, and now my ability to make babies. I feel so broken, so ugly.'

'Your breasts and your ovaries don't make you a woman, Sar.'

'I know, I know. I know it's wrong of me to feel this way, but I do.'

'It's not *wrong* of you. But when I look at you, I see a beautiful woman – strong, compassionate, selfless – those are all the things that make you a woman – not ovaries or breasts.'

Sarah lowers her eyes. 'We haven't had sex since the mastectomy. Nearly *a year and a half*. How terrible is that?'

'Maybe you're just not ready yet. That's perfectly OK, you know? I'm sure Tom understands.'

'Oh, he's super understanding, which just makes it worse. He says I'm just as beautiful as ever but he hasn't seen me naked. I lock the door when I have a shower, wear a top in bed.'

'Why haven't you told me about this?'

'Because I'm ashamed.'

'Oh Sar. You have nothing to be ashamed about.'

She pauses and then sits up in bed, a sense of urgency about her. 'Will you look?'

'Look?'

'Look at me naked. Tell me what you think. The truth, though. You have to promise you'll tell me the truth – the first thing that springs into your mind – shock, disgust – you promise you'll tell me.'

'I'm not going to be disgusted . . .'

'Promise. Or I will never tell you again when an outfit doesn't suit you and you'll be plagued with bad fashion choices for life.'

'My choices are not that bad.'

'You need my help sometimes,' Sarah jokes and although I'm scared that she'll sense my reaction, whatever it may be, and that it will upset her, I know that I have to do this for her.

'OK.'

'Total honesty.'

'OK.'

She uses her arms to push herself up and I can see the pain that she's in. I help her out of bed and she shuffles over to the floor-length mirror on her wall and then slowly struggles out of her joggers, keeping her knickers on.

'Will you help me with my top?'

I pull her T-shirt over her head and throw it on the bed and she stands there in just her knickers staring at the mirror before turning around to face me. At first my eyes are drawn to the see-through pads on the brand-new cuts around her pelvis, her tummy swollen from the gas that's been pumped into it. And then I let my eyes move up towards her chest, nervous about how I might feel to see my friend without her breasts – the breasts we've always so openly shown each other, from the early days when she

332

developed much sooner than me and I wanted to know what real boobs looked like, to our huge, swollen pregnancy breasts, our cracked-nipple breastfeeding breasts. But when I see her, the neat scars already starting to fade to a pale pink, I'm so glad that I don't have to pretend, not even slightly.

'You look beautiful.'

Sarah looks down at herself and then back up at me. 'You said you'd be honest.'

I move towards her and put my hands on her upper arms. 'I swear to God you look beautiful. I can't explain it. It's like without the distraction of breasts, I can see how gorgeous the tone of your skin is, your collar bone, and that stunning face of yours.'

Sarah starts to cry. 'You really mean it?'

'Look into my eyes and tell me whether I'm being honest with you. You see every emotion, even when I'm trying to hide it.'

'There's some sadness there.'

I smile. 'There is. Of course there is. Because looking at your scars, it hits me how much you've been through. I thought I knew but I'm not sure I really did. You're so strong and brave, you make it all seem like a walk in the park, but bloody hell . . .'

Along with her scars, you can see the slight discoloration of her skin on the one side, the cancer side, exactly where the radiotherapy blasted her.

She reaches over and grabs her T-shirt and I help her to put it back on and then sit back down on the bed.

'Thank you so much,' she says.

'I expect Tom will be thanking me soon too.'

She laughs and it makes me so happy. 'I couldn't have done any of this without you.'

'Trust me, I couldn't do anything without you.'

She climbs back into bed and pulls the cover over her and then taps the space beside her. 'There's one more thing I need to talk to you about.'

I snuggle in beside her, feeling suddenly terrified that she's going to tell me her cancer is back.

'What is it?'

'You know you're Thea's godmother?'

Sarah had Thea christened earlier this year. She doesn't go to church but she's always had a faith. It was a perfect day. It was March so it wasn't hot, but it stayed dry, and Thea looked adorable in the white embroidered dress Sarah had bought for her. She chose Luke to be godfather and it felt a little strange us posing for photos together, Sarah's gorgeous baby girl between us, a picture of how things might have been.

'Well, I was adding Thea to my will the other day . . .'

'Sarah.'

'It would be irresponsible not to have something in place, Laur. Anyway, I was thinking about who I would want to look after her if anything happened to me and Tom, and I was going to put Mum, but then I thought . . . well, I'd rather it was you. If you're happy with that, that is? It's perfectly fine to say no. I know you already have a lot on your plate with Dylan.'

'But nothing's going to happen to you.'

'I know, but if it did . . . Just think about it, will you?'

'Are you sure you want to ask me? I'm disaster mum compared to you.'

Sarah is the mum I wish I was. She always brings healthy snacks for Thea, usually lovingly made by her own fair hands. She doesn't allow Thea any screen time but she doesn't preach about it. She's always got some creative activity set up in every corner of her house – sensory play in the kitchen, arts and crafts in the dining room, construction and learning tools in the lounge.

'Are you crazy? Look at Dylan. If Thea turns out half as well as him, I'll be happy.'

'He's not bad.'

'He's *awesome*.'

'I'd do it in a heartbeat. Of course I would. But I won't need to, because you and Tom are going to be there.'

'Will you help him for me? If I'm not there? He's fantastic, but I think a girl needs a woman's touch. And not just any woman. A strong, badass woman like you.'

I put my hand on her arm. 'She's going to have a strong, badass woman called *you*. It's gone, Sar. That bastard cancer is gone.'

'I know. But if it comes back. I know you think I'm being morbid, but it gives me comfort to think she'd have you as a replacement mum. I mean, I'd rather you didn't sleep with Tom, but I'd want you to be here, all the time, like a real mum. And if that means you and Tom ending up together, I'd rather that than Thea not having you every day.'

'This conversation is getting seriously twisted – you do realize that, don't you?'

'You know what I mean.'

'I do. But for the record, I will never sleep with Tom. As much as I love him, it'd be like having sex with my brother.

And besides, you're going to be with him until you're both grey and old, so that just makes it even more weird because you'd be in the bed with us.'

Although she forces a smile, I can see that she's not completely reassured by my response.

'I don't want to even imagine a hypothetical time when you're not there,' I continue.

'I know. But I need you to. Just for now, and then I promise I'll never mention it again if you don't want me to.'

I turn to face her. 'If anything were to happen to you, which *it's not going to*, I would see Thea every single day. I would teach her to tie her shoelaces, and I'd plait her hair, and I'd read her all the best books about superhero women who never give up on their dreams, and I'd make sure that she respects her body and knows how beautiful she is, that she never feels she has to change for anyone, especially not a partner, that she always seeks adventure. And most of all, I'd tell her about her mummy every single day, about how she was the best person I've ever known in my life.'

Sarah wipes at the tears on her cheeks and I lean forward and hold her.

'Now we're not playing any more of your hypothetical games, OK? They stink.'

Sarah sits back and smiles through the tears, but this time it's a proper smile, her beautiful smile that lights up her eyes. 'I love you.'

'I love you too.'

I'm not sure if it's a date or not. Sam and I see each other a lot, but it's never on our own and we've certainly never been out for dinner unless Pizza Hut with the boys counts.

But when I told him Dylan had asked whether Noah could have a sleepover with him at Luke's, Sam suggested we go out and get some food together, so here we are. We've just finished our main courses and are waiting for our desserts.

'I'm sorry. I thought it would be quieter than this in the week.'

The restaurant is packed – great long tables of people all wearing party hats and pulling crackers and talking in overly loud voices to colleagues they probably barely speak to for the rest of the year.

'The joy of eating out in December.'

'So, I forgot to ask, how was the party? Did Dylan freak out when you explained the PlayStation was a joint birthday and Christmas present?'

I smile. 'He was actually pretty good about it. I did feel a bit bad, as Luke and I always made a promise that we'd never do the whole combined-present thing. It's shit enough having your birthday so close to Christmas. But then he went and asked for a three-hundred-pound present, so he only has himself to blame really.'

'Does he still believe?'

'In the big FC? I think so. But I think this could be the last year.'

'Yeah, same as Noah.'

'Sad, isn't it?'

Sam holds out a cracker. 'Want to pull my cracker?'

'I'd be delighted.'

I yank it as hard as I can and am glad when I win. I take out the gift (a mini-ruler) and then retrieve the joke.

'Ready for this?'

Sam nods.

'What do you call buying a piano for the holidays?'

Sam strokes his chin. 'Hmm, I don't know. Tell me.'

'Christmas Chopin,' I read. 'I don't get it.'

'Christmas shopping,' Sam explains.

'Oh. But it's pronounced show-pan, not bloody shoppin'.'

'I'm not sure they were worried about being that precise.'

'Well, they should be.'

Sam laughs and then the waitress arrives with our puddings – a chocolate brownie for me and sticky toffee pudding for Sam.

'Looks amazing. Thanks for suggesting this. It's been so nice to have a meal cooked for me for once.'

'You're welcome. And I'll cook for you anytime. You only have to ask.'

'Thank you.'

'So did you tell Luke about the midwife thing?'

'Yeah. He was really supportive. Happy to help out with Dylan.'

'That's good. You guys are still close, aren't you? Going on holiday together last year and stuff? Sam and I are like total strangers now.'

'Luke and I aren't really close any more. I suppose it's different now he's settled with Abby. I mean, it shouldn't be different. We were only friends anyway. But I guess he's busy with Partners in Crime so, rightly, his little free time is spent with her.'

'Have you met her yet?'

I nod. 'This afternoon, actually. She seems nice. Good for him.'

Sam goes quiet, eating mouthfuls of his dessert in quick

succession. Then he puts down his spoon. 'So, it's definitely over between you then?'

'Of course it is. It's been over for years.'

'I know, but when I've seen you together and when you talk about him, I don't know – it's always felt like there's unfinished business between you.'

I shake my head, despite always feeling that's exactly how it is. Well, until now, that is. It's how I know he's happy with Abby – there's no longer that feeling between us when I'm with him, not from his side anyway. 'It's definitely over.'

Sam smiles subtly and then picks his spoon back up and finishes his dessert. I do the same and then we pay the bill.

'Want to walk back to mine and then I can call you a taxi from there?'

I picture my empty house, the silence, and then I picture Dylan playing Mario Kart with Abby and Luke, the sound of laughter filling the room.

'Yeah, sure.'

We lie in bed not talking, a noticeable gap between us. I want to put on my clothes, but I know I can't do so without looking rude. I knew it would feel odd – it's been five years. *Five years.* Luke's body is the only man's body I can recall in any detail, his touch the only one I can remember, but I didn't expect to have to stop halfway through, Sam noticing the tears in my eyes.

'I know it's a cliché, but it's honestly me and not you.'

Sam laughs. 'Nice guys always finish last, right?'

'It's not like that at all. I actually think in a different time you're exactly what I would choose. But I just don't feel . . .'

I'm about to say ready and then realize how utterly

ridiculous that would sound. How can I not be ready after five years?

'You know, I mean this in the nicest possible way, but if you really do believe he's moved on then maybe you should allow yourself to as well.'

'It's not that.'

'Come on, Laura. I credit myself with a fair bit of emotional intelligence. In fact, I shouldn't have invited you back, but I guess I wanted to believe I was wrong.'

I feel like such an idiot when I sense my eyes filling with tears again, but I can't help the truth spilling out of my mouth. 'I wish I knew how to move on.'

I get the feeling Sam would cuddle me if we weren't still naked, but instead he turns on to his side to face me. 'You need to allow yourself to feel something for someone again. And of course the wisest option would be to let that person be me.' He smiles. 'But either way just allow yourself.'

I lean towards him and kiss him. And even though it might not end up going any further, right now it's exactly what I need.

16th December 2016

LUKE

I scribble out the words in my notebook and try again. Ever since I've been travelling with the lads, I've had this restlessness, an itch I can't quite scratch. And I know exactly what it is. When I see them up on the stage, the crowd singing their songs – I want that to be me again. I know I'm probably too old and I'm sure the songs I'm writing will never see the light of day, but it's felt good to be creating again.

I've been trying to get the song I'm working on today right for weeks. I've got the melody sorted; that's been the easy bit. But the *lyrics*. For some strange reason all the songs I write seem to end up being about Laura. I don't know why, as I never even see her any more. She's busy with her midwifery course and works odd hours. And I'm away a lot with Seb and the boys, so we have to carefully schedule our time around who's having Dylan and it means we've become ships that pass in the night. But it's like my subconscious is holding on to something I worked hard to let go of some time ago and it just seems to spill out when I'm writing.

I put down my pad of paper and go downstairs to see Abby, who is in the kitchen drinking a very green smoothie and listening to a podcast.

'I'm just not sure it's right to be drinking something the colour of cut grass,' I tease her.

She holds up her finger to her mouth. 'Shh. Listen. He's right, isn't he? We don't need all this *stuff* in our lives. We're drowning in it.'

I look around at Abby's kitchen – it still doesn't quite feel like *our* kitchen yet, even though I've been living here for nearly nine months – and I wouldn't say it feels like we're exactly *drowning* in stuff. There's nothing out on the surfaces except for the kettle and toaster, a utensils jar and a single wooden reindeer that she allowed me to put out on the shelf above the breakfast bar, all the other reindeers in my collection being relegated to a cardboard box in the loft. There are a few subtle abstract paintings on the walls – sort of imitation Rothkos (Abby's) – and a row of three red pillar candles on the windowsill. On the dining table, Abby's created this classy centrepiece – all fresh greenery and berries – but other than that it's positively *bare*.

'Shall we have a huge throw-out? You've got all those CDs in the study that are practically obsolete now. I've still got a load of Seb's stuff from when he was younger that needs to go. He doesn't even live here any more and I've still got boxes of his Meccano and Lego clogging up the shelves in his room.'

'But Dylan likes playing with those when he stays. Couldn't we just move them into his room?'

'Oh yes, of course, sorry. If he'd like them, he's welcome to them.'

Abby is wonderful with Dylan. When I moved in, she spent a whole weekend with him decorating his room to make it feel like his. She took him down to B&Q to choose the paint and treated him to extras like a Minecraft lamp he wanted and a brightly coloured Lego brick rug. She never tried to inflict her own tastes on him, arguing that his space should be a reflection of him, not her. But sometimes, just sometimes, it feels a bit like she's playing the part of perfect stepmother. Occasionally, I think I see a fleck of resentment in her eyes when we talk about him, or maybe not resentment but the sense that me having a young son is a bit *inconvenient*. But if I ever challenged her on it, I know she'd be distraught that I would ever think that of her.

'But your stuff – we've not really had a proper sort-out since you moved in, have we? I'll get rid of loads of my stuff too. It'll be freeing, don't you think?'

She looks so motivated that I can't bring myself to tell her that, actually, I like my 'stuff' – my hardback books that impractically take up tons of room on the shelf and that I will never read again, my CDs full of music that I could just stream, my old clothes that I'll never choose to put on but that have sentimental value because they remind me of the gig I wore them for or the holiday or one of the million other little moments that make up a life.

'Yeah, sure.'

'Great. Maybe when I'm back from my classes we could get started.'

Abby teaches yoga four days a week to, in her words, 'wealthy women who want to look like they're doing something useful with their time'. To her, yoga is a very serious and challenging practice so these people who just turn up with no intention to break out a sweat drive her mad.

'Sure. Just remember I've got to get Dylan from school and hold on to him until Laura finishes her shift. I think she's promised to take him to the Lego store once she's finished. But I can go through some of my stuff after that.'

'The Lego store? But that's miles. Can't she just order online?'

'Laura promised she'd take him. He wants to go in and actually choose something for his birthday. You know how particular he is.'

'She's a good mum, isn't she? I'm not sure I would've been that dedicated. Especially after a tiring shift.'

It's one of those fake compliments she often gives Laura. Ever since Laura turned down Abby's offer of spending Christmas with us last year, it's been a bit frosty between them. They're always civil with each other when Laura drops Dylan off or picks him up, but I don't think there's much love lost between them.

'Possibly making a rod for her own back, though,' she adds, finishing her oddly green smoothie and gathering the things she needs for her classes. She digs around in the freezer and gets some sort of nut roast out, putting it on a plate to defrost. 'I'll prepare you a nice meal this evening before that son of mine steals you away from me again.'

'Sounds great. Thank you.'

I'm off to Amsterdam tomorrow followed by a couple of other dates in the Netherlands and then on to Belgium before returning home the day after Boxing Day.

'I better send you off with some nutrients in your system, hadn't I? I know you'll be living on burgers for the next ten days whilst you're away.'

'I'll ask for extra gherkins.'

Abby smiles. 'We still on for Las Vegas at the end of the month? I thought we could book something tonight?'

'Definitely. It'll be a cool way to bring in the new year.'

'We could always go crazy and get married there.'

I laugh but then look at Abby and, from the expression on her face, I wonder if she's serious.

'OK, maybe not in Las Vegas,' she continues. 'I'm not sure that's really us. But we *could* get married. I mean, it's 2016, I can get away with asking you, can't I?'

'*Are* you asking me?'

'Well, we're not spring chickens any more, are we? I love you and I do want to spend the rest of my life with you so yes, I guess I am.'

I look at my hands, struggling to meet her eyes. 'Well, this is unexpected. Especially today.'

I can't help thinking of my two proposals to Laura, the wedding date I cocked up.

'Sorry. It's Dylan's day today, isn't it? Let's talk about it another time.'

'I'm not saying that. I . . .'

My phone rings so I pick it up off the worktop. 'Sorry, it's Mum. One minute.'

As soon as I answer the phone, I can hear that Mum is crying. Her words are garbled, rushed, things in the wrong order so it's hard to make sense of what she's saying. But I get enough of the gist.

'I'll go now.'

I put the phone down and Abby looks at me expectantly. 'What is it?'

'It's my dad,' I say. 'He's had a heart attack.'

As soon as I enter Dad's hospital room, it feels like my throat's constricting and I'm struggling to breathe. A woman, who I'm guessing is Sandy, is facing the window, rearranging flowers in a vase. Dad's wired up to all sorts of machines. He looks so much slighter than I remember him.

'So this is what I had to do to get you to come and see me?' Dad's voice is strained, quiet, but he has a hint of a smile on his face.

Sandy turns around. 'Oh, hi Luke. It's lovely to meet you.' She comes and gives me a hug and I'm not sure how to respond so I just stand there like a board. I can't help examining her, wondering what she has that Mum didn't. She's nowhere near as attractive as Mum but she has a sweet, girl-next-door face and there's a warmth that radiates off her. 'Well, I'll go and get some coffees. Give you two time to catch up.'

'Thanks, love,' Dad says, and Sandy puts her hand on his and then leaves the room.

'How are you?' I say, sitting in the chair beside Dad.

'I've been better.' Dad smiles and it's the face of my childhood. He was always smiling. 'But I'm not going to die if that's what you mean. Not yet anyway.'

'I'm so sorry,' I say. 'For blanking your calls.'

He shakes his head or attempts to but then thinks better of it. 'I'm the one who should be sorry.'

'The past is in the past. Don't trouble yourself about that now. I've been an idiot for holding on to it for so long.'

'I meant for having a heart attack on your son's birthday. That's a bit shit of me.'

'Oh. Well, it could've been worse. It could've been Christmas Day.'

'True. You always did love Christmas.'

'That was your influence, I think. You must have been

the only dad in the world who actually woke his kid up on Christmas morning.'

'I was excited to see if Santa had been.'

We both laugh and then Dad sounds breathless and I start to panic. 'Are you OK?'

'Yeah, I'm OK.' Dad pushes himself a bit further up the pillow so he's slightly more upright. 'Look, son. Before we go any further, I totally get why you blanked my calls. I should've bitten your hand off when you offered to meet up.'

'It doesn't matter now,' I say, waving away his concern.

'Things with Sandy weren't good at the time. We'd just had a massive argument about the twins and she was hassling me to get off the phone because she thought it was a work call and I'd promised to spend the day giving my undivided attention to her and the kids. But I never want you to think that it was because I didn't want to hear from you.' Dad looks directly into my eyes. 'I have always wanted to see you, Luke.'

'I know.'

'No, you don't. And it's the truth.'

I look away because I'm scared I'm about to cry.

'And you were right what you said that afternoon – I never should've given up on trying to get in touch with you. You were just a kid.'

I quickly wipe at my cheeks. 'Let's just put it behind us, OK? I want you in my life. In Dylan's life. That's all that matters now.'

'Maybe it was worth having a heart attack after all, then.'

The guilt makes my chest feel so tight it feels like *I'm* having a heart attack. And then Sandy comes back in carrying a coffee.

'I just need to make a phone call. I'll be back.'

I leave the room for a breather, sitting on a chair outside and checking my phone. There's a message from Abby to say she'll collect Dylan from school but before I reply, I find Laura's name and press call. It rings and rings but she doesn't answer, so I put the phone down and try again. Still nothing, so I leave her a message to tell her what's happened. It's weird to think she's in the women's centre on the other side of the hospital. I can't help longing for her to be here.

Then I look up to see Mum walking towards me carrying a bunch of flowers. I immediately jump up and give her a hug.

'I'm so glad you came,' she says as we release and sit down. 'Have you been in yet?'

'Yeah. He looks quite weak but he's OK.'

'Good.'

'You know Sandy is in there, don't you? Is she going to be OK with you being here?'

Mum waves her hand. 'Oh, we're all friends.'

'Really? So, it's just me that's held on to the grudge all these years.'

'I did tell you I was past it all, Luke.'

'I know. I just didn't realize it was *that* cosy.'

Mum laughs. 'Don't be silly. It's not exactly cosy, but we're fine. It was a long, long time ago.'

I nod and then I feel my eyes filling with tears. 'I've wasted so much time, Mum.'

I think Mum hears the emotion in my voice because she looks at me and then wraps her arms around me and I sob into her shoulder. 'Oh, Luke. It's OK. It's OK.'

LAURA

The woman that I'm helping to look after was making all the right noises and I was hopeful that today was going to be my day, but I've just examined her and she's still only three centimetres dilated. I can't believe it. I need to start ticking off some births on this placement, but it's like the babies sense me and think, bloody hell, I'm not coming out on her shift.

I finish at three today. Luke said he'd get Dylan from school and then I've promised him I'll take him to the Lego store because he wants to choose his birthday present. I look at the clock. A quarter past two. Unless my lady gets a move on, it's going to be yet another birth that I just closely miss out on. I mean, I love the rest of it. Getting to know the women. Supporting them through their excitement and anxiety. And afterwards – visiting the babies and seeing how they turn lives upside down but in the very best way. But I just want to experience the birth bit again like I did with Sarah. The magic of sharing that with someone. It is the reason I wanted to get into the profession in the first place after all.

'I was hoping room six was going to be my first birth,' I say to Heidi, the midwife I'm shadowing. She is amazing at her job but I get the sense I'm a bit of an inconvenience to her and she'd rather just get on with it without having to teach me stuff.

'You might be lucky. I don't think she's far off. Sometimes they go from three to ten really quickly, especially as it's her second baby. You can always stay on a bit later?'

'It's my son's birthday. He was asleep when I left this morning so I haven't seen him yet, and I promised I'd take him to the Lego store so he can choose his gift. We've not been yet and he's desperate to go. He wants to do this "pick a brick" thing or something.'

'Well, it's up to you.'

I can tell by the way she says it that she thinks I lack commitment. Her children are all grown up but she often tells me she made sure they understood that they didn't automatically come first just because she'd given birth to them. I admire her in a way – that ability to put herself at the top of her to-do list guilt-free – because as much as I am loving the training, I feel terrible that I'm not there for Dylan as much. That I can no longer help out on every school trip or always be there to greet him at the end of a hard day at school. Often I'm not even there to put him to bed. So there's no way I'm breaking the promise I made him and missing his birthday.

'Thank you for the offer though.'

We wander along the ward, Heidi supporting a mother who is in tears because she can't get her baby to latch on, and it takes me back to the early days with Dylan – after the ease of the initial few attempts, every feed became a battle and I can still remember the shame and anguish I felt at struggling to do something that was supposed to come so naturally. Heidi takes the woman's baby and rocks him gently, calming both mother and baby down so that they can have another attempt at feeding. With Heidi's help, the woman manages to get her baby to feed, a wave of relief and gratitude flooding her face.

Another one of the midwives catches us as we continue our rounds. 'I know you're desperate to see a birth, Laura. I think you might be in luck. Things are progressing quickly in room six.'

I check my watch. It's twenty minutes until the end of my shift. Maybe, just maybe if I stay a tiny bit late, I might get to see my first birth.

We hurry along to room six where the mother (Louise) is on all fours panting heavily. Heidi kneels down beside her.

'Try to breathe a little more deeply,' Heidi says, demonstrating a few deep, slow breaths. 'Use the gas and air, if you want, to just ease you through each contraction.'

'I can't bloody ease through them,' Louise shouts and then she says, 'Sorry. I'm just so fucking angry that bastard has left me to do this all on my own.'

'It's OK. I understand. I won't take anything you say in the midst of labour personally.'

Louise manages a smile but then her face contorts with pain and she yells out as another contraction comes over her. Heidi stands up and goes across the room to grab something, probably the Doppler.

'I can't do it. I can't do it,' Louise yells as the contraction begins to pass and she can manage to form words. 'I don't want to do it alone.'

And then she starts to sob and there's something so infantile about her that I want to reach out and take her in my arms. Instead, I kneel down beside her.

'You're not alone. We're here, OK? And we're not going anywhere.'

'Promise?' she says, looking up into my eyes.

'Promise.'

And then another contraction comes that makes her arms give way so that her head touches the floor, her bum stuck up in the air.

'I can't do it.'

'You haven't got a choice, darling,' Heidi calls over. 'But as Laura says, you are definitely not alone.'

She smiles at me, and I hope that perhaps I've said the right thing, that she thinks I'm doing OK.

We support Louise through her contractions and then suddenly she starts tearing off the baggy T-shirt she's been wearing and howling. 'I think I need to push.'

'OK, go with it,' Heidi says. 'Whatever your body is telling you to do, just go with it.'

Louise grabs the gas and air and starts puffing on it frantically.

'Try to slow your breathing down just a bit, darling. Baby needs you to be getting enough oxygen.'

Louise doesn't seem to hear as she continues with her short, quick breaths until she's nearly hyperventilating. I get down in front of her so that our eyes are level and model how to breathe, squeezing her hand every time I want her to take a deep breath in. It takes a few moments but gradually her breathing starts to slow and then she growls again, her whole body tightening with the force of her push.

This goes on for quite some time before Heidi gives me a look and I know that something's not right.

'I just need to examine you, OK, Louise?'

Louise doesn't respond, totally lost in her pain, but Heidi nods her head and I go over to join her.

Heidi examines her, Louise wincing with the pain. 'No progress is being made from all the pushing,' Heidi says in a hushed voice. Then she uses the Doppler to listen to baby's heart and it's clear straight away that it's in distress, so she presses the emergency button and then starts to speak to Louise whilst I go back to be next to her face and hold her hand.

'We need to get you up on to the bed and then another midwife is just going to come and check what's happening with baby. Baby is getting a little distressed and I think we might need to give you some help to get baby out,' Heidi says in a calm but firm voice.

'What's happening?' Louise says to me, her eyes wild. 'I can tell by your face that something's wrong.'

I curse myself for not being able to hide my concern better. 'It's going to be fine. You are surrounded by the best people. They are going to get your baby out safely, OK?'

I'm not sure if I'm really allowed to promise that, but I can't just sit here and watch her panic. I have to tell her it's going to be OK, even if in the end it's not.

'You have to understand. This baby and my little girl at home, they're all I've got. And I'm all they've got. So we have to be OK.'

'You will be.'

'I'm scared.' She says it so weakly I can barely hear her over the noise of all the rushing around, lifting her on to a bed, the other midwife, Sally, rushing in.

'It's OK. I'm right here with you. We've got this, OK?'

She nods and then I have to let go of her hand and move out the way as those who are far more qualified than I am take over and do their job. The rest is a bit of a blur – consent forms are signed and then Louise is rushed in for a caesarean. At first, I'm not sure if I'm allowed to accompany her but Sally nods when I give her a questioning look and I go into the operating room with them. Louise is given a spinal and within ten minutes or so she looks like a different person – her whole body no longer contorted with the pain. She still looks terrified, though, so I stay beside her and hold her hand.

'So your notes say you didn't find out the sex? You said you've got a little girl at home though, right?'

She nods. 'She's three. She asked Santa for a little sister for Christmas but I'd quite like a little boy. One of each, you know?'

'Well, we're going to find out which it is really soon.'

'I don't care as long as he or she is healthy.'

'We're going to have one last try to get baby out with forceps if we can, OK, Louise?' the doctor says, holding up the forceps, which, in the cold light of day instead of a textbook, look like some sort of torture instrument. 'When I tell you to push, I know you can't feel it but just try your best to push down into your bottom, OK?'

He looks at the monitor that is attached to Louise's tummy and when he can see that she is having a contraction, he shouts, 'Push. That's it. Keep going.'

Louise pushes with all her might until she's totally out of breath.

'That was fantastic. Just take deep breaths and I'll tell you when to push again.'

They go through this pattern about three or four times until suddenly Louise's baby is here and after a quick rub with a towel, it starts to cry.

'What is it?' she says to me and then the doctor puts the baby on to Louise's chest. Louise lifts her head to look down at her new baby. 'A little boy. Oh, look at him.'

'He's perfect.'

She starts to cry. 'I'm going to be OK. I have my babies. I'm going to be OK.'

She's saying it more to herself than anybody else, so I just nod and smile at her. And I know exactly how she feels. Because as much as I'd love to have someone in my life, a partner, I know that I'll always be OK because I have Dylan. And then I look at the clock. It's half six. It feels like my stomach hits the floor as I realize that I've missed Dylan's birthday. I was supposed to pick him up about three hours ago.

Whilst Louise is busy looking into her son's eyes, I go over to Heidi. 'Can I just pop out and make a phone call? I lost track of time and I'm supposed to be getting my son from his dad's.'

'Of course. You go. You did a great job, by the way. Most students just sit there open-mouthed in that sort of situation, but you really supported the mother.'

I try not to show her how much her praise means to me. 'Thanks.'

I rush along to the staff room and find my bag. Pulling out my phone, I notice there's six missed calls and a couple of messages from Luke, the first one asking where I am and the second one telling me Abby has taken Dylan to the Lego shop and to call him. Why the hell has Abby taken him? I don't want Abby stepping in to save the day and taking my son for his birthday treat.

I text Luke to apologize and to tell him that I'll be

leaving in about twenty minutes and then go back to check on Louise. They've already moved her back on to the ward where she is lying looking extremely sleepy whilst Sally and Heidi do a few checks on baby.

'Hey,' Louise says as she notices me coming in.

'How you feeling?'

'So much better now.'

'Good. Have you come up with a name yet?' I ask, nodding in the direction of her little boy.

'I'm going to call him Laurie. I figure Laura would sound a bit strange on a boy.'

The lump that forms in my throat is so large I find when I open my mouth to speak the words can't make it through.

'I couldn't have done it without you.'

I clear my throat. 'Rubbish. You were doing it the whole time. You were amazing.'

'Thank you.'

'My shift ended a while back and it's actually *my* son's birthday today too so I'm going to have to go in a minute, but Heidi and Sally will take good care of you. I hope your daughter is happy with her early Christmas present. I'm sure she'll be smitten.'

'Thank you. I hope so. And I'm sorry I made you finish late.'

'Don't be silly. It was an honour to share it with you.'

'I can't believe our sons share a birthday. How old is yours?'

'He's eleven today.'

'Wow, you don't look old enough.'

'Thanks. I definitely *feel* old enough.'

Louise looks over at her little boy, who has just been

weighed and is being wrapped in a blanket ready to be given back to her. 'Does it get any easier? Parenting, I mean. My three-year-old is adorable but, God, it's exhausting and I still feel like I have no idea what the hell I'm doing.'

'Physically, it gets easier for sure, but I still feel like I'm learning on a daily basis. I'm not sure you ever get to the point where you think, oh, motherhood. Yeah, cracked it.'

I sense the desperation in her eyes, a need for reassurance.

'But he's now my best friend in the world,' I continue. 'So it's definitely worth it.'

Louise smiles and then her baby is back so I leave them to bond and say my goodbyes to Heidi and Sally and then hurry out. And as I look at my phone again, I notice an answerphone message I didn't see before. As soon as I hear Luke's voice, I know something bad has happened. I run back across the car park as I listen, heading away from my car and towards the other side of the hospital.

Just as I reach the correct building, I see Luke sitting on a bench outside. He looks so exhausted, like he has weights hanging off every limb. When he sees me, his face crumples and he stands up and I run up to him and put my arms around him.

'I didn't think you'd come.'

'I'm sorry, I didn't notice your answerphone message at first.' I hold him for what feels like a long time and then eventually we release and sit down beside each other. 'How is he?'

'He's going to be OK. But . . .' Luke clenches his jaw and swallows.

'You regret not getting in touch sooner?'

Luke nods and I put my hand on his leg.

'I get it. But you have to focus on now, yeah? And on your future in each other's lives, having him in Dylan's life.'

'I know. Thank you.' He puts his hand on top of mine. 'I knew there was a reason you were the first person I thought to call. Seeing you always makes me feel better.'

I slip my hand out from under his, scared that if I sit here much longer, I'm going to fall back into the well of emotions I've been working so hard to climb out of. 'I'm really sorry but I need to go and see Dylan. Can you tell Abby I'm on my way?'

'Of course. Thank you for coming. I knew you'd be desperate to get back to him.'

'I feel I've let him down.'

'You've never let him down. You're the best mum, Laur.'

I shrug and stand up. 'I'm glad your dad is OK and that you're back in touch.'

'Thank you.'

I start to walk away until Luke calls out, 'I've missed you this year, you know? Us being friends, I mean.'

There's not a day goes by that I don't miss him. But I can't let him go if I'm still seeing him all the time. It's easier this way. 'We're still friends. See you soon, Luke.'

He looks like he wants to say more but instead he nods. 'See you soon.'

When I get home, Abby's waiting in the car outside. I let her and Dylan in, trying to push the completely unfair resentment I'm feeling to the side.

'Wait until you see what I've got,' Dylan says, a huge Lego bag in his hand. 'It's really cool, isn't it, Abby?'

'Well, I hope you are going to enjoy it.'

'Do you want a cuppa?' I ask, dumping my bags and taking off my coat.

'No, it's OK. I'm going to go and see Luke.'

'Of course.'

'I'll get some bowls to empty the Lego into,' Dylan says, putting his bag on the sofa and hurrying off to the kitchen.

'I'm so sorry that you had to take Dylan all that way,' I say to Abby. 'It's not like me. I've never let him down like that before, I really haven't.'

'Laura, you don't have to explain anything to me. Once, I actually left Seb in a supermarket and drove off. I totally forgot I had him with me.'

I smile, grateful for her generosity of spirit. 'Well, thanks for coming to the rescue. I really appreciate it. And give Luke my love.'

I don't know if he will tell her about me seeing him at the hospital earlier and I don't feel it's my place to say anything.

'Will do.' Abby turns to go but then she pauses with her hand on the door handle and turns back to me. It's odd because normally she seems so confident. So *perfect*. But now she looks almost scared. 'Do you think he's happy?'

'Of course he is. Didn't you see him? You made his day stepping in and taking him.'

'No, sorry, I meant Luke. Does he seem happy to you? You probably know him better than anyone. I mean, Jenny says he seems really happy, but I'm not always sure.'

It surprises me how much it hurts that Abby has clearly developed a relationship with Jenny. I barely see her these days. 'I'm not sure I know him better than anyone any more. I'm sure Jenny has a better handle on his emotions.'

'OK. It's just I asked him to marry me earlier.' Abby laughs awkwardly and I feel a tightness in my chest that makes it feel hard to breathe.

'Oh wow. What did he say?'

'Jenny called to say his dad was in the hospital so he didn't have chance to answer.'

'Oh right. Well, I'm sure you can talk about it later.'

She nods and opens the door but I can tell how disappointed she is, how she was clearly desperate for my reassurance.

'For what it's worth,' I continue, 'he seems really happy, yeah.'

Abby is unable to hide her smile and I have to force myself to remember that, for the most part, I'm happy too. That Luke and I moving on from each other is how it's supposed to be.

'Are you sure you know that I love you?'

Dylan and I are sitting on the floor of the lounge, surrounded by bowls of Lego, the smell of the 'Christmas Cookie' candle I lit earlier filling the room.

'Yes, Mummy,' he says with a tone of exasperation.

'But, like, really sure? You are the most important thing in my life and always will be. You do know that, don't you?'

'Of course I know.'

'But I feel like I let you down. I promised I'd always be there for your birthday and then I wasn't.'

I can hear the strain in my voice, the tears threatening.

'It's fine, Mummy. It's still my birthday now, isn't it?' He hands me the instruction booklet. 'You do know you're supposed to be passing me the pieces?'

'Great, so I get the boring bit.'

'You're good at finding the pieces. I'm better at building. We make a good team.'

I laugh. 'I make a good servant, more like.'

'Well, you do owe it to me for missing my birthday.'

'Hey, you,' I elbow him gently in the side.

'Just joking.'

I start sorting the pieces Dylan needs for the first few steps. 'I'm sorry Daddy couldn't take you to the Lego shop either.'

'It's OK. It was fun with Abby.'

'That's good. It was nice of her to take you.'

'Yeah, she's really nice. Not as nice as you, don't worry.' He smiles – my compassionate, knowing boy.

'Well, that's a given.'

'She's teaching me to cook. We made spaghetti bolognaise the other day.'

'You didn't tell me that.'

'I can't tell you *everything*, Mummy. I do forget stuff, you know.'

'Of course. Sorry.' Dylan's nearly used up all the pieces I've given him, so I have a quick look on the next couple of pages and find the bits he needs next.

'Is that man that dropped you off the other night your boyfriend?' he asks, pausing with a piece of Lego in his hand.

'Which man? I thought you were asleep.'

In a moment of loneliness a few months ago, I joined Tinder, but it wasn't until last week that I actually agreed to meet up with someone. I can't see me doing it again anytime soon.

'I was pretending,' Dylan says. 'I came out of my room and peeked.'

'Cheeky monkey.'

Dylan smiles but then he looks more serious. 'I didn't like him. He had a weird beard and a boring voice.'

It's an accurate description.

'I agree,' I say in a hushed voice and Dylan laughs. Then I reach over and ruffle his hair. 'I won't be seeing him again. And just know that whatever happens, you'll always be my number one, OK?'

'I know,' Dylan says. 'You're my number one too, Mummy.'

16th December 2017

LUKE

'Do you want some breakfast?' Abby asks, bouncing out of bed.

The strange thing about Abby is that she never expects an orgasm in return. If it happens before or during sex, then great. But if it doesn't, she doesn't hang around after the act expecting me to repay the favour. At first, I was relieved about that. Sometimes it can feel like a bit of a chore when you're spent and you still have to put in a shift. But it's like sex for Abby is more about the health benefits, the exercise element, rather than any real passion for me. Like having sex with me is her morning workout before her superfood smoothie and her yoga.

And that's another thing. Her *routine*. I feel like I know what is going to happen every hour of my life until the day I die. *Why don't we just stay in bed until twelve today? Why don't we change our plans completely and go to the beach?* It's not that we don't do exciting things together. We travel, we go to art exhibitions and see shows. But it all has to be planned in. There's so much *order* and I feel like I just want to rebel, like a teenager who's told they have to be in at a certain time or to keep their room straight.

'No, I'm OK, thanks. I'll grab a coffee in a bit.'

'OK.' She kisses me on the cheek and then bounds out of the room. How can anyone be so *alive* first thing in the morning? It's not natural.

I force myself to get up, shower and throw on some jeans and a jumper. Then just as I'm about to head downstairs, my phone buzzes. When I see it's a message from Laura, it's ridiculous, but I feel a flutter of excitement. It's the same every time. Even though I know it's probably only going to be about the fact Dylan's worn through another pair of trainers or he has some sort of assembly/play/presentation/sports fixture/bear hunt at school that I'm welcome to attend.

Dylan doesn't want to spend his birthday with me this year.

She follows her first message with about a thousand crying face emojis and although she's making light of it, it wouldn't surprise me if she really is lying on her bed in floods of tears.

I start to message her back but then pick up the phone and call her. When she answers, she doesn't even say 'hello', just launches in.

'I asked him if he wanted to do something really cool today. Said he could choose anything he wanted and he gave me this sad look and said, "I'd really just like to go to the cinema and McDonald's with my friends." Maccy Ds beat an awesome cool activity with me.'

I can't help but laugh. 'Beaten by a Big Mac. Hard times.'

'It's not funny.'

'A tiny bit funny.'

'No, not funny at all,' Laura says, but I can hear the slight amusement in her voice. 'Everyone always said when he went to secondary school he'd forget about me, but I was like, "No, we're different. Our relationship is unbreakable", and then, wham, he's gone and smashed it into tiny little pieces.'

'I think your relationship is still intact.'

'How can it be? It's his *birthday*. And he doesn't want to spend it with me. All the times I've sacrificed stuff for him. The guilt I felt last year when I was a bit late, even though I was bringing new bloody life into the world.'

I laugh. 'Ungrateful little shit.' And then I don't know where it comes from as I'm supposed to be spending the day with Abby, meeting up with her friends who look at me as if I'm the devil incarnate when I order something that, God forbid, contains *meat*, but I say, 'How about we do something together? If our son is being a meanie and doesn't want to see us, we'll do something super exciting and then talk about it in detail in front of him and make him jealous.'

'Genius.'

'So what do you want to do?'

'Eat chocolate and lament how my son no longer loves, wants or needs me.'

'That doesn't sound very exciting.'

'You're very sweet, but I can't expect you to give up your Saturday to deal with my neuroses. I'll get over it. I might eat my weight in cake in the process, but I'll get over it.'

'I'm coming over. I'll think of what we can do. No argument.'

'But . . .'

'I said no argument. I'll see you in about an hour.'

I put the phone down before she has a chance to convince me it's not a good idea and go downstairs, wondering how to break the news to Abby.

I find her in the kitchen wiping the worktops.

'Um, that was Laura on the phone.'

She looks up at the sound of my voice. 'Oh right. Everything OK?'

'Well, yeah. Sort of. I mean, she's feeling sad because Dylan's decided he doesn't want to spend his birthday with her.'

'Well, he's twelve. That's perfectly normal, isn't it?'

'I know it is. But it's still hard, isn't it? The process of letting go. I'm sure you felt it with Seb.'

'Yeah, I guess. But I expected it, so I was prepared.'

Abby has a way of viewing the world that I often admire. But sometimes I wonder if she actually feels anything deeply, whether she's *ever* felt torn apart.

'Well, I said I'd go over there, cheer her up a bit.'

'Why you? Can't she call Sarah or her mum or any of her other friends?'

'Well, it's our son, isn't it? Just because we're no longer together doesn't mean I shouldn't be there to support her through these transitions. We're still co-parents.'

Abby puts the cloth she's been using into the sink and then starts rearranging the jars in the cupboard. 'OK. Just remember we're having lunch with Suzie and Nick at one o'clock.'

'Oh shit, I totally forgot,' I lie. 'I was actually going to stick around there to see Dylan when he gets back from the cinema. I'm sure Suzie and Nick won't miss me. I'm not even sure they like me very much.' I laugh.

'Of course they like you.'

'Well, I'll see them soon. I'm sorry. It *is* Dylan's birthday.'

'Which you knew when we arranged it.'

'I didn't know Laura was going to be this upset, did I? I can't just leave her on her own. I'm sorry if that makes me a terrible person.'

'Of course it doesn't. I'm sorry. You're right. Go and see her.'

Abby is entirely reasonable nearly all the time and therefore it is impossible to argue with her because you always end up looking like a dick. But sometimes I wish she'd shout about stuff, be irrational, just show me some sort of emotion. Otherwise, it feels like you're forever on an even keel and life has no peaks or troughs, which might explain the lethargy that's developed when I'm around her. Although I'm not stupid enough to think the fact that Laura and I have become close again doesn't have something to do with it.

'Thank you. And please apologize to Suzie and Nick for me.'

'Will do. Wish Dylan a happy birthday from me. And tell him I'm going to make him a birthday cake for when he's here next weekend.'

'That's really sweet of you. Thank you.' I collect my wallet and car keys out of the little dish Abby makes me keep them in. 'I shouldn't be late.'

'Good, because remember we're sorting the guest list tonight. We need to get the wedding invitations out or we'll end up with no one being able to make it.'

'Sure. I'll get my thinking cap on.' I give Abby a kiss on the cheek and then leave, knowing in my heart that there's no way I can walk down that aisle.

'We could've just gone to the cinema, sat at the back, spied on Dylan and his mates,' Laura says as she pulls her water shoes on.

'Oh yeah, I'm sure he would've loved you for that.'

'I don't know. Lunch then. But this?' She runs her hand over her life jacket and wetsuit. 'I'm never sure about activities that involve wearing a helmet.'

'You do look quite funny.'

'Have you looked in the mirror?'

We traipse further up the mountain, the two stragglers at the back of the group. I get a funny look from one of the twenty-something girls in front of us and I wonder if she recognizes me from Paradigm, but it might just be because we're so much slower than everyone else.

'I can't believe it's only four degrees. I feel like I'm going to pass out in all this gear,' Laura says, wiping the sweat off her forehead.

'Just wait until you're in the freezing cold water. You won't be cursing all these layers then.'

'You're really selling it to me.'

'It's payback for the hot air balloon ride.'

'*You* booked that,' Laura says, exasperated.

'That's true. I did. But I did it for you.'

'I know you did.'

After what feels like a thousand miles, we get to the ghyll. It's a ridiculous activity to do in December, but Laura did always ask me to take her out of her comfort zone.

'Right, guys,' the instructor announces. 'We're going to climb this rock and then we're going to jump in, OK?'

Laura looks at me like she might kill me, and I laugh.

'It'll be fun,' I mouth.

Laura narrows her eyes and then the group starts to move so we follow, me behind Laura. When she starts to slip, I grab her, pushing her up by her bottom.

'I can see you're using me falling as an excuse to cop a feel back there.'

'I saved your life, I'll have you know.'

'Yeah, yeah.'

Once we get to the top, I try to pretend it's not really high up and that I'm not terrified.

'Will you jump first?' Laura says, pushing me in front of her. 'I want to see if you survive.'

'Thanks,' I laugh.

'Well, you know, I mean if you break a leg or anything.'

'Not really much better.'

'Just go.' She pushes me in the back and I inch forward towards the edge.

'Ready?' the instructor says. And although my heart is in my throat and everything in my body is telling me to turn and go in the opposite direction, I launch myself off, feeling every second of the fall before I splash into the water, sinking to the depths before bobbing back up.

When I surface, I push my hair off my face and look up to see Laura peering down at me from the rock ledge. I give her a thumbs up and then, with a little run up, she throws herself off the rock into the water. It felt much longer when I was the one doing the jumping – but, in seconds, she's hitting the water near me and then swimming over. When she reaches me, she grips on to stop herself from being pulled along with the current.

'Swim me to the edge,' she says, her hands gripped around my neck. So I swim to the edge of the gyhll with Laura on my back, releasing her when she can grab on to the rock.

'That was so much fun,' she says, standing up now that it's shallow enough. 'Dylan is going to be so jealous.'

I reach down into my wetsuit and pull my phone out of the waterproof case I've got it in. 'Let's take a selfie and send it to him.'

I put my arm around Laura and we pose for a selfie, both of us with our tongues stuck out, and then I forward it to Dylan's phone.

'Right, follow me,' the instructor shouts so I tuck my phone back in to the case around my neck and we float down on our backs.

'It's really beautiful, isn't it?' Laura says, looking up at the sky.

'It really is.'

'Thank you. For suggesting it. For not thinking I'm a neurotic weirdo because I can't handle our son growing up and becoming independent of me.'

'You're not a weirdo. Well, maybe a little bit.'

Laura scoops her hand into the water and splashes me in the face.

'Hey.' I repay the favour and Laura squeals.

'Keep up back there,' the instructor calls and Laura and I look at each other and giggle like naughty school kids.

We continue to float down, staring up at the sky. 'So how come you called me and not Sarah?'

'She's sunning herself in Mauritius, isn't she? Bloody cancer. She's never here any more now she's "making the most of every day".'

I laugh. 'I hope I'm not too poor a substitute.'

'You're doing OK.'

We get to the next rock elevation, and I climb up first and then help pull Laura up to stand beside me. As the cold air hits my dripping wetsuit I start to shiver, my teeth chattering.

'Come on,' I say. 'Let's jump in. It's weirdly warmer in the water.'

Laura peers over the ledge. 'I'm scared. This one's higher than before.'

'Me too. Let's do it together. We'll hold hands, yeah?'

'OK.'

I grab Laura's hand and then look over the edge and then back at her. 'Ready?'

She nods, and we shuffle a little closer to the rock face so we can jump out far enough not to hit our backs on the way down.

'One, two, three, jump!'

LAURA

'Favourite of Dylan's birthdays so far?'

'Got to be the private dinner on the beach,' Luke says. 'You?'

I wrap my arms around my knees. We're sitting on my sofa warming up with hot chocolates. 'I don't know. This one's been pretty good actually. Is that really awful when he's not even here?'

Luke laughs. 'It *has* been a really good day.'

'I really liked last year in the end too. Dylan and I sat up for ages chatting. It was nice to do nothing and just talk to him, you know?'

'My dad having a heart attack was a bit of a low though.'

'Oh yeah, sorry. But I guess it brought you two back together, so there was a silver lining. And Dylan adores him now. He was talking about him for ages the other day – telling me all about the time you guys went fishing in the summer and your dad taught him how to light a piece of paper using a magnifying glass and the light of the sun.'

'That was a great trip.' Luke smiles. 'And you're right – I'm strangely grateful for Dad ending up in the hospital. Seeing him and Dylan together – it's amazing. The way Dylan so clearly looks up to him like I always did. I just wish it hadn't taken me so long.'

'Well, you guys are definitely making up for lost time.'

I watch the reflection of the Christmas tree lights dancing in the window.

'Favourite age so far?' Luke asks.

'I can't say that. It feels wrong to say he was better at one age than another. And besides, they all have their good and bad parts.'

'He was a bit of a shit aged seven though, wasn't he? Let's be honest here.'

I can't help but laugh. 'Luke, you can't say that.'

'You know it's what you're thinking. And the first year was a bit dull.'

'Oh no, he was so cute and cuddly.'

'But he didn't really *do* anything, did he?'

'I liked that he needed me for his very survival. I mean, I'm not sure I liked it at the time. It felt like a bit of a weight on my shoulders. But now that he doesn't need me, I miss those days. I mean, I am loving doing something for me. Training to be a midwife is so fulfilling, but I do miss him.'

Luke lifts his legs up on to the sofa and crosses them. 'He still needs you, you know?'

'Really?'

'Of course. Who's the first person he told when that teacher gave him a behaviour point because his shirt was untucked?'

'Well, I think he hoped I'd go in and smack him in the face or something.'

'I'm surprised you didn't to be fair. But who did he turn to when that kid in his class started taking the piss out of him because he didn't play Fortnite?'

'Well, yeah, but . . .'

'Who does he message every lunchtime just to tell what

he's had for dinner or which club he's signed up for or the fact he's got a house point? I know I'm on your little group WhatsApp, but the messages are always aimed at you.'

'They're to both of us.'

'Fine, to *us*. My point is you're the safe haven he always returns to. The reason he has the confidence to step away, to make new friends, to try different things – that's all because he has such a secure base to return to.'

'Thank you. I guess it's hard not to grab on to his hand and say, "Don't go".'

'I know it is. But you don't do that. You set him free, and that's why he will always return. And he *will* always return.'

Luke reaches out and takes my hand and I swallow down the lump in my throat.

'You know he no longer believes in Santa, don't you? He was talking about making Thea a stocking and I said, "Well, Santa will do that," and he laughed and then he looked really guilty.'

Luke looks down. 'He knew last year. He just didn't want to tell you because he thought you'd be upset.'

'Oh. Is there a lot of stuff he tells you that he doesn't tell me?'

'Of course not. You know you're his number one.'

'He adores you too,' I tell him because I'm not sure that he knows.

Luke shrugs. 'I'm happy with second place. Or maybe third place after Sarah.' He smiles. 'I know that's more than I deserve.'

I shake my head. 'You are a great dad, Luke. I know I used to make you feel bad when you went away and stuff, but you were providing for us.'

'It wasn't always entirely selfless.'

'I know. But there's nothing wrong with following your passion. And I get that it can be hard being the one missing out on stuff at home. I feel it a lot now I'm working such long shifts. I think I was jealous a lot of the time and to be honest, I just really missed you.'

'I missed you too. I used to put the phone down and lie in my empty bed and just long for you to be there.'

'I always imagined you were having too much fun to be thinking about me.'

'Not at all.' Luke puts his mug on the side. 'You know, I was supposed to be going out for lunch with Abby and her friends today.'

'Oh, Luke. You shouldn't have let her down for *me*. I would've been OK. Ten stone heavier, maybe, but OK.'

Luke doesn't laugh and I feel a heaviness between us that both scares and excites me. 'I told her that we were co-parents. That it's my role to support you.'

'Well, I guess that's true, but you really didn't have to . . .'

'It's not the reason. I wanted to spend the day with you.'

'Oh?'

'She was right to be jealous.'

'What are you trying to say, Luke?'

Luke uncrosses his legs and puts his feet down on the floor. 'Come on, Laura. Do I really need to spell it out?'

It feels like he's getting angry and it makes me feel angry too. 'Yes, you do. Because you're *engaged to someone else*. You do remember that, don't you? You moved on.'

'I moved on because I *had* to. Because you stopped loving me. And I spent every single day for years hoping that maybe I'd win you back, that you'd start to remember what you loved about me in the first place, but you never did. So I had to let you go.'

I nod, so full of regret and sadness and hurt and anger that I don't know what to say. But I know there's one thing I need to make clear.

'I never stopped loving you.'

'OK, I mean, stopped being *in* love with me.'

I shake my head. 'I've never stopped being *in* love with you.'

Luke screws up his face in confusion. 'So why did you leave me? Why did you push me away all those years ago? Or ask if I was genuinely happy for you to move on when we spoke about it in Lapland?'

'I wanted you to hold me, to love me, not to try to have sex with me. And I asked you if you really meant it because I wanted you to tell me that you didn't, not to bloody encourage me to get with someone else. You said we were better as friends. How was I supposed to tell you I was still in love with you after you said that?'

'Well, there you go. I get everything wrong. You're better off without me.'

'No, Luke. Don't do that. Don't play the "I'm not good enough" card.'

'Well, I'm clearly not.'

He stands up, his back to me, ready to leave, and I drag my hands through my hair. 'Then why have I never found anyone who comes close to you? Why have I spent my life feeling that I've had my one true love – that that's it? I found you. I lost you. I threw you away and my punishment is living the rest of my life never feeling anything close to what I feel when I'm with you.'

He turns around and I can see he has tears in his eyes. 'You really feel like that?'

I nod.

He puts his hands on my cheeks, wiping the tears I hadn't realized I was crying with his thumbs. 'Then I'm going to kiss you. Unless you don't want me to?' He leans towards me, but just before our lips touch, I open mine to speak.

'Why didn't you want a baby with me, Luke?'

'I told you at the time. Things were better between us, I didn't want to see you so exhausted again . . .'

'I don't mean a second child,' I interrupt. 'I mean Dylan.'

'Oh, Laur. I was just young and scared. It wasn't about you. It was about me.'

'I was young and scared too, you know?'

'But we both know you're an infinitely better person than me.'

'That's not what I'm saying. It's just that I was always sure about you. So having a baby with you – I was always sure about that too.'

Luke looks me right in the eyes. 'Is that what you think? That it was that I didn't want a baby with *you*?'

I bite my lip and nod.

'I always knew you'd be the mother of my child. From the first time I saw you walking into the pub next to Sarah – your baggy jeans and crop top. Those killer abs . . .'

I roll my eyes – the knowledge that beneath my woolly jumper today, you definitely wouldn't describe my abs as 'killer' – how I wish it didn't always come back to that.

'Hold on,' Luke continues, holding up his hands in defence. 'It wasn't the abs that made me know you'd be the mother of my child. It was the way you kept looking yourself up and down as if you weren't sure you'd chosen the right outfit. The way you couldn't see how stunning you were. The way you didn't fall for my "I'm the lead singer in a band" spiel.'

'I totally fell for that really,' I admit.

'Well, I liked that you didn't show it. That you kept me on my toes. And I liked how you loved Sarah – does that sound stupid? I remember thinking, if I can ever convince her to love *me* like that then that's going to be the best feeling in the world. There was so much going on behind those eyes of yours and I'd never met anyone like that. So I always knew you were going to be the love of my life. My only doubts were about having a baby at that particular time. And part of that was because I knew that little person would take you away from me and selfishly I wanted to keep you all to myself.'

'You promise?'

'Cross my heart and hope to die.' He puts his hand on my leg. 'You know, I always thought the issue was that you hated me for even considering ending Dylan's life before it began. I hated me for that.'

'I never hated you. It just made me feel you didn't really love me.'

'Oh God, Laur. I wish you'd told me. I have tried so very hard not to love you.'

I put my hand on his face – this man I've loved for as long as I can remember. 'Me too.'

And then *I* lean towards *him*, the feel of his lips on mine like going home.

All of a sudden, there's a bang. We jump apart and I

open my eyes to see Dylan standing there, staring at us as if he's just caught us snorting hard drugs off the coffee table.

'What's going on?'

'Nothing. Your dad and I went ghyll scrambling because, well . . .'

'Does Abby know you're here, Dad?'

'Yes.'

'Does she know you're here like *this*?' He practically spits the last word out.

Luke stands up but Dylan steps back. 'I'm going to talk to her. It's complicated.'

'Complicated?' It surprises me to hear not the voice of a child but a young adult. 'You told me to always be honest, Dad. You're supposed to be getting married in a few months.'

'I know. Sit down. Let's talk.'

Dylan shakes his head so fast it looks like it might fall off. 'I have nothing to say to you, Dad. You're a liar and a cheat and I hate you.' He suddenly looks like a toddler again, in the middle of a why-don't-you-understand-me meltdown. 'I'm going to Marcus'.'

'Dylan,' Luke says, trying to grab his arm, but he storms off, luckily not towards the front door. After a minute, the patio door slams and the cold air sweeps in from outside.

'I'll go and talk to him,' Luke says.

'You've booked a venue? I didn't even realize you'd set a date.'

'It's not like you think. I got swept up in Abby's enthusiasm and I didn't know how to tell her that it's not what I want.'

'When is it? The wedding day?'

'There's not going to be a wedding day. Not with Abby.'

'When is it booked for?'

Luke sighs. 'March the seventeenth.'

'You never managed to commit to booking anywhere with me.'

'Laura.'

'I need to go and speak to Dylan. It'd probably be best for you to go.'

'Don't do this, Laur. I'm going to go straight home and finish things with Abby.'

'It doesn't matter right now. Right now, I need to be with our son.'

'So let me come and talk to him with you.'

I shake my head. 'I think he needs some time. I'll get him to call you.'

'OK.' He goes to kiss me but I turn my head away. 'Tell him I love him and I'm sorry, will you?'

'Will do.'

As he leaves, I want to beg him to stay, but instead I go out to the garden where Dylan is sitting on our little swing seat, pushing himself back and forth, his breath coming out of his mouth in white wisps. The swing seat we've had so many conversations on over the years – about the shape of the clouds, what he's played at school, the project he's planning with his Lego. I walk over and he purposely turns his head to the side so that he doesn't have to look at me.

'Come back inside. It's freezing.'

Dylan remains where he is, still looking away from me.

'Well, can I join you, then?'

He still doesn't respond but I grab a throw out of the garden box.

'I'm going to take that as a yes.'

He slows the swinging slightly to allow me to sit down, so I do, putting the throw over both of our legs.

'I understand you're confused about what you saw.'

'Are you getting back together?'

'No. I mean, we haven't even spoken about that. We just got talking about the past and stuff and we felt sad, I guess, that we hadn't always told each other how we really feel. We hadn't always been honest with each other.'

'I like Abby, Mum. I told you that. I don't want to move house *again*. I don't want to listen to you arguing again. Things have been better. I've been happy.'

'You're getting ahead of yourself, love. We haven't talked about anything like that.'

'But I don't want things to *change*. I want you and Dad to be best friends.'

'We will be. Always.'

'You won't. If you get back together, you'll make each other sad again.'

It's strange when your twelve-year-old voices your own fears. Kissing Luke, it felt impossible that that wasn't exactly where I should be. But now that he's gone, the doubts creep back in. I was so miserable a lot of the time. What if Dylan's right and we tear each other apart again? How can I put Dylan through that? And besides, if Luke's heart is truly with me, then why has he planned to marry someone else in three months' time?

'I just want things to stay as they are.' With a stab to my heart, Dylan starts to cry. Recently, when I've looked at him, I've been disturbed to notice very much a young man looking back at me. The shape of him is changing, his face, the way he holds himself. But right now, he looks like my baby boy and I feel an unfaltering desire to protect him.

I put my arm around his shoulder and draw him in close to me then wrap the throw around the two of us. 'Then they'll stay just as they are.'

'Really?'

I nod. 'Dad and I will just stay as best friends, OK? It's you and me always. I'll never do anything to hurt you.' I rest my head on top of Dylan's. 'Even though you decided not to spend your birthday with me,' I tease.

'I just wanted to go to the cinema with my friends.'

'I know. I'm winding you up. I'm glad you had a wonderful time with your friends.'

'I'm jealous of you and Dad doing the ghyll scrambling though. That looked awesome.'

'It was. That's why we went, you know? To make you jealous. Because silly Mummy was sad that I was losing you. To be fair to your dad, he just wanted to cheer me up. I was being stupid by the way. You did absolutely nothing wrong.'

'Shall we light a fire and do marshmallows? It's still my birthday now.'

'I know it is. And I'd love to. I'll go and get us hot chocolates. Unless you want beer now you're a tween?'

Dylan laughs. 'No. Yuck. Definitely hot chocolate. Shall I go and get some wood out the shed?'

'Yeah, you do that and I'll make the hot chocolate and fetch the marshmallows.'

'Bring the biscuits out too so we can make s'mores.'

'All right, boss.'

Dylan smiles and then gets up and walks over to the

shed. I head inside, finding my phone to see a couple of messages from Luke asking if Dylan is OK. I start to write him a message, unsure how best to phrase what I need to say.

> Dylan's fine. Today was lovely. But I think we both probably know deep down that it was a mistake. I hope you can sort things out with Abby.

I keep checking for a reply while I make hot chocolate but one doesn't come. I take our drinks, a bag of marshmallows and the box of biscuits outside and put them on the table. Dylan is piling up logs and paper and squirting it all with lighter fluid. I go back inside to the hall to grab us both coats, hats and gloves, and just as I'm walking back through the kitchen to go back outside to Dylan, my phone buzzes. My throat feels tight as I put in my pin code and then click on the message from Luke. And when I read it, the disappointment feels overwhelming. I'm not sure what I wanted it to say, but it just says, *OK*.

'Hurry up, Mum,' Dylan calls from outside.

So I put down my phone and paint on a brave face. 'Coming.'

16th December 2018

LUKE

'What are you guys doing here?'

Sarah pushes Dylan in and then follows, nearly bashing into the giant metal reindeer in the hall as they go through to the lounge.

'Dylan called me and said I had to pick him up from the shop around the corner from Laura's and bring him here.'

I furrow my eyebrows. 'Does your mum know where you are?'

Dylan shakes his head.

'Then I need to call her. She'll be worried sick.'

'No,' Dylan shouts, pulling me back. 'I told her I was going to get fish and chips with Marcus. She won't be worried, but I don't want her to know why I'm here.'

'So why *are* you here?'

I look at Sarah to see if she can offer any more clarity.

'Don't ask me. He just told me he needed to see you and that he'd explain when he got here. We've been sat in silence in the car.'

Dylan looks down at his hands and starts picking at the skin around his fingernails.

'I think you better come and sit down.' I sit on the sofa and pat the cushion beside me.

'I'll go and get us all a drink,' Sarah says. 'Tea? Coffee? Squash?'

'Can I have a can of Coke?' Dylan says, slumping beside me. 'Dad always has a load in the fridge.'

'Luke?'

'Coffee, thanks.'

'With a bucketful of sugar as usual? Coming right up.'

Sarah goes into the kitchen and I look at Dylan, who is still refusing to meet my eyes.

'Mum's talking about moving away,' he blurts out.

'What do you mean?' My throat feels tight.

'She said a fresh start could be good for us.'

'Well, she's not allowed to make that decision without me. It's up to her what she does with *her* life, but you belong to me too.'

'Oh, she's going to talk to you about it. And she said that whatever happens, I'd still see you every other week-end and in the holidays and stuff.'

'And what about what *you* want? Do *you* want to move away?'

'I've given her strict instructions that she's not going anywhere,' Sarah says, coming in with a can of Coke and handing it to Dylan.

'Surely she'd never leave you,' I say to Sarah. 'Has she had a job offer or something?'

Sarah shakes her head.

'So what is it, then?' I ask, feeling exasperated that they both seem to be hiding something from me.

'It's because of you, Dad.'

'She said that?'

'She doesn't have to,' Sarah chips in. Then she goes back into the kitchen, presumably to get the coffee.

'She loves you. She's miserable without you,' Dylan says,

and he looks like he's carrying so much on his young shoulders and that makes me feel terrible.

'I don't know what you know, what your mum's told you, but it was her decision for us to be apart, so I'm not sure you're right about this one.'

'He *is* right,' Sarah shouts through from the kitchen.

'It was my fault. I'm sorry.' He runs his hand through his hair – he has that typical teenage floppy fringe haircut so it's always in his eyes. 'I told her on my birthday last year that I didn't want you to get back together. I just didn't want things to change because you were friends and I didn't want you or Mum to be sad again.'

'Well, maybe you were right. What's changed?'

'I was a silly kid.'

I laugh. 'And now you're a grown man.'

'Well, yeah, sort of.'

I look at my son sitting on the sofa beside me. And it's amazing, but in the past few months he *has* completely changed. His body has become lankier, his limbs looking oddly stretched, his face now looks more like a young man's than a little boy's, and his voice is losing its childhood pitch.

'And now you're not friends any more anyway and you're both even sadder than you were before and it's all my fault.'

I put my arm around him. 'I'm not sad,' I lie. 'And it's definitely not your fault.'

'It *is* my fault. Mum's always trying to make me happy. She forgets about herself.'

He shuffles away slightly as if now, at thirteen, he can only cope with a small amount of affection at a time.

'The thing is, Dylan, with no disrespect to your mum,

even if you did tell her you didn't want us to be together, she's a grown-up and can make her own decisions. Of course your opinion is important and I'll always listen to you, but I think in the end if she really wanted to work things out, she would have done.'

Sarah comes in and hands me a mug of coffee, sitting down on the armchair with hers. 'Dylan, there's a cupboard full of biscuits in there. Why don't you go and work your way through them?'

Dylan has a look on his face that says, 'I know you're just trying to get rid of me', but because it's Sarah asking and not me, he does as he's told.

'And shut the door, will you?' Sarah says.

Dylan narrows his eyes but then closes the door.

'You know how proud she is,' Sarah says quietly.

'That's no excuse, Sar. She's had a whole year to talk to me, to get over that, but she barely even looks at me now.'

'She thinks you don't feel the same.'

'You're right. I don't feel the same as she does. I actually give a shit.'

Sarah puts her fingers to her lips and I curse myself for raising my voice.

'Dylan was right,' I say in a lowered voice. 'He doesn't need this in his life. This constant bloody heartache. Maybe she *should* move away. Maybe that would be the best for all of us.'

'You know you don't mean that.'

'Don't I?'

'She really does love you.'

'If she really loved me, we wouldn't be here.'

Sarah sighs and I can tell she's getting fed up with me,

but it's the truth. I put everything on the line that day and she threw it back in my face.

'She was distraught that you didn't fight for her.'

'What?'

'When she sent you the message that night, you just said "OK".'

'She told me it was a mistake, Sar. That she hoped I'd sort things out with Abby. I mean, seriously?'

'You set a date to marry someone else, Luke.'

'Because she rejected me time and time again and even *you* told me to move on. To let her go so that I could be a decent friend, a decent father. Holding on to Laura was ruining me.'

'I know. But just remember she never moved on. Even when you were engaged, she kept on loving you. That's a pretty scary place to be.'

I let out a deep sigh. 'But if she'd just told me that . . .'

'You know how rubbish she is at saying how she feels. It's a terrible character flaw.'

Sarah smiles and I find myself smiling back.

'But she's also the best person I know,' Sarah continues. 'And I hate seeing her like this. To consider moving away from *me*, it's clear she's not right in the head.' She sits back down. 'I realized a long time ago that I can't tell either of you what to do. Well, I can, but neither of you will listen. But the fact that Dylan called me up to ask me to bring him here . . .'

'I know.' I let my head fall into my hands. 'But we can't keep making decisions based on Dylan. I really hate that this is hurting him, but I just think Laura and I had our time and it's gone now. It's all too late.'

'Don't say that,' Dylan says, coming in from the kitchen.

I look up at him, feeling a sense of pride for the young man he has become, probably more *in spite* of me than because of me.

I get up and wrap my arms around him. 'Whatever happens, I'm always going to be here for you. If I have to travel across the country, I'm still going to see you all the time. I'm going to be in your life forever, whether you like it or not.'

'I know.'

'And I'm going to love your mum forever too. I've tried so hard *not* to over the years that I know now it's an impossible task. But that doesn't necessarily mean we're best off together. I've realized that too.'

I let go of Dylan and he nods his head.

'But I will try to make sure we get our friendship back. I'm sorry about that. I hadn't realized that it was affecting you, because we haven't been arguing, but I know we haven't been close either.'

'I think I preferred the arguing.'

'You don't mean that. But I'm sorry. I'll give her a call and talk to her. We'll sort it out.'

'OK.'

'Let me get your present. You can pretend you found it on your doorstep if she asks.'

'OK, thanks, Dad.'

I go upstairs and find the present I've wrapped for him.

'I'm just going to wash up these cups,' Sarah says, collecting our empty drinks cups and taking them into the kitchen.

'Thanks, Sar.'

As Dylan pulls off the wrapping paper, I can tell by his confused expression that he has no idea what it is.

'It's a taekwondo outfit. Remember I told you I used to go with Granddad.'

'Your trophies.'

'Exactly, yeah. I thought you might want to learn too. I've booked you lessons, and I thought I could take you each week and I think Granddad would like to come too, but if you don't want to do it, I can cancel them, or if you and your mum move away, I can find you lessons nearer to where you live.'

'I'd love to do it. Thanks, Dad. But I'd like to go with you. And Granddad, of course.'

'OK. Well, we'll start the lessons I've booked you here and if you do move, we'll sort it somehow, OK? If I have to come to you to take you to one near you each week then I will. You're my priority, you know that, don't you?'

'I know.'

Sarah comes through from the kitchen. 'Ready?' she asks us and we both nod. 'Come on then. Let's get you home before Mum starts getting worried about where you are.'

They move towards the door and I get up to see them out.

'She's coming to your gig tonight. We all are,' Sarah whispers into my ear, patting me on the back as I hug her goodbye. 'It's up to you what you decide to do with that.'

I put Mum's coffee on the table and sit down at the breakfast bar beside her. She came to drop off Dylan's present, but I think she could tell something was up because she didn't just drop and leave, automatically putting the kettle on and getting out the mugs.

'So am I going to have to beat it out of you?'

'I'm just nervous about tonight.'

'I've known you your whole life, Luke. You are not just nervous about tonight.'

I take a sip of my coffee. 'She's moving away.'

'Laura?'

I nod.

'What about Dylan?'

'He'll go with her, of course.'

Mum looks like I've just turned out all her lights. 'Where are they going? Far?'

I shrug. 'I don't know. I think it's just an idea at the moment. Dylan turned up with Sarah this morning to basically ask me to beg her to stay.'

'She's moving because of you.' It's more of a statement than a question.

'Why does everyone think I've somehow driven her away? She's always known where I am.'

Mum nods, her eyes staring into the depths of her coffee. 'What?'

'Do you know what I think the problem is? And I might be wrong because, well, what do I know? I don't think she's ever been able to believe that you love her. And I get it. You know, with your dad, I knew that he'd leave one day.'

'What do you mean?'

'It wasn't a surprise. I knew that in the end I wouldn't be enough for him. That he'd want more. I should've done what Laura did and got out first, but I guess a part of me hoped I'd be proven wrong.'

'Do you seriously think that, Mum? That you weren't good enough for him?'

'I'm not saying *good* enough. Just not *enough*. I was a simple housewife. I liked nothing more than looking after you and your dad, putting healthy meals on the table, making sure you both had clean clothes, that sort of thing. God, it does sound bloody boring when I put it like that.'

'You're an amazing mum. You were an amazing wife. I love Dad to bits, but he definitely made a very big mistake leaving you.'

'Did he? He seems pretty happy to me.'

I can't argue with that. Now that I've spent more time with Dad, seen him with Sandy and his boys, there's no doubt that he's content.

'My point is, I think Laura felt like she wasn't enough even though she is. I mean, that girl is more than enough. And you're my only son who I adore.'

'Don't you think I know that, Mum? But I've tried my best to show her that. I know I've not been perfect, but I've really tried.'

'I'm not saying it's your fault. I'm just telling you how I see it.'

'Well, maybe she *should* move away. Find someone who makes her feel loved and secure. Maybe that's the best for both of us.'

'Maybe.' Mum puts her hand on my arm. 'Or maybe you should try one more time to show her how you really feel about her.'

LAURA

'So Lanmouth's not good enough for you now, then? Now you're a *professional*?'

I roll my eyes. 'You wanted me to make something of my life.'

'But not to *leave*.' Mum takes a bauble out of the cardboard box and puts it on the tree. I haven't felt like decorating this year, but Dylan started moaning this morning that we always have the tree up by the time it's his birthday, so I popped out and bought one. Not that he's helping decorate it; he's too busy playing Mario Kart with Dad, both of them with eyes fixed on the screen, steering wheels in their hands moving back and forth manically.

'You can make something of yourself *here*,' Mum continues. 'There are hospitals here, you know?'

'It's not about Lanmouth.'

'So what's it about, then?'

'I need a *change*, Mum. A fresh start.'

'But what about Dylan? He's settled at secondary school. You know how hard a transition that one is. And you might not like the new place. What if you can't make friends? What if you're lonely?'

I throw the bauble I'm holding back in the box, lucky that it doesn't smash. 'Why do you *always* see the negatives?'

Dad and Dylan look over at me, their trance broken by the sound of my raised voice.

Mum pulls me into the kitchen and shuts the door and we sit opposite each other at the dining table. 'I'm just looking out for you. Raising things you might not have thought of.'

'Of course I've thought of them. I've spent my life being scared to do *anything* in case it goes wrong or I get hurt or it disappoints you.'

'Disappoints me? When have *I* ever factored into any of your decisions?'

'Are you kidding me? You've factored into *every* one of my decisions. Uni's too expensive, Luke's going to break my heart, a baby is going to ruin my life, being a midwife means I can't be a good mother . . .'

'I never said that.' Mum pushes her chair back, emitting a loud screech as it scrapes on the floor. 'Look, I'm sorry I've obviously been such a terrible mother. I'm sure you'll be much happier living miles away from me.' She stands up.

'Don't be silly, Mum. Sit down.'

'I don't want to sit here and be told everything I've done wrong, Laura. I know I'm not a perfect mother, that you're ten times the mother I was, ten times the *person*. But I tried my best and it only ever came from a place of love.'

'I know. I'm sorry. Please sit down.'

Reluctantly, Mum removes her cardigan, hooks it on to the back of the chair and sits down.

'I love you, Mum. I just want you to think I've made some all right decisions. That I've been a half-decent mother. A half-decent *daughter*. Because it feels like I've made a bit of a mess of my life and I'm trying to do better, but I'm not sure I'm getting it right.'

'Are you crazy? Look at you – you're best mother I

know. You're following your dream of becoming a mid-wife. You're going to move away to somewhere so much bigger and better than here. I wish I had even an ounce of your bravery.'

I put my head in my hands. 'But I'm *not* brave. I'm scared all the time.'

'I'm sorry.'

I look up at Mum and shake my head. 'It's not your fault.'

Mum wrings her hands. 'Actually, I think it might be. I'm sorry I let my fear hold you back, that I unwittingly caused you to be plagued in the same way. I don't want you to end up like me; full of regrets for all the things I was too scared to do.' Mum puts her hand on mine. 'Move away, darling. Start afresh. I'll be here cheering you on every step of the way.'

I smile, but the truth is I'm not sure moving away is the brave thing to do at all.

'Come on. Let's get you ready.' Sarah thrusts the hanger with my dress on in my face as I stand there in my hoodie and joggers.

'But why do we have to go?'

'I've told you. Because it's Dylan's birthday and he wants to go to his first gig, and because it's been five years and I'm still here. I'm alive,' Sarah shouts and I smile.

'I know. It's amazing. But I could take you out for a nice meal instead.'

'I want to go to the gig. And so does Dylan.'

I sigh, taking the hanger off her and placing it on the bed. Reluctantly, I start to remove my hoodie.

'It'll be like we're twenty-two again. Remember when we went to see them? When you two first started dating?'

'Of course I remember.'

'Let's relive our youth.'

'Except we're taking my thirteen-year-old with us, which makes me feel a hundred.'

'You'll be like the super-cool mum who takes your kid to gigs and all his mates fancy you.'

'Eurgh, that's just weird.'

Sarah laughs, and then she sits down on the bed and I notice she has tears in her eyes.

I sit down beside her, wearing just my joggers and a bra. 'What is it? Are you OK?'

'I did it, Laur. I survived.'

'What do you mean? Of course you did.'

'I never told you because I didn't want to worry you, but once my treatment had finished, I had an appointment with Dr Bennett and I said to him, "So what am I now? Am I in remission? Am I cured?" and he said, "Because of the aggressive nature of your cancer, if you're still OK in five years, we'll consider you cured." As soon as I got out the door I burst into tears.'

'You should have told me that, Sar. What an arse.'

'He was just being honest, I guess. Not the most tactful, but honest. Anyway, the point is – I did it. I got to five years. I never ever thought I would.'

I can't tell her that I didn't think she would either. That I've been waiting for bad news every time she's said she has something to tell me or she's been a little quiet or she's cancelled our plans. And the relief to know this is it, that she's beaten it, feels overwhelming.

I pull her into a hug and we just stay there for ages, neither of us able to let go.

403

Eventually, I sit up straight. 'Right. Well then, we are going to party like it's 1999.'

Sarah laughs. 'That's the spirit. Let's get you dolled up.'

'I'm not sure who I'm dressing up for. I don't think I'm going to pull with my thirteen-year-old son in tow.'

'Pull? God, I haven't heard that word in years.'

'See, even my lingo is ancient. I'm so past it I'm never going to meet anyone.'

'Don't be ridiculous. You're not over the hill just yet.'

I pull the dress over my head and flatten it out over my body. 'Seriously though. What if this is it? What if I'm alone for the rest of my life?'

'You can come and join me and Tom. I'm sure he could get into polygamy.'

'I'm being serious.'

'So am I.'

'Sarah.'

'Fine. Look in that bloody mirror. There is no way in hell you are going to be alone for the rest of your life.'

'But will I ever meet anyone that . . .' I tail off and Sarah takes hold of my hands.

'Yes, but I don't think moving away is the answer. Plus, I will barricade all the roads so you can't leave Lanmouth. I know it's a boring, dowdy, small town and you have to drive over an hour away to find any real sign of life, but it's our boring, dowdy, small town and if you leave it'll be like taking out the Costa.'

'I'm as much of a highlight as Costa?'

'We were very excited when that Costa was built, I'll have you remember.'

'Leaving you would be like losing my appendix.'

404

'Unbearably painful?'

'The only part of me that has absolutely no useful purpose.'

Sarah bumps me with her shoulder. 'Shut it, you.'

'You know it would be like cutting out my heart.' My voice starts to break. 'But I don't know how to get over everything if I'm still here.'

'And by everything you mean Luke?'

'Not just Luke. Everything that went along with it. It's our whole *history*. It's everywhere. I feel like I can't escape it.'

'Maybe you don't need to escape it.'

'Oh, Sar. Come on, we've been through this. If he really wanted me, he wouldn't have just given up. He wouldn't have booked a date to marry someone else.' I shake my head. 'There's just too much crap between us.'

'He didn't marry her, did he? He called it off the second he got home after Dylan's birthday last year. I know it's hard for you to believe, but I know his heart was never in it.'

'It's all too late now.'

'But you still love him?'

I give her a look. 'Whether I love him or not is really irrelevant.'

'How can it possibly be irrelevant? Love is *everything*.'

'Oh, you're such a romantic.'

'Sorry, I didn't realize you'd become such a stone heart.'

I point to my heart. 'Solid rock.'

Sarah smiles. 'Come on. Let's do your make-up.'

I let Sarah drag me into the bathroom. 'If we must.'

'Wait until you see our accessories.'

*

405

The pub is practically empty when we arrive. I spot Luke in the corner, tuning his guitar. He's got his head down but occasionally he'll glance up and is unable to hide the look of disappointment on his face when he sees no one else has arrived. He hasn't noticed us yet and I feel like running outside and grabbing people off the streets to come and fill the space. I don't want him to have to perform to just a few of us; I don't want him to feel like this whole solo project is a total waste of time.

'Hey Dad,' Dylan shouts. 'When are you starting?'

Luke turns around, a mixture of shock first and then amusement filling his features.

'You guys look . . . awesome.'

I'd almost forgotten that I'm sporting reindeer ears, Dylan's wearing a Christmas hat and Sarah looks like her head is stuffed up a turkey's bum. Tom and Thea are the only ones that look relatively normal – Tom's nod to Christmas being a sparkly bow tie and Thea wearing a pretty red party dress.

'It was Sarah's idea,' I say, rolling my eyes.

'Because you love Christmas,' Sarah says to him, giving him a hug. I stay where I am, feeling awkward.

'Nice venue,' I say, even though it's a bit dumpy.

Luke looks around. 'Yeah, maybe it's just the poster of me on the door putting the punters off.'

'It'll get busier. It says eight on the posters.'

Luke looks at his watch. 'Let's hope people round here like to be fashionably late.'

'Well, *we're* here, aren't we?' Sarah says. 'Surely we're the only important ones.'

'Of course,' Luke says.

'Can I have a Coke?' Dylan asks, reaching into my hand-bag for my purse.

I slap his hand. 'Not unless you develop some manners. You can't go putting your hand in women's handbags.'

'Please, Mum. It *is* my birthday.'

'Can you believe you have a snotty teenager?' Sarah says to Luke and me.

'I'm not snotty.'

'Sorry, I meant stinky. Can you believe you have a *stinky* teenager?'

Dylan gives Sarah a faux dirty look and then takes my card off me to go and buy himself a drink.

'Two glasses of champagne as well, please, Dylan.' She hands Dylan her card. 'Luke, Tom, do you want anything?'

'I'll have a cider, please, babe,' Tom says.

'I'm OK. Thanks, Sarah.' Luke adds, 'I've got a bottle of water over there with my stuff.'

'Just two glasses of champagne then, please, Dylan. In fact, get us a bottle.'

'You do realize you're asking a thirteen-year-old to buy you alcohol,' I say.

'Oh yeah, shit.' She covers her mouth.

'The kids at school say a lot worse,' Dylan says.

'I can imagine. Right, let me come with you.'

They go to the bar and Tom and Thea find a table near the stage, leaving Luke and me alone. I can't help feeling it was one of Sarah's clever ploys.

'I actually can't believe we have a teenager, can you?'

Luke shakes his head. 'Not really. As teenagers go, he's a pretty good one though, isn't he?'

I look over at Dylan chatting away to Sarah. I keep waiting

for him to become moody and closed off, as teenagers are known to be, but I'm glad that so far the transformation hasn't happened.

'He is.'

'He said you were thinking of moving away.' He says it casually, like it's small talk, but I know he's going to be pissed off I haven't mentioned it to him. I just wanted to have a proper plan in place before I told him.

'I was going to talk to you about it. I mean, I'm just in the planning process at the moment. No decisions have been made. I'd obviously discuss it all with you first.'

'I don't want you to go.'

'Well, I know you won't want Dylan to be far away. I'd make sure I . . .'

'I'm not talking about Dylan,' Luke interrupts.

'Oh.'

'I don't want *you* to go.'

Dylan comes over with his Coke in one hand and a glass of champagne in the other.

'Here you go, Mum,' he says, handing it to me, and Sarah follows behind with her glass and the bottle and we all go and sit down with Tom and Thea.

'Right, shall we make a toast?' Sarah says. 'Happy birthday to Dylan, the best teenager on the planet.'

We clink our glasses together and Luke goes and gets his bottle of water and then raises his arm to join in.

'And to you,' I say to Sarah. 'For being so stubborn there was no way you were going to let a pesky little thing like cancer beat you.'

We all raise our glasses again. 'To Sarah.'

'To Laura, for qualifying to become a midwife,' Sarah

says. 'I can't think of a better face for those babies to see when they first enter this world.'

I smile and join in the toast.

'And Luke,' Sarah continues, 'for being brave enough to start out on this solo endeavour. You are going to be a huge success, again.'

'Looking around here, I'm not so sure about that.'

It's much busier than it was when we arrived, but it's certainly nothing compared to the packed stadiums Luke is used to.

'But I really don't want all that again,' Luke continues. 'I just want to be able to do what I love and for people to hear my stuff and think it's OK.'

'*I've* heard it, Dad. It's pretty good for an old bloke like you.'

Luke squeezes his neck. 'Enough of the "old", mister. You're catching up with me, you know?'

Dylan furrows his eyebrows. 'You know that's not possible, Dad.'

Luke smiles. 'I do.'

'And to Tom and Thea, for always being the light when the world felt black,' Sarah says, and she and Tom look at each other with such devotion it brings tears to my eyes.

'Now come on, Luke,' she continues. 'Go and get this party started.'

He downs the rest of his water. 'I'm not sure about that but I'll try my best.'

'You'll be great,' I say.

'Thanks,' he smiles, but he looks terrified and I wish I could hold him.

Luke grabs his guitar and then goes up on to the little

stage. He pulls the stool into the middle and sits down. He looks so gorgeous in his jeans and white T-shirt, his leather hoodie jacket open over the top. It's strange seeing him up there on his own with only his guitar for company. He looks so lonely. If I had a musical bone in my body, I'd be tempted to go up there and pose as a backing singer.

'Right, well, hello. I'm Luke Jenkins.'

'Woo hoo,' Sarah shouts and a couple of people laugh.

'Thank you all for coming. A few of you might know me from a little band I used to be in called Paradigm, but most of you are probably too young.'

More laughter from the audience as the majority of them certainly wouldn't be classed as 'young'.

'This is my first solo gig so I hope you'll all be kind. I've been working on this stuff for a little while now but I've only really played it to my living room wall.'

'And me,' Dylan shouts.

'Oh yes, and to my son, who is at the front here. In fact, it's his birthday. Maybe we should start with singing "Happy Birthday"?'

The room starts to cheer and then Luke starts to play 'Happy Birthday' on his guitar and the whole room joins in. It's actually a really great ice-breaker, and when it's finished it feels like the audience are on side. So, when Luke sings his first song, they all listen rather than chat to each other and afterwards he gets good applause.

The set is beautiful – a mix of upbeat numbers that get the audience tapping their feet and nodding their heads and some slower numbers where the room goes so quiet the atmosphere is electric, and listening to the lyrics, I can't help but wonder if some of the songs are about me and the heartache I've unwittingly caused him.

'Right, you'll be glad to know this is the last song of the night. I hope you've enjoyed the rest of the set. I'm hoping to get the chance to get back in the studio soon so who knows, perhaps you'll see my new album in the shops at some point.'

A loud cheer circles the room, led by Sarah and Dylan who are whooping loudly and frantically clapping their hands.

'Thank you, everyone. You've been an amazing audience. Now this last song is actually an old song. I wrote it many years ago to say thank you to the mother of my child for giving me my wonderful son. The son who is now thirteen years old.' He pulls a 'how has that happened?' face and there are warm smiles from the audience. 'She'll hate me for pointing her out, but the mother of this wonderful son of mine is also sat here in front of me.'

I feel a lump in my throat.

'Before you get the sick buckets out, this isn't actually a sugar-sweet love story. Because I royally messed the whole thing up. Something I will regret for as long as I live. But I don't want to regret not telling her how I feel now, because I'm not sure that she really knows.'

Now he looks directly at me. 'Laura, this song is for you, and I still mean every word. You and Dylan are the best part of me. I know I drive you insane sometimes. I can't promise we won't argue, because I think that's just us. We're fireworks, right?'

I nod, tears streaming down my face.

'But if you'll have me, I will love you fiercely, passionately, with every fibre of my being.'

He starts to play the first few notes of the song he wrote for me, the song he sang to me in that hotel bedroom all those years ago, and the crowd erupts. And then he sings – his voice so beautiful, every word hitting me in the chest – and I glance over at Dylan with a questioning look and he nods so I nod back.

When I turn to look into Luke's deep brown eyes, it feels like I'm twenty-two again – the same butterflies, the same awe – and I mouth 'I love you' and he beams at me as he plays the last few notes of the song. And then when he's finished, he puts down his guitar and runs over to me, picking me up, and I wrap my body around him. Then he places me on the floor and gets down on one knee.

'I'm sorry I haven't got a ring. I didn't exactly plan this. But will you marry me? And I mean really marry me this time – actually walk down the aisle?'

I find myself bursting into tears, and I think Luke can tell they're not entirely happy tears as he stands up and guides me over to the table where we sit down – the rest of the room sensing this might not be the fairytale ending they first thought and breaking off into quiet conversations amongst themselves. Tom picks Thea up with the excuse that he's taking her to the toilet and Sarah grabs Dylan, escorting him over to the bar with her.

'What is it?' Luke says, taking my face in his hands, but I can't stop crying long enough to get the words out. 'Don't you want to marry me? It's OK if you don't. I'll still always be your best friend.'

I shake my head. 'It's not that. It's just – Dylan's thirteen. *Thirteen*. And every one of the years we've been apart I was in love with you, but I was too scared to tell you. I thought you didn't love me as much as I loved you and I couldn't handle that. And now I see that you do. You do and we could've been together all this time. We both could've seen Dylan every day. He could've had a home that was still intact. We could have been a proper family.'

Luke grips my hands in his. 'We've always been a proper family, Laur. Look at that boy. He couldn't have turned out any better.'

I turn and look at Dylan who is chatting animatedly to Sarah. Then she leans forward and asks the barmaid for something.

'I know. But by being apart we missed so much of it.'

'I get that. But maybe everything happens for a reason. Maybe we had to go through all that for things to be better. For you to find your passion. For me to grow up. I don't know. I know we can't change the past. But please don't let that ruin our future. Because I still plan on having quite a few years on this planet and I don't want to spend a single one of them without you.'

Sarah and Dylan rush over and Dylan hands Luke a packet of Hula Hoops, which he takes with a bemused expression.

'Because you haven't got a ring,' Sarah says through gritted teeth.

Luke laughs, opens the packet, sifts through until he finds a Hula Hoop of a decent size and then holds it out to me, getting back down on one knee. 'Let's not waste another second being apart. Please marry me.'

I wipe away the tears from my cheeks and nod and Luke forces the salty crisp on to the end of my ring finger.

'She said yes,' Luke shouts. 'Eventually.'

The whole room starts cheering and laughing and then the owner of the pub appears at the table with a huge plate of mince pies, a bottle of champagne and four glasses.

'On the house. Congratulations and Merry Christmas, everyone.'

Luke surveys the large collection of my 'beloved' Christmas snack and stifles a giggle. 'Thank you.'

'Best mince pies in the country – made by my wife.'

The landlord walks off and I pick one up.

'No way,' Sarah says, looking at me.

'Well, it's not Christmas without a mince pie, is it?' I take a tentative bite and am amazed to discover that it's delicious.

Tom and Thea appear back at the table, helping themselves from the plate before Dylan pulls Thea on to his knee and Tom sits next to Sarah.

'I've actually got an announcement myself,' Sarah says, looking over at Tom.

'What is it?' I ask.

'Well, it's obviously not that I'm pregnant,' Sarah says and Tom reaches over and puts his hand on her leg. 'I got a job at the theatre. I'm going to be writing the music for their next show. It's only running for three nights, but it's a start.'

'That's amazing,' Luke and I say together and then Luke raises his glass and we all follow. 'Congratulations.'

We're all quiet for a while whilst everyone tucks in and then Sarah says, 'Remember Dylan's birthday when we sat in the deckchairs and I said, "May all of Dylan's birthdays be as wonderful as this." Well, I think this one tops it.'

Before anyone can reply, the landlord turns the music

up – the opening bars of 'All I Want for Christmas Is You' getting everyone out of their seats. Tom pushes our table to the side of the room and then takes Sarah in his arms, her hands clasped around the back of his neck as they sway in time to the music. Dylan grabs Thea's hands and twirls her around, making her giggle.

And when Luke holds his hand out to me, we dance too, singing the words to each other. And then, as the song comes to an end, we kiss. Just like we did all those Decembers ago.

Acknowledgements

By the time you get to your fourth book (how is it possible I've written and published four books?!), this section can start to feel a little repetitive, so I'll keep it brief.

To my editor, Clio Cornish – I'm so grateful for that day we were having lunch and you said, 'I had this crazy idea but how about making this a Christmas book?' I adore Christmas (definitely in Luke's camp on this one) and I love how it changed the book for the better. You are always a pleasure to work with. To my agent, Alice Lutyens, for your unwavering support and for just generally being the best agent in the business and an all-round brilliant human. To Ciara Berry and Courtney Barclay for all your hard work to get the book into as many hands as possible. And Sarah Bance for always making the copyedit process such a dream.

To my fellow warriors – for sharing your stories with me and for understanding the cancer 'journey' in a way that no one else can. I have tried to get a little bit of all our different experiences in there as I know no two journeys are the same and we all have different issues and insecurities about what we've been through. I hope Sarah's story feels authentic and that in some part of it, you all feel 'seen'. I wish I'd met you ladies in different circumstances but I'm so glad I met you. I'm so proud of us all x

To my wonderful friends – I see this book as a celebration

of female friendship. It really is something beautiful and I know without it my world would be a much more dismal place. Thank you for the love and the laughter, the acceptance and the support. It's so hard to list names when it comes to friendship because it is an ever-changing thing – people move away, or get busy with work or life 'stuff', and friendships fluctuate but I hope you all know who you are. A special mention to Etta, Alice and Laura – my absolute constants in a busy world. I love you and thank you.

To my brilliant friend and midwife extraordinaire, Kirsty, for all the midwife info. Any errors here are entirely mine. I'll have to have midwives in all my books as it gives me an excuse to invite myself over for a cuppa and a catch-up!

And to my other constants – my family. Mum, Dad, Emily and Pete – we've had another crap year (cancer, you can f-off now) but we always pull together when it matters and I love you all more than I could ever put into words. I'm so grateful that I was born into this passionate, loving family. Dad – 'cursed' gene or no gene – I would still choose you as my Dad, without question, any day of the week and twice on Sundays. I hope you know that.

Carl, Jacob, Dylan and Coco – like Sarah says in the book – you are my light when the world feels dark. Can't wait to see where our next adventure takes us. Dylan – I know you had to wait until book 4 for the dedication (it's tricky when you have so many children and there *were* specific reasons!) BUT you did also get a main character named after you so I feel (hope) that makes up for the wait.

Last but not least, to my readers. I hope you like this one as much as the others and thank you so much for sharing the love – it honestly means the world to me.

Turn over for an extract from *Hello, Stranger*

Available to buy now

LUCY

'You know this has to happen, don't you? That there's no alternative.'

We are lying in bed eating croissants, sharing the same tray – leaning towards each other so as not to spill crumbs on the quilt – our foreheads nearly touching, and in many ways it feels just like any other Sunday morning. Radio 2 is blaring out from the kitchen – we spend our lives with Jamie turning it off and me turning it back on – him enjoying the silence and me needing background noise. He has covered my croissant in Nutella, just how I like it, neither too little nor too much, and drowned his in jam so that it constantly spills out the sides and runs down his fingers. Normally, once he's finished, I'll grab his hands playfully and start to lick the jam off and he'll try to push me away with his legs, until we inevitably end up back under the covers.

But I don't think that will happen today. Because today I am leaving our relationship, the best relationship I've ever had in my life, knowing that it will be the relationship I will compare all others against. That one day I will walk down the aisle and there will be another man standing at the end waiting for me and amidst the joy I will feel a flutter catch in my chest as I picture Jamie at the altar and wonder *what if?*

'There's not no alternative. The alternative is that we don't split up.'

We're talking about it in the way we might discuss a story in the paper or on the evening news, both starting by calmly presenting our argument, using well-thought-out examples to back ourselves up, listening to each other's point of view whilst knowing we are never going to agree. I'm a complete nightmare for backing down – we both know that – and he loves me anyway for which I love *him* immensely. I know that this conversation will probably go the same way as all our others do – with me storming off in frustration that he won't accept that I'm right and then, when he needs space, me following him around not understanding why he can't *just see* my side. But at the moment all is reasonable and calm.

'So we don't split up and you spend your life regretting it, resenting me . . .' I can hear the emotion filtering its way into my voice and take a deep breath, trying to remain measured so that he knows that I'm not just jumping on some spur-of-the-moment worry and blowing it out of proportion. That I've thought this through for the past two months or so – well, in many ways, since the moment I met him and realized how amazing he was. I've tried it every which way in my head, listed all possibilities, all outcomes, and I know that there is no other option.

'If I'm making the decision then I'd never resent you. That wouldn't be fair.'

I push the tray on to his lap and stand up, putting on the joggers and T-shirt that I left on the floor beside the bed when I took them off last night. He hates that I scatter my clothes around the bedroom floor, spending his life picking them up and dumping them in one huge pile, as if that's somehow making the room tidy.

'You wouldn't do it on purpose. Resentment isn't something you *choose*, or something that you can choose *not* to feel. It creeps up on you slowly and eats into you until it eats the love too.'

'Like a monster? Or a moth?' A hint of a smile creeps across Jamie's lips and I know exactly what he's doing – trying to remind me of all the wonderful things about him so that I change my mind and stay. But I don't need reminding. And I can't allow myself to soften.

'You're not taking me seriously.'

His face falls suddenly. 'I am. I just don't want you to be right on this occasion.'

I want to sit back on the bed, to take his face in my hands and kiss him.

'What if I promise to let you be right about everything else for the rest of our lives and you just let me have this one thing?' he continues, looking up at me with his big brown eyes, his hair a beautiful mess, as it always is after he's woken up, and I wish I *could* let him be right about this. I wish with all my heart that he *was* right, but I know that if I climb back into that bed with him and pretend that everything is going to be OK, it's going to ruin both our lives.

'I'm going to move in with Amy for a bit. You keep the house for now and, when you're ready, I'll help you to sell it.'

'Lucy.'

'It's for the best.'

'So why does it feel like the worst day of my life?'

He looks so sad and I wish that he'd just shout at me, storm off into his man cave (the bathroom) and slam the door. Why does he have to be so bloody adorable? How am I supposed to leave him when he's like this? I try to think of something I can say to provoke him. But at the same time, deep down I know this isn't just another argument. There will be no make-up sex. And I don't want our last 'moment' to be us screaming at each other.

'It's going to be OK. I know it is.'

I say it as much for myself as for him. Because the longer I stand here, the less sure I am that it's true.

He just wanted a decent book to read ...

Not too much to ask, is it? It was in 1935 when Allen Lane, Managing Director of Bodley Head Publishers, stood on a platform at Exeter railway station looking for something good to read on his journey back to London. His choice was limited to popular magazines and poor-quality paperbacks – the same choice faced every day by the vast majority of readers, few of whom could afford hardbacks. Lane's disappointment and subsequent anger at the range of books generally available led him to found a company – and change the world.

'We believed in the existence in this country of a vast reading public for intelligent books at a low price, and staked everything on it'
Sir Allen Lane, 1902–1970, founder of Penguin Books

The quality paperback had arrived – and not just in bookshops. Lane was adamant that his Penguins should appear in chain stores and tobacconists, and should cost no more than a packet of cigarettes.

Reading habits (and cigarette prices) have changed since 1935, but Penguin still believes in publishing the best books for everybody to enjoy. We still believe that good design costs no more than bad design, and we still believe that quality books published passionately and responsibly make the world a better place.

So wherever you see the little bird – whether it's on a piece of prize-winning literary fiction or a celebrity autobiography, political tour de force or historical masterpiece, a serial-killer thriller, reference book, world classic or a piece of pure escapism – you can bet that it represents the very best that the genre has to offer.

Whatever you like to read – trust Penguin.